The
Skinless Face
and Other Horrors

The
Skinless Face
and Other Horrors

Donald Tyson

WEIRD
HOUSE

Trade Paperback Edition

"The Skinless Face." First published in *Black Wings* II, edited by S. T. Joshi. PS Publishing Ltd., 2012.

"Virgin's Island." First published in *A Mountain Walked,* edited by S. T. Joshi. Centipede Press, 2014.

"Curse of the House of Usher." First published in *Gothic Lovecraft,* edited by Lynn Jamneck and S. T. Joshi. Cycatrix Press, 2016.

"The Waves Beckon." First published in *Innsmouth Nightmares,* edited by Lois H. Gresh. PS Publishing Ltd., 2015.

"The Wall of Asshur-sin." First published in *Black Wings* IV, edited by S. T. Joshi. PS Publishing Ltd., 2015.

"The Organ of Chaos." First published in *Black Wings* V—New Tales of Lovecraftian Horror, edited by S. T. Joshi. PS Publishing Ltd., 2016.

All other stories appear herein for the first time.

ISBN: 978-1-888993-30-1

Editor & Publisher, Joe Morey
Co-editor, S. T. Joshi

Interior design by F. J. Bergmann

Weird House Press
Central Point, OR 97502
www.weirdhousepress.com

Special thanks to S. T. Joshi, without whose encouragement these stories would never have been written, and to Joe Morey, without whose unflagging determination they would never have been published in this collection.

Table of Contents

Introduction

When I made the deliberate decision to become a professional writer shortly after leaving university, I had it in mind that I would write fiction. I'd successfully completed all my course requirements for a Masters degree in English literature, but when the time came to write my thesis, I found that I just didn't have the heart to waste a year or so on a project in which I had no interest whatsoever. For a while I halfheartedly looked for a "real job," as some of my relatives liked to call it, and when my complete lack of enthusiasm failed to turn anything up, I committed myself to freelance writing as a career, do or die.

For almost ten years it appeared it would be *die.* I sold the odd thing here and the odd thing there. A radio script to CBC Radio. A television script for a series that never came to be. Short stories to various magazines. Some poetry. A few nonfiction articles. They were all professional sales, because I had decided from the first not to give my work away, but they were irregular sales with long gaps between them.

Life as an unsuccessful freelance writer is uniquely humiliating. There is never enough money coming in to actually buy anything, and never enough positive affirmation from professional editors and publishers to convince you that you haven't wasted your existence. I was able to live at the house my father had built with his own hands, a four-unit apartment building. I grew up there living on the main floor with my brother, my sister, and my parents. We rented three other apartments. After my father died, I took over the maintenance of the building, and watched my sister and brother, both of whom had "real jobs," go off to marry and make real lives for themselves. I didn't have enough money to support a relationship—I couldn't even afford my own car. But I considered myself fortunate to have a roof over my head, and time to write.

Part of my problem was my lack of direction. I tried writing all kinds of fiction, always looking for something that publishers might want. I tried mystery stories and science-fiction stories, both without success. My horror stories did sell, but not well enough to convince me I could make a living writing them. I placed a juvenile novel with Scholastic, but when the contract was ready to be signed, Scholastic abruptly backed out of the deal. Someone higher up in the corporate food chain didn't like the subject matter of my novel. So that was it for my juvenile-fiction career.

At this time I became fascinated by the occult and started to study not only the history of Western occultism, but the actual practice of modern Western magic, as exemplified in the teaching documents of the Hermetic Order of the Golden Dawn and other occult schools such as the Society of the Inner Light and the Builders of the Adytum. It never once occurred to me that I might want to write in this field. I was a fiction writer. In the course of my studies I compiled a set of notes for my own use in which I analyzed magic from a rational perspective. I was interested in figuring out how it could work, if indeed it did work, and explaining its working in a way that would not outrage common sense.

One day I looked at my binders of compiled notes and realized they were a book. I typed them up and offered them to a new publisher named Carl L. Weschcke who was just in the process of trying to get Llewellyn Publications off the ground in Minnesota. He liked the book and agreed to take it. We signed a contract. *Great,* I thought, *my writing career is finally taking off, even if it is in nonfiction.*

And then, for five full years, nothing. The time limit on the contract came and went. For a while Carl stopped responding to my letters (this was before the birth of the Internet). I guess he had nothing new to tell me. I could have withdrawn my manuscript and offered it to other publishers, but when Carl did write to me he expressed strong continuing interest, and promised the work would be published as soon as the company was on stable financial ground.

While waiting for this to happen, I wrote a second nonfiction occult book on the subject of the Germanic runes. I offered it to Samuel Weiser, an established occult publisher, but by a coincidence Weiser was just then bringing out a book about the runes authored by Stephen Flowers, and they didn't want two rune books on their list (this was very short-sighted of them, because in a few years the field of rune books exploded into dozens of titles).

Finally, I worked a bit of magic designed to end the stalemate at Llewellyn, and the same day received a letter telling me that my first nonfiction book, *The New Magus,* would be published. This is not unusual, by the way. Magic defies chronology. The letter from Llewellyn was sent before I worked the magic, but it precisely fulfilled the purpose of the magic.

As soon as I had the actual book in my hands, I submitted my rune manuscript to Llewellyn and Carl accepted it. *Rune Magic* was published fairly quickly, in less than a year. This was the beginning of my career as a writer of occult nonfiction, and the beginning of actually earning a living as a freelance writer. Llewellyn continued to accept most of the manuscripts I sent in to them, and my titles stayed in print for many years, so that the collective earnings from them accumulated.

I had fallen, seemingly by happenstance, into a nonfiction writing career (I am fully aware that many skeptically-minded individuals would consider my occult nonfiction to be fiction, but let that pass). Even had I wished to write in other genres, I wanted to earn a living, and occult nonfiction was accomplishing that goal for me.

As it happens, for anyone who may be wondering, I do believe in the efficacy of magic. My intense practical studies of all branches of both Western and Eastern occultism convinced me that magic was more than superstition, that it had a power that transcended the laws of physics. On two occasions, both of which were life-changing, this was proven to me beyond any shadow of doubt. All of my nonfiction occult works are completely sincere. I am a writer by trade, but my true calling in life is magic.

Mingled in with all the nonfiction titles from Llewellyn were two novels, one about the occult adventures of the Elizabethan sage Dr. John Dee and his psychic companion, the alchemist Edward Kelley, titled *The Tortuous Serpent* (1997), and another about the adventures of Abdul Alhazred, H.P. Lovecraft's fictional author of the *Necronomicon,* which was titled simply *Alhazred* (2006). In both works I promised readers that I would try to write more about these characters in future, and I kept my word.

After publishing several dozen occult nonfiction works with Llewellyn and other publishing houses, I realized one day, six or seven years ago, that if I was ever going to make an impression as a fiction writer, I needed to devote myself full-time to fiction writing. This insight came to me very clearly some time after the publication of my Lovecraft biography, *The Dream World of H.P. Lovecraft* (Llewellyn, 2010). I was not getting any younger, and few writers produce their best work in old age. Immediately I shifted all my energies over to writing fiction.

This might have come to nothing. I have always been terrible at marketing myself. I don't enjoy doing it, and I am bad at it. But by a stroke of good fortune S. T. Joshi was looking for stories for several of his anthology projects, and he expressed support for my horror fiction. My story "Virgin's Island," which is based on an idea in H.P. Lovecraft's *Commonplace Book,* was the first thing I wrote after deciding to devote myself wholly to fiction. Joshi took it for his mammoth anthology from Centipede Press, *A Mountain Walked.* This was eventually published in 2014. Soon after placing this story, Joshi accepted "The Skinless Face" for *Black Wings II,* published by PS Publishing in 2012.

Without the interest and support of S. T. Joshi, I can confidently state that the present book would not exist. A freelance writer works in a kind of vacuum jar, isolated not only from the readers of his work but also from the people who publish it. This is just the nature of writing. It is a lonely profession. Most writers do their very best to overcome this isolation by forming ties with other writers, editors, publishers and, as far as possible, with the fans of their work. I have not been able to do this. I am by nature a hermit. I use this word without qualification. Although I am married (one of the two life-changing magical events I mentioned earlier), I have no friends and very few acquaintances. My contacts in the field of publishing can be counted on the fingers of one hand.

These stories represent for me a significant part of my legacy as a writer of fiction. I have been devoted to horror literature as a reader since my early teens. Although my other tastes in fiction have changed—I find it very hard to read science fiction these days, for example, but devoured it when I was young—my love of horror stories has not been outgrown. However, over the decades my appreciation of the horror story has matured. I now admire and enjoy the slow build of atmosphere, the creation of an uncanny, claustrophobic sense that reality has been tipped on its ear, more than I do gross descriptions of blood and mutilation, or nasty little plot twists.

It is clear to me today that writing horror fiction has always been what I was destined to do as a fiction writer, but it took me almost forty years to realize it. My early successes in selling horror stories should have provided a clue, but I had no one to advise me and sometimes I am slow to see the obvious when it comes to my own work.

The tales in this book were written over approximately a five-year period, with a few exceptions. During that time I wrote other fiction. A collection of John Dee and Edward Kelley occult mysteries titled *The Ravener and Others* was published by Avalonia in 2011, and in 2014 Hippocampus Press brought out my novella *The Lovecraft Coven*, which was combined under the same cover with another novella, *Iron Chain*. A collection of Abdul Alhazred stories, *Tales of Alhazred*, was published by Dark Renaissance Books in a very handsome illustrated edition in 2015.

In all of the stories in this collection I have had one underlying purpose—to create a unique atmosphere of mounting dread. The horror story succeeds best when it creeps upon the reader by slow but relentless increments until, with sudden awareness, the reader feels its cold, bony fingers around his throat. By then it is too late to stop reading. He must continue to the end. The most successful horror stories will stay with the reader after they have been read, returning to his mind at quiet moments throughout the days and weeks that follow. I very much hope that I have succeeded in instilling this lingering unease with at least a few of these tales.

H.P. Lovecraft liked to mingle facts into his fiction. He used reality the way a good cook uses spice. This practice has always struck me as sound, and I have followed it in my own stories. Astute readers will notice that many of the background details in the stories are historically or geographically accurate. This doesn't make them better stories in itself, but it seems to me that it lends an air of plausibility that contributes to the overall effect.

To cite a few examples from the gothic novella "The Lament Horror," there was a a canal on the Blackstone River that runs through Massachusetts prior to the building of the railroads, and it did take a full day for the canal packet boat to travel with its passengers from Providence to the stopover town of Uxbridge. Limited coal mining did take place in that region during the 1830s. The poor houses of Massachusetts did sell the poor as laborers to farmers and tradesmen for a set period, selling to the lowest bidder—the one who would supply food and lodging to the indentured poor at the least expense to the county. There was a poor farm in Grafton at the time. Massive steam engines three stories tall were indeed used to dewater mines in Cornwall during that period. And so on.

Stephen King observed in one of his interviews that he did not believe it was necessary for a fiction writer to be historically accurate. Well, he is correct, of course—it is not necessary. The writer can always rely on the majority of his readers being ignorant of his factual mistakes. Even so, it seems to me disrespectful to readers not to at least attempt accuracy in background details, where it is possible to achieve it. There is a certain pleasure in separating out the real from the imaginary, the factual from the fanciful. At least, I have always found it so when reading Lovecraft and other writers who have interwoven the real and unreal.

If anything ties these stories together, it is their Lovecraftian tone. I have tried to achieve the same broad goals that Lovecraft sought without ever seeking to imitate his style or his work. The horror in my stories is not concerned with good and evil, as understood by human beings. It arises from the sheer otherness that confronts ordinary people without warning, an otherness that causes them to question not only their sanity but the reality of the very ground upon which they crouch quaking in terror.

A theme that runs through a number of the stories—"Virgin's Island," "The Wall of Asshur-sin," "The Colonids," and "The Skinless Face," for example—is the presence just beyond the frame of events related in the story of some vast and ancient chaos that has extended the merest tip of its little finger into our sane, comfortable world. Even this slight, indifferent touch of the otherness threatens to send our globe spinning out of its orbit. There is no remedy, no recourse, and the only escape lies in oblivion.

This book would never have been published without the sustained interest and support of Joe Morey of Dark Renaissance Books. In spite of serious personal setbacks in his own life, he persevered in ushering it through the press. For this I am eternally grateful.

—Donald Tyson
Cape Breton, Nova Scotia
2017

The Skinless Face

1.

The side window of the UAZ-452 was so coated with dust, Howard Amundson could barely distinguish the brick-colored desert from the cloudless blue sky above its flat horizon. Not that there was much of interest to look at from the jolting, grinding minibus, he admitted to himself. Over the past ten hours the scenery had transitioned from the grassy plain that lay just outside of Mandalgovi to red dirt with only the occasional trace of green to show that anything was alive in the desolation.

There was no question in Amundson's mind that the Gobi Desert was the most desolate place he had ever seen. The sheer bleakness of it held its own strange grandeur. It was nothing like the deserts in Hollywood movies, with their rolling sand dunes. The Gobi was carpeted with rocks. They lay scattered everywhere, ranging in size from pebbles to Volkswagens. For the most part the empty landscape was flat, but here and there a low ridge broke the monotony.

A jolt beneath his seat clicked his teeth together on the corner of his tongue. He tasted blood and cursed. The ruts in the track the driver followed were so deep that they bottomed out even the Russian UAZ in spite of its spectacular ground clearance.

The Mongolian in the front passenger seat turned and grinned, then spoke a few words to the driver, who glanced back at Amundson and laughed. Neither of them understood English, so there was no point in talking to them. They had been hired to transport him to Kel-tepu, and obviously were not concerned about what condition he might be in when he arrived.

The Skinless Face

He wrinkled his nose. The inside of the minibus smelled like a mixture of oil, sweat, and camel piss. God alone knows what it had transported before Baby Huey. Amundson twisted in his seat to study the straps that held the canary-yellow case of the multispectral electromagnetic imager on its pallet. The machine was the only reason he was in this desert. When Alan Hendricks, the acting dean of the Massachusetts Institute of Technology, had offered him the chance to give it a field test, he had jumped at the opportunity. A successful trial would clinch the grant of tenure he had been lobbying for over the past two years.

Only later had he paused to consider what would be involved in moving Baby Huey halfway around the world to the backside of nowhere. The machine was as small and as light as modern electronics could make it, but even so, it took a lot of energy output to make electromagnetic waves penetrate solid rock, and Huey tipped the scale at more than a quarter of a ton. Beside it sat the generator he had demanded from the Mongolian authorities. He had made it clear to them that there was no way he would take Huey into the desert without its own power supply. The government had agreed to his demand. The Mongolians wanted the test to be a success almost as much as Amundson.

I should be back at MIT going over term papers, he thought, scowling through the dirty window. *If this thing runs into some glitch and fails, I'm going to look like a fool, and there won't be anyone else to blame. I'm naked out here—no assistant, no colleagues, no one to cover my ass.*

It was not a comforting thought. He had been quick to claim credit for the basic design work on Huey, even though the initial concept had come from one of his graduate students, a bright Chinese man named Yun. The grad student had kept his mouth shut—he wanted his doctorate, and knew better than to try to upset the natural order of things at the university. But that only meant that if Huey failed, Amundson would have to shoulder all the blame.

The UAZ-452 lurched and shuddered to a stop as the driver killed the engine. Amundson pushed himself halfway out of his seat and saw through the windows on the opposite side of the minibus that they were not far from a cluster of khaki field tents, beside which were parked several trucks.

"Are we there yet?" he demanded of the driver.

The Mongolian grinned and jabbered in his own language. He threw open the side door and gestured for the lanky engineer to get out. Hot desert air rolled into the air-conditioned interior. Amundson unfolded himself with difficulty. After sitting for so long on the uncomfortable seat, stiffness had found its way into his very bones.

From the open door of the largest tent, a group of Westerners and a single Mongolian emerged. The leader, a white-haired man with a potbelly and a bearded face, extended his hand. He was a head shorter than Amundson and had to look up to meet the engineer's gray eyes.

"You must be Amundson from MIT," he said in a resonant voice. "I'm Joseph Laski, and I rule in hell." He let out a booming laugh at his own joke.

Amundson accepted the callused hand and shook it, surprised by its strength. There was soil under the fingernails.

"This is my wife, Anna, my assistant, James Sikes, Professor Tsakhia Ganzorig from the National Museum of Mongolia at Ulaanbaatar, and the head of the American student team, Luther White."

"From Pittsburgh," the athletic young black man said with a grin. "You'll meet the rest of the students at dinner."

"Supper," Anna Laski corrected with a slight smile. "We dine late."

"No point in wasting the light," her husband explained.

"Pleased to meet you," Sikes said. "I can 'ardly wait to get a look at that machine of yours." He was a small man with narrow shoulders and a bald patch at the crown of his head.

"You're English," Amundson said with surprise.

"Cockney by birth, but I've been with the Smithsonian for near on twenty years."

The Smithsonian had put up the bulk of the money to finance the Kel-tepu dig, which was named after a local geological feature. Satellite photographs had revealed the faint outline of buried ruins on the track of an ancient silk road. They were invisible from the ground, but had looked promising enough for the Smithsonian to gather a team of archaeologists. The students were all unpaid volunteers, of course—they always were. They worked for the experience of being part of an important expedition, and for the improvement of their résumés. From what Amundson had read about the find at Kel-tepu, they had all hit the jackpot.

A loud bang from the open rear of the minibus drew his attention. He made an apologetic face to Laski and stalked around the vehicle.

"Be careful with that!" he said in irritation.

The two Mongolians were hunched over the imager, using a kind of wrench to release the buckles on the tight straps that held it to its pallet. Another strap let go and hit the side of the minibus.

Ganzorig came around the edge of the door and spoke to his countrymen in a quiet voice. The grins fell from their faces, and they nodded seriously.

"I'm sure they'll be careful," he told Amundson. "I have explained how valuable this equipment is to the expedition."

"Thank you," the engineer said. "If it gets knocked out of calibration, it will take me a week to put it right again."

Laski approached. The others had gone back into the tent.

"Let me show you around the site," he said, putting his hand on Amundson's shoulder.

He allowed the archaeologist to lead him behind the tents, where some distance away from the camp the ground had been excavated in a series of trenches and holes. From a distance it resembled a gopher village.

"You'd never know this is a river valley, would you?" Laski said companionably. "It looks flat. Even so, satellite photographs and topographic measurements show that an ancient river once ran through here, very close to where we are digging. It dried up fifty or sixty thousand years ago."

They stopped in front of a wall of canvas erected in a rectangle some ten yards wide and forty yards long.

"We keep our prize behind this barrier to exclude windblown dust and desert animals. You'd be surprised how many creatures live in the desert. Some say there are even wolves."

Drawing aside a flap in the wall at the near end of the enclosure, he gestured for Amundson to enter and followed close behind him. The engineer stopped and stared in amazement.

"It's quite a sight, isn't it?" Laski said with a dry chuckle. "I always like to watch the reaction the first time someone sees it."

The ground had been excavated just inside the barrier on all sides, so that only a perimeter strip a few feet wide remained of the original desert surface. The rest of the enclosure was an elongated hole, but it was not empty. Within it lay a black stone statue. It reminded Amundson of the statues of Easter Island, but was not quite like anything he had ever seen. The lines of its primitive form exhaled brute strength. It was humanoid but not quite human in its proportions. The massive erect phallus that

4

lay flat along its lower belly was certainly not human. It seemed vaguely aquatic in some indefinable way—perhaps it was the thickness of the neck or the webbing between the impossibly long fingers.

The covering of soil had preserved the sharp edges of the stone carving, with a single exception. The face of the statue was no more than a featureless mask. No trace of a nose, lips or eye sockets remained, if indeed they had ever existed.

"Have you identified the stone?" the engineer asked.

"Some kind of basalt," Laski told him. "We're not yet sure exactly what it is, to be honest. It has resisted identification."

"You mean it's not local," Amundson said as he began to slowly walk around the hole.

"Not local, no."

"So the statue wasn't carved *in situ*."

"Good heavens, no. The stone of the desert is too fractured to carve out a figure of this size. You're thinking it's like the recumbent statues on Easter Island."

"The thought had crossed my mind," Amundson murmured. He bent over to study the surface of the head.

"No, impossible. This statue was transported here from far away—how far, we can't even guess, but there is no stone like this for hundreds of miles. And it was upright—we've found its pedestal buried at its base. At some point it was toppled off its support into a hole and covered with dirt."

The burial of ancient stone carvings and ancient religious sites was not unknown. Amundson remembered reading about such a site.

"You mean like Göbekli Tepe?"

Göbekli Tepe was a twelve-thousand-year-old archaeological site in Turkey consisting of carven stone monoliths and other structures that at some point in its long history had been completely buried, but was in every other way intact.

"Yes," Laski said, pleased at the reference. "Something like that."

The engineer crouched and leaned over the edge of the hole as far as he could reach. He was just able to touch the corner of the smooth face of the giant.

"You're certain it wasn't buried face down."

"Quite certain," Laski said firmly. "The position of the arms and hands, to say nothing of the phallus, clearly shows that it is lying on its back facing the heavens. Even so, we excavated beneath the head. There is no face on the other side."

"I think I see the chisel marks," Amundson murmured, stroking the black stone lightly with his fingertips.

"You can see them better in early morning. The low angle of the sun accentuates them."

The archaeologist waited in silence while Amundson studied the enigmatic, featureless mask. The engineer straightened his knees and turned. Lights of excitement danced in his pale gray eyes.

"It will work, I'm sure of it."

Laski clapped him on the shoulder.

"Excellent! We'll get started tomorrow."

2.

Dinner—*no, supper,* he corrected himself—was better than he expected. Sikes did the cooking chores, and he did them purely from choice, Anna Laski explained to Amundson. The little Cockney had an innate talent for cooking. It was usual on an archaeological dig to eat the local cuisine, but at Kel-tepu it was the local diggers who sampled what was to them exotic dining—roast beef, pudding, dumplings, fish-and-chips, meat pies, stews, bangers-and-mash.

"The first night of the dig, the local man assigned by Gani to do the cooking made khorkhog and khuushuur—goat meat and deep-fried dumplings," Anna told him. "I didn't think it tasted that bad, really, but Sikes was beside himself. He practically begged Joe to make him camp cook."

The conversation around the long dining table in the main tent was lively and free of the tensions that so often plagued academic gatherings. In part this was due to Professor Laski's dominating personality—his enthusiasm and good spirits were infectious. In part it was also due to his gracious wife who acted as hostess at the table. But mainly it was the general atmosphere of success that pervaded the entire team. Those participating in the dig knew they were making history, and at the same time ensuring the future prosperity of their academic careers. This left them with little to complain about.

Two conversations were taking place at the same time across the table, one in English among the Americans, and the other in Mongolian among the local diggers. Gani, as Anna Laski called Tsakhia Ganzorig, acted as translator at those infrequent intervals when a member of one group had something to say to a member of the other.

Amundson noticed several of the Mongolians toying with small carved stone disks around the size of a silver dollar. When the opportunity arose, he turned to the young woman seated on his right, a blond graduate student from the University of Southern California named Luce Henders.

"Could you tell me, what are those objects?" he murmured.

She followed his eyes, fork poised before her lips, and smiled. "You mean our good-luck charms? That's what Professor Laski calls them. We've been finding them all over the place, inside the graves."

"Graves?"

Luce chewed and nodded at the same time.

"This whole site is really one huge graveyard. There are graves all around the colossus—that's what we call the statue. Hundreds, maybe thousands of them. The bones are gone, but when we dig we find stone ossuaries that must have held them, with those carved disks inside."

"What happened to the bones?"

"Time happened. Thousands of years ago this was a wet river valley. Bones don't last under those conditions unless they petrify."

"Is the stone of the tokens the same as the stone of the colossus?"

"We're pretty sure it is," she answered. "It's not local stone."

"I wonder if I might have one," Amundson said apologetically. "I can use it to adjust my projector before I set it into place."

"I don't see why not; we've got dozens. Everyone's got one. Give me a minute."

She stood and left the tent. Amundson continued his meal. In a few minutes she resumed her seat and with a smile pressed something cold and hard into his hand. He studied it.

The black stone was surprisingly heavy, and not quite circular, he noticed, but ovoid, some two inches across on its longest dimension and half an inch thick. Its edges were rounded like those of a beach stone. Into one face a simple geometric figure had been deeply carved. It was a kind of spiral with four arms. Amundson realized that it was a primitive form of sun wheel or swastika.

"Thank you," he told Luce Henders. "This will be very useful."

One of the grads, a red-haired Irishman from Boston College named

Jimmy Dolan, noticed the black stone and pointed at it across the table with his fork.

"I see you've joined the cult of Oko-boko," he said. Several other students laughed, including Luce.

"When we first started finding these stones, we noticed that they were going missing," she explained to the engineer. "Professor Laski was upset because he thought we had a thief in the camp. He and Gani started to question everybody, and it turned out that the Mongolian diggers were taking them for good luck charms. This valley is supposed to be real bad luck or something, according to local superstition, and the Mongolians believed that the stones would protect them from the evil whatever-it-is. They got upset when the Professor tried to take the stones back, so he realized he'd better let them keep them or he'd have a mutiny on his hands and we would never get any work done. Anyway, Gani made all the local diggers promise to give the stones back when the dig is finished. You'll have to give yours back, too."

Amundson dropped the black stone into the vest pocket of his shirt and laid his hand across it.

"I do solemnly swear to return it," he said.

Luce laughed, her blue eyes sparkling with something a little brighter than the table wine. *Things are looking up,* Amundson thought to himself, *things are definitely looking up.*

3.

The engineering problem was simple. The imager had to be positioned directly above the face of the colossus, and no more than three feet away. Since the statue could not be moved, it was necessary to build a structure above it to support the machine.

When Amundson mentioned the problem to Sikes, the little Englishman said he had just what was needed, and came back with two aluminum ladders. The ladders easily spanned the sides of the trench in which the colossus lay. It was necessary to support them from below with diagonal bracing so that they would bear the weight of Baby Huey without buckling, but this was not difficult.

Within an hour the framework was ready and the squat yellow machine in position beside the hole. Amundson had already spent the previous evening setting its sensors for the density of the black stone, which appeared identical in every respect to the stone of the statue. It was surprisingly easy to skid the imager along the ladders, and only a bit more taxing to get it positioned precisely above the face using the built-in camera as a guide.

Laski had been right, Amundson thought as he looked at the camera image of the blank face on his monitor. The statue was oriented with its head in the west, and the beams of the morning sun slanting along its body highlighted the marks of the chisels that had been used to cut away its features. He wondered idly what strange compulsion had caused a primitive people to cast down the statue and mutilate it. Perhaps they were some warring tribe, and thought they were defeating the god of their enemies. He shrugged. He was an engineer, not an archaeologist. There was no need to bother his mind with such questions, which were probably unanswerable.

Amundson found himself less nervous than he expected, considering that his future career at MIT was riding on the performance of the imager. He smiled to himself. Not all of last night had been spent on work. The latter part of the evening he had devoted to the relaxing task of exploring Luce Henders. She was interested in him only because he was the first unfamiliar male to walk into the camp in months—that much was obvious—but it had not diminished his pleasure.

Why make life complicated when it could be simple? That was his personal motto. It had served him well enough through the first half of his life, and he saw no reason why it should not serve equally well through the second half.

This morning, Luce was away from the camp with Laski and his wife, Gani, and most of the others, excavating an artificial passage that had been found amid the graves. The discovery had been made by chance, while digging exploratory holes. When first found, the passage had been completely choked with rubble and its entrance covered with dirt. Laski was removing the rubble slowly so as not to miss any objects that might lie in it. He had the students screening the dirt and gravel as it was taken out of the passage by the diggers.

Amundson noticed Luther White across the trench. When he looked at the black grad student, White turned his head away. He had worn the same sullen expression all morning, and had failed to respond when Amundson greeted him at breakfast. Apparently it was impossible to

9

keep anything secret in so small a camp. He wondered if Luce had even tried to conceal her late-night visit to his tent? Or had she taken some perverse pleasure in relating the details to Luther?

After a few minutes dithering around, White found his way around the hole and approached Amundson. All the cheerfulness of the previous day had vanished.

"Stay away from Luce," he said in a low voice.

"What?" The engineer smiled disarmingly. "What did you say?"

"You heard me," White snarled. "I'm not going to tell you again. Luce is mine, not yours."

He backed away before Amundson could think of a response. Sikes, working nearby on the wires that connected the imager to the data processing unit, gave no sign that he had heard the exchange, although he must have heard every word.

"I'm ready to switch on," Amundson told the Englishman in a neutral tone.

Sikes nodded. He started the generator with its pull cord. It fired on the second pull and ran smoothly. With his laptop computer across his knees, Amundson put Baby Huey through its paces. The scanner hummed and stopped at the end of each pass, moving slowly back and forth like a farmer ploughing a field. Its beam was invisible, but a red laser cast a spot on the stone below it to act as a guide.

Sikes approached behind him and peered over his shoulder.

"You mind telling me 'ow this works?" he asked.

Amundson didn't mind. He had the time. The scan of the machine was largely automatic, once its parameters were programmed in.

"You know how it's possible to recover a serial number on a gun, when the number has been completely filed off?"

Sikes nodded. "They use acid," he said. "The metal is 'arder under the place where the numbers are stamped in, so the acid eats the surrounding metal quicker, and the 'arder numbers show up in what they call bas-relief."

Amundson nodded in agreement. "It's the same with stone. When stone is carved using a chisel, the repeated impact of the blade aligns the molecules in the stone. The harder the impact, the greater the alignment; or the more frequent the impact, the greater the alignment—same thing, it's the total impact on the stone that determines the degree of stress."

"You mean a few 'ard 'its is the same as a lot of little 'its," Sikes said.

"You've got it. What this machine does is to project energy down into the stone and then read the resonance that energy produces in the aligned molecules. The greater the alignment, the stronger the resonance. A computer assembles the data into an image."

"It's sort of like ground-penetrating radar," Sikes said.

"It uses a completely different band of projected energy, but the overall idea is similar."

"So you can use this 'ere machine to recover any image that was ever impressed on any stone surface, even after it gets worn away by erosion?"

"In theory," Amundson said. "In practice, it's not so simple. Some images are carved using regular pressure instead of struck using hammers. Some types of stone work better than others—usually the denser stone yields a better result."

"Why won't the impacts of the chisel from when the face was cut away spoil the image?"

Amundson raised his eyebrows and glanced over his shoulder at Sikes. The little man was no fool.

"Because they were all uniform, more or less. They will be picked up by the scanner, but they will be like a curtain of background noise. The computer will be able—should be able—to strip away that curtain and reveal what lies beneath it."

"Won't that be a sight," Sikes said, staring at the little red dot of the laser as it scanned back and forth across the face. "We'll be the first people for thousands of years to see what it looked like."

Amundson shrugged. The excitement for him was in the technical challenge of recovering a clear image. A face was a face. Undoubtedly the image on the colossus would be strange and uncouth, like most primitive art, but what would it signify in the scheme of things? The world was littered with old statues, each bearing unique features. What was one more such image, more or less? He only hoped it would be grotesque enough to catch the eye when printed in the newspapers.

"How long is it going to take?" Sikes asked.

"About two hours to scan. Then the computer will need another four hours or so to process the data into a coherent image. It should be ready by late afternoon."

"I can 'ardly wait," Sikes said with sincerity.

You and me both, Amundson thought. Everything in his life was riding on the outcome of this test. If it failed, he could always run it a few more times, but he knew that the imager would either yield a result on the first scan, or it would never yield a good result. Conditions were perfect.

4.

"We'll know in a second," Amundson said.

He had moved his processing computer into the main tent and set it up on the cleared dining table. Almost everyone in the camp was waiting to see the image when it finally formed on the monitor screen. Laski stood behind him, with his wife and Gani close on either side. The grads milled behind them, and the Mongolians clustered on the other side of the long table, their faces curiously apprehensive. Many of them fingered the small stone disks as though they really were protective talismans. Amundson got the impression that were it up to the superstitious diggers, he would never be permitted to display the image of the face.

"It will be in black and white," he said to those behind his chair.

A buzzer sounded in the bowels of the computer.

"Here it comes," he said, unable to prevent his voice from rising in pitch.

The image began to appear on the monitor in horizontal strips, painting itself across the screen from top to bottom. When it was about a fifth of the way down, Amundson released the breath he had been holding unconsciously and relaxed the knotted muscles in his abdomen. It was going to be all right. He couldn't see what the image was yet, but he could see that it was a clear, coherent image, and for him that was all that mattered. The test was a success. It was not quite as sharp as a photograph, but he had never expected that degree of clarity.

They waited in silence as the gray bands continued to paint themselves onto the screen.

"It's human," Gani said.

"So it is," Laski said with excitement. "I was expecting something monstrous, but it's human."

"It looks female," Anna Laski murmured.

"No, it's male," Sikes said.

"It looks female to me," Luce told him.

Amundson wondered what she was seeing. The face, which by now was more than half visible on the screen, was clearly the face of a man.

It was startling in its sheer ordinariness. It might as well have been a contemporary snapshot of anyone in the tent. Indeed, the more he looked at it, the more it seemed familiar to him. He wondered where he had seen the face before.

Luce laughed nervously. "This is a joke," she said.

Amundson turned in his chair to look at her.

"What do you mean?" Laski asked.

"Well, look at it. It's a joke, that's all. You got me, Professor Amundson. You got me good, guys; you really had me going. I thought this was a real test."

"What are you talking about?" Amundson demanded.

She stared at him with wide blue eyes, the half-smirk frozen in place on her lips. She looked at the others.

"Come on, guys, funny is fun, but this is enough."

They all stared at her. She pointed at the screen.

"You used a picture of my face. Good one, you got me. Now turn it off."

Laski glanced at the computer screen, then back at the blond grad student. "Are you feeling quite well, Luce? Perhaps you had better go to your tent to lie down."

"It's my face," she said loudly. "Do you think I don't recognize my own face?"

"My God," Anna Laski said. Her fingers rose to her lips. "My God."

Amundson looked back at the screen. The face had almost completely formed itself in grayscale. It was a lifelike representation of a middle-aged man with short hair.

"My God," Anna Laski said more loudly, backing away from the screen.

"Jesus, I see it now," Sikes said.

"See what?" Laski demanded. He turned to his wife. "Anna, what do you see?"

"It's my face," she said. "I didn't recognize it at first, but it's my face."

Her husband looked at the image. "It is a man's face, my dear. If nothing else, the beard should tell you that."

"Look again," Sikes told him in a faint voice. "Look 'arder."

Amundson wondered if they had all suddenly gone mad. There was no question about the gender of the face. It was definitely male, but clean-shaven. There was something maddeningly familiar about it.

"You say you see a beard, Professor?" Sikes asked him.

13

"Yes, a short beard much like my own."

"I see no beard," Sikes said.

"That's absurd," Laski said. "It's right there. You see it, don't you, Gani?"

The Mongolian shook his head. He was strangely silent, but there was fear in his eyes. The same fear was mirrored in the faces his countrymen on the other side of the table. The tent had fallen still.

"It's my face," Joseph Laski said in a leaden voice.

"It is all our faces," Gani said.

Amundson stared at the screen. Recognition leapt out at him. How could he have missed it? The image on the screen was his own face, its eyes staring impassively back into his. It was like looking into a mirror—or better to say, like looking at a black-and-white photograph of himself. A mirror reversed his face from left to right, and he had became accustomed to seeing it that way. That was why he had failed to recognize himself instantly.

"It can't be all our faces," he said, his voice lifeless in his own ears. "I never scanned any of our faces. In any case, it's only one image—it can't be all our faces at the same time."

"But it is," Sikes said.

One of the Mongolian diggers began to jabber in his own language at Gani, who responded in a soothing tone, but the man was in no mood to be placated. Gathering his courage, he walked quickly around the table and stared at the image on the monitor. For a few seconds he did not react. Then he screamed and began to babble at the other diggers. Gani put a hand on his shoulders and the man flinched as though burned with hot iron. He backed away from the monitor, unable to take his eyes from it until he back pressed against the side of the tent. The touch of canvas on his shoulders galvanized him. With a cry he ran from the tent. The other Mongolian diggers quickly followed, leaving only the archaeologists beside the table.

"There has to be a scientific explanation," Amundson said, his eyes captivated by the image on the monitor.

"Mass hallucination," Luce said.

"I've been on LSD, I know what it feels like," Dolan said with a shake of his red head. "This is no hallucination."

"But how is the image being formed?" Amundson asked. "How can it be different for each of us?"

"Maybe it isn't an image at all," Sikes suggested. "Maybe it's something that makes an image in our minds when we look at it."

Amundson bent over one of the machines on the table.

"What are you doing?" Sikes asked.

"I'm printing out a hard copy," the engineer murmured. "I want to see if it has the same effect as the image on the monitor."

The printer generated the black and white copy in a matter of seconds. Amundson took it from the rack and held it up for the others to view. They unconsciously backed away a step when he extended it toward them.

"It's the same, still my face," Luce said.

"And mine," Anna agreed.

"Mine, too," Sikes said.

Amundson stared at them, barely able to contain his excitement. "Do you know what this means?" he demanded.

They gave him blank stares.

"It means we're all going to be famous."

5.

The sound of banging from outside the tent drew their attention away from the sheet of paper.

"I'll go see," Gani told Laski.

He left the tent. After a minute or so they heard excited shouting in Mongolian, followed by the sound of a single gunshot. When they rushed to the door, they were in time to see the three camp trucks speed away across the desert, leaving fantails of dust in their wakes.

"They've taken all the trucks," Luce said in bewilderment.

Gani staggered from the communications tent. There was a patch of redness on his left thigh.

"Those bastards shot him," Sikes said. He hurried over to support the archeologist beneath the arm.

"They smashed the radio," Gani told Laski, pain in his voice. "I couldn't stop them."

"Well, they're gone," Laski said.

The reality of their situation slowly sank home. Without a radio there was no way to call Mandalgovi and report the incident, and without the trucks there was no way to leave the camp. It might be days before anyone in the town sent a truck to investigate the radio silence. On the plus side of things, there was no shortage of food and water in the camp. The main concern was for Gani. They managed to stop the bleeding from the bullet wound, but it was a serious injury. He needed a hospital.

Anna Laski moved the injured man onto the bed in her tent, which was larger than the camp cots. She appointed one of the grads, a quiet girl in glasses named Maria Striva, as his nurse. He had collapsed almost immediately after leaving the communications tent, and continued to lapse in and out of consciousness, but whether from pain, shock or loss of blood, none of them was qualified to tell.

As dusk gathered, the others returned to the main tent and sat around the table with Laski at its head. Sikes silently served them coffee while they talked.

"We might as well go on with our work," the archaeologist told the students. "This dig is too important to abandon over one incident. In any case, there's not much else that we can do."

"It will be difficult without the diggers," White pointed out.

Laski nodded.

"Which is why we will go slowly. We don't want to miss anything or, God forbid, have an accident. As you all know, we've almost finished clearing the tunnel of rubble. The echo gear indicates a sizeable chamber beyond. We should be able to break through to it tomorrow, even without the diggers."

White nodded and looked around at the other grads to gauge their mood. "We're game," he said.

"Good." Laski turned to Amundson, who sat with the printout of the scanner image face down on the table in front of him.

"Run another scan," he said.

"The result will be the same," Amundson told him.

"Run another scan anyway. We need to be absolutely certain this isn't some kind of chance artifact of the machine itself."

Amundson did not argue. The order made sense. In any case, what else was he going to do with his time? He was not a trained archaeologist, and therefore could not help with the excavation, even had he felt inclined to offer his services as a digger.

"You'll have to work alone tomorrow, I'm afraid," Laski told him. "I need every person at the tunnel."

"Now that the imager is in place, that won't be a problem."

He was rechecking his test results at the desk in his tent an hour later when Luce entered, wearing only a yellow silk robe tied at her waist. Her short blond hair was immaculate, but the powder on her cheek could not completely hide the bruise beneath.

Amundson stared at her from his chair without rising. He had not expected a return visit, given the tense circumstances. Sex was not high on his list of priorities tonight.

"He hit you?"

She touched her cheek gently and winced. "What does it matter? I do what I want, when I want."

She approached the desk and picked up the printout, turning it over to stare at the image with fascination as though mesmerized by a serpent.

"What does it mean?" she asked in a low tone that was barely audible.

"It means we are all going to be famous, and quite possibly rich. No discovery like this has ever been made before."

She shook her head with annoyance. "But what does it mean? Why our own faces?"

"I have no idea," Amundson said, wishing she would just turn around and walk out of the tent so that he could get his work done. "That's something you archaeologists will have to determine. I'm an engineer."

"Do you suppose the original face of the colossus, before it was chiseled off, had the same effect? Did everyone who looked at the statue see themselves?"

"Yes, I think so," Amundson told her. "What my imager generated is an accurate reproduction of whatever was on the original face of the statue. I don't see why the effect would be any different."

"That's why they cut it off," she murmured with conviction. "They couldn't stand seeing themselves, so they toppled the statue and struck off its face before burying it."

"I expect you are right," Amundson said, shuffling the printouts of readings from the machine. "Look, Luce, I'm really quite busy now—"

She sat across his thighs, her arms around his shoulders, and forced her tongue into his mouth before he could finish the sentence. Her robe fell open, and the erect nipples of her firm young breasts pressed against his shirtfront. She arched her back to raise herself and slide her breasts from side to side over his face. With a moan of desire, she dug her hand between his legs.

Amundson found himself thrusting into her as she lay diagonally

17

across his cot. With part of his mind he realized she was naked, and that he wore only his open shirt. He had no memory of moving across the tent, or of taking off his pants. He shrugged out of the shirt with annoyance, relishing the freedom from its encumbrance. He felt wholly alive, like some powerful beast awakened from long sleep. When she bit his shoulder, he slapped her across the face, back and forth, until her upper lip split and blood marked her barred white teeth.

Only when he had exhausted his lust and lay panting across her did she push him off and leave the cot. Her eyes held a restless look, sliding over him as though he were of no further interest. Neither spoke. Shame mingled with regret welled inside Amundson when he looked at the blood on her lip. He might be many things but he had never hit a woman. She bent to pick up her silk robe and slid into it, then flipped it closed and tied it with a sharp tug of its sash. Without a backward glance she left the tent.

Amundson lay naked across the cot, listening to the sound of his own breathing. What the hell had just happened? In an instant he had gone from bored indifference to white-hot lust mingled with violence. The sight of blood on the girl's face had excited him. That had never happened before. Sex had always been good for him, but nobody would have ever described it as anything other than white-bread. The outburst of passion had left him drained. Suddenly, it was all he could do to keep his eyes open. He shifted himself on the cot into a more comfortable posture and knew nothing more until the following morning.

6.

When he left his tent, the sun was already well above the eastern horizon and the morning chill had been driven from the stones that lay scattered across the pebbly ground. He was almost glad to discover that he had overslept, and that the rest of the camp, with the sole exception of Sikes, had already left for the passage excavation. In the main tent, Sikes gave him scrambled eggs and toast, with black coffee. He sipped the bitter liquid with gratitude. A headache throbbed between his temples, making it hard to focus his eyes.

Sikes must have had a rough night of his own. The little Englishman was uncommonly quiet and seemed to perform his housekeeping duties in a meditative daze. After he finished clearing away the breakfast dishes and silverware, he announced to Amundson that he was leaving to help with the excavation work.

The engineer nodded absently at him and did not turn his head to watch him go. His thoughts were preoccupied by the question Luce had asked the night before. Why their own faces? What did it mean to see oneself, to have one's essential pattern exposed?

He had brought the printout into the dining hall with him. It rested on the table beside his coffee cup, face down. Turning it over, he held it up and studied it. The face, which was most definitely his own, stared back at him. There was a trace of amusement at the corners of its lips—or was that only his imagination? The longer he stared into the eyes of the image, the more variable the expression of the face seemed to become. It shifted from wry amusement to arrogance to lip-curling contempt. Its mouth trembled as though it were trying to speak to him.

Amundson set the sheet of paper down and rubbed his eyelids with his thumb and index finger. Little wonder his mind was playing tricks, given the stress he had been under for the past few days.

He took up the paper and regarded it again, striving to separate himself from it. This could not be an image. It had to be some sort of symbolic code series designed to affect the human mind at the deepest level, and provoke the same illusion in every person who looked at it. He was not seeing the code, he was seeing only the effect of the code, but the code itself must be printed on the paper in his hand, just as it had been impressed onto the stone face of the colossus so many thousands of years in the past.

There was a popular name for self-executing code that reproduced itself from one medium to another. Virus. What he was looking at on the paper, without actually being able to see it, must be some form of symbolic mind-virus, transmitted through the visual sense.

He turned the paper face down, his fingers trembling. The sophistication required to produce such code was terrifying in its implications. No ancient human culture could have designed it, or at least no culture recognized by science. Unless the code had been generated by some intuitive process, or channeled from some higher external source. Perhaps if he divided the code into parts, he could analyze it without being affected by it.

He slammed the flat of his hand against the table and pushed himself to his feet. It was pointless to speculate in the absence of data. He would run another scan, varying the parameters from the first scan to see if it achieved a different result. It would probably be best to do an entire series of scans under as many conditions as possible.

Bright spots of light danced before his eyes as he left the main tent. He gathered up the processing computer and the laptop from his own tent and carried them toward the canvas enclosure around the colossus, where he busied himself connecting wires and preparing the scan for the imager. His mind was not on his work.

If a copy of the face were published in major world newspapers and shown around the globe on the nightly television news, in a single day it would imprint itself on the minds of perhaps a billion human beings. That was a sobering thought. Before releasing it to the press he would have to assure himself that the coding of the image was not harmful.

Thus far, it had not caused any damage. His thinking was still clear. It was absurd to even consider withholding the results of the test from the media—once it became public, his fame and prosperity were assured. He would write a book and it would become a best-seller. He wondered why the idea of withholding the results had even crossed his mind and laughed to himself. The eerie chuckle startled him, until he realized that it had proceeded from his own mouth.

The desert was filled with strange sounds this morning. On the other side of the canvas barrier, he heard a distant barking. It was followed by a series of drawn-out howls, like those of a wolf. He wondered idly if there really were wolves in the Gobi. It would be a fine state of affairs if the archaeologists returned to camp at the end of the day and discovered his wolf-mauled corpse. He couldn't let that happen. Was there a weapon in the camp? He decided to look for a knife or a gun, even a good solid club.

The ghosts were waiting for him when he emerged from the enclosure. They stood silent and motionless all over the open ground, watching him with dead eyes. Their bodies were translucent and colorless, but they wore some kind of ancient apparel that resembled none he had ever seen before. There were soldiers, priests, merchants, slaves, maidens, matrons, whores. Some were even children, but they stood as impassively as the rest.

The weight of their dead eyes on Amundson was like a physical force, compelling him to do something, but he knew not what. It produced an unpleasant twisting sensation in his lower belly. Coupled with his headache, it made him irritable.

"I don't know what you want," he muttered to them. "You'll have to be clearer; I don't know what you want."

He walked through them on his way to Laski's tent. He needed to acquire a weapon before the wolves reached the camp and tore him apart. The touch of the dead against his skin was similar to the brush of cool silk. The ghosts made no attempt to stop him, but merely turned to regard him with mute accusation.

Inside Laski's tent, the sweet-sick smell of fresh blood struck him in the face. He blinked in the dimness. The Mongolian archaeologist lay on his back on the bed with his throat torn out. *Damn wolves,* Amundson thought. The shy grad student, Maria Striva, crouched on his chest, naked, her body streaked with blood. She glared at the engineer, blood and bits of flesh clotting her teeth, her nose, the corners of her mouth and her chin. Her bloodshot eyes were so wide open that he could see their whites all the way around their brown irises. There was no sanity there.

With some part of his mind Amundson realized that she had become a wolf. The desert was filled with wolves. Why didn't the Mongolians kill the verminous creatures? If the wolves were permitted to roam free in this way, sooner or later everyone would be attacked.

The woman threw herself off the bed, her blood-covered fingers clawing for his throat, but her feet became tangled together and she fell heavily onto her face and breast, knocking the wind from her lungs with a sharp yelp. Calmly, Amundson stepped across her body and picked up a short-handled pickaxe that rested on the floor next to a travel trunk. As the woman pressed herself up on her hands, he sank the point of the pickaxe into the top of her skull. She collapsed, dead.

One less wolf to deal with, he thought with satisfaction. He remembered why he had entered the tent and rummaged through the trunk. At the bottom he found a revolver. When he left the tent, the ghosts nodded their heads at him with satisfaction.

7.

As an experiment, he shot one of the ghosts. The report of the revolver rolled across the desert and lost itself on the dusty wind. As expected, the bullet did nothing. The ghost merely smiled at him, and its translucent head became a naked, grinning skull. That was to be expected, but he was a scientist after all, and of what use was surmise without verification? Thereafter, he ignored the ghosts, even though they followed him all the way to the entrance of the passage.

He recognized the two corpses that lay near a mound of tailings, not far from a black hole in the ground, bodies grotesquely twisted in their death throes. One was the red-headed grad, Jimmy Dolan, and the other was Sikes. Amundson tilted his head as he studied the tableau. It appeared that Dolan had stabbed Sikes in the back with a tent spike, and that Sikes—plucky little man that he was—had managed to bash in Dolan's brains with a rock before he died. *Two more wolves taken care of,* the engineer thought with satisfaction.

He climbed down the aluminum ladder into the pit and entered the mouth of the slanting passage, which descended into the solid bedrock at a downward angle of around twenty degrees. The light soon failed behind him, but he saw a tiny square of brightness at the end of the long, straight tunnel, and continued on, feeling his way along the wall with his left hand. The stone felt smooth beneath his fingertips, almost like polished marble.

At the end, Amundson had to pick his steps with care over uncleared rubble. An opening had been made that was large enough to crawl through. He emerged into a vaulted chamber of thick, square pillars. The portion of it near the tunnel entrance was illuminated by the glowing mantle of a propane lantern. From the corners of his eyes, Amundson saw carved statues resembling animals and manlike beasts. They nodded their heads at him in approval, but he paid scant attention.

On the open floor lay the bodies of Laski and his wife, horribly mutilated. Between them, a naked Luther White, his muscular dark body glistening with sweat in the light from the lantern, stretched across the corpse of Luce Henders. She also was naked and lay face down on a low platform of polished stone. With scientific detachment, Amundson noticed that her head was missing. He glanced around but failed to locate it.

White was busy thrusting his erect member into the dead girl's pale, blood-streaked backside, and did not notice the intrusion. With each thrust he grunted, "ugh-ugh-ugh," and the headless body jerked on the altar as though by some undead animation. From the darkness beyond the reach of the lantern, ghosts began to gather. Amundson threw back his head and howled.

"She's mine," White snarled at him. "You can't have her."

He thrust himself away from the corpse of the girl and stood up, still impressively erect, his penis coated with blood. Between the buttocks of the headless corpse there was only a mass of chewed flesh that resembled raw beef. White looked around with quick jerks of his head from side to side. He lunged and grabbed up a shovel with a short D-handle. Holding it like an axe, he advanced with cautious steps toward the engineer.

Amundson shot the black man in the chest. White looked down at the hole until it began to ooze blood, then laughed.

"Bullets can't kill me," he cried through lips caked with dried blood.

Amundson howled again and shot White two more times. The second bullet found his heart. The black grad student dropped like a marionette with its strings cut. The ghosts clustered close and nodded, their translucent eyes shining in the lantern glow like pearls.

The engineer thrust the revolver into his belt. The sharp tang of gunpowder cut through the cloying scent of blood. He felt strong. More powerful and more potent than he had ever felt before. His mind was clear, his thoughts ordered and supremely rational. He realized that his sexual organ was engorged with blood, and gazed down at the headless corpse with a speculative eye.

"No, *mine*," he murmured to himself, and began to giggle.

Something drew him more strongly than his lust. In the darkness beyond the circle of the lantern light he sensed a vast space that extended downward, like the inverted vault of starry heaven. That was what the ghosts were trying to tell him. He must explore that space. It was his destiny, the only thing for which he had been born into this world. He listened, and now he could almost hear the whispers of the ghosts. If he remained in the darkness with them, it would not be long before they could talk to him and teach him. He could remain here a long time. There was ample food. Was that his own thought, or the thought of the ghosts?

As he started forward, his boot slipped in White's blood, and he fell heavily to the floor, the back of his head striking and rebounding from the polished stone. Something rolled beneath his hand when he struggled to get up. He blinked and held it to the light. Recognition entered his thoughts—the oval black stone he had put into his shirt pocket and then forgotten about.

As he held up the stone, a kind of sigh arose from the throng of the dead. Acting on some impulse below the level of thought, Amundson extended the stone toward the ghosts. The pallid forms withdrew like mist from flame. He blinked heavily and shook his head. What was he doing here in this dark cavern? The vague memory of leaving the camp and climbing down into the passage came into his mind. He tried again to stand, then cursed and began to crawl toward the lantern with the stone clutched firmly in his left hand.

Awareness came to him in flashes, between which there was oblivion. He was in the tunnel. He stumbled across the loose stones of the desert. He pushed through the resistless ghosts in the camp. Then he was sitting at the table in the main tent. Everything looked completely normal. He picked up his half-emptied coffee mug, and felt a faint trace of warmth, or perhaps it was only his imagination. The printout of the face lay beside him on the table. He turned it over and looked at it. Fame. Fortune. Prestige. Success. Acclaim.

He let it drop from his hand. It drifted under the table. He realized with surprise that he still held the oval talisman clutched in his left fist and laid it with care on the table. He sat staring at the doorway of the tent. Through the opening he could see the ancient ghosts walking to and fro in their eternal procession of the damned.

With quick, economical motions he drew the revolver, cocked the hammer, put the muzzle into his mouth, and pulled the trigger.

8.

General Goppik surveyed the corpse of the American with distaste. Blood and brains had splattered the wall of the tent around the hole left by the departing bullet. The man's pale eyes stared sightlessly, already starting to shrivel in the dry desert air. He picked up the black stone that lay on the table and regarded its carved surface with curiosity before putting it into his pocket. A keepsake for his young son, he thought.

There were corpses everywhere. The more his soldiers searched, the more bodies they found. Evidently the entire party of foreigners had gone mad and murdered each other with extreme violence—all except this one, who had taken his own life. It was a propaganda nightmare. The Western press would never stop talking about it. The archaeological dig at Kel-tepu would have to be closed down, naturally. There was no other course of action to follow. The entire site would have to be sanitized, and some story invented to account for the massacre. Terrorists, perhaps. Yes, terrorists were always useful.

Noticing a sheet of paper on the floor beneath the table, he bent and retrieved it. The paper bore some sort of computer printout of a black and white photograph, not a very clear one at that, showing a Mongolian man. He frowned and squinted at the image. There was something familiar about this face. He had seen it before, perhaps in some rogue's gallery of wanted criminals.

Grunting in dismissal, he started to crumple the paper in his hand, then thought better of it and smoothed it out on the table before folding it and putting it into his inner vest pocket. More than likely it held no importance, but it was evidence at a crime scene. He would take it back with him when he returned to Ulaanbaatar. If the face were publicized in the newspapers, perhaps someone would recognize it.

Virgin's Island

The enclosed transcriptions were made from documents discovered among the effects of Jeremy Neeley, a 34-year-old Anglican minister of Dartmouth, Nova Scotia, who is presently missing and presumed drowned. They were discovered the morning of May 27, 1935, in a sealed leather portfolio case found floating on the surface of the sea near the rock known locally as Virgin's Island, an unusual geological formation in the open Atlantic some 21 miles south from the mouth of Halifax harbor, and separated from the mainland by seven miles. Thomas Campbell, a lobster fisherman from the small fishing community of Hackett's Cove, spotted the portfolio while en route to examine his lobster traps and drew it out of the water on the end of a boat hook. Not knowing what to do with the leather case or its water-sodden contents, he turned them in to the nearest detachment of the Royal Canadian Mounted Police, who had them conveyed to the Public Archives at Dalhousie University for examination.

In this way the documents came into my possession. As a conservator who has frequently had to deal with mildewed or water-damaged papers over the years, I must admit that the initial appearance of the matted mass did not seem promising. I was unable to offer any assurances of success to RCMP Constable Henry Harris, who deposited the portfolio in my office here at the Archives Building, but I made the promise that I would do what lay within my power to render the documents readable. I am happy to report to the board that almost three-fourths of the leaves in the portfolio, amounting to 37 items, were salvageable. By good fortune Mr. Neeley used in his pen a permanent black ink that is uncommonly resistant to blurring.

The members of the board will find my transcriptions of the documents bundled in the same order they occupied in the portfolio.

The originals have been returned to the RCMP along with the leather case that held them and a copy of these transcriptions. Some of them are newspaper cuttings from various papers such as the Halifax *Morning Herald* and the *New York Times*. Other items are letters of correspondence with local historian and folklorist Dorothy Shriff, and with Clyde Evans, an amateur mountaineer and a resident of Montreal who achieved some notoriety towards the end of the last decade for his mountain-climbing expedition to the kingdom of Nepal. Evans has been reported missing and must be presumed to have perished in the sea along with Neeley. The rest of the documents consist of sundry notes made by Neeley in pencil on loose letter-sized sheets with a high linen rag content, and a kind of journal written in a hard-backed bound notebook, which I was forced to disassemble during my conservation efforts—individual leaves are counted as separate items.

The only other object in the portfolio was a bas-relief carving on one side of a thin ivory tablet approximately six inches tall and two inches wide (refer to the photograph enclosed with the transcripts). The back of the tablet is blank. Our biology department here at the university has been unable to identify the animal source for the ivory. The anthropology department reports that the carving resembles some of the religious art found among the tribes inhabiting the northern coast of Greenland that were discovered during Rasmussen's Second Thule Expedition of 1916—however, the resemblance is not exact. This carving was returned with the conserved documents and is presently in the hands of the RCMP in Halifax.

As to the full significance of these documents, I confess myself to be at a loss to offer an explanation. It is evident that Neeley suffered from some form of hallucination or delusion, perhaps brought on or at least exacerbated by exposure to the elements. Although the account in his journal is coherent, the subject matter itself demonstrates a lapse of sanity. There is an indication in one of the letters that for many years he was obsessed with Virgin's Island. From the point of view of local folklore the material is of sufficient interest that it is my recommendation to this board that efforts be made to secure the original documents and the ivory carving, along with the leather portfolio, from the Neeley family when the police have exhausted their efforts to locate Neeley's remains.

Written this day of June 9, 1935, by Herbert Moore, chief conservator of the Public Archives of Nova Scotia, Dalhousie University, Halifax.

Virgin's Island

Newspaper filler item clipped from the May 3, 1935, edition of the *New York Times:*

> Halifax, N. S.—Etched deeply into the face of an island which rises from the Atlantic surges off the S. coast of Nova Scotia 20 m. from Halifax is the strangest rock phenomenon that Canada boasts. Storm, sea and frost have graven into the solid cliff of what has come to be known as Virgin's Island an almost perfect outline of the Madonna with the Christ Child in her arms.
>
> The island has sheer and wave-bound sides, is a danger to ships, and is absolutely uninhabited. So far as is known, no human being has ever set foot on its shores.

Human interest piece from the Halifax *Morning Herald,* December 11, 1933:

> "Saluting the Lady" by Tom Thumm
>
> No one knows when the quaint practice of "saluting the Lady" began among the fishermen on this rugged part of our Nova Scotian coast, but one old Bluenoser reports hearing tales of the custom from his grandfather when he sat on the old man's knee. It appears to be a unique bit of the kind of local colour for which this Maritime Province is so justly famed, steeped in the past as we are by virtue of being one of the oldest settled regions in North America. Some say an Irish schooner captain named Burke started the custom around the middle of the last century, but other authorities stoutly maintain that it has been going on for at least two hundred years. Whatever its origins, it is a reality of the sea that no Maritime boat or ship will pass by the sheer east cliff face of Virgin's Island without sounding her horn in tribute. The direst misfortune is said to befall any scoffer foolish enough to ignore the salute. One long blast, three short blasts, and again one long—this our sea-faring men call "saluting the Lady," and they would no more omit this duty than they would give up their hot rum toddy.

Newspaper item from the *Yarmouth Telegram,* September 24, 1934:

> Longliner *Seaking* returning to Yarmouth from the Grand
> Banks, lost with all hands on the night of September 21 off
> the rock known as Virgin's Island, some 20 miles southeast
> of Halifax. Other ships in the area reported moderate seas
> and a wind from the northeast of seven knots. Skies were
> clear. A schooner, the *Mary Mae* out of Bangor bound for
> Sydney, reported strange lights on the uninhabited rock near
> where the misfortune is presumed to have occurred, but
> no connection between these lights and the sinking of the
> *Seaking* has been established. Further notices of this tragedy
> will be printed if more information becomes available.

Hand-written letter from Nova Scotian historian and author Dorothy
Shriff to Jeremy Neeley, dated March 29, 1935 [much of the text,
particularly on the second leaf, is blurred beyond recognition and
unrecoverable—*recommendation:* attempt to procure a clear copy from
the records of Dorothy Shriff]:

[first leaf]

> ... afraid that there is little more I can tell you concerning
> the folklore of the ocean oddity known locally as the Virgin's
> Island, but officially named Story Rock after Captain James
> Story of the Royal Navy, who discovered the island in 1681.
> Story reported that his ship, HMS *Antelope,* a 48-gun frigate
> of some 516 long tons, was making its way cautiously through
> a bank of fog when the sheer cliff of the island reared up
> immediately in front of her bow, extending higher than even
> the lookout on the mainmast could follow with his eyes.
> Story later would remark that "it seemed as though we had
> reached the very end of the world itself."
>
> He made immediate and strenuous efforts to turn the
> ship. One of the ordinary seamen, Jack Beckker by name, was
> lost over the side in the confusion and sank like a stone before
> anyone could throw him a line. Fortunately for the captain
> and his crew, the wind was on the port bow and he was able
> to tack off the cliff just in time to avoid a wreck. He wrote in

his ship's log, "The rock rises sheer from the sea, and when the wind is from the south-west the waves breaking upon it make scarce a sound that can be heard from further than thirty yards. Consequently the rock poses considerable danger to His Majesty's ships should they steer this course with greater frequency in the future, as seems likely given the prosperity of the Providence Plantations and Massachusetts Bay ..."

[second leaf]

... became broken-down with drink in later life, so his words are to be viewed with skepticism. Story's grandson averred that his grandfather never was able to get a full night of sleep after his near encounter with the rock, but that in his dreams he would return to that dreadful morning and watch as something unnatural that matched the color of the sea took Jack Beckker under the waves, while he stood (in the dream) paralyzed and unable to cry out or offer assistance ... [there is a considerable lacuna here]

... legend of the Micmac Indians reporting sightings from the mainland of strange lights on the wind-blown summit of the rock, lights that danced and ascended into the heavens ... Glooscap, their great hero, climbed the cliffs and fought such a fierce battle with an evil spirit that it made the island capsize and sink, but it rose again because the sea would not receive it ...

[the remainder of the two-page letter is illegible]

Carbon copy of a typed letter from Neeley to Clyde Evans dated November 1, 1934:

Dear Clyde,

It filled my heart with joy to read in your last letter that you wish to accompany me on my little expedition. When I wrote asking your expert advice concerning the equipment I would need to scale the cliff, I did not dare hope that you would offer to come along. It is a poor affair compared with your towering achievement in Nepal, to say nothing of your triumphs in the Andes three years ago. I confess, I was not looking forward to attempting the climb on my own, given my scant practical experience on sheer rock faces. You've put my mind at rest about reaching the top, and I can now turn my thoughts to what I must do when we get there.

In gratitude,
Jeremy Neeley

Typed letter from Clyde Evans to Neeley, dated November 7, 1934:

My dear chum,

You didn't think I'd let you attempt this harebrained stunt on your own? It would have been the same as murder. How could I live with myself if one of my old schoolmates came to grief only because I wouldn't lift a helping hand? To be honest, you've got my imagination working in top gear. This climb won't be such a snap as you seem to think, not even with me at the top of the rope. There's a reason Virgin's Island has never been climbed, you know, and it isn't just because the federal government has made it a bird sanctuary and declared it off limits. It's a damned difficult climb!

I've been looking at the photographs of the cliffs you sent, and I agree that the easiest route will probably be up the eastern face of the island, the side that bears the image—it's a little higher, but the fractured condition of the rock should provide better purchase. The real trick, you know, is going to be in transferring everything from the boat to the cliff. I'll get my affairs in order here in Montreal, and I'll let you know in a few months by post if I have a break in my schedule in the spring when we can attempt this mad expedition of yours, which you are so hell-bent on trying.

Your friend,
Clyde

Virgin's Island

Carbon copy of a typed letter from Neeley to Clyde Evans, dated January 30, 1935:

Dear Clyde,

In response to the curiosity expressed in your last missive as to my motivations, let me only say that Virgin's Island has become something of an obsession. I've been fascinated by the island since childhood. My uncle used to tell me fisherman's tales about its ghost lights and the evil misfortunes they brought unwary mariners who neglected to salute the Lady. For the past two years I've been studying everything ever written about the rock. I've even had dreams about it—real doozies, let me tell you. I can never remember them clearly when I wake up but I'm always covered in sweat and trembling like a leaf in a gale.

There's a family connection with the island, did you know? I'm a descendant on my mother's side of its discoverer, Captain James Story, whose grandson settled in Boston. At the time of the American Revolution, he and his family fled New England with the other Loyalists and came to Yarmouth. Eventually one of his descendants found his way to the Halifax region, where they've been ever since.

The truth of the matter is that I can't tell you why I must make this climb, because I don't know myself. Think of it as a kind of spiritual pilgrimage. In every man's life there are things he feels he must do, and this is one of mine. Ever since hearing the legends of Virgin's Island as a boy I've felt drawn to the place. I'm hoping that after I've climbed the cliff and walked around on top of the rock, I'll get it out of my system for good and all. It will be a relief not to be plagued any longer by these damned nightmares, which I believe are produced by the frustration of wanting to explore the rock but not being able to reach it.

I hope I haven't said too much—I don't want you to think that your old school chum's brain has turned mystical. We Anglican ministers are a hard-headed bunch, and more skeptical than most when it comes to superstitions.

Faithfully yours,
Jeremy

Handwritten letter in ink from Clyde Evans to Neeley, dated March 17, 1935:

Jerry,

Good news, old sport. I can positively guarantee two weeks of liberty in May, beginning on the 7th. How does this suit your plans? It better suit, because it's the only time I can find between my lecture tour and the Alaskan climb I've promised to lead. It's too bad it is so early in the year. The winds on that cliff are apt to be damned cold, and God help us if we tumble into the sea. But it's all I've got, old chap—let me know if it suits.

Clyde

The following two leaves of penciled notes in Neeley's hand were attached by a paper clip to three 9-inch by 12-inch aerial survey photographs of Virgin's Island showing the top of the island and the eastern and southern faces.

[notes, first leaf]

Island's overall shape is a surprisingly regular rectangle, apart from an indentation in the northern side, with the longest diagonal extending roughly from the southeast to the northwest. Total area, approximately eleven acres. Elevation above sea level, 956 feet along the eastern edge, declining to 795 feet on the western edge. All sides descend sheer into the ocean—there is no boat landing of any kind. The surface is too boulder-strewn and uneven to allow access by small aeroplane, and the unpredictable winds would preclude approach by dirigible, were anyone wealthy enough and foolish enough to try it.

Ecology consists of hardy low-lying plants, grasses and lichens in which numerous species of seabirds, chiefly razorbills, northern gannets, auks, puffins and herring gulls, make their nests. These birds also nest in fissures and on ledges of the vertical cliffs, and such is their variety and abundance that the island has been declared the most important Eastern Canadian seabird habitat south of Labrador.

Virgin's Island

Toward the centre of the island there is considerable rubble in the form of massive stones of roughly cubical dimensions that are tumbled together, giving the impression of some sort of intelligent pattern; however the sheer enormity of the stones seems to preclude this notion, which has been advanced by several writers of sensationalistic books on ancient civilizations, one of them James Churchward, author of well-known work *The Lost Continent of Mu*. (*Re:* Churchward's response to my letter of inquiry on October 3 of last year.)

[notes, second leaf]

The highest cliffs are oriented almost due east. (*Query:* Can this be coincidence?) When approached by sea from the east, the island rises above the horizon like a vast obelisk, and in the early morning light, shines red with the color of newly-splashed blood. The image of the Virgin fills two-thirds of the cliff surface, but it is only visible when the rays of the sun strike the rock from a more southerly direction, enhancing the irregularities in the stone with highlights and shadows. In the afternoon hours the image becomes entirely obscured by shadow.

Geologists dismiss the image as an optical illusion—James Churchward is of the contrary opinion that it was carved on the rock some 20,000 to 30,000 years in the past by an advanced civilization using some form of heat ray that fused the rock. (*Query:* Was the image made by Atlanteans? and if so, for what purpose?)

Image shows a seated woman in a hood and flowing robe, cradling a babe on her knee and gazing down at it. (*Item:* some fishermen have reported that on the day of the summer solstice, when the light is at precisely the correct angle, the face of the figure changes to resemble a skull, and the babe becomes something inhuman. Only a handful of the many thousands who have viewed the image claim to have witnessed this effect, which is rudely denied by other fishermen for whom the image is sacred, or at least forbidden to criticize.)

Typed letter from James Churchward to Jeremy Neeley, dated October 3, 1934:

Dear Mr. Neeley,

Many thanks for your kind praise regarding my books. A writer is always gratified when his work meets with the approval of readers, particularly when they display a grasp of the subject matter as you have done.

As to your specific question about the origin of the astonishing icon known as the Madonna of the Atlantic— yes, I do believe that the image was artificially created at some period in the prehistoric past, and that it long antedates the Pyramids of Giza, and even the Sphinx which is so much older than the Pyramids. We can only speculate as to how such an enormous image might be created, but I believe that it was done by means of chromatic rays that had as their power source energized crystals with the property of magnifying the light of the sun.

To us, it is an image of the Madonna with Child, but you must realize that to the ancient Egyptians it would have appeared to be Isis holding on her knee the babe Horus; the Hindus might have interpreted it as Krishna in the arms of Devaki. The image is not Christian as such, but is a universal image of nurture and motherhood. We tend to interpret it as the Virgin Mary with the baby Jesus only because we have been conditioned by religious art to think of it in these terms.

At some time in the future I hope to make a closer study of Virgin's Island for a book dealing with the ancient lost civilization of Greenland. Perhaps we will meet in your native city of Halifax. In the meantime, I do thank you again for you interest in my work.

Yours sincerely,
James Churchward

Virgin's Island

Single leaf of sundry notes in pencil. They appear to be random jottings.

Propitiation: the act of pacifying, appeasing, or conciliating a god with offerings and sacrifices, in order to win the favor of the god, or to regain the good will of the deity.

Euphemism: an auspicious term substituted in place of an inauspicious term. Example—the Greek Furies were called the *Erinyes* (Angry Ones), but were often referred to euphemistically as the *Eumenides* (Gracious Ones) as a superstitious way of turning aside their wrath.

Second example—the fairies of Celtic mythology were greatly feared and dreaded, but were sometimes addressed aloud as the "Good Folk" as a way of pacifying their malice.

High Places: gods of the pagan world were often worshipped on high places such as treeless mountaintops. Witches assembled on sabbat festivals on high places. Refer to the Brocken, Hartz Mountain Range; also the Blocksberg; Heuberg; Lyderhorn in Norway; refer to "Night on Bald Mountain" by Mussorgsky.

Oracular dreaming: the practice of receiving oracles in the form of dream images or messages. It was believed that the gods communicated with men through their dreams, and that to be chosen for such messages was a singular blessing.

Mother Goddess forms: Isis; Astarte; Ceres; Virgin Mary; Matronit; Shakti
Mother of monsters: Tiamat
Mother of abortions: Lilith; Hecate

The remaining document is a dated journal of the climbing expedition to Virgin's Island, written in Reverend Neeley's own hand in a hardback bound notebook. The paper is of excellent quality, and the permanent black ink has not blurred to any appreciable degree. I will refrain from commenting about the contents of the journal, as it is not my place to do so, but will observe that folklorists may find the material fascinating, should the board determine to acquire the notebook for the Archives.

Journal of Rev. Jeremy Neeley

May 9

We set out for Virgin's Island from the small fishing port of East Dover before first light. The boat had sat tied to the dock, prepared and waiting for the run, for the past five days. No one was up and about when we left due to the early hour, but the villagers will see my black Packard coupé parked up the road and notice that the boat is missing. I've told nobody where I'm going, and gave a false name when renting the boat. What Clyde and I intend to do is against federal law, and because of my position as a member of the clergy I couldn't risk being betrayed to the Mounties. I doubt any of the villagers would talk—they engage in a fair amount of smuggling and are not fond of the police—but it pays to be cautious.

Had another of those damned dreams with the deep, throbbing roars and menacing shadows last night but said nothing about it to Clyde at breakfast. His mind was filled with the details of the expedition and I daresay he didn't even notice my subdued manner. He's the least introspective human being I've ever known, and lives as much in the present moment as any of his Viking ancestors. I let him take the tiller of the Johnson Sea Horse outboard and we putted out of the harbour over water as flat as a pane of glass, the little four-horsepower engine moving us smartly along. The outboard is only a few years old and should be reliable—the owner of the boat assured me that it would not quit on us.

Conditions couldn't have been more benign. The air was warm for this time in the spring and there was almost no wind. Both of us were dressed for the worst the Atlantic could throw at us. I suppose the East Dover fishermen would have laughed to see us go out, bundled up as we were, but they wouldn't have known that we intended to stay overnight, and perhaps longer, on an exposed rock in all kinds of weather.

When we hit the swell of the open ocean the breeze freshened. I was glad I had let Clyde handle the boat. I concentrated on not losing my sausages and scrambled eggs, and kept us pointed in the right direction with my liquid-filled pocket compass. Virgin's Island can be seen from the heights of some points on the mainland, but not from our port of departure. I confess, my heart thundered in my chest when it came into view. It is impressive enough in photographs, but when first seen with the naked eye it almost appears supernatural, so strangely does it rise up from the deep, like the lone tombstone of some giant in an endless watery graveyard.

We had to round the shoulder of the island to reach the eastern face. As we did so, we saw the towering expanse of the cliff blood red in the rising sun. A thrill went through me such as I have never before experienced, a mingling of expectation with dread, and a kind of fatalistic relief that the long waiting was at last over. The image of the Madonna and Child was not yet visible, which was a pity, I reflected to myself, since by the time it became highlighted by the angle of the rising sun we would be too close to the cliff to really appreciate its beauty. White-feathered gulls dipped and wheeled above us as we approached the monolith, the air filled with their indignant cries. I was glad that I had decided to wear my canvas fishing hat.

As agreed, we selected the most likely landing spot and worked the boat in with the emergency oars to secure it to the rock face. The rise and fall of the boat on the gentle swell made me queasy again but I tried to give no sign of it. Below the high mark of the waves the cliff was cloaked in a thick mat of dark-green seaweed that smelled strongly of salt. Clyde deftly transferred himself to the rock and clung on its side like a fly, with his left hand wedged in a fissure. With the other hand he inserted steel eye-loops into narrow cracks in the stone, and drove them home with a hammer that was lashed by a cord around his wrist.

Never was I more thankful that he had decided to accompany me. I doubt I could have done what he did. At last the lines were attached to the bow and stern, and the rubber tires draped over the landward side of the boat to absorb the inevitable shocks when the waves sent it against the rock. It was impossible to moor the boat firmly against the rock due to the rise and fall of the waves, to say nothing of the tides, but we did the best we could to make it secure and safe.

As I write these words sitting in the stern, Clyde is working his way up the first pitch, driving in pitons and trailing hemp rope behind him. Soon I will begin to inch my way up the cliff. We both have heavy packs, but plan to pull them up on lines as we go. Clyde is completely at home on the rock face. I can hear him whistling to himself, so still is the sea. The wind must be from another direction, for there isn't a trace of it in the boat. It really is a fine morning. Even so, I have checked the floatation compartments to make certain they are tight. This boat will not sink, even should the waves capsize it. Just as well, since it is our only way back to the mainland.

(later)

We completed the climb without mishap. As I sit here cross-legged on the top of the cliff, facing the open ocean with my journal on my knee, my pen so trembles with excitement that I can scarce still it enough to write these words. The object of my enthusiasm is before my eyes, resting in the crease between the pages of my journal. It scarcely seems real, yet there it is. But I must record its finding in proper order and not let my wonder and delight carry me away.

I found the climb arduous but manageable. I have often climbed the mountains of Cape Breton as a recreation, but have seldom faced sheer walls such as this one, and I confess that I was nervous at the beginning, but this soon passed thanks to Clyde's expert lead. As the sun rose and began to move more southwardly in the heavens, shadows showed themselves on the warming rock face. By bracing my feet against the cliff and leaning backward on the rope, I could make out above me the curve of the Virgin's shoulder and the rounded head of the Christ child. At that distance there was no definition in the features of the infant's face.

What people think they see in the features is mostly an illusion, I think, similar to the illusion of the so-called man in the moon, which looks nothing like a man. Psychologists have determined that our minds are ordered in such a way that we automatically seek to perceive the human face and the human form in abstract patterns and textures. The detail that passersby on ships think they see in the image of the Madonna is a product of their own expectations, projected onto the random patches of light and shade on the cliff.

The birds proved a constant distraction. Their shrill cries never ceased, and they swooped and soared quite near to us as they passed, agitated by our inexplicable presence in their world, where no human being had ventured before, or at the very least, where no human had ventured for many centuries, if the legend of Glooscap is to be given credence. Following with my gaze one uncommonly aggressive northern gannet that flew close over my head, I saw it vanish, seemingly into the face of the cliff above. I knew this could not be, and fixed the location in my memory, then as I ascended, worked my way across toward the spot, insofar as the rope set in the stone by Clyde would allow lateral progress.

In this way I found the recess in the cliff that Clyde had missed, for he had made his ascent some three yards to the left of the opening. When I pulled myself up level with it I got a bad fright. I had forgotten the bird in my excitement. Of course it was still in the recess, hidden by shadow. It exploded out at my face with a thunder of wings and a shrill scream. My grip on the rope faltered and I slipped several feet before I caught myself. The abrupt drop had the useful consequence of sending the bird harmlessly over the top of my hat, but it made my heart freeze for a full beat.

Pulling myself back up, I peered into the shadowed opening. It was curiously regular, as though it had been cut or bored into the rock by some artificial means. In size it was some two feet high and eight or nine inches across. I glanced up. Clyde had stopped and was gazing down on me with curiosity, his face framed against the sky in the golden halo of his curling blond hair. I waved to show that nothing was wrong, and put my hand into the opening. Amid the bird droppings and bits of browning grasses I felt a nest that was deep enough to be concealed from sight. It was not the sort of nest we encounter in our walks through the woods on the mainland, but was merely an irregular mat of fibers. My fingers brushed an egg, still warm from the breast of the absent and very annoyed mother.

With care I extended my arm as far into the cavity as I could reach and felt beyond the prickly twigs and straw of the nest to the space behind it. I thought it was empty and was about to withdraw my hand, when I brushed something that felt like a flat piece of wood. I drew it out and saw that it was, of all things, a small ivory carving! You may imagine my astonishment. Several times I turned it in my hand, then realized the risk I was taking and with the greatest care slid it into the deep pocket of my trousers. Had it slipped from my fingers, it would have been lost forever. I spent several minutes feeling around blindly in the cavity but discovered nothing else, not even beneath the nest, which I felt obliged to move since I could not risk missing anything that might be beneath it. Apart from the carving and the nest, the recess was empty.

Busy with the packs, Clyde had not noticed me draw forth the ivory tablet. I decided to refrain from mentioning the find until we could examine it together. Twenty minutes later, I found myself standing on the comparatively level stone surface of the summit, which in that wind-blown place was bare of grasses. Clyde was hauling up my pack. I did not disturb his work, but leaned out and gazed down at the boat, no larger than a postage stamp against the emerald-green waves of the sea. A few puffy clouds hung along the distant eastern horizon, but otherwise, the sky was a glorious blue vault.

The panoramic view was extraordinary, made all the more so with the knowledge that I was only the second man to see it in modern history—Clyde having seen it first. To the east and south stretched the uninterrupted rim of the Atlantic. I turned in a slow circle and gazed across the island, its green expanse descending gradually to the western edge. Beyond, I could see the misty coastline of Nova Scotia, diminishing to invisibility as it extended northward. It had a bluish coloring. The island itself was a jumble of irregular stones covered with green grasses, lichen, and scatterings of white and blue wild flowers, over which hopped and walked and sat such a profusion of seabirds as I had never seen before. Every so often a flock of them would rise up into the air and mill about before settling once more. As they did so, the squawking swelled to a deafening level, then diminished, resembling the sound of a wave breaking on the rocks of a beach.

Toward the center of the island I saw the mounds of tumbled stone blocks that were so evident in the aerial survey photographs. I confess my disappointment, for at this near distance they bore no resemblance to any habitation, not even one fallen to ruin, but merely appeared to be a natural formation. White droppings from the birds frosted their planes and angles like drifts of snow. I might have wandered down among them immediately, but my mind was still on the carving, and on who could have placed it into the high recess of the cliff, which was almost 500 feet above the sea.

Stepping away from the edge, I drew the carved piece of greenish ivory from my pocket. The top of the tablet was tapered in the form of a shallow pointed arch, so that in overall shape and proportion it somewhat resembled a Gothic church window, although no Gothic architecture ever used an arch that flat. The elongated aperture of the recess in the cliff had also had an arched top with similar proportions.

"Hullo? What have you got there, old chap?" Clyde asked, coming over.

I told him how I had discovered the little carving. He took it and held it up to the sun, then tossed it in his hand in a way that made me cringe.

"Be careful," I warned him. "It's absolutely priceless."

With an easy smile he gave it back to me and clapped me good-naturedly on the shoulder.

"A little souvenir to remember the expedition, eh?"

He left me to ponder the tablet and went back to the packs. Looking at it now as it rests like a little ivory bookmarker on the page of the open journal spread across my right knee, I am filled with a sense of sacred reverence. It depicts in bas-relief a highly stylized version of the tableau that adorns the cliff face, and appears to my judgment to be none other than the Madonna seated on a high-backed throne with the Christ child on her knee. The two human figures are delineated with uncouth angles and strange proportions, yet their general posture can be puzzled out after some squinting. However, the bone structure of their faces is very badly executed, so that they almost seem two distorted masks. Across the square back of the Holy Virgin's throne, which projects some distance above her head, are engraved markings, quite deeply incised as though with a jeweler's wheel. They seem to be some sort of hieroglyphic writing, but they are like no script I have ever seen.

The style of the bas-relief image, with its rounded limbs and conventionalized features, reminds me of Eskimaux soapstone carving, but it is not Eskimaux art, or the art of any other primitive culture that I recognize. It seems to be completely new—or rather, very old. It is almost abstract, like some pagan Picasso. The ivory resembles elephant tusk and is uncommonly hard, like glass under my fingernail. It shines in the sunlight with a satiny greenish lustre, semi-translucent. The tablet is more weighty than I would expect of ordinary ivory.

It's a curious thing to relate in the chill rationality of written words, but when I look away from it, the memory of it in my mind appears to dance. That is, the memory of the image seems to show a standing figure frozen in the act of some sort of ritual dance. Yet when I return my gaze to the carving, I cannot make out any trace of a dancing figure, only the enthroned Madonna and Child. I must put the carving away safely in my pocket. I tremble to think of its value to anthropology. My guess is that it represents some hitherto unknown native culture, unless perchance it is an artifact from lost Atlantis. The thought makes me smile, but I do not entirely dismiss the possibility.

(later)

Clyde and I have explored the island. With one exception there is little enough to see. We first walked the perimeter, which drops sheer to the sea like the eastern cliff, and is swept clean for several yards in from the edge by the wind and rain, giving a secure enough footing for those who are not inclined to vertigo. But the stench—there are bird droppings everywhere. We thought we had smelled the worst of it during the climb up the face, but once we descended from the height of the eastern ridge and put the body of the island between our noses and the sea breeze, the full odour of the place became evident. I don't believe I've ever breathed in anything quite so foul. Or in this instance, so fowl, if you will forgive my pun.

When we turned our progress toward the center of the island, we had to watch our feet and take care to step around the nests. For the most part the birds behaved well and got out of our way, although they gave shrill voice to their disapproval. Thank heavens not all the species are nesting. It was only when we drew near the stone blocks and I looked up at them that I began to realize how large they were. Each was the size of a small house. I could almost fancy that I saw signs of tool marks on their lichen-mottled sides, but the impressions were too widely spaced to have been made by any chisels used by men, so I dismissed the notion.

We found that we could walk through gaps under and amid the stones. They leaned at crazy angles above our heads, forming a maze of passages and grassy open courtyards. They gave shelter from the wind and muted the cries of the birds, which for some reason did not descend to the grass between them. The dark shadows and abrupt turns began to play on my nerves. Clyde may have felt it also, for he was uncommonly silent. The sensation was almost palpable, a kind of dream that is sometimes felt when entering an ancient tomb or holy place.

Toward the midst of the great stones the ground opened into a kind of meadow that was shaped like a boat, narrow at each end and wider in the centre, where we saw there was a sizeable hole. We approached its edge cautiously.

"Watch where you put your feet," Clyde said. "The lip may be undercut."

I inched forward beside him, leaning out and craning my neck to see the bottom of the depression. The realization grew on me that it did not have a discernible bottom. It dropped straight down like a well, its rim almost a perfect circle. With Clyde holding onto my wrist with both hands, I leaned further out over the edge. The most perfect blackness greeted my gaze.

"I don't see a bottom," I told him. My voice echoed up from the dark into my ears.

He pulled me back, looked around in the grass for a pebble, and flipped it into the hole. It ticked once against the side. We listened for half a minute but never heard it again.

"Why doesn't this show up on the aerial photograph?" he mused.

"It probably does," I said. "The centre of the island is a patchwork of shadows cast by the blocks."

When I went back later to fetch my leather folder, I took out the aerial photo and examined it. Sure enough, the mouth of the hole was readily visible, once I knew where to look and what I was looking for. It was partially obscured by a spear-like shadow from the corner of one of the blocks.

As leader, Clyde decided that it would be best for us to set up camp in the central clearing in the midst of the blocks. I didn't argue, since it was a sensible course. The blocks provided shelter from the wind, which began to increase as the afternoon wore on. It howled in the most dismal manner through the accidental channels and archways. Privately, however, I was unhappy at the plan, and would have preferred to erect the tent somewhere else. The clearing and the hole gave me the willies. Every time I turned my back on the pit, I got the irrational crawling sensation between my shoulder blades that something was climbing out.

May 10
Early morning. The air is still chilly, and the jagged shadows keep the dew from drying on the grass. I'm worried. Clyde has decided to descend into the hole to explore its depths. I should have seen it coming. How could he resist the challenge? He absolutely refuses to allow me to descend with him, so I will have to wait on the surface for him to emerge. Right now he's fixing breakfast on the little alcohol stove.

A plane just went past overhead, very high up. I doubt its pilot spotted our tent, lost as it is amid the shadows. We are very tiny on this vast rock, itself only a speck in the immensity of the Atlantic. Greater than the mighty ocean is the sea of time on which we float, unbounded and infinite. Who knows what wonders, what horrors, may have transpired in the dim past, before our race stood erect? Who can guess at the mysteries of the future, when we and all our works are passed away and the sun itself grows old?

The morbidity of my musings destroys my appetite, which should be ravenous, but I will force myself to eat something so that Clyde does not notice how morose his old school friend has become. What, you ask, set my mind on such a depressing train of thought?

Last night in the tent my dreams were troubled. This is often the case lately, but last night it was much worse. The cliff face loomed over me as I clung to it like a spider on a thread, and the inhuman faces carved into its surface became animated with some kind of malign awareness. They glared down at me as though in outrage at my hubris. I can't remember what they looked like, but their eyes burned with a kind of balefire, and they had teeth, or rather fangs, that were needle-sharp and extended inward around the perimeter of their circular mouths. I realized with dread that the teeth were in the sides of the pit and reached over to wake Clyde, but his sleeping bag was filled with dry bones that rattled under my touch.

In the midst of this nightmare, suddenly I knew why the little ivory carving had provoked the impression of a dancing figure. The awareness woke me. I lay in the dark, shivering and covered in cold sweat. Clyde's soft snores sounded beside me through the blackness. With care so as not to wake him, I found the tablet where I had put it between the pages of my journal, then located my flashlight. I hunched my back to Clyde to shield the light and switched it on, masking most of its brightness with my fingers. I let the light play across the carving. In the moving beam, it seems alive. The outline of the Madonna and Christ child were clearly delineated by the glancing shadows.

With great deliberation, my fingers trembling, I angled the beam from the flashlight to the side and rotated the carving upside down. What I saw made me unconsciously stop my breath. It leapt forth in perfect clarity. There could be no doubt—it was a solitary standing figure, but not that of a human being. The bas-relief contours of its body danced before my eyes with a kind of obscene glee. As I gazed upon it in the glow from the flashlight, I could not have said with any assurance what it represented—perhaps a mythological creature with something resembling legs and a head, but the upper limbs, if they were limbs, were oddly angled and did not come from the torso at the shoulders.

The figure stood hunched over, as though crouching or stooping on a small stone pedestal carved beneath its bent legs, though exactly where its legs ended and its feet began, I could not discern. What I had earlier mistaken for the projecting high back of a throne upon which the Madonna sat was actually this cubic pedestal, its exposed side covered with the hieroglyphics of some forgotten language. After comparing the two images in the light, I began to suspect that the Madonna and Child was no more than an optical illusion, a chance occurrence of lines that the mind seized upon and transformed into the familiar icon when the true image was inverted.

I have kept this revelation to myself thus far this morning. Why, I don't really know, but I am reluctant to talk about it. Even the thought of what the image on the eastern cliff of this island would be, were it somehow possible to rotate and invert the cliff, causes a kind of sickness inside me. What would the passing fishermen do, I wonder, if they realized the kind of horror they are saluting with their boat whistles? Would they continue in the superstition, or would they creep past in fearful silence?

There is a strangeness in the birds. Yesterday my mind was elsewhere and I failed to notice, but this morning it is all too obvious. They watch. Their tiny eyes hold an unnatural awareness, a kind of ancient, wicked knowing that I do not like because it reminds me of my nightmares. What strange sights have been seen by the countless generations of their distant ancestors? What things once crept between these massive stone blocks that were so terrifying, they still refuse to alight amid the grass?

As eager as I was to get onto this island, I think I will be even more eager to leave it, when I can persuade Clyde that he has done enough exploring. The lure of the hole is irresistible to him. No point in even suggesting that we return to the boat before he descends into it, but once he has had a good look around, I will bring up the subject of going back to the mainland at the earliest opportunity. Something informs me that it will be best not to linger here on this island. The foreboding that prickles on the back of my neck will not go away, but only becomes stronger.

(later)

Clyde is lost. There is no other reasonable conclusion to reach. I blame myself for not speaking out about my misgivings, or trying to prevent his descent into this accursed abyss. I could have stopped him had I tried strenuously enough, and he would still be alive, but I said nothing because I did not wish to seem like an old woman in his eyes, and now he is dead. The best friend of my childhood, dead because of my indecisiveness and pride. I will always blame myself.

The descent began well enough. Clyde started down the rope in good spirits around nine o'clock. He had let down 300 feet, and had another 200 coiled at his waist. We both knew his camp flashlight was inadequate to the task, but it was better than mine. He promised that if he found anything interesting, we would climb down together to examine it. I did not respond, but at that moment there was nothing in the world that filled me with such horror as the thought of descending into that black hole. The birds perched on the stone blocks watched him disappear below the rim into darkness with their alien, evil gaze. They began to cackle softly among themselves, fluttering their wings in the breeze, and I thought of vultures that sit so patiently and wait for death.

An hour passed before I began to feel nervous about

Clyde's situation. Going to the black mouth of the hole, I shouted his name down into it. My voice echoed from the walls, giving me reason to believe that it had penetrated to a great depth. There was no answering call. When I tried the rope, I found it slack. I did not dare to pull it up, since I did not wish Clyde to return to it and find it missing. I waited another two hours while the sky became increasingly overcast. Around noon it started to rain. I took refuge beneath the overhanging side of a tilted stone block and watched the mouth of the hole, my heart as cold as the rain itself.

Even had he found something of great interest in the depths, it seemed unlikely that he would remain below for more than three hours. He would realize that I would become worried, and would not wish me to start down after him. This was the line of my reasoning. Odds were that he had suffered an accident, or at least a difficulty of some sort. It was time for me to investigate. At this point my assumption was that Clyde had been injured—that it might be far worse had not yet occurred to me. Stiffening my resolve, I forced myself back to the edge of the abyss. First I reeled up the rope to determine if it had been cut by a sharp edge of rock. It was uncut and was its full 300 feet in length. After measuring it with the span of my arms, I let it fall back into the hole, and set about preparing myself for the rappel into the darkness.

As is true of all forms of climbing, going down is easier than going up, at least when ropes are used. The rappel is a technique wherein the climber allows the rope to slip slowly through loops in his harness in a controlled fashion, while walking backwards down the sheer face with his body in a prone position. It can be done rapidly in a series of kicks by an expert, but I took my time, not knowing what mishap might have befallen Clyde, who was so much more skilled than myself. Every ten yards, I stopped and shined my camp flashlight around on the rock walls of the hole, which was almost a perfect cylinder, broken only at intervals by small fissures and hollows where the rock had sheeted away, probably due to the cumulative action of expanding ice during the winters.

The flashlight proved woefully inadequate. Its beam seemed to simply fade to nothingness beyond a range of thirty feet or so. I became conscious of a dull moaning or roaring sound that rose and fell with an irregular rhythm. It crossed my thoughts that it might be Clyde's voice, distorted by echoes, but I dismissed the idea immediately—the moan was too deep to be made by a human throat. A chill penetrated my entire body as I realized its source—it was the island itself that moaned, the sound generated by the action of moving water or wind in some deep channel. This hole was the island's throat, and the sound was its voice.

By this time I was soaked to the skin by the rain. It did not fall directly on me once I had descended a few dozen yards, for it was falling at a slight angle, but it ran down the sides of the hole, and down the rope, and I found it impossible not to come into contact with it. It was a miserable situation, but my thoughts were on Clyde, not on myself. At a hundred yards, I came to the end of my rope. I need hardly say that the end had a knot tied in it, so that it was impossible that it could slip through my climbing harness. Clyde would never have fallen in such a fashion, and I did not entertain the notion for an instant.

The beam of the flashlight revealed a gleaming piton hammered into one of the fissures in the rock, and tied to its eye-loop, another length of climbing rope—the 200-foot-long line Clyde had taken on his belt. Transferring myself from one to the other rope was not an easy task, particularly since there was no purchase of any kind other than the steel spike to which the second line was tied. I managed it awkwardly, after coming quite near to falling on one occasion. I continued down the second line. At spaced intervals I shouted Clyde's name at the top of my lungs. There was no point in calling for him continuously—I would have gone hoarse in the space of a few minutes. I saved my voice, and when I called, I called with all the volume I could muster. The echoes dancing around my head were the only response, apart from the deep, almost subsonic moan of the island, which became louder as I climbed down.

At some point I became aware that the air was moving. I felt it against my dripping face when I looked into the blackness below. Looking up was like looking at the full moon in a night sky with no stars. The roaring moan seemed close. It beat rhythmically on my eardrums and in my chest. I continued the descent, and very nearly came to a bad end. The rope had no knot at its termination. By chance I felt its smooth end slide through my fingers before it reached my harness, and stopped myself in time. I knotted the end with one hand, then took out my flashlight and switched it on.

My thoughts were chaotic. How could Clyde have failed to knot the end of the second line? Was it possible that he had simply slipped off into the darkness below? It was incredible to me that so skilled an expert could make such an error. I refused to believe it. Shining the beam of my flashlight downward, for a few moments I saw only the same unvarying darkness. Then something massive rushed toward me from the depths, driving the air before it into a rising wind. It was dark and amorphous, and filled the shaft from side to side. Before I could react, with a groan it just as rapidly withdrew, leaving the featureless black behind. My mind was frozen with fear, so that I did not think to try to climb. After the passage of fifteen or twenty seconds, it came rushing up again, and I realized that it was the sea.

Some opening at the base of the island, probably beneath the surface of the waves since no opening showed up in survey photographs, was funneling water into the middle of the island under pressure. As the passage which led to the base of the hole narrowed, the pressure of the water increased, so that it was forced upwards in the hole for a considerable distance at each wave, or each flux of sea current, whichever drove the phenomenon.

The reason I was able to make this deduction so quickly is that we have a similar thing in Nova Scotia, though on a much smaller scale, at a series of sea caves that are called the Ovens. The waves drive into the cave, and as the cave narrows, the air is trapped in the rear and creates a curious booming roar, like the discharge of a cannon. The movement of the water causes a kind of wind that is felt by those who stand on the lookout inside the largest of these sea caves. The water rising and falling in the hole was driven by a similar mechanism, though on a much larger scale.

There had to be more at work that just the action of the waves and ocean currents, I realized upon reflection. The column of water was rising several hundred feet above sea level. Perhaps some undersea vent released bursts of superheated steam at regular intervals that drove the water into the narrowing channel, then upward along the vertical cylinder of the hole. Whatever the cause, it was surely one of the most extraordinary natural wonders in the world, and until now had been completely unknown.

The surge upward of the sea was hypnotic. It did not always rise to the same level, but varied in height to a considerable degree. I wondered if Clyde had been caught by an unusually high surge and pulled from his line? Shining the flashlight around, I almost missed the opening in the far side of the hole, somewhat above the level of my head. It was a kind of doorway with a pointed and very shallow arch at the top. Even though badly weathered, it was obvious that it must be artificial. The dimensions of the opening were unnaturally tall and narrow. There was a kind of writing around the carved frame of the opening. My excitement intensified as I recognized the same hieroglyphic script that was on the ivory tablet. Indeed, the shape of the tablet resembled the shape of the archway.

Clyde's flashlight was more powerful than mine—he would have seen the opening much more readily. I shone my light around the walls, and saw the gleam of polished steel. A series of pitons had been set into the wall of the hole at roughly the same level leading from the rope to the archway. My friend's work. He had reasoned that it was easier for him to set the spikes into the wall, than it would be to climb out of the hole, move the first rope to the other side, and climb back down. The mystery of the missing knot was solved. He must have untied it to slide the rope out of his harness once he was hanging from the eye-loop of the first piton.

The traverse which my friend would have found a simple exercise was for me fraught with difficulty and considerable danger. I ascended back up the rope to the level of the archway and began the arduous transfer from the rope to the steel spikes. It took me a full twenty minutes to cross the ten yards of spikes, whereas Clyde could probably have done it in less than two minutes, once the spikes were set in the wall.

Only when I stood upright in the high-roofed passage leading into the rock did I pause to consider the possible meaning of the archway. Someone, or something, had built it. The dimensions did not seem suited to the human form, but might be well adapted to the crouching thing on the ivory tablet. Those inhabiting this island must have used the opening to gain access to the island's moaning throat, where its gorge rose and fell. For what possible purpose? Perhaps it was only because I have served before the altar of the Anglican Church for almost a decade, with its rich tradition of ritual observances, but my mind turned immediately to sacrifice. Could this tunnel have a religious significance? At the time I could not imagine any other purpose for which it might have been carved.

I had come to this island as a Christian pilgrim seeking to offer, in my own small way, homage to the Madonna and her precious gift to the world, only to discover that this was a pagan place, or perhaps even a place alien to this world, for what was the thing depicted on the ivory tablet, and on the inverted cliff face, if not an alien being? In past centuries it would have been called a demon or devil, but the enlightenment of our present age admits no such nomenclature. Yet its sheer otherness is evident in every line of its image.

My arms trembled with fatigue but I did not pause to rest. If Clyde was somewhere down the passage, injured, he would need immediate attention. I went along it as quickly as I dared by flashlight. The batteries were new, but would not last forever. The floor of the passage sloped downward— by how much was impossible to determine, since I had no reference, but it was not enough to sweep me off my feet. I noticed that the floor was free of dust, which puzzled me for a time, until I reasoned that during storms, the water in the hole might rise high enough to flood the tunnel, and would run down the slope carrying the dust with it. This had not occurred recently since the walls and floor were quite dry.

The passage ended on a Y-intersection with two other passages of similar dimensions, one that sloped downward to the left, and the other upward to the right. I stood perplexed, wondering which way to search, and realized that I would have to search both sides. I took the left way and soon found myself confronted by another branching. The sense of dread that I had pushed deep into the background of my thoughts over concern for Clyde's safety surged forth. What if I became lost in a warren of diverging passageways? Was that the fate that had befallen my friend?

The obvious precaution was to mark my route as I went, so that I could find my way back to the hole. I took out my climbing ax and looked around for a suitable place to strike a distinguishing mark on the lip of the passage from which I had emerged. My heart leapt with hope when I saw a chip in the stone that had been newly-made by a sharp steel point. Clyde had thought of the same precaution and had acted on it. There was no need to mark my way—I had only to follow his markings, and they would lead me to him.

I took the left passage and followed it to a blank wall of stone, where the workers digging it had simply stopped for whatever reason and abandoned it. Retracing my steps, I took the right passage and was rewarded by another of Clyde's marks at the next junction. In this way I progressed deeper into the intestines of the island, as I fancifully called the passageways. Clyde had chosen a downward course. The need to search back and forth to locate his marks on the stone proved increasingly frustrating, as my apprehension for my own safety mounted, and I'm afraid that I found myself cursing him under my breath for venturing so deep into the belly of the beast.

The air grew moist and warm, with a warmth that seemed artificial. It occurred to me that it might be geothermal in origin, part of the same process that drove the column of sea water so far up the islands's throat. I began to encounter side chambers showing signs of former habitation, some of them containing strange furnishings the function of which I could not conceive. One item I paused to examine might have been a bed, or a chair, or a table, or none of these things. The lingering scents on the air made my stomach roll. They were not bad smells, merely unfamiliar, with a depth of unfamiliarity that I have never before experienced. They called forth no image, real or imagined, in my thoughts. It was impossible to tell whether the rooms had been abandoned for five minutes or five centuries, but it was evident that the water making its way from the surge in the hole during storms must be diverted elsewhere by the slopes of the intervening passages, for there was no sign of flooding.

When I noticed that the beam of my flashlight was not so bright as before, my nerve almost failed me. I could never hope to find my way up through the maze of passages without a light. Just as I was about to turn back in despair, I heard faintly in the distance before me a cry that sounded human.

"Clyde! Steady, old man," I shouted. "I'm on my way."

I started forward, when something happened that drained all strength from my legs, so that I collapsed to my knee. The beam of my flashlight dimmed to a fraction of its brightness, and then for a few terrible seconds, failed utterly, leaving me in a darkness that was blacker than anything I had ever experienced or could have imagined possible. I found myself making noises in the depths of my throat as I shook the flashlight. It flared to a dim and unstable yellow glow. Regaining my footing, I stood with my back braced against a wall of the passage, gasping shallow breaths, icy sweat sprouting from my armpits, a kind of sickness twisting my groin and making my stones draw upward.

Again came the cry—weak, distant. I took a step toward the sound, and the flashlight flickered once, just once, for half a second. My nerve broke. I found myself running wildly back the way I had come, searching desperately for the marks in the stone Clyde had made, my breaths clicking in my throat. I'm embarrassed to say that I may have gone a little mad for a time. The next think I knew, I was climbing, climbing, up the ropes, climbing out of the mouth of hell with Clyde's weak cry still in my ears. Surely, I am damned for this act of cowardice. There is no doubt in my mind but that I am damned for eternity.

I write this in my journal alone in the tent, the rain falling with soft pats on the canvas. Night descends. The birds that were perched on the great stone blocks have vanished—they must withdraw to places of refuge when darkness approaches. I only wish there were a refuge for my soul.

(later)

A nightmare woke me. In it I saw Clyde's face, covered in blood, his blue eyes staring at me with mute accusation. There were shadow beings surrounding him, and they were doing things to his body, unspeakable and monstrous things that my mind refuses to remember. In my memory is the image of a blood-stained lute—but it is not a lute, it is some part of Clyde stretched and spread upon a metal frame, and one of the horrors is stroking the strings of the lute with a chitinous appendage, and Clyde is screaming, his cries breaking into different tones almost like a kind of Satanic music. When I woke, I thought I could hear them echoing from the hole, but I believe it was only a dream memory. I write by the light of my flashlight, in which I replaced the old batteries with new ones.

I have been thinking about the inverted image on the carving. Why would those who made the larger image on the east cliff have carved it upside down? It makes no sense—unless, it was carved into the cliff upright, and some titanic geological upheaval inverted the entire island. I'm not a geologist, so I don't even know if such a thing is possible, but if it were so, it would mean that the top of the island is really the bottom, and that by climbing down into the hole Clyde was really climbing upward to its former summit. The idea makes my head spin.

(later)

Something is moving outside the tent. The crackle of dried grasses woke me. It is early morning and the sky has a faint glow in the east, enough for me to glimpse a large shadow sliding between the stone blocks that surround the tent. I thought it might be Clyde and called out to him but received no response. I have no weapon. Well, let it come. As one of the damned I do not deserve salvation. These may be my last written words.

May 11

In the morning I sat in the tent, afraid to open the flap, paralyzed with doubt as to which course of action to follow. The thing, whatever it may have been, that I glimpsed, or thought I had glimpsed, in the early morning hours did not attack the tent, but for all I knew it was still outside, waiting for me to emerge. Assuming that it had withdrawn—or had been no more than a figment of my tormented imagination—I wondered what to do next. Should I descend once again into the hole with fresh batteries in my flashlight, and try to find Clyde? Or would the best course be to go down to the boat and seek help for Clyde from the mainland?

After all, I reasoned to myself, if Clyde were injured, as seemed almost certain, how could I get him out of the hole? It was impossible, absurd to even imagine making the attempt. I had barely managed the climb up from the opening in the side of the shaft myself, with no burden. Could I even sway Clyde across to the second rope on the pitons? No, the best course would be to go for help. And yet, the nagging voice of my conscience spoke to me, and said that Clyde might only be trapped beneath a fallen stone, or with his foot wedged in a crevasse, but otherwise well enough to manage the ropes himself. By taking the time to return to the mainland, I might be condemning him to slow death, whereas prompt action on my part might still save him.

Some of the rooms that opened from the deeper passageways had not appeared abandoned. Was this merely an illusion, or is it possible that a race of creatures still lives within this damned island? That this is a damned place I no longer have any doubt, and I am one of its damned. But not like the others here. No, Clyde and I are nothing like those who made the passages in the stone deep beneath its grassy surface. My mind wrestled to visualize the image on the ivory tablet, but as in previous attempts, it was defeated by uncouth angles and proportions that exist only in nightmare.

(later)

After finally screwing up my courage sufficiently to open the flap of the tent, I crossed the island to the east side and discovered that the boat is no longer there. There is no sign of wreckage, it is simply gone. In a kind of frenzy I walked around the entire island, peering over its edge to see if the boat was drifting on the waves. What good I thought this might accomplish, I cannot now imagine, since even had I spied the boat there was no way to reach it. Eventually I returned to the tent. Where else is there to go?

I have been thinking my situation out with a serious mind. Fishing boats and ships pass by this island, saluting the damned inverted image on its flank, and if I stand upon the very edge of the eastern cliff and wave my jacket or sleeping bag in the air, eventually I am sure to be noticed. However, it may take days, or even weeks. Clyde, if he is lying injured in the depths of this hellish place, cannot survive for so long a span. Therefore I am determined to descend into the hole once more and search for him.

Before I make the descent, I will set up a kind of scarecrow on the edge of the cliff, which if I am fortunate will be noticed from the sea. It must be something man-made or it will not attract serious attention, and the only man-made thing large enough to be seen from passing ships is the tent. My worry is that the winds may increase and rip it off the cliff before it is spotted. I wish it were a bright color but it is dull brown.

I will take a pack down into the hole with some food and water for Clyde, and extra batteries for my flashlight—I brought four sets to the island, so they should last long enough. I will take my journal as well, since I don't know how long it will take me to search the passageways and I may want to record my thoughts. It would make me feel better if I had a revolver, but all I have for a weapon is my climbing hammer, and as formidable as it may be against a human foe, I fear that what I may face in the depths of this island will not be impressed by it. Whatever happens, I mean to find Clyde, or find his corpse. I will not desert him again.

One thing puzzles me. How did that shadowy thing I saw in the night make its way up the hole? It could not have climbed the ropes, because in my madness and terror, I pulled up the top rope after me when I emerged onto the surface. Do they possess some sort of science that allows them to rise through the air? Or are they winged? If they wander the surface, what must they make of the boats and ships that salute as they pass the island? Do they ignore the salutes, or do they accept them as some sort of tribute? What would they do if confronted suddenly in their own warren by one of the beings from the ships? Would they study us, or kill us? Would their reaction even be comprehensible to the human mind? These questions I asked myself, but found no answers.

(later)

I have been down the passages, and I found poor Clyde, what remains of him. I tell myself that he must have been already beyond help when I fancied that I heard his cry, but I cannot make my mind believe it. But let me start at the beginning, so I can tell it all.

It took me several hours to get the tent erected on the edge of the eastern cliff. The sun was high in the heavens when I began my second descent into that hellish black void. I let the top rope down on the opposite side of the opening, where I judged the passage to be located. Because I had done the descent once before, it was easier, although the pack on my back began to tire me a little by the time I reached the end of the first rope. It took me some time to seat an anchor spike for the fresh second rope I had brought with me—Clyde's second rope was still attached to the opposite side of the shaft. Transferring from one rope to the other was awkward but I managed it. As I went deeper, the moaning of the sea as it rose and fell in the hole beneath me exerted an almost hypnotic effect, so that I had to shake my head and blink my eyes to maintain my concentration.

My thinking was that if Clyde still lived, and I could get him back to the entrance to the passageway, it would be easier to help him ascend if the ropes were directly above the entrance. On the other hand, if I found him incapacitated, my chances of getting him out of the hole were practically zero. If I found his corpse, I would be forced to leave it behind. Perhaps a team of his climbing partners could at some later date recover it, assuming the government gave them access to the island for this purpose. I refused to consider for the present the complications that might arise should whatever lived within the belly of the island make its presence known.

I followed with care the marks Clyde had blazed on the entrances to the branching passages, and eventually found myself in a part of the warren I did not recognize. The alien scent was strong in my nostrils, causing me to sneer in involuntary revulsion. I would have preferred the stench of the birds above, which at least was a thing of this world. All of the rooms I passed had objects in them at this level, but it was impossible to conceive their functions. Although I went quietly and saw no other living thing, I could not shake a conviction that I was being watched. It made the skin crawl between my shoulders beneath the weight of my pack.

The first indication that I was nearing Clyde's location was a subtle change in the odor of the tunnels. The alien scents became overlaid with something familiar that I could not identify. It grew stronger as I proceeded toward the end of the passage, which opened into a chamber. There were no sounds other than the distant moan of the sea in the hole and the harsh rasp of my shallow breaths. To say that I was frightened would be the height of understatement. I was so terrified that I could scarcely force one foot in front of another, and expected to black out from moment to moment.

The familiar smell should have forewarned me what sight would greet my eyes in the chamber, but it was only after I saw what was left of poor Clyde that I recognized it. Blood. It was everywhere, on the walls, the floor, even some splashed on the ceiling, but most of it was concentrated on a kind of long, low stone table, or altar—I don't know which it was, if it was either of these things. Dimly, I noted metal cylinders and oblong boxes in the corners that may have been machines, although there were no wires or external knobs or dials. Some of the tissues and fluids had been collected in transparent spheres supported by tripods. Whether they were specimens, or trophies, or some obscene form of relics, I did not attempt to guess. I was too busy vomiting.

The worst thing was Clyde's head. It rested on a carved pedestal that was made from a massive piece of the same kind of greenish ivory as the little tablet I had found on the cliff, with its severed neck supported by some sort of collar or socket. The entire face and scalp had been removed, exposing red muscle tissue and veins that are never meant to exist in the open air, and my friend's lidless blue eyes stared forward with such a fixed gaze of horror as I have never seen on another human being. The pedestal was cylindrical, carved all over its curved surface with a bewildering pattern of strangely angled lines and overlapping curves, so that it almost resembled a geometrical diagram.

I noticed for the first time that there was a second archway in the chamber, leading to a passage beyond. Wiping the acid taste of vomit from my lips with the back of my hand, I approached the pedestal and touched its side. It felt warm beneath my fingers, and vibrated as though alive. The surface of Clyde's corneas appeared to be coated with some sort of clear gel. They stared fixedly forward like the eyes of a fish. I positioned myself in front of the head and crouched at the knees to bring my face level with that of my former friend, so that my gaze would meet his. There was no movement in the eyes, yet I could not dispel the disturbing conviction that they were aware. I passed the beam of my torch directly over the face, and saw the pupils contract.

What I might have done next I cannot imagine, but before I could take any action, a rustling sound came from the dark archway across the chamber. I covered the glass of my flashlight with my hand to mask most of its light and listened intently with Clyde's staring eyes still fixed upon my face. Silence. Then I heard a kind of buzzing, followed by several clicks. This was answered by a second buzzing in a higher tone at some greater distance. It did not sound mechanical. Rather, it reminded me of the sounds made by insects when they rub their legs or wings together. A faint blue glow flickered in the depths of the corridor beyond the arch, and the rustling recommenced, coming nearer.

I looked back at Clyde and laid my hand gently on his bloody, hairless skull. There was no sign to show that he felt the touch, or that any sanity or even awareness remained behind those eyes, but somehow I sensed that he was present in some form. Taking my climbing hammer from my belt, I drove its spike through the top of his skull and deep into his brain. The crunch of breaking bone was followed by silence for several moments, then the buzzing came again from the archway, more insistent than before, and the dragging rustle quickened.

No longer even trying to hide the beam of my flashlight, I ran back the way I had come. My sole thought was to get above ground as quickly as I could manage it, though I see now that I was a fool to fancy I would be any safer on the surface of the island than I was beneath it. When I reached the first bifurcation of the passages, I looked for Clyde's mark and stopped dead in my place—for there were two marks that were almost identical, one on each of the branching stone archways leading to other passages.

There was no time to consider. The chitinous buzzing sounded not far behind. I guessed at the mark made by Clyde's hammer and took that way. When I reached the next intersection, I found that the same trick had been played. The deception would have proved completely effective had the passages been level, but in my progress into the maze of tunnels I had noticed that Clyde had taken a descending route, choosing those passages that slanted downward. With this in mind, I took the way that inclined upward, and continued this practice. Every conjunction of the passages had been baited with false scratches on the stones intended to mislead me, but I ignored all the marks and paid sole attention to the slope of the floor.

In this way, I soon outdistanced the buzzing, rustling sounds of pursuit. It was evident that the monsters could not move as rapidly as a human being. My relief when I found myself back at the archway that opened onto the hole was intense, but it quickly vanished as I searched for my rope, which I had left dangling just to the right of the opening. With one hand grasping the frame of the arch, I leaned dangerously far out over the surging column of water and shone my flashlight on both sides. The rope was gone.

A sense of despair sapped my strength. I slid to the floor with my pack pressed against the stone wall of the passage and sat there for a time, empty of thought, empty even of feeling. Then a glimmer of hope stirred in my heart and brought me back to my feet. I could move around the cylinder wall of the hole on the pitons Clyde had driven in, and climb Clyde's second rope, which was still attached. True, that would leave a hundred yards of sheer rock face, but by using and reusing the pitons on my harness, together with the rope, I could probably work my way back to the surface.

I felt with my hand at my harness, and it was only then that I finally realized that I was lost. My climbing hammer— it was still embedded in Clyde's skull. There was no way I could drive the pitons home in the sheer rock face without a hammer. I had nothing else with which to strike them, nothing but my fists, and they would quickly have turned to bloody stumps were I to try to use them in this way. Through my head ran that absurd little nursery rhyme:

> For want of a nail the shoe was lost,
> For want of a shoe the horse was lost,
> For want of a horse the rider was lost,
> And all for the loss of a horseshoe nail.

Presently, I am sitting with my legs crossed at the mouth of the passage, the abyss of the hole in front of me, horrors unimaginable behind. I have just heard that hellish buzzing again. It is coming nearer. Before it reaches me I intend to hurl myself into the darkness below, and let the surging water take me to wherever it goes when it recedes. I will not suffer the same abominable fate as poor Clyde.

You who read these words, in the event that this journal is ever found, tell everyone that Virgin's Island is accursed, and must never be disturbed. Make up whatever story you can imagine to keep them away, but never allow anyone else to come here. This evil has slumbered for a very long time, perhaps tens of thousands of years, and if we are fortunate, it may slumber for a few years still. I only wish there were some way to stop those damned boats from saluting the cliff with their horns. It may attract the attention of these things, and that could be very bad for the future of our race. Make no attempt to find my corpse. Leave this hateful rock to the birds that roost here, and to the horrors that crawl within.

Lake Mist

Until a few years ago I spent all of my summer vacations in a rented cabin on a sheltered inlet of the Bras d'Or Lake in Cape Breton. It was then, and I suppose still is, a beautiful place for those who love their solitude. The inlet almost forms its own separate lake. The highway and the nearest town are miles away. A scattering of summer homes around the lakeshore add a touch of color without being obtrusive. Hoary old spruce march down the mist-shrouded hills to the water's edge. Their boughs team with songbirds in the early morning, and deer come out from between them to bow their long necks and drink the crystal-clear water.

My rustic log cabin is on the eastern shore of this bay, which gave me an extra measure of isolation since most of the newer summer houses are clustered across the water to the west, where there's a better access road. They form a little seasonal community that gives over the rest of the bay to the dozen or so solitaries like myself who prefer it that way. My cabin is almost a century old, and was originally built as a fishing cottage, or so the present owner told me. It's older than the tall, dark spruce that press close to its sides and back, a consideration that I found appealing when I stayed there.

I suppose most people would think it strange that an attractive woman in her late twenties would prefer to spend her summers alone in an isolated cabin in the deep woods, without electricity or indoor plumbing. Amenities consisted of a hand pump for cold water in the kitchen, and a refrigerator that ran on propane. I didn't mind roughing it—welcomed it, in fact. There was nothing fancy about the cabin, but at least it was honest, and real.

At that time, I worked as an editor in the art department of a fashion magazine based in Toronto. My work days were filled with painted faces, brainless chatter, and the ceaseless rush to meet deadlines. I went through the motions of social interaction. I had my tastefully decorated studio apartment, my circle of acquaintances, and my love affairs, but it was just a charade. None of my friends were close, and my lovers always found reasons to leave after a few weeks.

Each lover gave a different reason for breaking things off, but it all came down to the same thing. I've been told that there is something otherworldly about my personality. I've been called distant and fey. It intrigues men at first, who regard it as a challenge, but over time when it doesn't go away it makes them uneasy, and they find excuses to end the relationship. You might assume this has embittered me toward men, but the truth is that I simply have no strong feelings toward other human beings. I don't dislike them, but neither do I yearn for their company.

Society was the least of my concerns during those lazy vacations in Cape Breton. I read or listened to classical music on my earbuds, perfectly content to spend three weeks alone with my thoughts. Sometimes I just lay in my black one-piece bathing suit on the front porch of the cabin and watched the fly fishermen in their boats cast their sun-gilded threads across the water. I felt no urge to be in the boats with them. While on the lake I remained a strict observer, divorced from life with all its cares and coils.

In retrospect, it seems painfully naïve to imagine that I could separate myself from the loom of fate so easily. By the very act of living we weave the threads of change within ourselves, and the only genuine solitude for us comes at the end of days. Knowing these truths, the lake has lost its appeal. I doubt I will ever go back.

The machinery of my own personal revelation was turning long before I arrived at the cabin that final summer, but it was several days before I engaged the fatal mechanism.

It happened this way. On the third morning after my arrival I lay sunning myself in the canvas lounger on my front porch while reading a Stephen King paperback. I had just finished settling in at the cabin, and was beginning to relax and take notice of my surroundings. Looking up from the page to rest my eyes, I spotted a rowboat drifting near the center of the bay with a solitary old man in it. I judged he must be elderly because the hair of his uncovered head gleamed like a patch of snow in the sun. Other than that, his body posture just looked old and tired. The boat was too far away for me to make out any details.

I thought nothing about it and went back to my book. Even on the sparsely-populated eastern shore of the broad inlet there were often fishermen. But more than an hour later, when I happened to glance up again, the boat was still there. It had not moved. The tiny white-haired figure sat motionless with his shoulders hunched, gazing steadily over the side into the blue water as though searching for something.

This lack of activity on his part made little impression. A boat on the lake is an ideal place for private thought. It was only after noticing him in the same spot on several consecutive days that I began to watch for him. In the mornings after I got out of bed, I started to look for his boat out my bedroom window. When I left the cottage for a walk, my eyes automatically scanned across the water for a moment to check whether the boat was still there. It became a kind of touchstone.

I discovered through observation that its white-haired pilot was my nearest neighbor. He lived in a blue cabin not far around the heel of the bay, and seemed to be keeping some sort of personal vigil. Each dawn he rowed out through the mists with slow, even strokes to the middle of the lake, then shipped his oars and sat motionless, gazing at the rippled surface of the water for hours, until the sun began to decline. When the spruce trees lengthened their black afternoon shadows across the water, but before the twilight mist descended from the hills, he rowed back to his cabin with the same measured strokes and vanished from sight.

Undoubtedly he was an eccentric old bird. With the aid of a pair of binoculars I was able to observe him talking to himself in the boat, making little gestures with his hands on his knees while his lips moved. It crossed my mind that he might be an alcoholic, but never once did I see the glint of a bottle in his hand. Nor did he smoke, so marijuana wasn't the reason for his excursions upon the water. The puzzle of the man's daily routine preyed on my mind. In the isolation of my cabin there was nothing to distract my curiosity.

My vacation ran its usual placid course and neared its end, and my body, aware of this timetable, begun to readjust itself to a faster city pace. With only a few days left, I began to feel restless, sitting around the cabin with nothing to do, and impulsively decided to hike over and get at least one close look at my mysterious neighbor before leaving him behind.

I waited until late afternoon, when he turned the bow of his boat and

Lake Mist

put it away on shore for the night. My canoe would have been a faster and easier way to reach his cabin than walking, but I told myself that the walk would be a chance to stretch my legs. Besides, being on foot provided an excuse for passing close to the old man's door. A path of sorts wound all around the lake, never wandering far from the water's edge. At this point, I had not entirely made up my mind to talk to him. I just wanted a closer look at where he lived.

This is what I told myself, but thinking back, I realize that the real reason I did not take the canoe was the lake mist. It is a peculiar feature of this inlet of the Bras d'Or Lake that on certain summer days, when conditions are right, it acquires a covering of mist in the early mornings and at twilight. On some days the mist is thicker than on others, and on rare occasions it remains over the water from sunup to sundown, looking like a white, down-filled coverlet.

Years before, I once made the mistake of taking the canoe out very early in the morning and was caught by the mist. I found that I could not see the shore in any direction. Even the sun was hidden in its uniform whiteness. The mist muffled the usual sounds of the lake, so that I had no sense of direction. I'm ashamed to admit that I panicked, and thrashed the water with my paddle in a futile effort to find the shore. Eventually I was able to fight down this irrational terror. I forced myself to sit and wait for the rising sun to burn the mist away before returning with badly shaken nerves to my cabin. This experience made me reluctant to take the canoe out on the water when there was even the slightest risk that I might be caught by the mist.

After almost an hour hiking along the vague path, pushing through waist-high saplings that had grown up in the middle of it, stumbling over uneven ruts and loose stones, and being eaten alive by mosquitoes, I bitterly regretted my decision to walk. I realized that I had misjudged the difficulty of the path, which in places was so overgrown as to be invisible. The sun drooped ever nearer the western hills, and even my untrained eye told me that it would be dark before I could manage to return to my cabin by foot. There was no moon that night. I cursed myself for my nosiness, and for not bringing a flashlight.

Now I would have to speak to the old man, whether I wanted to or not, if only to beg him to row me back across the bay in his boat. Otherwise, I would find myself alone in the woods in utter blackness, and that meant a long cold night under a tree. Only a complete idiot tries to walk through the woods in total darkness. It's a sure way to lose an eye on some projecting tree branch, or sprain an ankle by stepping into a hole.

When I finally emerged from the spruce trees beside the blue cabin, my spirits lifted a little. It was a trim, ordinary-looking little structure. The patch of lawn surrounding it was four or five weeks uncut, and the cabin needed a coat of paint, but aside from these details it looked like any other cottage on the lake. I stepped up onto the low porch and knocked at the screen door. The inner door stood open. The room beyond exhaled a musty smell through the screen, and in the shadows beyond I heard the buzzing of a fly.

I knocked again, louder. There was no response. The screen door was latched from the inside. I made my way around the house, moving cautiously. A trace of my earlier nervousness had returned. It was probably for this reason that he did not hear my approach. Or at least, he failed to look up when I came into view around the corner.

He sat on the rough-cut slab of stone that formed the back step of the cabin, eating cold Graves Beans out of a can with a spoon. I saw with surprise that he could not have been more than forty. It was his snow-white hair and the rounded stoop to his broad shoulders that had deceived me in the distance. He was a big man, but haggard and thin. Several weeks of whitish stubble frosted his chin. His distant blue eyes were set in a wide face that bore an expression of detached simplicity.

I stood motionless, feeling like an intruder. When he seemed not to notice me, I cleared my throat. "I knocked on the front door but nobody answered."

He stopped eating and raised his head. "I don't much use the front of the house," he said, his voice resonant.

He went back to his meal.

"I live across the inlet. You can see my log cabin from here. I was out walking, and I went farther than I'd intended. It was a stupid thing to do. Now it's almost dark, and I don't think I can get back before—"

"What do you want?"

Usually when men see me, they respond with interest. As I mentioned before, I'm reasonably attractive. Their eyes move from my face to my breasts, then to my hips, then back to my breasts. His emotionless blue eyes never left my face.

"Well, really," I said, taken up short, "I'd be grateful for a row across the water in your boat. Otherwise I'll get stuck in the woods overnight."

He seemed to consider this. It was as if small lights of awareness turned on in his mind one by one. His face hardened, becoming more human. "I guess I have to take you back. You were careless to come so far this close to dark."

"It was stupid," I agreed, inwardly annoyed at my eagerness to deprecate myself. His presence was intimidating.

He set the can and spoon on the granite step and got up with the easy motion that is a sure sign of great physical strength.

"I'll get the boat. Have to take you across right now or it'll be dark before I get back."

I moved aside and trailed after him down the slope to the water's edge, watching his shoulders flex under the thin material of the sweat-stained red-and-white checkered shirt he wore. By this time, the crickets were singing in the grass. The breeze had died and the surface of the inlet bore that glassy smoothness that always comes just at dusk. A descending curtain of mist cloaked the trees on the hillsides, so that only their tops projected above it. It was quiet and beautiful, yet in my present state of mind, disturbingly dreamlike.

He picked up the bow of the little boat from where it rested on the grass and silently dragged it down to the water. Then he went back and got the oars, a noiseless shadow.

"Do you live here all year round?" I asked to cover my nervousness.

"I'm on vacation with my boy."

"You must be fond of the water. I see you every day out there in your boat."

He paused to look at me. Even though his expression was obscured by the half-light, I felt a malignancy in the air. It was gone in an instant. He climbed into the boat and steadied it with an oar on the grass, waiting for me to follow. There was no time to consider. The first stars glowed faintly in the purple vault overhead. I stepped into the bow and settled onto the plank seat. He pushed us away from the mud with an oar, then fitted it to its lock and began to row with the slow powerful rhythm I had come to know so well.

I had not really gotten a good look at the boat in the dulling light. My sudden awareness of its condition did nothing to calm my unease. Gray boards showed naked beneath peeling white paint, curled and split from exposure to the weather. In the bottom, green mold encrusting the rotten shell.

I sat for a time watching the man's thick neck as he dipped the blades of the oars into the water. He was so familiar with the inlet that he did not even bother to glance around for a bearing, not even as the mist reached the shore and began to close over the mirror surface. As minutes dragged by, the silence began to prickle on my nerves. When two people are alone together without talking, the urge to say something becomes overpowering.

"By the way, my name's Dora Lee Harris."

"Ross Macintyre," he grunted.

"Do you come to the lake often, Mr. Macintyre? I don't remember seeing you around here before."

"Johnny and I keep to ourselves."

"That's your son?"

"Yeah."

"This is a good place for kids. How old is he?"

"Twelve last April."

"Is your wife here with you too?"

"Dead. Five years ago in a car crash."

"I'm sorry."

"Sure."

I didn't say anything else, but the reference to his son must have touched a response in him.

"I bought him a new fly rod last Christmas. He likes to fish. Good at it. Every morning out on the water before breakfast."

"How did he do?"

"Loves to fish," repeated Macintyre, not noticing. "Stands up and casts just as smooth as silk. Better than I ever could. No one taught him, neither. Damned good."

I was relieved he had decided to talk. It made him seem less grim.

"It's too bad he had to leave."

"What?" he asked distractedly.

"Your son. I said it was too bad he had to go home. Maybe we could have gotten together sometime."

"He's not home."

"Oh? When I didn't see him, I just assumed he'd gone home. Where is he?"

Without turning his head, Macintyre nodded across the open water.

"Over there."

Lake Mist

I strained my eyes to distinguish the tiny lighted windows of the cottages along the western shore. Already the mist was hiding them from view.

"You mean he's staying on the other side of the bay?"

He shook his head. "He never made it to the other side."

I stared for a moment at the gray mist that bordered the water. Even the obvious can be hard to grasp if it's horrible enough. A shock thrilled through my fingertips. The air was like crystal, perfectly still. Only the whisper of the oars and the tiny squeal of the turning brass locks broke the silence. Macintyre's muscular shoulders moved rhythmically forward and back, forward and back.

His tone was reasonable. "I told him, never stand up in the boat. He said he couldn't cast sitting down. He was proud of his cast. Should never have let him go out alone, but he was such a damned good swimmer. Must have hit his head. I waited for him to come back, just like always. When breakfast got cold, I went out to call him. Boat was upside down in the water."

He was talking to himself. His words had a wooden tone, as though he had spoken them a thousand times in his mind and exhausted their meaning.

The inside of my mouth felt dry against the tip of my tongue. I had to speak. "What about the body?"

He chuckled—an eerie sound that made my skin creep. "Damn lake got him. Sucked him down into the bottom slime. He's still there. I hear him at night moving around, fighting to breathe."

The water expanded endlessly on all sides. By this time, the gathering mist had covered the lights in the windows of the distant cottages. Even the trees on either side of the bay were ghostlike.

I stared at his thick neck with fascination, able to think of only one thing. I can't swim six strokes.

His toneless, dreaming voice droned on. "I'm going to get him free. Every day I watch him push against the rocks and weeds. He looks up through the water and begs me for help. I want to dive in, but I can't move. I almost drowned when I was a kid. I used to get nightmares. When I think of that cold water closing over my head and filling my lungs—"

He shivered. "I know what's down there, waiting. It wants the both of us. Black rotten filth that squeezes and sucks. Makes me sick to think about it. I can't face it, not yet. But Johnny knows I'm coming. It won't be much longer."

I took shallow breaths, trying not to attract his notice. His featureless back gave no clue to what was in his mind. If he became violent, his powerful arms could sweep me into the water like a child. I tried to brace my feet more firmly in the bottom of the boat. Something wet and cold touched my ankle. I made a little noise in my throat.

For the first time, he paused his rowing and turned on his seat to peer through the shadows at the bottom of the boat.

"It's just water," he said. "The boat leaks. Gets worse all the time. The bottom's rotted clean through—full of worm holes. One of these days it'll fall to pieces."

He recommenced his steady, even strokes.

I sat hugging my knees in the gathering darkness and listened to the liquid dip of the oars. Macintyre's pace had seemed quick enough a few moments before. Now I felt his arms to be moving with nightmare slowness, as though he were rowing through molasses. My awareness focused on the creeping wet that worked its way into both my hiking boots.

The mist hung all around the boat. It seemed to stay at a constant distance, just out of reach, but I knew this to be an illusion. It was over us, covering us with cool dampness, pressed to our faces, filling our lungs. Macintyre did not turn his head. I don't know how he knew which way to row in the mist and gathering darkness, but his strokes never faltered.

My muscles coiled like taut springs, ready to react in my defense. The human body protects itself with a mindless determination incredible to those who have never experienced it. The tyranny of his flesh had kept Macintyre a prisoner in the boat, calling up phantasms in his mind from his childhood nightmares of drowning to counter his love for his son, binding him helpless on a rack of need and fear.

A faint cry floated across the water. The mist made it impossible to determine its distance, or even its direction. Macintyre stopped rowing. We both sat and listened to the twilight silence.

"Johnny!" he shouted, voice hoarse with emotion.

The mist wrapped the name in soft cotton and smothered any echo.

"It was just a coyote," I murmured.

"Listen," he hissed.

Lake Mist

We sat straining our ears. I heard, or thought I heard, a faint splashing, like the rhythm of a swimmer moving his arms through the water.

Macintyre twisted on his seat to stare at me. In the gloom his face was no more than a gray mask. "My boy's free," he said. "He's coming for me. Listen."

The soft splashing was closer. I couldn't tell which direction it came from. It seemed to be all around the boat.

My nerve broke. I grabbed for one of the oars. I don't know what I intended to do with it, sitting in the bow of the boat, but I think I had some crazy idea that I would use it like a paddle. When Macintyre realized what I was trying to do, he held the oar down so that I couldn't pull it away from him. The boat began to rock from side to side.

"Here, son, I'm right here," he shouted.

Although I can't be certain what happened then, I think the boat capsized. It felt as though something lifted and tipped it from underneath, but I won't swear to that—it may have been just my panicked imagination. As it tipped, it came apart. The sides separated from the bottom and even the individual planks peeled away from the ribs. I went down into the cold water. It closed over my head. Something touched my legs and began to squeeze them. I felt it pull me downward. It must have been Macintyre in his madness, trying to drown me. After all, what else could it have been?

I kicked my legs free, and realized that I was still holding the oar in my hands. It offered enough buoyancy to keep my head above water. By this time, I had lost contact with the fragments of the capsized boat, which had drifted into the mist and been hidden from view. I began to try to swim away from that place, using my legs and my free arm. I didn't know where I was going, I only wanted to get away from whatever had tried to pull me under the water.

In real life, when you find yourself in a situation of extreme peril, no one comes to rescue you. I don't know how long I floundered around in the chill water. My body became entirely numb, and I started to shiver uncontrollably. I realize now that I was dying of hypothermia, but at the time all I felt was a dull determination to get away from the unseen swimmer. The mist cloaked everything in gray, and the gray became darker.

Something touched my foot. I shrieked and kicked at it with instinctive violence. Then I realized that it was the rocky bottom of the lake. I had managed to float to shore. I pulled myself wearily out of the water on legs that felt as if they were made of lead, and found that I was below my own cabin. My relief was so great, I fell to my knees in the grass, and couldn't stand back up, although I tried half a dozen times. In the end, I had to crawl up to my front door.

The next day I left the inlet, and never went back. Its mist-shrouded surface holds no attraction, now that I know what lies beneath. Macintyre's body was never found, nor was there ever any trace of his son. They are both still down there, under the mist, waiting together. Waiting for me.

The Alchemist's Assistant

1.

"Do not make me kill again," Andalia said in her strangely lilting accent.

Werther looked up at her from his book with a mixture of incredulity and calculating interest.

"What did you say?"

"I do not like to kill," she said, then paused, and more slowly formed the words, "I do not like to mur-der."

"Where did you learn that word?"

The ape-like creature dropped her eyes with an almost human shame.

"Have you been reading again?" he said more sharply.

She turned away and gazed out the uncurtained window at the flakes of falling snow that brushed the black glass. Night had stolen on like a quiet thief while Werther sat in his padded leather chair before the glowing fireplace, reading one of his old books. They were all old, older even than him, and he was as old as the hills themselves that surrounded the old house. They even smelled of age, just as he did. She wrinkled her blunt nose with distaste. Her large brown eyes rolled away from his disapproving stone-gray stare, colder than the snow beyond the many panes of glass. A log crackled in the fireplace.

"You know what I promised if you read again."

"Andalia knows," she said with resignation, her head bowed.

"The glamour will not hold without fresh infusions of human blood."

He put his book aside on the little table near the arm of his chair, first carefully marking his place with a hundred-dollar bill.

Why did he always use the money for a bookmark? she wondered, watching him from beneath the lashes of her lowered eyelids. It was a question that had never before arisen in her mind. The longer she lived, the more questions came forth like this one, from the nothingness inside her, to float unanswered before her awareness. She did not dare voice them aloud.

He arose from the chair with a surprising serpentine grace, uncoiling his long limbs effortlessly. The charcoal business suit that was his habitual attire lent him an air of gravity. His back was unbowed by age. Although his hair had lost most of its auburn coloration, it still grew thick on his head, and his elongated, pale face had few wrinkles.

The ape-thing took off her woollen dress of green plaid and folded it neatly on a window seat. She wore no undergarments. Lowering herself to her hands and knees on the oaken floorboards, which were blackened with age and centuries of use, she waited in resignation. The heat from the fireplace warmed her dangling breasts.

He took up his riding crop from the brass canister that stood on the tiles of the hearth and flexed its length between his slender fingers. She had never seen him on a horse, yet he always kept the crop close at hand. It was a lot like the master himself, she thought—straight and stiff and hard. Another of those pointless rising thoughts that would never be voiced.

The crop lashed across her hairy back with slow, methodical strokes. He used all of the strength of his arm, and he was uncannily strong for a man. She bore her punishment in silence. There was no resentment in her heart, only a sad resignation. Was this life? Was it for this that he had called her up from the void, using a few chemicals and some chanted words of the old arts? To be whipped like some dumb beast, or less than a beast? She felt a creeping in her heart, not for herself but for him. What was the emotion called? Shame. That was it.

"Put your dress back on. We are going into the town to hunt."

2.

The first time they had driven down from the hills to the small New England town of Camden, she had trembled with anticipation. It had all been new to her—the colored lights in front of the shops, the traffic noises, the smells of all the people who shuffled along the sidewalks, chattering and staring into plate glass windows at nameless things for sale. Werther had bought her something called an ice-cream Sunday. She had sat at the counter on the red padded stool in the ice-cream parlor, picking at it with her little silver spoon, terrified that she would make an error in the table manners he had taught her only the night before. But none of the humans paid any attention to her, other than to smile indulgently. She had forced her lips into an answering smile, as she had been trained.

The spell of glamour held strong that day. Those who looked at her saw only a shy young woman with large brown eyes and long, dark hair that hung over her slender shoulders in loose curls. Werther had called her his "niece" and explained to a man in a bookstore that she had come from Ecuador to visit with him and to assist with his research for his new book.

He was known to the humans in the town as an eccentric writer who liked to keep to himself in the ancient gambrel-roofed house that lay hidden among the forested hills. He had arranged to buy the house sight unseen on the strength of the description by the real-estate agent. That was before she had been conjured into existence, so she only knew about it from chance comments he made to her.

Camden was a tourist town. Apart from its small lobster fishing industry, it relied on the young people who came in summer for fishing and boating, and in winter for the ski slopes some fifteen or twenty miles inland. The motels were usually filled, and the sidewalks thronged with strangers. That was one reason Werther had chosen this place to live—a strange face was apt to attract less attention where so many outsiders came and went throughout the year.

He would stay here for a time, perhaps for as much as a decade, writing his novels under his assumed name and having them published in New York. He even had a literary agent whom Andalia had never smelled, apart from the scent that clung to the checks he mailed to his reclusive client. It was all a pose. Werther had no need to write for money. He had been a wealthy man for centuries. But it was necessary to maintain appearances, he had told her. He wore his mask and she wore hers. Both hid secrets that could not be exposed to the humans.

"They attacked me once in Mainz," he murmured as he guided the German-made car along the snow-covered, winding road.

She flinched, then deliberately forced herself to relax on the leather seat beside him. Sometimes, it was as though he could read her thoughts. She wondered if she murmured things aloud without realizing it?

"That was …" he paused in thought, "… that was more than two centuries ago. I was betrayed by a man I thought to be my friend. They were going to burn me alive. I barely escaped through the trees. They tore off my clothes and beat me with farm implements."

He chuckled at the memory, then turned his head and leaned forward.

"See where I lost part of my ear."

She gazed, not at the notch in the back edge of his right ear, but as his exposed neck, where the blood pulsed so near to the surface. She could almost taste it on her lips. The urge to tear into that soft, white flesh was close to overpowering, but she had been well conditioned.

"I see," she murmured.

The wipers on the windshield made a rhythmic *shelop-shelop* noise that calmed her nerves. The road had not been plowed yet, but the snow was new-fallen and no more than a few inches deep. It gave little hindrance to the wheels of the big black sedan.

"While we are in the town, you must stay as much as you can in the shadows," he murmured. "The spell will hold better under shadow. Maintain your concentration at all times. We will try for a young child tonight. That will give you a longer span before there is a need for your next infusion."

The younger the human, the more vitality its life held in potential. She had learned this herself, during her furtive reading of his alchemical texts while he slept.

"Maybe we will find a baby," she murmured.

He chuckled. "That's the spirit. Take joy in your hunt. Everything must eat to live. You are no different from these mortals in that regard. Even I must consume vital salts at intervals. It is the universal chain that binds us to the flesh."

"But I was not meant to be flesh," she said, and instantly regretted it.

He sat silent, staring out at the falling snow in the beams of the car's headlights, his index finger tapping the top of the steering wheel.

"That was a curious thing to say," he murmured. "I keep forgetting how long you have been alive. What is it? More than four years? I don't believe I've ever kept one of your kind alive for so long before. But you have been such an excellent assistant."

He laid his hand on her knee and slid it up the inside of her hairy thigh, pushing the hem of the woolen dress aside. She did not flinch or pull away. She was proud of her self-control. The touch of his hands raised a revulsion within her that grew steadily stronger with each passing day, but she took extreme care that she never showed so much as a trace of it. Her master held the power of life and death. He had called her up from the abyss and he could just as easily send her back. And he would send her back, as soon as she ceased to be useful to him.

"How is the spell holding?"

"It holds," she said.

He grunted at this terse response and removed his hand from her leg, but said no more.

3.

They stopped first at the Book Bank, a secondhand bookstore where Werther placed orders for obscure and out-of-print editions. The owner, a rotund balding man named Fennel, had proved expert at tracking down the rarest of titles, a task for which he was well compensated by her master. It was a satisfactory arrangement for both men. Fennel asked no questions, and Werther paid whatever price he demanded for his services without a quibble. Money meant nothing to Werther.

She hated entering the store. It smelled of dust and rat droppings and beetles. The owner smelled even worse. He used some kind of lotion to slick his few strands of dark hair to his pink scalp. It stank of alcohol and sandalwood, but it could not cover the odor of his flesh. The store was always too warm, and the air clogged her throat.

The bell above the front door alerted Fennel to their arrival. His round face flashed into a welcoming grin. He set down his pencil and brushed bits of eraser off the frayed cuffs of his tweed sports jacket with an unconscious, reflexive gesture.

"Well, speak of the Devil," he said with a heartiness that seemed to her hyper-sensitive ears both insincere and excessive. "I was just about to phone you. Your book came in this morning."

Werther said nothing, but held the door open for her to pass into the store.

"Don't get too near to him," he murmured in a voice so low that no human could have heard the words.

She nodded as she slid into the long, narrow space, which was lined with books on each wall and had a row of double-sided shelves running down its center that extended from the worn hardwood floor to the exposed beams of the ceiling. All the shelves overflowed, and more books were stacked everywhere on the floor, so that there was barely room to walk.

The owner eyed her keenly as she slid past the sales counter into the rear. "How are you feeling tonight, little miss?"

"Very good, sir," she murmured, lowering her eyes and turning her face away.

He watched her for a few seconds across the counter, the book in his hand. It was wrapped in brown paper held closed by packing tape. Werther said nothing, but merely stood and waited.

"Sorry, sorry," Fennel said. The grin returned to his round cheeks.

"Is something wrong?"

"No, course not." Fennel shook his head. "It's only that for a second there I thought I saw ..."

"Yes?"

Andalia watched through the crack above one of the middle row of shelves.

"Her skin ..." He shook his head again. "It's nothing, my eyes are just playing tricks on me. I must need a new set of glasses."

When they left the store, she took care to raise her hand to her face as she walked past the counter. She concentrated on holding the spell firmly in place, although she could feel it waver.

Werther took her hand and drew her from under the light of the red neon sign and around the corner of the brick building where there was darkness. None of the people hurrying along the sidewalk through the falling snow paid any attention to them.

"You are losing control. I feared as much. We came just in time."

"I could drink the man," she suggested quietly.

"Who? Fennel?" he laughed outright, something he rarely did. "No, my creature, he is too old for you. In any case, he still serves my needs."

He extended his head from the mouth of the alley and glanced quickly left and right.

"There, that child. You will abduct her while I distract her mother."

Andalia stepped nearer behind him and located the child on the opposite side of the street. It was a girl of some eight or nine years who

81

stood holding the hand of a woman as they stared into a plate-glass window. The window was decorated with a Christmas display. The girl wore a red felt coat and a black beret over her long blond hair, which was gathered into a single braid at the back. Andalia saw that her mother had tied the end of the braid with a red bow. The child laughed, and the sound of her laughter carried across the street, muted by the snow.

4.

They crossed the street at a diagonal, walking with a casual pace. There was almost no traffic. They had to pause only once to allow a truck to pass. The angle chosen by Werther placed them on the sidewalk a dozen yards in front of the girl and her mother, who had by this time left the brightly decorated window.

Werther held her hand in his. His fingers felt as cold as ice. He pretended to pause to study a chalkboard with a list of prices beside the door of a restaurant.

As always at such moments, she felt nothing. Her heart rate remained even and her breathing regular. A strange calm possessed her. The passing world seemed to slow down as time elongated itself.

Werther stepped into the middle of the sidewalk, drawing her out with him.

"Excuse me, good woman, perhaps you can assist us."

The woman stopped and stared at them with startled blue eyes. Instinctively she placed an arm around the shoulders of the child. They were mother and daughter, Andalia observed. The resemblance in their features could not be mistaken, and in any event, they smelled the same.

"My niece and I are looking for a dining establishment called the Lobster Palace. Would you happen to know of it?"

The woman thought for a moment and started to shake her head. "Why, no, I don't think I've ever heard of any—"

Her gaze wandered to Werther's pale eyes and remained fixed there as she stopped speaking.

"Take the child," he murmured.

Andalia extended her hand and removed the small fingers of the child from the clasp of her mother.

"Come with me, little one. I have something to show you."

The girl did not try to pull away, but she looked up at her mother's face questioningly.

"Go with her," the woman said in a dead voice. Never once did her gaze waver from Werther's eyes.

Moving quickly to get away from the brightly lit street, she drew the unresisting girl around a corner and hurried down an alley and into the unlit service road that gave delivery trucks access to the rears of the stores and restaurants. A loading bay lay deep under shadow. It was an ideal place to do what she must do. There was just enough light reflecting from the new-fallen snow to illuminate the upturned face of the girl. For the first time Andalia realized that she was pretty.

"What is your name, little one?"

"Mary."

"Stay very still, Mary, and do not be afraid."

She kept her hands on the girl's shoulders, but the girl did not attempt to run away.

"Are you going to hurt me?"

What a strange question, Andalia thought. None of her prey had ever asked it before. She thought of the last, a young man who had tried to kiss her and instead had died screaming, unable to break free from her inhumanly powerful embrace.

"You should close your eyes."

The girl did not close her eyes. She continued to stare up into her captor's face, blue eyes wide and lips ever so slightly parted.

"Are you a monster?" she asked in a tiny voice.

Andalia realized that her glamour had failed. The girl looked upon her true appearance. It was the first time in her four years of existence that the spell concealing her from the humans had failed completely.

The girl's question puzzled her. She let it play through her thoughts slowly, over and over until it became a kind of mantra. *Am I a monster? Am I a monster? Am I a monster?*

She straightened her back and released the child's shoulders. "No, little one, I am not a monster. Run back to your mother."

Without a word the girl turned and ran, following the tracks of their footsteps in the snow.

Andalia stood in the darkness. She felt—nothing. An emptiness. And then, something. Resolve.

"I am not a monster," she repeated aloud to herself.

Werther waited for her at the corner. His long face, as usual, bore no expression, but she could feel the anger inside him. Once more her spell of concealment masked her ape-like features.

"You failed," he said.

No, she thought, but she said, "Yes."

He hesitated for the merest fraction of a second, then shrugged. "It is of no importance. We will try again tomorrow night."

As they walked back along the alley toward the bright lights of the main street, she noticed a shadow lying partially concealed behind a trash barrel. Her nose caught the scent of fresh blood.

He became aware of her interest.

"Of course I had to kill the child. She saw your true face."

You lie, she thought.

"Of course," she said.

5.

On the drive back to the house, her master said little, and she made only the expected responses. He talked of the book and its importance to his work. She pretended to listen but her thoughts remained in the alley with the corpse of the little girl. She had never felt this way before. In place of her customary inner calm, her emotions rushed this way and that, like the ruffled surface of water beneath the blustering gusts of October.

He would attempt to kill her as soon as she entered the house. Of that much she was certain. She had disobeyed him. That was a sin her master would never allow to pass. In his mind she had proven herself an untrustworthy instrument, and many times she had seen him cast his broken tools into the fire. He would raise up another hairy monster to take her place.

I am not a monster, she said to herself, taking care not to move her lips.

"Did you say something?" he asked without turning his gaze from the falling snow highlighted in the car's high-beams.

"No."

The dark shadow of the old house reared its shoulder past the trees as they rounded the final curve of the road and turned up its long gravel drive. By this time the gathering snow lay half a foot deep, but it did not hinder the progress of the car. Werther guided it around the rim of the oval turning area of the drive and stopped in front of the door.

"Home once again," he said with a false cheerfulness.

She opened her door without haste, stepped around its edge, and sprinted across the snow-cloaked lawn for the edge of the trees.

Behind her, Werther spoke words of power on the night air, vibrating them deep in his chest so that they boomed out from his lips with unnatural force.

She felt the strength fail in her legs, and fell forward. The darkness of the forest lay only a few yards beyond her outstretched hands. She listened to the soft crunch of the snow beneath his boots as he approached behind her.

"You are a most astonishing creature," he said, bending to pick her up in his arms. He was much stronger than a mortal man. "I would never have believed you capable of such betrayal."

Was her throat paralyzed as well?

"I— I— " She swallowed and tried again. "I am not a monster."

He stared at her, his gray face without emotion. Then he turned and carried her into the house and down the stairs in the kitchen that led to the cellar.

A brightly painted pentacle covered most of the polished concrete floor of the cellar. Werner had modernized the windowless space soon after buying the house, or so he had once informed her while in a more expansive mood than usual, as they lay side by side in his bed. It was the perfect place, he had said, to work his arts uninterrupted. It also made an effective prison, she thought, as mutely testified by the chains that were set in the mortar between the stones of the wall.

He laid her down not ungently within the pentacle.

"I must get my book from the car," he murmured. "I don't want the pages to become damp. Wait for me, my dear; I won't be long."

He chuckled to himself as he went up the creaking flight of wooden steps and passed from her view. She heard the heavy steel bolt that secured the oak door in the kitchen slide into place.

With an intense effort of will, she found that she could move her arms, though not yet her legs. The enchantment he had placed over her was losing its force, as such things always did over time, but would he be gone long enough?

As she had hoped, he remained away from the cellar for almost fifteen minutes. It was natural that he would pause to examine his new book, and after all, why should he hurry back? He was sure that she could not escape.

When he returned, he found her lying where he had left her. She watched him approach. She had allowed the glamour that cloaked her features to fall away. There was no need to maintain it within the house. He was well accustomed to see her hairy body in the clothing of a mortal woman. His eyes strayed to the gap between her thighs, exposed where her dress had ridden up her legs, but he was not like other men—not so weak that he could be swayed from his purpose by lust.

"I may as well remove your dress," he said, more to himself than to her. "Otherwise the fire of your burning will destroy it, and I will have to buy another for my next assistant. I do so loathe shopping for dresses."

He stepped into the pentacle and began to strip off her green plaid dress with quick, businesslike motions.

She pretended that she was still paralyzed, until he bent over her, and she was able to grasp him in her arms. She bent his spine backwards like a bow. It broke with a sickening crunch of dislocated bone.

"Foolish creature, what are you doing? You know you can't kill me."

Even as he spoke his spine crackled and his back rippled as his vertebrae found their former places and unbent themselves. He started to push himself back to his feet.

With a swift strike of her hand, she crushed his throat. Blood welled from the corner of his mouth. He tried to speak and found that he could not utter a sound. Even so, he gave no sign of alarm. He merely shook his head at her in a way that was almost pitying.

She knew she had only a few precious seconds before his throat healed itself and he spoke the charm of dissolution. Sliding away from his grasping hands, she used her arms to pull herself out of the pentacle.

"You should never have let me learn to read," she told him.

In the manner she had practiced under the trees while he was away from the house, she began to vibrate the words of the charm of dissolution, which she had memorized months ago.

His expression of condescension turned to surprise, and then horror. Wisps of steam arose from his charcoal-gray suit as his blood began to boil, and a blue flame curled up from his hair. Countless other blue flames broke forth through his clothing all over his body. They were like the jets from a gas oven. They burned with an intense but localized heat, and almost no smoke. The result was what the humans knew as spontaneous combustion. Except, there was nothing spontaneous about it. Within minutes nothing remained on the concrete but a pile of gray ash with bits of bone glowing in it like live coals.

She wrinkled her flat nose in disgust at the oily, sooty smell. When she tried, she found that she was able to stand up and stagger across to the wall switch that activated the ventilation fans in the ceiling. They quickly cleared the air. For several minutes she stood looking down at the mound of ash. In the emptiness inside her an emotion stirred. Satisfaction. How many days of life remained to her, she could not guess, but each day would belong to her alone.

"I am not a monster," she said. "But you were."

She went up the stairs to get a dustpan and a broom.

Curse of the House of Usher

1.

I read Roderick Usher's letter in the sitting room of my Boston flat with conflicted emotions. We had been close friends during our student days at Miskatonic University, or perhaps allies would be a more accurate descriptive. We were both outsiders in a philosophical as well as a geographical sense, so it was natural that when we found ourselves roommates that we should spend much of our time together, shut out as we were from the unwelcoming social circles of the local Arkham youths.

In part this shunning by the locals was due to rumors of our occult rituals. Usher and I were alike in so many ways, both tall and athletic in body, both reserved in speech, but our greatest consonance lay in our mutual passion for the unseen. We experimented, as young men will, and earned the reputation of necromancers among the students of Miskatonic. Spiritualism was then at its height of interest, and the Theosophy of Madame Blavatsky was the subject of common discourse. We embraced this fad for the occult with uncritical enthusiasm. All our nights were spent summoning the dead and conversing with them, nor did we fail to achieve significant successes in these endeavors.

Yet after we left the bell jar atmosphere of academia for the seemingly unlimited horizons of the greater world, we seldom sought the other's company. I established myself outwardly as a writer of strange tales while pursuing my esoteric studies in the privacy of my own dreams. I became an explorer of the dreamlands, and gained a reputation there as a great dreamer. From time to time I would hear word of Usher's decadent extravagances in the fleshpots of Berlin and Prague. The last mention of his exploits, which I chanced to overhear several years ago spoken in casual conversation by a school acquaintance, placed him in a gaming house in Morocco, running up astronomical gambling debts while intoxicated on the lethal combination of opium and absinthe.

The letter requested that I visit his ancestral estate, which Usher had inherited following the death of his uncle. The tone of the letter was strangely mixed; part forced jocularity in which Usher asserted that I must need a vacation in the country after the assaults of the Bostonian bluestockings following the celebrity of my last published collection of stories, and part a touchingly sincere plea that we renew our old comradeship after so long a hiatus.

As it chanced, the letter arrived at a time when I had determined to take a break from my esoteric experiments in lucid dreaming. I was burnt out, as the vulgar saying goes, and could no longer enter the dreamlands at will, but struggled to transit even the first portal of deep sleep. The cynicism of my Boston literary acquaintances tainted my imagination, and I found myself eager to see if a separation from their world-weary ennui would revive my childhood wonder and once more open the gates of dreams for my explorations.

Also, it must be confessed, I felt curiosity to see the estate that Usher had so often alluded to during our late-night chats at the university. He had painted it as an otherworldly place, a house forgotten by time. As I held his letter folded in my hand and heard his words echo in my memory, it seemed the ideal retreat in which to set aside for a short while the burden of the practical concerns that had been imposed on my mind by my publisher and certain members of my family.

It would be less than honest to say that the memory of Usher's sister played no part in my decision to accede to his request. During his student days he always kept a photograph of her in the lid of his ornately engraved silver pocket watch, and at quiet times he would open the watch and gaze at her with an expression of melancholy affection. She was a strikingly beautiful young woman, very like to Usher himself in countenance, with lustrous gray eyes and fine, curling black hair that framed an alabaster brow. I even remembered her name. Madeline. Neither Usher nor I had married during the years of our separation. His bachelorhood was presumably due to his indulgence in the vices of the world, whereas mine was the result of an almost monkish asceticism.

It was with a bewildering brew of emotions that I drafted a reply to my friend agreeing to visit his estate within the fortnight, although I gave no promise as to the date on which I would arrive, or how long I intended to remain there as his guest. It was in my mind to see how the two of us got on together before binding myself to a prolonged sojourn.

2.

Usher's family estate lay some dozen miles inland from the ancient port of New Bedford. It nestled between the hills in a secluded stretch of Massachusetts countryside, remote from villages and farms. Whatever had impelled the first Usher who ventured his fortunes in the New World to choose so isolated a geography was a puzzle. When the house was erected more than two centuries ago, it must have been even more remote than it is today. That was before the railroads, before the automobile, even before the steamship. Usher had never explained why the house had been built where it stood, but he had often waxed eloquently about the rugged grandeur of the forested hills that guarded its solitude. The timber was old-growth that had never been logged.

The nearest habitation was the farming hamlet of Benton, some seven or eight miles distant from the Usher estate. Fortunately for me, it was serviced by a rail spur. The rustic residents were typical of our fair state— taciturn, suspicious of strangers, and surly of manner. My casual remark that I was a friend of Roderick Usher met with blank stares and pinched lips. By paying twice what the job was worth, I was able to induce the owner of the general store to allow his laboring-man to drive me to the Usher estate in the store truck, an aging and rust-eaten Ford of uncertain and variable coloration.

The man, who smelled strongly of horse manure and who wore a checkered flannel shirt so faded that it almost looked a dirty white, spoke fewer than a dozen words during the entire drive along the twisting, rutted forest road, which in places had been almost washed away by the floods of the previous spring. Six months later the damage still had not been repaired. We were forced to edge around places where the road fell away into the swiftly running creek that flowed beside it. At several points the creek bubbled and frothed beneath sagging covered bridges scarcely wide enough to accommodate the truck's fenders. Their rotted beams groaned ominously beneath our weight, and I had occasion to be thankful that the truck had been unloaded before our departure.

The trees that pressed close on either side of the narrow road were ancient sentinels, their twisted and blackened trunks half-covered in green moss and shelved with ledges of white fungi. Their drooping boughs met above our heads and shut out most of the gray afternoon light, so that it was impossible to see the piled leaden clouds that filled the October sky. Dead leaves covered the road-ruts with faded red and gold hearts, or hung trembling from the branches of the younger oaks and maples that struggled for life between the shoulders of the brooding evergreens. The dark masses of these ancient guardians muted the annual celebration of autumn.

At last the truck ground its gears wearily over the crest of a low rise, and the trees opened on either side of the road, affording me the first glimpse of my destination. It was the bleakest prospect over which I have ever gazed, and my heart fell to look upon it.

True to Usher's description, the house occupied a hollow between the low, forested hills that surrounded it. Autumn had browned the grasses of the poorly cut lawn that extended down a gentle slope from its left side. The right side of the property and part of the front were flooded with a tarn of black and stagnant water that pressed against the very foundation stones of the structure. From my elevation, scant though it was, I could see no inlet for this fetid pool, in which grew rank weeds and rushes, but a dry bed of pebbles showed where the water ran out when it overflowed during rains. Its surface was more than half-covered by a kind of scum or algae, but where the water was open it reflected the leaden sky and the mold-blackened stone blocks and sightless black windows of the house of Usher in the most dismal fashion that may be imagined.

I knew from Usher's reminiscences of the place at university that the house was built of locally quarried stone blocks, but my imagination had never conceived so uninviting a façade. Its architecture bore no resemblance to the conventional timber-frame houses of historic New England that I love so well. It stood taller than it was broad, and its chimney-pierced roofs were steeply pitched and covered in black slate. The windows, although quite lofty and framed in gothic arches, were narrow and infrequent in number, so that the walls I could see from the elevation of the road seemed expanses of all-but-unbroken stone. The house reminded me of illustrations of old Scottish keeps—miniature castles built by minor lords in the Highlands to serve as strongholds against warring clans and bands of outlaws.

Curse of the House of Usher

The road wound down across an open stretch of browning lawn to a wooden bridge that spanned part of the tarn. I could not resist thinking of it as a drawbridge, although there was no mechanism for raising it, and the door of the house, though uncommonly wide, was a conventional door and not a castle gate.

The truck wheels squealed in protest as my taciturn driver applied the brakes. He sat looking forward through the dusty windscreen, his callused hands tightly clenched on the steering wheel. The uneven idle of the engine seemed unnaturally loud.

"Why have you stopped?" I asked him.

"There's the house," he said in his thickly accented Yankee English.

"I know that. Drive me down to the bridge so that I can unload my trunk."

"This here's the turning place," he said.

I repressed the impulse to anger and kept my tone casual. "You can drive down to the house and let me off, then back the truck up the hill, if you don't wish to turn on the lawn. You cannot expect me to carry my trunk all that distance."

His hands tightened on the steering wheel until their big knuckles turned white. "I won't go no further. This here's the turning place."

Nothing I could say would induce him to change his mind. Even a bribe of money left him unmoved.

So that's the way it is, I thought to myself. *There is some feud between the locals of Benton and the Ushers, and the fools won't venture onto the Usher estate.*

When I realized the futility of arguing with the man, I dragged my travel trunk off the back of the truck and watched as he turned the rusting vehicle and drove away without so much as a backward glance. I sat upon the trunk lid in disgust, facing the house, and listened to the sound of the poorly tuned engine diminish down the road. At length there was silence.

No movement came from the house or its grounds. My expectation that the truck had been heard or seen soon faded.

"I've had warmer welcomes," I muttered to myself with a slight rueful smile.

Silence swallowed my words. Not a leaf rustled. Not a bird sang. It was the stillness of death.

Leaving my trunk in the middle of the road where I had dragged it, I made my way to the neglected strip of lawn and crossed the bridge, which I noted was in need of minor repairs and fresh white paint. The heels of my travel boots on the planks thudded in the gray quiet, but no nesting bird was frightened from the black waters of the tarn. Only a few bubbles arose and broke on its surface, emitting a foul stench.

As I came near the house, I noticed a crack in the stonework that ran up from the tarn all the way to the eave of the roof in a jagged line, like the path followed by a bolt of lightning, but a path of shadow rather than a path of light. It was barely wide enough to have slid in the tips of my fingers—but it seemed out of keeping with the general state of the house, which overall was in good repair, although it had evidently been neglected during the past ten years or so.

I grasped the verdigris-covered brass knocker on the massive front door and let it fall twice against its sounding plate. After half a minute, footfalls echoed within, and the door swung wide. A dignified and elderly servant in a black suit, his gray hair carefully brushed to one side of his head and his thin gray moustache waxed on the ends, regarded me through watery brown eyes with the complete lack of emotion of all good butlers. I handed him my card.

"Randolph Carter. Mr. Usher is expecting me."

The elderly servant bowed without a word and admitted me into the front hall. He withdrew through a set of double doors of age-blackened walnut, closing them behind him and leaving me to admire the sweeping marble staircase with its massive and ornately carved banister, and the enormous crystal chandelier that hung above my head. The black marble tiles of the floor were polished to such a high luster that they reflected, as in a mirror, the portraits hanging on the paneled walls.

I approached beneath a painting that appeared from its ebony frame to be the oldest, and studied the unforgiving visage captured in oils. He was dressed in the costume of the early eighteenth century, with a powdered wig on his head. The family resemblance to Roderick Usher was unmistakable. His dark eyes glittered with life-force, so that I found it disconcerting to gaze long upon them.

Here sits the patriarch of the Usher clan, looking like some Oriental potentate surveying his lands and slaves, I thought. It must have been an unpleasant experience to fall under the power of so pitiless a countenance. Yet here he was today, no more than a few daubs of paint on canvas. Such is the transient mortality of all living things.

93

3.

The walnut doors parted with more authority than they had closed, and between them stood Roderick Usher, dressed in a blue velvet smoking jacket and matching Turkish smoking cap with a tassel that hung down to his broad shoulder. A slender black Russian cigarette glowed between his fingers.

I recognized his familiar features at once, but found myself regarding them with more alarm than affection. It was the same high brow, the same gray, heavy-lidded eyes and hooked nose, the same strong jaw and sardonically curled lips, so familiar in my memory, but how changed they were! His eyes in their hollow sockets looked haunted, and the skin across his prominent cheekbones seemed stretched like dry parchment. His hair, once a glossy black, had turned to gray and hung in ragged disorder where it escaped his cap, so fine in texture that it seemed to float around his countenance like the smoke that rose from his cigarette.

He hesitated only a moment, then swept across the tiles and took my hand between his. "It was good of you to come, Randolph."

His tone held genuine warmth. At such closeness the signs of dissolute living were plain in the lines indelibly graven across his face—lines that only a youth wasted in vice can cut on living flesh. I detected a slight tremble in his hands before he released me. Moved by some impulse of remembered youth, I clapped him on the shoulder in a familiar way and squeezed his upper arm before dropping my hand.

"There's nowhere else I'd rather be," I said, and at that moment I truly meant the words.

He glanced up at the portrait in the ebony frame. "I see you've made the acquaintance of Uriah Usher, the builder of this house. He laid many of these stones with his own hands, did you know?"

"We were having a staring contest, but I lost."

He laughed lightly, in the way I remembered from our university days. "Well, well; come into the drawing room where we can talk. Where are your bags?"

I described the uncouth behavior of my driver. It raised no surprise in Usher's gray eyes. He ordered his man, whose name was Simmons, to have the trunk carried into the house and up to my room.

The cavernous drawing room boasted a dizzyingly high paneled ceiling and a great stone fireplace. A grand piano occupied a corner of the floor. Beside it, near the wall, stood a harp, and across the cushion of a chair rested a guitar.

Usher guided me to a padded French settee covered in pink silk and we sat together on it. Behind us, the weak light from the clouded sky came through three mullioned windows framed by long drapes of a deep burgundy. It illuminated with a kind of pallid glow the smoke that hung in the air and softened the edges of things, rendering the shadowed furnishings of the room vague. Opposite the settee, an open arch led into what I presumed to be the library, as I could see tall cases of books lining its walls.

"If only you'd informed me in advance of the day of your arrival, I might have arranged for your transportation from the village."

"I didn't know myself when I could get away from Boston. It's a matter of no importance."

He studied me with a smile on his lips, but in his eye lurked a calculating assessment that he failed to conceal, or perhaps did not attempt to conceal. It was hardly to be expected that his manner could be other than worldly, I told myself, given his globe-spanning travels and his varied experiences.

"I almost feel we've never been apart, I see your name so often in the literary magazines. You've gained a sizeable reputation as an artist."

I shrugged and made a deprecating gesture with my hand. "The critics need something to write about. Next year it will be somebody else."

"You are too modest. I have all your books, in there." He nodded toward the library.

For the better part of an hour we talked of Miskatonic and Arkham, each contributing scraps of information overheard during the intervening years about boys we had known there, since grown to men and making their way in the world with varying degrees of success. The expressionless butler, Simmons, brought in a silver tray with brandy glasses and a crystal decanter filled with an amber liquid. The drink warmed my blood and made me more animated in my storytelling, but I declined the offer of the Russian cigarettes that Usher continued to smoke as he listened, all the while watching me with his keen gaze.

A bit of white moving at the corner of my eye drew my attention through the arch to the library, where a woman stood before a set of shelves studying the polished leather spines of books. She drew down a slender volume and opened it, seemingly oblivious to my regard.

"Sister, our guest has arrived," Usher said without raising his voice. So silent was the house, it was scarce necessary to speak above a whisper.

She closed the book and turned with a bemused smile. Her gray eyes wandered for a moment before settling on my face.

"Come and join us, Sister."

She seemed to float rather than walk across the marble floor. The long and full white skirts of her dress concealed her shoes, adding to the illusion. The upper part covered her arms with white lace but left her hands and shoulders bare, creating a charming effect. She was even thinner than her brother, except for a portliness about the waist that her lacings could not entirely conceal. Her eyes seemed almost shining, they were so filled with vital spirits, but her lips, though fuller than her brother's, were pale as wax, and her cheekbones stood out sharply on the oval of her face, which was framed by long curling hair as black as the wing of a raven.

We stood as she entered, and Usher made the introductions.

"Madeline has been looking forward to having someone other than me to talk to," Usher said. His voice had a slight edge, and she glanced sharply at him.

"It is a pleasure to meet you at last, Randolph. My brother has told me so many of your adventures at Arkham."

Her fingers felt chill against mine, as though no blood flowed through them.

"Adventures?" I looked at Usher. "Did we have adventures, Roderick?"

Her laughter sounded hollow, as though it echoed in an empty room.

"The time you and my brother used an old book you found in the university library to summon a demon? Don't you remember?"

I forced laughter and cast a glance at Usher, surprised that he had spoken of the event, which I had uttered to no living human being.

"Our minds were filled with the spirit of inquiry, my dear. We were so young." Usher laid his hand on her arm. "Shall we play for our guest?"

She smiled and nodded. He went to the chair and took up the guitar from its seat. I expected her to sit at the grand piano, but instead she sat before the harp and tilted it back against her shoulder.

Usher noticed my gaze upon the piano. "I suffer from a rare affliction that causes any harsh sounds to be physically painful. I can no longer bear to hear the piano—a pity, for it is a fine instrument. The softer music of strings does not torment my ears."

I realized that since entering the house I had not heard a clock chime the quarter hours.

"Have you always suffered so?"

"In my youth the condition was much less severe, but as I grow long in years, it worsens."

They played several German folk songs while I listened and watched Madeline. Her beauty was ethereal, almost fairy-like. She seemed to inhabit another realm and this one at the same moment. I could see that she was Usher's twin. It was evident in the line of her shoulder, the length of her neck, the noble height of her brow, but all that was angular and harsh in his features was softened and beautified in hers.

"Wonderful," I said, applauding effusively when they indicated the performance was at an end. "I've never heard such beautiful playing."

Usher acknowledged the compliment with a slight bow of his head.

"My family has always been gifted in music, among other things."

"Brother, I grow tired. I must go to my room and lie down."

"Of course, Madeline. How thoughtless of me, let me help you to your feet." He called for his butler. "Simmons will help you up the stairs."

We watched the little gray man walk with her into the entrance hall and ascend the marble staircase.

"She is dying," Usher said to me without preamble.

I stared at him, uncertain if I had heard him correctly.

"It is a wasting illness, hereditary in nature. Nothing can be done in a medical way to cure it. The doctor was here in the morning. He told me in confidence that she may have as much as three months remaining, or she could take a seizure and die tomorrow."

I went to him and took his hand into mine. "Roderick, I am saddened beyond words. If there is anything I may do, you have only to ask."

"One thing you may do for me, old friend. Remain in this house and help me to find the source of the curse that has blighted my family for untold generations, and that now kills my dear sister."

4.

Taking a step back from him, I studied his face for signs of madness. "Curse?"

"You heard me rightly, Randolph. Do not look at me so. My reason remains sound, though for how much longer, I cannot predict. Come with me into the library."

We passed through the arch, and he closed its pocket doors, sealing us away from the rest of the house. A single window let in a pale grayness, for the days are short in October and the hour had grown late.

"It is unfortunate you did not arrive sooner, but we may still have enough time. I told you there was nothing that could be done medically, but there may be another way to save her."

"Why did you not mention this curse in your letter?"

He looked at me with a bitter smile on the corners of his lips.

"Would you have come?"

I hesitated only for an instant.

"To help your sister? I would have come immediately."

"I believe you," he said, nodding so that the cloud of fine gray hair around his brow rippled like seaweed in an invisible current. "But I could not take that chance, old friend. I've grown cynical over the years, and my faith in men has often been disappointed."

He went to a sideboard and used a Lucifer match to light the wick of a glass oil-lamp. The grayness from the window was replaced by a wavering golden glow, and the acrid tang of sulfur mingled with the smell of tobacco smoke.

"Come to the reading table and seat yourself," he told me.

Setting the lamp on the table, he went to a shelf behind me and drew down a leather-bound journal that was closed by means of a tied red ribbon. He tugged one end of the ribbon loose from its bow and opened the journal before me.

"This is our family record. My great-great-grandfather, Ezekiel Usher, began it, and various members of my family have added bits of lore to it over the generations."

I leafed through the journal without enthusiasm. The antique writing was in several different hands. It would take hours to read through the record from beginning to end, even if I were able to decipher all its pages.

"Tell me about this family curse."

His eyes widened with enthusiasm. There was a disturbing fanaticism in their depths. He shuffled the pages of the journal and pointed to a place near the beginning.

"The first mention of it occurs in this record, but I believe it to be as old as the house itself. Ezekiel wrote of a servant girl found drowned in the waters of the tarn. The explanation was that she had slipped off the bridge and hit her head on its edge, but my forebear never believed it. He writes here of various members of the household seeing movement in the water."

"Movement?"

"As though something were sliding beneath the surface. You may have noticed that the water is as black as ink. Nothing can be seen within it beyond a depth of a few inches, but sometimes I myself have observed ripples, and heard splashes."

"Fish, perhaps? Frogs?"

"The water is poisonous. Nothing of the animal kind lives in it."

"What has this to do with your family curse?"

He straightened up and paced to the other end of the reading table.

"I don't know. Perhaps nothing."

I gazed at the pages of the open journal in perplexity.

"How does this curse express itself?"

Usher sat abruptly in the chair at the opposite end of the table and leaned forward, staring into my eyes with disturbing intensity.

"It has been a peculiarity of my family line that it flourishes only in direct paternal descent, and only within the walls of this house."

"I'm not quite sure I understand you, old fellow."

He clenched his fist and brought it down on the table with a thud.

"The women of my family who marry and move away to live with their husbands are invariably childless. Either they are sterile, or the fruits of their wombs abort themselves."

"Always?" I was unable to keep a skeptical tone from my voice.

He nodded.

"That is most strange, I agree," I said at length. "Still, I hardly see how it affects the health of your sister."

"There is more, Randolph. Those of my family line who remain within these walls suffer a strange wasting of their vitality and are afflicted with all manner of uncommon infirmities. In my own case, it takes the form of my preternatural sensitivity to harsh noises. Suffice it to say that the Ushers do not live into old age, but shrivel and die in their prime of life, as though the very life-force of their souls were being drained away."

"You believe that Madeline's complaint is the result of this hereditary wasting of vital force?"

"I do indeed," he said with emphasis.

Spreading my hands in apology, I shook my head. "If the Usher family line suffers from some form of hereditary wasting disease, I fail to see how I can be of any use to you, Roderick. I am not a physician."

He ignored my attempt to placate him. "As I said before, I do not believe my sister's complaint to be medical."

"Then what is it?" I asked bluntly.

He looked from side to side as though expecting to see something in the shadows, but what that might have been I could not imagine, as we were quite alone in the library. Leaning still further forward, he lowered his voice. "I believe there is something in this house that feeds on the lives of my family. It has sapped my dearly beloved sister of her strength, and largely of her sanity, and unless we stop it, I am convinced that it will soon deprive her of life, as it has so many of my ancestors."

In the stillness my uneasy chuckle sounded ghoulish. "Then the solution is simple enough. You and your sister must move out of this house and return to it no more."

He closed his eyelids and sighed like a man whose heart is about to break from sorrow. "Do you think I haven't thought of that? If only it were so easy." He opened his eyes and studied me with a solemn gaze. "I cannot expect you to understand our situation. I am the last of my line. All of the Ushers are dead other than my dear sister. Were we to leave the house, it would pass into other hands, and that is unthinkable. This has been the seat of the Ushers for more than two centuries. How can you comprehend, you whose ancestry means so little to you? For the Ushers, family is everything. This house is our world. We cannot and will not abandon it."

His words made little sense. With the very life of his sister in the balance, what other considerations were there? Yet it was obvious from his sincerity that he believed what he told me, so I made no attempt to argue.

"Have you formed any conjecture as to the origin of this family curse?"

"Indeed I have. My forebear Ezekiel mentions in the journal a family legend that old Uriah Usher, who sailed from Ireland to America in 1747 and who built this house, erected it on the site of a circle of stones."

"A stone circle? Do you mean a ritual circle erected by the natives of this land?"

"A stone circle, yes, but as to who erected it—" He paused as though hesitant to finish the thought. "It was a circle of large stones. Uriah surveyed the surrounding hills and concluded that it was the best location to build upon. The legend says that he incorporated the stones of the circle into the foundations of the house itself. As for the rest of the blocks, he quarried them from nearby to save the cost of transport, which would have been considerable."

"Do you mean to say that the tarn is not a natural body of water, but a stone quarry?"

His eyes flashed with enthusiasm. "So I believe, although it is not written anywhere in the journal or in any other family account."

Usher's ancestor was a practical man, I thought. When building with stone, the greatest cost is often that of transporting the stones from the quarry to the construction site. Yet to deliberately create such a dismal pool of poisonous black water at the very foundation of the house itself seemed folly.

Usher read my thoughts. "We would drain the tarn were it possible to do so, but the terrain of the valley is against us. There is simply no lower-lying hollow into which to drain the water. My grandfather tried pumping it out with a stationary steam engine, but he could never lower the level by more than six or seven inches, and within a night it was back at its usual elevation, from which it never varies by more than an inch."

"Where do you suppose the water comes from?"

"When the quarry was excavated, the workers must have tapped into some concealed spring. The mass of the water above pressing down upon it keeps more water from issuing from its vent, but when the water level drops, the spring replenishes the tarn. At any rate, that is my surmise."

He fell into a brooding silence. I waited for him to speak at greater length, but he seemed lost in his interior ruminations.

"Is it your belief that this family curse is due to the desecration of the stone circle?"

"It must be," he snapped. "What else could it be?"

"If you are correct, then I suggest you consult the local Indian tribe. It may be that their medicine man— "

His harsh bark of laughter cut off my words. "Don't you think I've tried? I spent the better part of last summer talking to Indians, and do you know what I learned? They're dead, Randolph. The tribe that built that stone circle ceased to exist centuries ago, probably before the house was erected."

The silence lengthened between us. I found myself unable to think of any words that might comfort him, or humor his mania. That his mind was unbalanced by worry over Madeline's condition, there could be no doubt.

"You know the studies of our university days?" he said.

It took a few moments reflection before I understood his meaning.

"Do you mean our occult experiments?"

"Precisely those. It may be that they will serve us best when at last we are confronted by the source of my family curse."

"Is such a confrontation imminent?"

He looked at me across the table with dispassion, as though from some great eminence, and there was nothing of human emotion in his voice. "I feel it must be. My sister and I are the last of our line, and when she dies, I cannot imagine how I shall go on alone."

"What is it you expect me to do?" I asked, ignoring the implication of his words.

"I want you to inquire about the curse in the dreamlands, which I understand you have the power to enter at will. Seek there for an antidote, or at least an anodyne."

My expression caused him to fall silent. In a few words I told him of my inability to enter the dreamlands for the past several years, and my despair of ever regaining my former ability. Usher gave no outward sign, but I sensed the frustration within him.

"You must make the attempt. Everything I have, this house, its lands, my very life and that of my sister depend on it. Tell me that you will try."

To humor his mania, I assured him that I would attempt to inquire in the dreamworlds about his family curse.

5.

My bedroom was spacious and well appointed, but it still retained an odor of dust and mildew when I entered it to sleep. Not enough time had passed since my unexpected arrival to air it properly.

By way of compensation, the staff of the house had done their best to make me welcome. One of the servants had lit a glass oil lamp similar to the one in the library and placed it on the stand beside the bed, which was a massive edifice of carved mahogany with four tall spiral posts as thick through their middles as the leg of an elephant. My trunk rested in a corner out of the way. I discovered by inspection that my clothing had been taken from it and put into the drawers in the cedar-lined armoire, or hung from the hangers on its rod. My change of shoes was set neatly beside the door.

It had been my intention to read some of the Usher family journal before sleep, and for this purpose I had carried it up the stairs from the library, but I soon found that the train journey from Boston and the ride in the delivery truck had left me so fatigued that my thoughts kept wandering. After ten minutes of effort, I closed the leather cover of the journal with a sigh of frustration and went to bed. The sheets and pillowcase had been changed, and were newly laundered. For this small grace I gave silent thanks and turned down the wick of the lamp until the flame died within its glass shade.

The perversity of human nature is consistent and predictable. Now that I lay in bed, in total darkness, my fatigue lifted from my mind and the need for sleep abated. I found myself listening to the tiny sounds of the old house. The creak of a beam. The squeak of a mouse. The ticking of a beetle in the wall. Each small noise was like thunder in the silence. The clouds that all afternoon had blocked the rays of the sun at last unrolled from the darkened heavens and allowed silvery moonlight to paint itself across the foot of the bed quilt as I lay beneath it, staring upward at the dark ceiling, wide awake.

As a rule, my control over my ability to fall asleep is greater than that of the average person. Indeed, it might almost be called preternatural. This is a gift I was born with that I have honed through years of intense dream working. This night some inner governor refused to allow my awareness to relax into the arms of Morpheus. I even found myself holding my breath during long intervals of complete silence, when the only sound was my own heartbeat.

The crack of a twig came faintly to my ears from outside my window. For a time I continued to lie in bed, resolved to ignore it. Finally, curiosity got the better of me. I threw off the quilt and the sheet and went to the narrow mullioned window, which looked better suited to a Gothic church than a private dwelling. My room was on the second level, and the ceilings of the ground level were uncommonly high. This gave me an elevation from which to overlook the grounds.

My bedroom was located on the side of the house against which the main body of the tarn pressed. The black mirror of the water reflected the starry sky, for the clouds of the afternoon had completely vanished. A moon nearing its fullness rode high above, painting the ragged grass of the lawn at the water's edge, and the leaves of the shade trees beyond it, with a whiteness like frost. It was a convincing illusion, but the night was too mild for frost.

A figure moved with slow steps around the far edge of the tarn. It was a woman wrapped in a green cloak, her head bowed as she watched the path before her feet, which appeared to be naked. I recognized Usher's sister, Madeline.

The elevation of the nearly-full moon told me that the hour must be close to midnight. It occurred to me that Madeline might be walking in her sleep, and might be in danger of tumbling into the tarn and drowning. Then she turned her head to look behind, and I saw that her eyes were wide open. Another more insidious possibility forced its way into my thoughts—that she might have come to the decision to end her own life, before it was terminated against her will by her illness. If so, was it my place to intervene?

In the end, I did not descend to the lawn but continued to watch from my window. At times, she seemed to look directly at me, as though she could see me standing in the darkened room, but this must have been impossible. I kept my face out of the moonlight that shone through the glass.

She continued along the edge of the tarn until she came to a stone that jutted up from the grass at a crooked angle. Here she stopped and seemed to caress the stone with her hand before turning to face the star-shot black pool. An owl sounded its night call from the trees, but she did not turn her head. All her attention was directed at the tarn. She seemed entranced, as though mesmerized, and had her eyes not been wide open I would have judged her to sleepwalk.

She raised her slender white arms in a gesture of invocation and began to speak, but in so low a voice that I could not distinguish any words. Only a faint murmur reached my straining ears. When she had done, she stood and waited.

The stars in the tarn rippled and parted, and the very water itself rose and moved toward her. For the first time the thought occurred to me that I was the dreamer, and that I lay asleep in the bed, only imagining that I stood at my window. But when I glanced back to the bed, I found it empty. My years of experience as a traveler through the dreamlands gave me assurance that I was wide awake, and even though I could no longer dream-walk at will, I trusted the old instincts.

She did not cry out or try to flee. Instead, she took a step forward so that her naked feet entered the black water. Her long cloak fell open, and I saw that she stood naked beneath it. The moonlight caught the dome of her belly and her white thighs, but shadows preserved the modesty of her sex. They cloaked her skin like a garment, save for the parts I have mentioned and the tips of her breasts, which stood forth in vivid contrast to the darkness inside her open cloak.

Something from the tarn extended itself toward her. At first I thought it was a serpent raising its head from the bulge of black water that shivered and gleamed at her feet, but it was too long and thin to have supported its own weight as it touched and seemed to caress her belly. I felt the blood flush in my face as this snake-like tentacle moved lower and passed between her thighs. The sense that I witnessed a union forbidden by all the laws of God and nature surged within me. A mingling of outrage and shamefulness warred in my heart, but I could not turn my eyes away as she let her head fall back on her neck in a posture of ecstasy. The loose cloak slipped from her shoulders and fell behind her to the grass.

Her body shuddered and a soft moaning sounded through the night, like the cry of some forest creature mating in mingled pain and delight. In moments the serpentine extension of the water withdrew itself and the rounded bulge moved back to the center of the tarn and descended, leaving its surface again a starry mirror as the ripples settled.

For more than a minute Madeline stood motionless. Then she shook her head, as though to clear it, and turned to pick up and put back on her cloak. Without a backward glance she returned along the margin of the black pool the way she had come, making toward the bridge and the front door—but before she reached the bridge she passed around the corner of the house and was lost to my sight.

I stepped away from the window, badly shaken. When I drew my hand across my face, I discovered that it was covered in a chill sweat. Did Usher know about his sister's nocturnal visits to the tarn? I had no illusions that this was the first time—she had conducted herself with too much self-assurance. Had I seen what I thought I had seen or was it some trick of the moonlight?

When I returned to my bed, I anticipated a sleepless night, but it could not have been more than a few minutes before I drifted into unconsciousness, my fatigue at last overpowering the heated workings of my imagination.

6.

My next awareness was that of a housemaid, gently shaking me awake by the shoulder to inform me that Mr. Usher wished to see me in the drawing room at my earliest convenience. I washed in the basin of fresh water provided and quickly dressed myself before descending the stairs.

A short and rather corpulent man wearing gold-framed eyeglasses and a faded brown travel suit was in conversation with Usher in the hall. Both men turned at my approach, and Usher introduced me. The little fellow was William Hoffman, Usher's family physician. His round face bore an expression of watchful slyness, and there was an impudent smirk on the thick lips beneath his bristling salt-and-pepper moustache. With reluctance I accepted his hand and found it moist. I guessed his presence in the house so early in the morning could not bode any good thing, but held my silence as Usher finished his words of parting and allowed the physician to make his way out the door.

"It's bad, Randolph. It's very bad, I'm afraid."

His face was haggard. All the lines and hollows across it were accentuated by a new sorrow that left him like a damned soul, staring back at the fading shore from the boat of Charon.

"Madeline?"

"She's dead. Her maid found her this morning. We called Doctor Hoffman immediately, but it was quite pointless. Her body was already cold when she was discovered."

I put my hand on his shoulder but he did not seem to notice the touch. He seemed dazed, like a man not yet recovered from the stunning effect of some blow to the head.

"I am terribly sorry, Roderick. Did Hoffman venture an immediate cause for her sudden death?"

"A fit in the night, he called it, but I believe he was only guessing." His face hardened. "He wanted to take her body back to Benton for an autopsy, but I absolutely forbade it. I will not have my sister cut open for the puerile study of fools."

"What will you do?"

He blinked and seemed to see me for the first time. He attempted to force a smile but the effect was ghastly and I was glad when he ceased the effort.

"Her death was hardly unexpected, although it came sooner rather than later. I have her resting place prepared in the family crypt beneath this house. I even have her coffin. It arrived from the maker last week. If I might prevail on your good graces …"

"Of course, old friend, anything you need. You have but to ask."

"Will you help me to prepare her corpse, and carry the coffin into the crypt? I could have the servants do it, but somehow that seems too remote and heartless. She deserves better than to be handed off to servants, don't you think?"

To me it seemed that the tasks he mentioned were best left to the trained staff of a mortuary, but I held my tongue and nodded.

"You mean to inter her without embalming?"

"It was her wish. She had a morbid horror of being embalmed, and I shall respect it, as irrational as it may have been."

"Of course, as you should."

The corpse of Madeline still lay in her bed. Her cheeks were pale, but still so filled with life that I expected her breast beneath the cotton sheet to rise and fall. She was quite cold to the touch. I noted that after returning from her visit to the tarn, she had put on a nightdress of white silk.

We prepared the corpse as best we could. I withdrew to allow Usher to clothe his sister in her funeral dress, then returned to help him place her in the coffin. His cheeks were still wet with tears, but he seemed unaware of it. He informed me that Madeline had chosen the dress herself— an elegant garment of gray silk trimmed with black. Usher spent an inordinate amount of time brushing her hair with a silver hairbrush, and I received the impression that it was not the first time he had performed this function. At last he closed the lid of the coffin and latched it.

"Help me to carry it to the crypt."

"Is there to be no funeral service?" I asked in surprise.

He looked at me. It was like gazing at a skull with two dark eyes set deep in its sockets, and a mask of skin stretched across its bony ridges.

"What would be the point? I am the only family she had in the world, the only one left to mourn her. When I die, there will be no one at all."

It was not the time to discuss the matter. Usher's mind was less than wholly rational. I reasoned that it would do no harm should the corpse rest in the crypt for a few days, until he regained some of his composure. Then he might reconsider a more conventional funeral arrangement for her. But it would be folly to try to bring it up this day.

The coffin was well made and consequently quite heavy. Even so, Usher would not ask his servants for their help. They watched in silence as we wrestled the box down the main staircase and into the entrance to the cellars. It was fortunate for us that the silver handles at each end of the coffin had been fashioned for more than mere display.

By the time we got it to the crypt, I was covered in sweat and had to resist the impulse to curse in frustration. Usher seemed unperturbed. Despite his thinness, he retained the strength of limb that had distinguished him at Miskatonic. He bore up under the work much better than I, at least in a physical sense.

We set the sealed coffin upon a stone table that to my fanciful mind resembled an altar. There were other similar long boxes in recesses in the walls, presumably occupied by dead members of the family. Some of them showed signs of great age. The air in the crypt had a smell that was impossible to define, but in some way cloyingly repulsive. It was not the smell of decay. It may have been the lingering scent of long-dead flowers that had worked its way into the very stones of the place. It made my stomach roil.

"Usher, I must get out of this cellar. The smell …"

For the first time that morning, he looked at me with something resembling human feeling.

"Of course, old man. Thank you for your help. I couldn't have managed it without you."

He gripped my arm in his hands with sudden enthusiasm and drew me close, staring into my face. The light from the oil lamp gave it a ghoulish strangeness.

"You do see that I couldn't let that oily little fool, Hoffman, touch her? You don't know what foul creatures like him do with the dead. I'm a man of the world, and I've heard stories and seen things in Europe that would freeze your blood. He would have defiled her, Randolph. At least here she is safe from his touch."

What could I say in response to this? I pressed my lips into a smile and waited for him to release my arm.

"You go," he said, waving me out of the crypt with a flick of his pale fingers. "I will stay for a time and talk with my sister."

I left him standing over the coffin, staring down at it as though he could see through the polished rosewood planks of its lid. His lips moved silently, but whether in prayer or in speaking her name, I know not.

7.

In the late afternoon, while Usher lay asleep in his room from the effects of the laudanum given to him by Hoffman, I went outside and slowly traced a semicircle around the margin of the tarn, moving from the bridge at the front door around to the side overlooked by the window of my bedroom. There was a kind of path worn in the long grass, indicating light but regular traffic.

As I walked along, I was conscious of the water at my left side, like black oil. The sunlight penetrated it no more than a few inches. From the rotting vegetation that floated on its surface there arose a faint but vile odor of decay. It was the scent of funeral flowers left too long untended. I suddenly realized that it was the same scent I had detected in the crypt, only stronger. Occasional clusters of bubbles burst upward, as though from the exhalation of some submarine creature, but they may have been caused by expanding methane gas.

So I told myself, as I tried not to let my imagination get the bit between its teeth and run away with me. How a woman could follow this path in the depths of night was beyond my comprehension. It tried my nerves to the limit in broad daylight, having seen what I saw from my window. Nothing in the universe would have induced me to walk here after dark.

I came to the tilted stone and stopped to study it. In the soft mud at the edge of the water I saw the imprint of her naked feet, still quite clear. The stone was a kind of menhir or standing stone. It projected some four feet above the sod, though how much of it extended below the ground I have no way to know. On the side fronting the house I found markings that looked like writing of some sort, but the characters resembled no alphabet with which I was familiar, either in this world or the dreamlands. They were greatly worn by the action of the elements, and I judged them at least several centuries old.

I straightened my back and looked slowly around, with the distinct crawling sensation between my shoulder blades of being watched. There was no movement in the line of shade trees at the edge of the lawn other than a slight trembling of the golden and orange leaves in the mild breeze. I turned to study the black windows of the house. No face confronted me in their blind eyes, which seemed to gaze blankly down with an expression of startled surprise from under the gothic arches of their stone brows.

Movement drew my attention to the water at my feet. There was something in the water, just far enough below the surface that I could discern none of its details, other than that it was round and about the size of a dinner plate. It appeared and disappeared with regularity. A kind of yellowish-gray border surrounded a coal-black center the size of my clenched fist. Drawn by an irresistible curiosity, I leaned my face down toward the inky surface of the tarn, standing as far out over the water as I could manage without slipping into the wet mud.

The object rose nearer to the surface. I regarded it in silence for a minute or so, unable to place its vague outline with any object or water beast in my memory. It was then that it *blinked* at me, its broad lid descending slowly and then opening again with more quickness as the black circle in its center expanded in size.

I very nearly tumbled into the tarn when I jerked my head away. I did fall over backwards into the grass, and struck the back of my head against the corner of the standing stone. There was a flash of light inside my skull. When I opened my eyes on the cloudless blue sky, it was to the sound of my name being called. I sat up slowly, and my head began to pound with a vengeance. When I felt the back of it, there was a lump but fortunately no blood. I pushed myself to my feet, leaning on the stone for aid, and saw that the elderly butler, Simmons, was hailing me from the open front door, asking if I wished to take afternoon tea with Usher.

I waved my hand to show him that I was unhurt, and hollered that I would return to the house momentarily. He stood as though uncertain for several seconds, then withdrew and closed the door.

My vision was double. Blinking, I pressed my thumb and index finger to the corners of my closed eyelids, then focused my eyes on the surface of the water. The eye, if such a thing it was, had withdrawn. Was it possible that I had merely imagined it? Could a frog or a fish have caused such a bizarre fancy? The mind sees what it expects to see. I remembered in the past how often I had caught a glimpse of my cat from the corner of my vision, or seen her shape curled in the semi-darkness among the rumpled blankets at the foot of my bed, only to realize later that she was in another part of the house, and that I could not possibly have seen her. Such is the power of expectation. But why would I expect to see a gigantic eye in the tarn?

I looked again for the footprints of Madeline Usher, and to my surprise found that they had been obliterated. I must have scraped them out with my heels when I fell, I thought. Yet I saw that my shoes were not covered in wet mud. Leaving this riddle for later consideration, I returned to the house to take tea with my sorrowing host.

8.

Hoffman returned with his little black leather bag the next day to examine Usher. As he was leaving, he motioned me aside with a discreet wave of his chubby hand, and indicated with a jerk of his head that he wanted to speak with me outside the house. I told Usher that I would see the doctor off, and went with him to his automobile, which was parked on the lawn at the far end of the footbridge.

"It is most fortunate that Roderick has a friend visiting with him at this trying moment in his life," the little man began by way of preamble.

"I would rather my visit had taken place under more agreeable circumstances."

The sly face of the portly little man did not inspire me with confidence. I could well see why Usher distrusted him. He stared up at me with a sidelong tilt of his head, like a bird eyeing a worm.

"Roderick's mental state is most precarious. It stands balanced on a precipice above a fathomless abyss. He was never what one would call strong of mind, and his obsessive affection for his sister has only aggravated the shock of her loss."

"Obsessive affection?"

He smiled and licked his thick lips beneath his bristling moustache, which resembled a shaving brush.

"Roderick and his sister have been cut off in this house from the society of others of their social standing for many years. Her brother tells me that she has received no male admirers for a very long time, yet her physical condition at the time of her death speaks otherwise."

"What physical condition?" I asked with some heat. "See here, Doctor, what are you driving at?"

He shrugged and raised his thick eyebrows. "But surely you noticed when you saw her? Madeline Usher was with child."

I stared at him, shocked beyond words.

"She was pregnant?"

"About six months, I should say. Perhaps seven months."

I remembered noting the rounded dome of her lower abdomen, but nothing so outrageous as pregnancy had even entered my thoughts. I could not find words.

"The servants have told me that Madeline received no male callers for over a year. The butler and the two other male servants are well advanced in years. I suppose it is possible that one or the other of them could be the father, but it seems unlikely."

Outrage built slowly within me, as I stared at his toad-like, smiling face, so knowing in its slyness. What he suggested was unthinkable. The effort to hold myself back from striking him down made my entire body shake.

"Leave this estate immediately," I said in a low tone. "If you delay, I will not be responsible for my actions."

He blinked in owlish surprise. "What do you mean?"

"If you don't leave at once I shall throw you into the tarn."

A look of sudden fear passed over his features. It was oddly intense, and seemed more extreme than was justified by my very real threat. Without uttering another word, he rounded the rear bumper of his Nash and almost leapt into the driver's seat. The rear tires spun on the gravel, casting several stones into the black water, and he vanished in a cloud of dust over the crest of the hill and in among the trees.

9.

By this time I wanted nothing more fervently than to leave this ghastly house of sorrows, with its black tarn and looming evergreens, behind me forever. I stayed on as Usher's guest. I could not desert him at so tragic a passage in his life. He had no one except the servants, and after two days, not even them, because all of them—even the silent, silver-haired Simmons—turned in their resignations and left the Usher estate.

I found myself cooking for both Usher and myself. He was in no fit state to do anything. The death of his sister almost unhinged his finely balanced brain. He wandered through the rooms of the empty house like a ghost, seldom speaking to me. I feared that the slightest obstruction in his life might cast him into complete madness. He did not say why the servants had left the house. Perhaps he did not know the reason himself. I wondered if it had anything to do with the creature in the tarn. Had they known about the creature? Did Usher himself know about it? On the day of my arrival he had alluded to seeing something stir beneath the black waters. I dared not mention the matter lest I sever his last link with reality.

I think it was four days after the death of Madeline, or it may have been five, that I was awakened in the night by a crash of thunder that shook the stone walls of the house to its foundations. I blinked the colors from my eyes and sat up in bed. A lightning flash while I lay asleep had impressed itself through my closed eyelids. For several minutes I sat in the darkness, blinking the spots from my vision and listening to the wind throw the raindrops against my window like sheets of hailstones.

It came to me that the lightning might have struck some portion of the house, and that it would be prudent to investigate since there was no one within its walls but Usher and myself, and Usher was in no mental condition to do any kind of practical work. I put on my dressing gown and slippers, and made my way by touch along the walls out the door of my room. My night vision began to return, and I was able to distinguish the hallway and the banister at its middle section that marked the upper landing of the main stairs.

I walked the length of the hall, sniffing for smoke. This may seem an insufficient precaution but my sense of smell is uncommonly keen. I felt confident that if anything were burning above, I would detect the odor. There was no scent of smoke. I made my way toward the stairs, meaning to descend and go outside to examine the roofs and chimney pots of the house for damage. The lightning flashed periodically, giving me confidence that I would get brief but clear views of the roofs.

The door to Usher's bedroom was shut. I paused outside it and listened for the sound of movement, but heard nothing above the intermittent thunder but the gusts of wind against the walls and the rattle of rain against the windows. There seemed no reason to disturb the sleep of my troubled friend.

Curse of the House of Usher

When I reached the hall, a noise drew my attention to the rear of the house, where the kitchen and storeroom were located. I stood listening at the foot of the stairs, but it did not come again, and I could not imagine what might have caused it. I wondered if Usher had been awakened by a crash of thunder, and had himself descended to investigate before I left my room.

I walked toward the kitchen, moving cautiously through the darkness, which was infrequently broken by flashes from the windows. To my surprise, the door to the cellar stood open. Usher often descended to the crypt to mourn over the coffin of his sister, but insofar as I knew, he had never done so in the middle of the night, even though it was perfectly possible that he went to her while I slept. It was not a topic I dared raise with him in his present unbalanced state.

For a time I hesitated, unsure which course to follow. I had no wish to intrude on my friend's mourning, but neither did I dare leave him alone in the cellars at night given his fragile condition. At last I descended the stones of the cellar stair and made my way along the damp lower corridor toward the crypt. A thin band of lamplight shone from under its ironbound door.

While I was still a dozen paces from the door, strange noises from within the crypt made me stop and advance more slowly. The windowless door stood shut, but the gap beneath it was wide enough to permit the transmission of sounds. I laid my fingers on the chill iron of the latch, but hesitated. The noises continued. There was the rhythmic creak of wood, as though something were rocking back and forth. An image came to me of Usher, kneeling on the stone floor, rocking back and forth in the extremity of his mourning. Then I heard his grunt. It was a bestial sound, like that of a boar rooting in the mud with its snout. Without pausing to think, I pressed down on the latch and opened the door.

You may know the common expression, one's heart grew cold. It is more than mere words. As I stood before the door with my hand on the latch, the blood drained from my chest, and I felt a tangible chillness under my ribs, as though cool well water were being poured over my heart. My head began to spin, and it was only my grip on the latch that prevented me from falling. I swallowed and licked my lips that had suddenly grown numb. With greater care than I had used to approach, I withdrew from the door, walking backward, as though from the very gateway of hell.

10.

I was in the library when Usher found me. I needed time to think. He entered through the hall door and stopped when he saw me sitting at the reading table, my head in my hands, my fingers laced through my hair, the flame of the lamp fluttering wildly within its glass shade because in my confusion I had neglected to set the height of the wick after lighting it.

We stared at each other through the dancing shadows. Neither of us spoke. I could find no words, and Usher's tongue seemed frozen to the roof of his mouth. But his dark eyes spoke volumes in those voiceless minutes. I saw there shame, regret, self-loathing, remorse, frustration, anger, and defiance.

"You cannot understand," he said at last, his clear voice ringing out like rifle shots above the howl of the wind, for the storm was increasing in its fury.

"Usher, how could you— "

"I am the last of my line, Randolph. For the Ushers, family is everything. This house is everything. Its walls are our skin, its windows our eyes. It has endured for more than two centuries but when I die, as I shall soon enough, there is no other of my blood to receive it or care for it."

My glare of revulsion softened with compassion. "But surely there are other women."

"There have been many other women. But I loved none of them. All my life I have loved only one."

"Such an abomination cannot be called love."

His laughter horrified me. It had in it the ring of madness.

"You are like a child, Randolph. You have explored the strange land of dreams, but you have never seen the things I have seen, or done what I have done. What I have with my sister is pure compared to those things. Vile, disgusting things."

"Your sister is dead, Roderick."

He stared at me, wild-eyed, as though unable to comprehend my words.

"Madeline is dead," I repeated more slowly, emphasizing each word.

"Yes," he said, nodding vigorously. A bit of spittle gleamed at the corner of his mouth. "But we came so close, Randolph, so very close, she and I."

A crash of thunder outside the front windows of the house made us both turn at the same instant toward the sitting room. She stood framed in the dividing archway. Her white limbs were naked save for a few scraps of her burial dress which she had torn away with her fingernails. Her belly, rounded no longer, was rent by a ragged gash that streamed blood and other effluvia over her thighs and shins. The severed umbilical cord hung down between her legs. In the hooked claws of her blood-soaked hands she held something small and red that wriggled feebly and waved its tiny arms in the air. A kind of mewing sound came from its tiny lips, weak but already demanding attention.

In an instantaneous flash of lightning I saw more clearly that the premature fruit of her womb had other moving appendages beside its wriggling arms and legs. The motions of these false limbs were insect-like, too quick and skittering to be human. For some reason I cannot conceive I was reminded of the waving legs of a live lobster when it is dropped into a pot of boiling water. From its sloped forehead something projected that was like a single great bloodstained horn, and I knew how Madeline's belly had been opened.

Thunder crashed with deafening force, shaking the entire house under our feet. In the wildly fluttering shadows from the lamp Usher took a step forward and reached out his hands.

"What miracle is this?" he asked with bursting joy. "Madeline, my dear love, you live."

Her eyes stood open so wide their whites were visible all around their edges, and she smiled horribly, showing her teeth. A growling noise began deep in her throat and became progressively louder. As Usher took another step, she raised the writhing horror in her hands and brought it to her face as though to kiss it. A keening screech burst from its tiny mouth. With a violent jerk of her head, Madeline tore away its throat and began to chew its flesh, its blood glistening on her grinning lips and running down her chin.

Usher screamed like a damned soul and rushed toward her. She threw the monstrous infant at his face, and when he paused to brush it aside, she darted at him with inhuman quickness and fastened her long fingers around his neck. The two struggled. Usher seemed dazed, but Madeline was possessed of an unnatural strength. She pulled her brother's face toward hers and bit him on the cheek while his arms flailed impotently over her hunched naked shoulders.

It was the snapping of Usher's neck that roused me from my trance.

I made no effort to speak to this mad thing that was no longer human but ran past her through the drawing room and into the hall, where I tore open the front door and dashed into the rain and the wind. So great was the fury of the storm that I could not hear my slippered feet as they pounded across the bridge. I did not pause or look behind until I had reached the crest of the hill at the edge of the forest. Only then did I collapse to the road and turn to view the house.

The flashes of lighting and crashing of thunder were almost continuous. By this hellish illumination I watched the main roof of the house of the Ushers fall slowly in upon itself, and after it the walls collapse inward. I blinked the rain from my eyes and squinted against the electric glare. It seemed to me that something extended itself up from the boiling waters of the tarn, which were whipped by the gusts of wind. Whatever it may have been, it was long and black, so that it was almost invisible to my sight save where the lightning reflected from its gleaming curves. It wrapped around a chimney that still remained and with a wrench that I heard from the hill, hurled it down into the tarn with the other building rubble.

It is long to write of this destruction, which took only a few heartbeats to accomplish. I sat for a while in the rain, staring at the low pile of jumbled stones that had once been the ancient home of a proud family, but was now returned forever to its primal chaos. The curse of Usher was fulfilled, and the house of Usher stood no more.

Witchery Boy

1.

The boy approached the log cabin with caution, moving silent as a ghost beneath the sugar maples and shading beech trees that filled the belly of the ravine. He heard the liquid chuckle of the brook as it ran over broken rock slabs but could not see the water. His sandy hair hung ragged over his prominent sunburned ears, his freckled skin was peeling across the bridge of his nose. He crouched behind a low-hanging pine bough and squinted at the single window in the front of the cabin with his clear gray eyes.

The door opened inward and an old woman stepped out on the porch with a pump shotgun cradled under her arm. Her white hair was tied behind her head in a bun. She wore a shapeless dress of unbleached cotton that hung flat over her chest and straight at her hips. "Might as well show yourself. I know you're there."

He straightened and stepped forward across the carpet of brown pine needles. The sun warmed his neck when he left the shadow of the trees. He continued to the foot of the porch and just stood with his hands dangling awkwardly at his sides.

She eyed him up and down, a frown creasing the corners of her bloodless lips. What she saw was an undernourished child of about fifteen years in worn-out jeans and a tattered white cotton shirt. The sneakers on his feet had holes in their toes. Scratches streaked his forehead and the backs of his hands.

"Speak your mind, boy."

"This here the place they call Leitch Creek?"

"Suppose it is?"

"You the one they call Ginty Crowe?"

"What if I am?"

"If you're her, I expect we're kin."

She raised her wrinkled, hairless eyebrows and regarded him with wry amusement. Her small, deep-set eyes were the same clear gray as his.

"How you figure that?"

"They say you and my ma's ma was sisters."

She studied him again, this time with more shrewdness. "You're Sara White's cub?"

He felt other eyes watching him from the four-paned window but did not turn to look. He nodded.

The old woman spat off the edge of the porch. "That girl's plumb dead."

The boy's eyelid twitched at the corner but he gave no other sign. "I know that. I watched her die."

"Why are you come to me? Why ain't you home with your pa?"

He straightened his back and stared at her with defiance. "Pa got no use for me, now that ma's dead. He throwed me out."

"Even so, why you come to me?"

"I come for you to teach me to witch."

Her dry, lipless mouth spread slowly into a wicked grin and her eyes glittered. "Don't know what you're talking about, boy."

"Everyone up northways say you're the powerfulest granny woman in these hills."

"Is that what they say."

"I got the sight," he said quickly. "I see visions."

She grunted. "Any fool can see visions. All it takes is a jar of white lightning."

"I know how to find water with a branch, and I see ghosts sometimes."

"You ever speak in tongues?"

He shook his head.

"Did your mother talk about me afore she died?"

"She been telling me stories about Granny Ginty since I was a pup. I want to be just like you."

His gaze wandered to the window. In the dimness beyond, a pale oval face regarded him without expression. It drew back and faded as he looked at it.

The old woman closed her wrinkled eyelids and began to mumble to herself, too low for the boy to catch her words. He wondered if she was knocked in the head. When she regarded him again, it was with speculation.

"What name they call you?"

"My name is Lucas. They call me Luke."

She turned and spat again. "If you're staying for dinner, you'll have to work for it. There's a pile of wood out back by the stump. Chop it into kindling and tote some in to the cook stove."

She turned and went into the cabin, shutting the door.

2.

He worked his way around the cabin. Not far from a chicken coop he found a massive stump of what had once been a beech tree. No other trace of the tree remained. A hatchet was embedded in its surface. Beside the stump, short blocks of birch, maple, and hemlock were piled up haphazardly where they had landed, probably after being thrown from the back of a pickup truck.

He looked around. Beside the cabin was a shed. Through its open doors he saw the south end of a cow. Nearby was an old motorcycle with a sidecar half-covered by a canvas tarp that had holes in it. The yard sloped down to a creek that splashed and bubbled white foam over large boulders. He followed it with his eye where it wound away between the steep, tree-cloaked hills. There was no sign of a house or a road for as far between the hills as he could see.

He picked up a block of wood and used the hatchet to begin splitting off kindling. It was work he had done before. After a while, he found a length of maple thin enough to grip in his hand, and used it like a club to hammer the hatchet blade into the hardwood.

As he worked, a girl slipped out the back door of the cabin and wandered toward him. He pretended not to notice her. She stood with one hand gripping her thin upper arm across her breasts, staring at him intently. She was taller than the boy and slender, with honey-blond hair sun-faded into streaks and soft brown eyes. She wore a red halter top and white shorts. Her feet were bare. He judged she was a few years older than him. He started thinking about her breasts and put the hatchet in the wrong place. It got stuck in a knot. Cursing, he worked the handle back and forth to worry it out.

"My name's Nora," the girl said.

"I'm Luke," he said without looking at her.

"Granny Ginty's my gran. That makes us second cousins."

"How you figure that?"

"I heared what you said. My ma and your ma was cousins. That makes us second cousins."

He considered the matter. "I expect so."

She bent and picked up a block of wood. He took it from her and centered it on the stump. Birds sang overhead in the trees. A cool breeze blew up along the course of the creek, carrying dampness with it. He smelled a scent from her that was something like vanilla. He became aware of the sweat dripping from his nose and wiped it away.

"Is your gran teaching you to witch?"

She shook her head, and her wavy hair danced against her cheeks. "Gran says I ain't got the sight. Gran says you can't make a lemon taste like a peach no matter how hard you squeeze it."

"You ain't no lemon."

A blush came to her cheeks and she smiled.

"How is it you come to live here?"

She shrugged. "Pa left when I was little. Ma got sent to state prison. They say she tried to kill some banker's son with a straight razor."

"That's hard."

"Way it is, is all."

They worked together for a while in silence. She handed him the blocks, he chopped, and she gathered up the pieces from around the base of the stump and carried several armloads into the cabin.

"How'd your face and hands get all scratched up?"

"I been living rough the past few weeks, sleeping under trees, stealing food."

"Well you're home now."

"That's for Granny Ginty to decide, ain't it?"

Nora glanced at the cabin. "She won't turn away her own kin. 'Specially not one who's got the sight. She been waiting for you for a long, long time."

He stopped with the hatchet raised in his hand and looked at her. "What do you mean, waiting for me?"

The girl shrugged. "Well, maybe not for you in special, but for someone like you. She got some work she been preparing for years, but she can't do it alone."

"What kind of work?"

"She won't tell me. Some kind of witch work."

This revelation raised hope in the boy's heart that he would be allowed to remain, but he did not show it.

"It sure will be good to have someone to talk to around here."

"You got your gran."

"She don't talk much, 'cept to the spirits at the rock."

"What rock?"

"I expect you'll see it, by and by."

3.

Granny Ginty spread a worn linen cloth over the rough boards of the kitchen table. She went to a cupboard that hung on the wall and took out a rusting coffee can. Looking at the boy seated across the table, she shook it so that its contents rattled like double-ought buckshot against its sides.

"Before I make up my mind whether you stay, I needs to know more about you," she said.

"Ask what you want. I got nothing to hide."

"The black beans'll tell me better than you." She chuckled. "Black beans tell ol' Ginty everything."

Nora stood in a corner of the kitchen, watching silently. Luke glanced at her and she smiled encouragement.

He'd eaten better than he had for the last three days. His belly was full of chicken stew and brown bread, washed down with the white whiskey the old woman brewed in her own still. He only wanted to close his eyes and sleep. Outside the tiny kitchen window, dusk collected shadows between the trees. He couldn't even remember the last time he'd slept more than an hour at a stretch. Twice on the way south he'd been beaten and robbed. The first time, they'd taken the stash he'd carried away from his father's farm. The second time, they took the food and clothes he himself had stolen from barns and backyards along the road. He was bone-weary.

Granny Ginty opened the coffee tin and held it across the table toward him.

"Spit in it."

He looked at her, wondering if he'd heard her right. She shook the tin impatiently. He leaned forward. A faint aroma of coffee still clung to the inside of the old can. He gathered saliva by sucking on his tongue and spat into it.

She slapped the lid back on and shook the can, then opened it and tipped it over the white cloth. As she did this, she muttered words under her breath. Black beans cascaded from the can onto the cloth and bounced and rolled. One bean rolled onto the floor. Nora picked it up and laid it carefully on the corner of the table. The old woman ignored it and set the can down, then peered intently at the pattern the beans made on the cloth. Her head tilted to the side, like the head of a puzzled bird. She seemed to listen to the silence.

Luke looked at Nora. The girl met his gaze but her expression did not change.

"What do you see?"

"Shut up. The beans is talking to me."

She bent her face close to the beans and turned her head so that her ear was only a few inches above the table. A long hiss of air escaped her throat. Somewhere outside in a tree, an owl hooted. The boy looked hard at the scattered black beans, but he saw only beans.

"You got an old soul, boy. That's good. No one can do witch work 'less they got an old soul. You been here afore many a time, but always you died with your task unfinished."

"What's my task?"

"Hush. I'm telling you, ain't I?"

The owl hooted again, a drawn out, mournful sound.

"There be some powerful spirits watching over you. They gave you the sight so you would finish your task this time around."

Luke bit his lower lip to keep from asking the same question again.

"They want you to learn to witch. They want you to learn real good." She bent her ear to the table. "They want me to learn you the witchery ways."

Relief made him relax and sit back. She was going to let him stay.

"I'm to learn you to raise the dead out of the stone, and to make them do what you tell them to do."

She bent still closer, until her ear almost touched the table.

"You got a powerful strong gift, but you are willful and contrary. Pride

123

goeth before a fall, boy. Best you remember that."

The black beans on the table began to tremble and spin around. One by one, they stood on end and danced. She stared down at them from the corner of one eye, her hollow cheek no more than an inch away from them.

"Beware the stone," she said in a strange voice that wasn't hers. "Make peace with the dead. Awaken the day. The eye of the hawk watches you from the east. Shimvanu, Imlanu, Vuloovua, Ova, Taxova, Hamimannu."

Luke looked at Nora, but the girl merely shook her head. The words meant nothing to her.

"The unwinding of the sun one by one, and two by two, but three by three must never be."

A great gust of wind shook the walls of the cabin and made a sound like a passing freight train in the stone fireplace. The old woman cried out and jerked back her head. At the same moment, the black beans scattered from the table across the floor of the kitchen.

They spent the next quarter hour hunting for them and putting them back in the can. At the end of it, Luke was so sleepy, he swayed on his feet where he stood and his eyelids drooped shut unless he blinked hard.

"You can sleep in the loft in Nora's bed. Nora will sleep with me."

The girl made no objection. She showed Luke the ladder that led up to the loft at one end of the front room. Below the loft, a bed was built into the wall in a kind of box that held a lumpy-looking mattress covered in a worn quilt.

"That where the old woman sleeps?" he asked her.

"Well you don't see no other beds in here."

He looked around. The cabin only had two rooms, the front room and the kitchen in the back with its pantry.

"Expect I don't."

He climbed the ladder, found a straw-filled mattress in the loft, and was asleep face down across it before he could summon the strength to unlace his sneakers.

4.

For three days Luke gathered and chopped the wood for the cookstove and the whiskey still, fed the chickens and cleaned out their coop, pulled weeds in the garden, mowed the grass around the house with a scythe, milked the cow in the shed, swept the cabin floors, emptied the night-time piss from the china chamber pot, and limed the outhouse. He did it without complaint. It was the same kind of work he had done up north after the death of his mother.

The outhouse was on the bank near the creek, downstream from where he used a wooden bucket to draw water from a bubbling, frothing pool between the rocks. Granny Ginty left the back door of the cabin and made for the outhouse. She used a crooked walking staff to support herself on the uneven grass-covered slope. Luke didn't look at her. For three days she had ignored him. He felt her flinty gray eyes on him, though.

He carried the bucket of water up to the cabin and emptied it into the tin cistern in the kitchen, then went back to the creek for another bucketful. The old woman stood waiting for him, her fingers folded together over the knobbed head of her staff.

"How you suppose little critters in the grass keep from getting ate up by the hawks?"

He stopped in surprise and looked at her.

"They crouch down and keep still," he said.

She nodded. "That's part of it. Them that don't want to be seen gets real still. But stillness in the body ain't enough. You got to be still here, and here." She touched her index finger to her forehead and her flat chest.

He set his empty bucket down on the bank. "Is this you teaching me how to witch?"

"Close your mouth and open your ears, boy."

He stood looking at her.

"Rabbit moves, hawk sees it out the corner of its eye. Rabbit rustles the grass, fox hears and comes a-running. How many big rocks got their heads above the water behind you?"

He started to turn around to count them.

"Don't look. How many?"

"I don't remember."

"Why not?"

"I never paid much notice to them."

She nodded her white head, watching him with glittering eyes.

"Rocks know how to be still. Not only out here." She made a circle with the motion of her hand. "In here, and in here." She touched him on the forehead and the chest. "You practice that. You make yourself still all through like them rocks out in the creek."

Another time, early in the morning, when he was lying on his back on the mattress in the loft with his hands behind his head, staring at the bark-covered rafters that held up the roof, she called to him from below.

"Think you can come on down here without leaving your bed?"

He thought about it. He was learning not to answer the old woman too quickly. When he did, he usually put his foot wrong and she mocked him.

"I don't rightly see how I can do that."

"You can close your eyes, can't you? You can make pictures in your head about what it looks like down here, can't you?"

"I expect so."

"Do it, then put yourself into the picture you make in your head."

She walked off and left him lying there. He didn't move for another hour, and she didn't bother him.

Another time, when he was coming back to the cabin, she met him under the trees on the path. He was not surprised to see her. In spite of the stick she used to help her balance, she could walk for miles and never get tired.

"That's a fine boomer you got there, boy."

He held up the dead red squirrel with a feeling of pride.

"Got him with a slingshot over yonder."

"Slingshot's good," she said with a nod. "But slingshot's not the only way to hunt boomers."

"I could use a rifle if you get me one."

She waved her hand in disgust. "Boomer's all about fast. Why is he hard to catch? Because he's so damn quick. Even a fox has trouble catching him. Now suppose you could slow things down."

She looked at him. He shook his head.

"Slow what things?"

"Everything, boy. Suppose you could slow everything down, and that includes Mr. Boomer here. Think you could catch him then?"

"Ain't nobody can do such a thing," he scoffed.

"You real sure about that?"

She was mocking him, as she often did. He was sure, but he didn't say anything, he just stood frowning at her, stubborn as a bulldog.

She tilted back her head, closed her eyelids, and muttered to herself. For an instant her body seemed to jump and blur, then he saw that a dead red squirrel dangled from her hand. He looked down and realized the squirrel he had been holding was gone.

She laughed, making a sound like a rusty saw. "You didn't move any faster than Mr. Boomer here, and he's dead."

That was her way, to come on him unawares and say something to challenge him and make him feel like a fool. At first it made him angry and frustrated. He thought about leaving, but he had nowhere to go. Besides, he had come to like Nora's company. She was the first friend he'd ever had. After a while, he started to pick up witchery ways of doing things from the old woman. She didn't so much teach him as challenge him to figure out things for himself.

5.

One Monday morning he prepared to take the old woman's Indian motorcycle into town to buy supplies. She usually went herself, but she said her back was bothering her. Nora didn't know how to ride the machine. He stripped off its canvas tarp and loaded six boxes of mason jars full of white whiskey into the sidecar. Nora helped him get the ancient bike started. She had watched her gran do it countless times and knew the things to do. To the boy's surprise, the bike fired up on the second kick of the starter.

He knew how to ride a motorcycle but not one with a sidecar. The first mile along the winding road through the hills was interesting. It was all he could do to keep the contrary bike out of the ditch. Lucky for him, there was no traffic on the road. By the time he reached the little town of Hagtree he was getting the way of it.

The owner of the general store was named Bradford. He and the old woman had an agreement. In exchange for her moonshine, he gave her what she needed to live—flour, beans, tea, lard, kerosene, cloth for dresses, shot shells for her gun, and whatever else she ran out of.

Luke pulled up behind the store. Bradford came to the rear door when he recognized the familiar sound of the Indian's engine. He was tall and skinny, with round eyeglasses and thinning gray hair that was combed straight back from his forehead and plastered into place with hair oil. He wore a long white apron that tied around his neck. It was stained in front with patches of blood from the fresh cuts of meat he sold.

He carried the boxes of mason jars into the store, and came out with a sack of flour and the other necessities on the boy's list. When it was all loaded into the sidecar, he stared at the boy in silence for a time, as though undecided about something.

"Best you take your poke of flour and get out of here real quick," he said at last.

"I ain't planning on staying."

"People got the idea that Ginty Crowe threw a witch ball at Blanche Isaacs a while back, a few days before she died. I don't believe that myself, but it don't matter because they believe it. They been watching for her. I expect they seed you ride into town. They know this old Indian belongs to her."

"What's a witch ball?"

The man looked at him with surprise.

"Don't you know? It's like a little ball of beeswax with some hair inside it."

"I never seed nothing like that."

"It won't matter. They'll know you're with her. You need to get out of here."

"I heared what you said," the boy muttered. "I got no other business."

"Good." The store owner nodded. "I wouldn't want to lose my supply of white. It's the best in these here hills."

The boy kicked the motorcycle into life and rode it around the store and back onto the street.

They were waiting for him where the road narrowed just outside of the town. Two pickup trucks parked grille to grille blocked his way. Two more trucks pulled into the road behind him, shutting him in between them. He saw there was nowhere to go and turned off the bike's engine.

"I don't want no trouble," he said.

"You're living with her, ain't you, peckerwood?" a bearded man with a shotgun demanded.

The boy nodded. He swung his leg casually over the back fender of the bike and stood up.

"They say you're her kin," an older woman with a pinched face said.

"That's true."

"We don't want your kind here," another man said.

"She's in league with the Devil," said a young woman in a long black dress with a silver cross around her neck, who stood in the bed of one of the pickup trucks. "She's evil."

"I'll be sure to tell her that," Luke said. From the corner of his eye he noticed a narrow lane leading off the main road under the trees.

A woman standing in the road bent and picked up a stone, then threw it at him. He batted it aside, and it stung the palm of his hand. Others jumped down from the trucks and picked up more rocks from the shoulder of the road. They began flying through the air. He put up his arms to shield his head.

"Thou shalt not suffer a witch to live!" someone shouted.

He didn't wait. He bolted between the trucks for the side road and ran down it with the mob behind him. No one thought to use the trucks—they followed him on foot and continued to throw rocks at him. A few hit him in the back.

The forest opened into a clearing. He saw that it was an old gravel quarry. It had not been used for decades. Young trees grew here and there between the rocks. The excavated walls were steep and their soil too loose to climb. He realized he had run himself into a trap. Maybe the people following him had wanted him to come here. It was the perfect place to stone him to death, and he knew that was their intention. There was no doubting the murder in their eyes.

He had a few seconds to hide. The mob was still around a bend in the access road, concealed behind trees. He looked for a direction to run but there was none. The ground rose on all sides and overhung at the top. There was no way he could scramble out of the quarry. He crouched behind a large boulder.

Closing his eyes, he took a deep breath, then let it out slow. In his mind he heard the voice of Granny Ginty.

"Rocks know how to be still. Not only out here, but in here, and in here."

He heard them approach, their boots clattering over the loose gravel, their angry out-of-breath voices like the snarls of hungry dogs. He turned his mind away from the sounds and didn't engage with them. He made himself into air and let the voices pass through him without touching him. He felt no fear, no hope, no purpose. He just was, in that moment, and the next, and the next.

After a while, they went away. He stayed put for the better part of an hour before returning cautiously to where he'd left the motorcycle. He expected someone to be watching for him, but the old bike stood alone in the road. The big headlight was broken out. Someone else had slashed the sack of flour, but not much flour had spilled. He looked up and down the road as he adjusted the sack in the sidecar so the cut would be on the top, then started the motorcycle and rode back to the cabin.

6.

It was toward the end of October when the old woman took the boy to the black rock. Luke had seen it from a distance more than once while out hunting boomers and checking his rabbit snares. Some instinct had kept him from going close. It was in a clearing on a kind of ledge at the base of a rounded mountain, with hills rising up on both sides so that it was only open to the east.

A strange silence hung over the clearing. The forested slopes on three sides blocked most of the wind, and the shadows of their tall trees rippled like black bars across the ground. The weirdest thing was the lack of birdsong. The air seemed to hold its breath, everything was so still.

The rock itself was the size of a dining-room table, and partially embedded in the ground. It stood up some four feet from the grass that grew around its base, and its surface was flat but irregular.

Luke laid his hand on it and found it cold and heavy. It felt like metal. The sun shone on it between the shadows of the trees, but it sucked the heat from his palm like ice.

"Why'd you bring me here?"

The old woman ignored his question.

"Ages agone when the world was young, this stone fell from the sky and landed right here. The Indians claim it was thrown down by the Red Man. That's what they call their god of lightning. They say he felt something in his throat and coughed it up, and out come this here stone."

"Like a meteor?"

Again, the old woman ignored him.

"It ain't like other rocks. All you need to do is feel it to know that. It's a whole lot heavier, and colder. The Indians used it like a jail for the souls of their most powerful medicine men after they died, so their souls wouldn't wander back to their camps and eat the flesh of their younguns.

Later on, when the white man came, those who witched for evil ends was locked up in here, along with the souls of them Indians."

"You mean it's some kind of graveyard?" Luke asked.

"Why do you think graves always have big slabs of stone over 'em?"

"To carve on the names of the dead, I expect."

"They don't need a big, heavy piece of marble or granite for that. No, the stones is over the graves to keep the ghosts of the dead from wandering the earth, and going back to visit with their families. When a dead soul goes back to its family, it's always hungry."

Luke thought about this.

"So this here rock is like a giant headstone for a grave?"

Granny Ginty nodded her head, watching him narrowly with her small gray eyes.

"It keeps souls trapped inside it, a whole lot of powerful souls of medicine men and granny women from a long time ago."

He regarded the rock nervously and stepped back, wishing he had not touched it. The old woman laughed.

"It ain't gonna bite you, boy."

"Why'd you bring me here?" he asked again.

She drew a breath, let it out slowly through the flared nostrils of her nose while looking at the sky, then stared at him hard.

"If some of them powerful souls locked up in this here rock is set free with the right kind of magic at the right time of the year, then all their power flows into the one who frees them."

He thought about this. It did not seem impossible to him but it sounded dangerous.

"If that's so, why ain't you already done it?"

"Only a man can work this witching. No woman can do it. That's why I ain't done it."

"Nora once told me you was waiting for me a long time afore I come here," he said. "Was it for this work you was waiting?"

She nodded, smiling horribly.

"I trained you up to know the witch ways, and now you're ready. You'll set three of the great ones free of the rock, and their power will become your power."

"When?"

"The night of All Hallows. That's the night when the dead walk the earth and move amongst the living."

Luke had a sense that the old woman was not telling him everything. He didn't resent it especially because she never told him everything. It was her way to make him reflect and figure out the truth of things by himself.

"Is it dangerous?"

She laughed. "Don't worry none, boy. I'll be here to watch over you."

He spoke before thinking, without even intending to ask the question.

"Is it true you once threw a witch ball at Blanche Isaacs?"

The grin left her lined face. "Who told you that lie?"

He repeated what Bradford at the general store had said. Her face darkened further.

"When they is ailing or lovesick, they comes to Granny Ginty, but when some evil happens they is quick to turn their backs."

She left him alone in the clearing, staring at the black rock, lost in thought.

7.

"What are you thinking about, Luke?"

He blinked and turned.

Nora stood watching him with her hands behind her back. She wore a blue print dress with orange blossoms all over it, and had her wavy blond hair tied behind her head in a short ponytail. She looked clean, like she'd just been swimming in the creek, but her hair wasn't wet.

"Not much, I expect." He looked at the sun. It was higher in the sky. At least an hour had passed without him noticing it.

"I brought you something."

She came forward and showed what she held behind her back. It was a large red apple.

"I got it from a high branch on that apple tree t'other side of the creek. All them apples is coming ripe about now."

He took it and started to bite, then noticed a worm weaving its head back and forth near the stem. He flicked it off with his finger and threw the apple back to her.

"I'm not hungry. You eat it."

She bit into the soft skin of the fruit and chewed with apple juice running from the corner of her mouth.

"Your gran ever tell you about this here rock?"

She shook her head. "She don't talk to me much about things with magic in them. I only know she comes up here sometimes at night and witches round it."

"How do you know that?"

"I snuck out of the house and followed her a couple of times, and I watched from over there behind them trees."

"What was she doing?"

"Don't know. It didn't make no sense. She talked to herself and did a kind of dance around the rock, like some kind of Indian medicine-man dance. She had a little drum and she beat it with a stick and danced and muttered some words I couldn't make out."

"I think maybe she's crazy. They all hate her down at the town."

"I know they do."

"They say she made a witch ball and threw it at a woman and killed her."

"She did," Nora said. "Leastwise, she made the witch ball. I watched her make it out of some beeswax I got from a hive in the woods. I never seed her throw it at anyone, though."

"She's powerful wise in them witch ways, but she ain't a good woman."

"I know that, too."

"Why do you stay with her?'

She threw the apple core into the trees at the edge of the clearing and turned to him with a smile.

"Do you want me to go away?"

"No, but before I come here, why did you stay with her?"

"She needs me. When I was young she took care of me, so I guess it's my time to take care of her."

He spat in the grass.

"That old woman is tough as an army mule. She don't need no one taking care of her."

She ran forward and climbed up on top of the black rock. She stood there, legs parted and arms lifted, looking up at the sky.

"Hey, you'd best get off of there, girl."

"I don't want to get off."

"That rock is bad luck. Get down before you catch it."

"You make me," she said in a playful voice.

He reached up to take her hand but she snatched it away and danced

133

to the back of the rock. He started to circle it but she kept moving sideways and backward, keeping just beyond his touch. She laughed at him, her face flushed. Finally, he climbed up on the rock and grabbed her in his arms. She fought to get free, but not too hard, and before long they were locked in a kiss. It was the first time he had kissed her. It was the first time he had kissed anybody.

She lay back on the rock, drawing him down on top of her, and helping him get out of his jeans. He found that she wore nothing under her dress. Her hands kept caressing him and pressing different parts of his body. When he hesitated, she showed him what to do.

As he thrust into her, the chill of the rock seemed to rise right through her body and into him, making him hard and cold as flint. When he came, it was stronger than when he did it with his hand, and different somehow.

He lay on her breasts, panting for breath, and waited for the earth to stop spinning. Then he pushed himself up on his elbows and gazed into her brown eyes.

"I think I love you."

"I know you do, Luke."

"We should leave here."

"Where would we go?"

"Don't matter. I can make a living. I know how to witch away warts, and how to take the heat out of fire. I can find water in the ground or anything that's been lost. I can make love charms and money charms. I can heal by laying on my hands."

"Gran taught you all those things," she said.

"That's so."

"Do you think it's decent to just leave her by herself and go off like that?"

He frowned. It was clear Nora didn't want to leave her grandmother. She had lived with the old woman most of her life. He decided not to press things. Let her come to the decision to leave on her own, he thought. He could wait. Anyway, there was more the old woman could teach him.

"I'll stay here, if that's what you want."

She drew his face down between her chill fingers and kissed his mouth. He tasted apple on her flicking tongue.

8.

The night of Halloween, the moon was nearly full. It rode high in the starry sky at midnight, when Luke and Granny Ginty climbed the slope to the clearing that held the black stone. She had prepared him for days to do the ritual, making him memorize the words he must chant and the things he must do to cast a magic circle around the rock. He felt nervous but ready. He was naked, his body smeared with an ointment that left black streaks on his white skin. She carried her bent staff, and a canvas bag on a long strap over her shoulder. Whatever was in the bag clinked when she walked.

"The spirits is close tonight. Can you feel 'em, boy?"

Luke stood and smelled the air. It was chill but not freezing. There was something in it, a kind of crackling force that felt like lightning about to strike. It made the hairs on his arms and legs stand up.

"When do I start?"

"First you need to drink this potion."

She took a narrow bottle out of her bag and twisted the cork out of its neck with her teeth. He smelled it and pulled his head back, wrinkling his nose.

"What's in it?"

"Never you mind what's in it. Drink, and it will make you strong and hard for the work tonight."

He took the bottle, hesitated only a second, then swallowed its contents. The taste was bad. He resisted the urge to spit as he handed the bottle back.

After a few minutes, his body began to feel warm all over, and his heartbeat quickened. His flaccid penis thickened and rose up to press against his belly. As it did so, its rubicund head emerged from the hood of its foreskin. He touched himself in embarrassment. It felt as hard as iron.

"Now you're ready," she said with a chuckle, staring at his groin.

He put his hand down there and turned half away from her, feeling himself blush with shame.

She reached into the bag on her hip and took out a large mason jar filled with a liquid that looked black in the moonlight.

"Mind you don't drop it," she said.

He accepted the jar and held it up close to study it. Whatever it contained was still warm.

"Ghosts of the dead is hungry," she said. "If you want them to come near, you got to feed them what they like. You get over to the rock and pour what's in the jar over the top of it."

"Is this blood?" he asked.

"It ain't milk."

A horrible suspicion came over him. He stared at her. In the slanting moonlight her deep-set eyes were concealed in shadows, so that her face looked like a skull.

"How come I ain't seed Nora since early morning?"

"Maybe you never looked in the right places."

"Where'd this here blood come from?"

"Never you mind about that. You just do as I told you."

"Where's Nora?"

"She's around someplace."

"Where is she?"

"Best you keep your thoughts on what you got to do, boy."

He set the mason jar in the grass.

"I ain't doing nothing until I know what you did to her."

He took a menacing step toward the old woman. She stood her ground.

"You kilt her, didn't you? You needed blood for this ritual and you kilt her for it."

"You don't know much, boy."

"I know you kilt your own kin."

"Nora's not dead."

"You're lying. You kilt her, I know you did."

"She can't have been killed, you fool, on account she weren't never alive."

He stared at her skull-like face. She drew her thin lips into a grin and revealed her rotting yellow teeth.

"What are you talking about?"

"If you must know it, I didn't want you to take it into your head to leave, so I made Nora for to keep you company. You saw her when I wanted you to see her."

He shook his head in denial, remembering the afternoon with the girl atop the black rock.

"You're lying. I touched her more than once."

Granny Ginty laughed a dirty laugh.

"You did a sight more than touch her."

"She's real."

"Sometimes she were just a vision I put in your head. She were real when I needed her to be real, but she weren't no Nora."

The moonlight wavered in front of her, and Nora stood before him in her blue dress with the orange blossoms. She stared at him with innocent eyes. "Was I good for you, Luke?"

He reached out his hand to touch her cheek, but before he could reach her, the moonlight wavered again, and Granny Ginty stood grinning at him.

"Why'd you do it?" he asked in a small voice.

"For a witch to pass on power to somebody else, the two got to be of the same blood, and it got to be done by coupling. No other way. I needed to pass my power to you afore you could do this ritual we're doing here tonight."

"I ain't doing no ritual tonight nor any other night. You used me and lied to me. I don't trust you no more."

"You will do the ritual." She reached into her poke and took something out. "Know what this is?"

He looked at the small sphere on the palm of her hand. It caught the moonlight and glittered like amber glass. He saw strands of hair locked inside it.

"This here's a witch ball. If I throw this and it hits you, you'll be dead, but if I throw it and miss, you'll wish you was dead."

He thought about knocking her down, but she was a lot stronger than she looked. What if what she said about the witch ball was true?

"What do you want from me?"

"Just do what we studied for you to do, and do it quick afore the potion wears off."

9.

He poured the thick contents of the mason jar over the surface of the black stone, making a cross as the old woman had directed. The metallic scent of blood filled his nose and sickened him. Granny Ginty stood watching at the edge of the clearing, a black shadow as motionless as the trees behind her.

"Three be called, three come forth, by the power of the cross," he recited. He uttered the string of meaningless words he had memorized. They buzzed in his ears as he sounded them. Turning his back on the stone, he walked toward the east nine paces and stood with his arms raised.

"The way is open. Drink of the life that is in the blood."

Again he chanted meaningless but ancient words that held power in their very shapes and sounds. When he faced the stone, three figures sat upon its edge with their backs to each other. They had no color but seemed to be formed out of shadow and moonlight. They sat motionless, staring outward.

One was an old Indian woman with a hunch in her back between her shoulders and a nose like the blade of a hatchet. The second was an Indian chief by the look of his headdress and clothes. He sat back straight, head high, proud in bearing. The third was a white man who was dressed in antique clothes. To the boy, he looked a bit like pictures he had seen in books of George Washington, but there was an evil twist to his mouth.

None of the three turned to look at him. He glanced over at Granny Ginty but she might as well have been carved from stone. He began to walk in a large circle around the black rock. He went in the direction the old woman called widdershins, against the course of the sun in the heavens, her remembered words in his mind.

"Widdershins be for drawing things out, boy. It unravels threads and unwinds bindings. It loosens knots and bends what's straight. It draws out splinters and opens locks. The sun's got his way, and the way of the moon be widdershins."

As he walked, the old Indian woman got up from the stone and began to walk behind him. He didn't dare to turn his head to look at her for fear that she might meet his eyes with hers, but he could feel her following behind him, almost near enough for her to reach out and brush his naked back with her long fingernails.

At the beginning of the second circle, the Indian chief stood up and fell into step behind the old Indian woman. The boy sensed an eagerness in him. The blood from the jar had not satisfied him, but had only awakened his hunger. Luke thought about bolting for the edge of the clearing, but when he looked at Granny Ginty, he saw that she had raised her right fist in the air over her head, as though ready to throw something.

As he began the third circle, the antiquely-dressed white man in the powdered wig and buckle shoes stood and fell into step behind the chief. Luke completed the third circle and stopped, then walked three paces toward the stone, as the old woman had told him to do, before turning to face the spirits. They stood shoulder to shoulder, watching him with intense awareness.

"The cross and he that hung on it have drawn you forth from the stone," he recited. "The blood of sacrifice has drawn you forth by your thirst. The circling has drawn you forth beneath the moon."

He stopped speaking. This was all Granny Ginty had told him to do and say. He waited for her to do something, but she remained at the edge of the trees, well outside the circle. The three spirits stared at him, their eyes burning like sparks from a fire. They took a slow step toward him.

Instinct made him step backward. He could see their thirst, their hunger, and all three looked only at him, at his naked flesh. They continued to step toward him, and he continued to back away, until the edge of the cold black rock pressed against his buttocks.

"Quick, Luke, climb up on the rock. They can't take you if you stand on the rock."

He recognized the voice and twisted his head. Nora stood atop the flat surface of the rock wearing her blue dress with the orange blossoms. He saw that her throat had been cut, and that her blood had streamed over her face, and he realized she must have been hung upside down from her heels when she was murdered, like a slaughtered sow.

The three hungry ghosts were close. He scrambled up onto the rock to avoid their reaching fingers, and stared at the girl.

"Are you real?"

She smiled, and the blood on her face faded away, and the wound in her long white throat closed.

"As real as you."

He reached to embrace her, but his hands passed through her body.

"I can't stay long, Luke. The blood brought me back, but I can't stay long. I ain't as strong as the others."

"That old bitch lied to me."

"She always lies; you know that."

He looked across the clearing, but couldn't see the old woman. The three raised spirits surrounded the rock and reached over its surface toward his legs. He felt their fingers rake across his skin, and saw their fingernails draw blood. It flowed down his shins and seemed to make them stronger. He kicked at their hands and danced out of the way of their grasping clutch.

"What do I do, Nora? I don't know what to do."

"You know what to do, Luke," she said with such certainty that it calmed him. "I got to leave now. You know what to do."

She dissolved into moonlight within the circle of his arms and they closed on empty air. Suddenly, he did know what to do. It was the widdershins circle that held the three he had drawn from the rock. He stood in the center, ignoring the slashes of their fingernails against his legs, and closed his eyes. The potion Granny Ginty had given him still worked its power within him. He drew upon its fire to fortify his purpose. He muttered to himself, then raised his arms and opened his eyes.

The stars began to move in the night sky. The moon circled after them, sliding toward the west to disappear behind the dark shoulder of the round mountain at his back. The sky in the east paled, then turned pink.

"What are you doing, boy? Stop it. I'm warning you, stop it now."

The voice of the old woman seemed to sound in his head, but he ignored it. He knew she was a liar. Nothing could come out of her mouth but lies.

From the hollow of the hills to the east, a blinding ray of light struck across the clearing like the blade of a knife. It cut through the widdershins circle, slicing it in two like the halves of an apple. The three spirits around the rock cried out with a single voice of despair and vanished like shadows.

Luke turned slowly on the rock, looking for danger, but saw only the clear light of morning. All Hallows Eve had passed in the span of a few brief moments. The old woman had taught him how to slow time down, but what was slowed down could also be sped up. The circle of the moon he had made by walking widdershins could not endure the thrusting radiance of the sun.

He climbed off the rock, his bare feet sticky on their soles with drying blood that was both his own and Nora's, and went to where the old woman lay in the grass. Her eyes started from their deep sockets and her tongue hung out the corner of her open mouth. She had taken some kind of fit or stroke, but was still alive. Short, quick little breaths made her chest rise and fall. Near her outstretched hand lay the witch ball. He picked it up and studied its making.

Bending down until his face was close to that of the old woman, he stared into her cold gray eyes, so like his own eyes.

"You shouldn't of kilt Nora, and you shouldn't of lied to me."

He put the witch ball into her mouth and used his fingers to shove it deep into her throat.

The Waves Beckon

1.

"If you ask me, this is a terrible idea," Nurse Eunice Waite said to Head Nurse Sarah Cork.

"It's the Director's idea," Sarah told her with a thin smile. "Why don't you tell him how terrible it is?"

Eunice sniffed and squared her shoulders. She was a big woman. Her enormous breasts jiggled beneath her white top in spite of her orthopedic brassiere.

"I thought not," Sarah said. "Now get back to work and let me do my job."

Eunice leaned over the desk and glared down at the round, fleshy face of her supervisor. "I'll say only this—nothing good comes from hiring outsiders."

She turned on the low heel of her sensible white nurse's shoe and stalked out of the office, slamming the door behind her.

After allowing a decorous interval of silence, Sarah got up and opened the door. "You can come in now, Miss Bowers. I'm ready for your interview."

The woman who walked in from the waiting room was tall and thin, with a long face and a small mouth bracketed by habitual frown lines. Her dark hair was pulled back from her ears in a severe bun. She wore no makeup to accentuate her brown eyes, which were her best feature in Sarah's opinion. Her drab gray dress looked handmade. A small silver crucifix hung around her neck on a delicate chain. That was her only piece of jewelery. When Sarah accepted her hand in greeting, she felt the fingers of the other woman tremble.

"Sit down, Miss Bowers."

"Please, call me Ruth."

"If you wish."

She returned to her place behind the desk while the woman in gray perched on the edge of the chair indicated. She kept her small black leather purse balanced upright on her knees in both hands.

"I've been going over your résumé," Sarah said, indicating the open brown file folder on her desk. "It says you had five years of experience caring for the severely disabled at Arkham Hospital."

"That's right." The other woman's voice was surprisingly mild.

"You didn't indicate why you left."

The woman shifted in her chair and dropped her gaze. "I just felt it was time to expand my horizons and move on. I didn't want my life to stagnate."

Sarah nodded, watching her. "One of my cousins works at Arkham Hospital. She told me you left under a black cloud. She said there were charges made of gross incompetence."

"No formal charge was ever laid," Ruth said sharply.

"No, of course not, or you wouldn't still have your nursing license, would you?"

The other woman met her gaze defiantly. Sarah heaved a sigh and closed the file folder. She laced her chubby fingers together over it.

"I'm going to be honest with you, Ruth. The Marsh Care Facility is grossly understaffed. We need more nurses, and it is hard to lure them away from the bright lights of the big cities to work in a small town such as Innsmouth, where there is so little to do for recreation."

"I imagine that would be the case," Ruth said.

"You're here because no one else will hire you, isn't that the truth?"

After a moment's hesitation, the other woman nodded.

"Now we understand each other. We need nurses and you need a job. I'm willing to overlook the rumors surrounding your resignation from Arkham Hospital and give you a chance."

The other woman's dour face flickered briefly into a shy smile. "Thank you, Miss Cork. You won't regret this decision, I promise."

"I'll be watching you closely for the first few weeks, so don't screw up, or out you go. There's no second chance for you."

"I understand."

Sarah stood up. "Come with me. I'll give you a quick tour of the Facility."

She left the administration office and walked briskly down the hall on her short legs, with Ruth at her side and half a pace behind.

"This Facility exists in its present form because of the generous bequest of Obed Marsh, who funded the construction of the original building on this very site in the mid-nineteen hundreds. When the original building burned down after a lightning strike, the present structure was erected in the nineteen twenties to replace it."

"It's very impressive," Ruth murmured.

Sarah gave no sign that she had heard the other woman speak.

"We have three wards. All our patients are funded by the yearly investment income from the Marsh endowment. Some have been abandoned by their families and are wards of the institution. Others have families too poor to pay for private medical care."

She stopped beside a double door, which stood open.

"This is Ward One. The patients here all suffer from mental disabilities such as severe retardation. In almost every case the disability is congenital."

Ruth peered into the ward, and had to resist the urge to flinch back. Men and women of various ages sat on the beds or at small tables, rocking back and forth. A few stood leaning against the wall. There was a curious similarity in the appearance of their vacant faces, a flatness of the nose and a prominence of the eyes. Their mouths appeared unnaturally wide and their necks were short.

"What you are observing is referred to as the Innsmouth Look. It's been the subject of several articles in prominent medical journals."

"What causes it?" Ruth asked.

"When Innsmouth was a fishing village, many generations ago, it was isolated from the rest of Massachusetts by the poor roads that served the community. There was a tendency for the inhabitants to intermarry, and eventually this produced the curious facial deformities that you will encounter throughout the Facility." She laughed lightly. "You'll even see it among some of the staff."

Now that she mentioned it, Ruth noticed that the head nurse had uncommonly protuberant eyes, round and heavy-lidded, like those of a frog, and her thick neck was quite short.

"I have some Innsmouth blood myself," Sarah said.

"I never would have known," Ruth murmured.

They continued down the hall and stopped again at the next doorway.

"Ward Two is occupied by those with more severe physical deformities.

Some of these patients also have mental problems, but they are not so limiting as those in the first ward. They can feed themselves, those that have the use of their hands, and some can even go to the toilet unattended."

The deformities seemed to consist of a general thickening of the neck and torso, and a distortion in the legs that prevented walking upright. Some of the patients were missing limbs or parts of limbs. Their facial disfigurements were more severe than those in the first ward.

She hurried after the head nurse, who had started down the hall without waiting for her. They stopped at the third doorway and looked into the room beyond.

"Ward Three contains the most severe cases of congenital deformity," Sarah said calmly, pretending not to notice Ruth's grimace of horror. "These poor people can't walk. Some of them are able to crawl or hop along the floor on their stumps. We encourage them to be as active as their physical condition allows."

Ruth stared at the things that sat on the beds or crawled on the floor. She had cared for the severely disabled, but she had never looked after the needs of monsters. She wondered if she had made the right decision, coming to Innsmouth.

"Let's go upstairs," Sarah said. "I'll show you the nurses' cafeteria and lounge, and the apartments for residents. You'll be living here at the Facility, is that right?"

"Well, I hadn't really thought about it, but I assumed I'd be taking a room somewhere in town."

The little head nurse laughed.

"You don't know Innsmouth, Ruth. The people here are wonderful, but they are suspicious of strangers. I doubt anyone would rent you a room. As for the Gilman House, stay away from that hotel. It's in a terrible state of disrepair. You're much better off living here with us, and the rent is very reasonable."

"There are no wards on the upper floor, are there?"

"No, all the patients live down here. Our resident nurses and attendants live upstairs. It's like night and day. You won't even know you're still in the building."

2.

Ruth unpacked her suitcase in her apartment, which consisted of a kitchenette, a combined living room and bedroom, and a full bathroom. She was surprised how nice it was. The entire second level of the Marsh Facility was decorated in bright colors and lively patterns, as though in an attempt to deny what lurked below, and to a large extent it succeeded. True, there was still the smell of antiseptic in the air, and it was possible to hear the public address system echoing up through the floor when things were quiet, but overall she might as well have been in her own apartment building. It was much better than the single room she had imagined renting in the town.

About two dozen nurses and orderlies lived on the second level with her. They were standoffish, but that was to be expected in so small a place as Innsmouth. Many of them had the Look, but not in its advanced stages. They would probably warm up to her after she worked with them for a few weeks, she decided.

She took out her Bible and placed it on the bureau, then took her crucifix and hung it over her bed, where the previous occupant had hung a dreary painting of a storm at sea. She slid the small painting behind the bureau to get it out of the way. The Facility was located not far from the coastline, but she didn't need to be reminded of that every minute. It seemed that the halls of the Facility, both lower and upper floors, were filled with pictures and carvings related to sailing ships and fishing boats and the ocean. It was almost obsessive. She had always hated the ocean. Fortunately, her windows faced the hills. At least in her own apartment she could avoid looking at the Atlantic.

Kneeling at the side of her bed, she folded her hands together and began to pray.

"O Lord, watch over me, your foolish daughter in faith, and keep me from harm. Strengthen my resolve to do your work so that I remain steadfast when the moment of crisis comes. Inform me of your will, O Lord, that I may be your instrument of mercy on this earth. Amen."

The prayer was her own composition, and she recited it three times a day—on waking, at noon, and before going to bed. She had evolved past the need to use more conventional forms of prayer. The guiding hand of Jesus was upon her and she felt it as a physical touch upon the top of her head.

Since she had not been assigned any work on her first day at the Marsh Facility, she decided to take a walking tour of Innsmouth and acquaint herself with its streets. She put on her good pair of hiking shoes. They were the most expensive article of clothing she owned, but nurses were always careful about protecting their feet. On the average nursing shift they walked for miles and spent hours standing. She couldn't afford feet that hurt.

The Facility was no great distance beyond the outskirts of Innsmouth. She followed its tree-lined drive and found herself in the town. What a shocking experience it was. She had heard that Innsmouth was one of the more depressed communities of Massachusetts, but she had not imagined such advanced decay. It might as well have been a suburb of Detroit. The houses constructed in the grand Victorian style looked ready to collapse under their own weight. There were holes in the roofs, tumbled chimneys, broken and boarded up windows. None of those she passed had seen a new coat of paint in decades.

It was a singular feature of Innsmouth that a small river ran through the town, crossed at intervals by quaint wooden bridges. In between these bridges, the water fell over a series of geological faults in the landscape that produced cascades. She traced the river down toward the harbor, enjoying the sound of the rushing water. Now and then she saw a curtain move in the window of a house as she passed. Innsmouth was not uninhabited; it only appeared so. When she stopped and looked across the town, she could see only three figures on the streets. One of them appeared hardly human, it was so bent over, and it moved with a kind of hopping motion, but it was too far away to see clearly. She squinted at it, shading her eyes from glare of the sun, until the curious figure moved behind the corner of a building and was lost from view.

As she drew nearer the waterfront of the town, the houses became smaller and meaner in appearance. The smells of salt and fish grew stronger. A flock of seagulls filled the air, their frantic screams sounding almost human. They hovered over a dirty fishing trawler that made its tortuous way into the harbor along the narrow dredged channel. It seemed to be the only active fishing boat on the wharf, although several other run-down vessels were tied up there.

She passed a large, brooding building that was shuttered up. Weathered lettering on the front above the doors read *Marsh Refinery*. There was no activity around the building, which did not appear to have been used

147

for years, or even decades. This must be where the Marshes had smelted down the gold the family was reputed to have brought to Innsmouth in trading schooners from the South Seas or, as some folklore asserted, from the depths of the sea itself. But that was long ago.

As she stood in front of the refinery, the sound of a conversation drifted up the alley at its side. It was in some guttural foreign language she did not recognize. Listening to it, she wondered how such gulping, slopping sounds could issue from a normal human throat. Curiosity drew her toward the mouth of the alley. As she reached it, at the far end something large and close to the ground flopped its way around the corner of the old brickwork. She caught no more than a glimpse of its shadow, and wasn't sure whether it was a man with his back hunched or a large dog with a bad leg.

She started to go down the alley to investigate, but caution got the better of her curiosity. This was a rough section of town, even for so rough a town as this. She had no wish to be trapped in some enclosed courtyard by tramps or criminals. She decided that she had seen enough of Innsmouth for one day, and backed out of the alley.

3.

Ruth's life soon fell into a predictable routine. She was assigned to work in Ward Two under the oversight of Nurse Eunice Waite, a large and very loud woman who made her dislike of Ruth clear on their first shift together. Sarah Cork appeared to derive some sort of amusement from ordering Eunice to teach Ruth the routine. The corners of her broad slit of a mouth twitched and her froggy eyes sparkled as she spoke to the other nurse. Eunice was sullen to work beside, but to her credit she did not neglect her duties and was an excellent nurse. She had the muscle mass to lift and roll over the heavier patients who could not help themselves in their beds.

Most of the work was boring and repetitive, but Ruth had never minded repetition. Her father had been a strict disciplinarian, and had used his belt to teach her the virtue of honest toil. She washed her patients, helped them to the bathroom when they could walk or gave them bedpans when they could not, and tended to their bedsores, which were a chronic problem throughout the second and third wards.

It was surprising how quickly she became accustomed to their deformities. Some of them had strange flaps of skin in rows on the sides of their necks, and the texture of their skin was moist and almost scaly. The skin flaked off in patches, as though shedding, when she scrubbed them with a washcloth. Between the fingers and toes of many of them there was a kind of webbing, and the toes were oddly elongated, making normal walking very difficult when coupled with their bent backs.

On Friday afternoon she was summoned into the administration office. Head Nurse Sarah Cork flashed her a momentary smile of greeting across the desk and motioned for her to sit.

"How has your first week with us been going, Ruth?"

"Very well. Eunice has been teaching me the way things are done at the Marsh Facility."

"I'm delighted to hear it." She folded her chubby fingers together on the desk and her face became more serious. "The reason I called you in here today was to inform you that the family members of our patients will be visiting this evening. Friday is visiting night."

As yet, Ruth had not encountered a single family member visiting a patent. "Only Friday night?"

"That's right. It may seem unduly restrictive, but we find that the patients accept the routine of the Facility better when not disrupted by frequent visitors."

"They come in the evening?"

"After dark, yes."

"My shift will be over by then."

"I know, but there is something you need to know. It's our policy to allow the family members complete privacy with the patients. Under no circumstances are you to go down to the first floor after dark. Do you understand?"

Ruth blinked at the emphatic tone in the other woman's voice.

"Yes, I understand."

"What are you to do?"

"I'm not to go down to the first floor after dark."

"For any reason."

"For any reason," Ruth repeated.

Sarah Cork sat back in her chair and relaxed. She smiled again, and Ruth could not help thinking of a bullfrog that had just swallowed a fly.

"That will be all."

Ruth returned to Ward Two. Eunice eyed her up and down. "Did Cork tell you about visitors' night?"

Ruth nodded. "Doesn't it seem a little strange to you?" she asked the big woman.

Eunice shook her head.

"Only one visiting night a week, after dark, and we're not even allowed to be there in case anyone needs anything?"

"The families have been coming here for years. They know what to do if one of the patients needs anything."

"What if there's an emergency, like a Code Red?"

Eunice shrugged. "The night doctor would take care of it, I expect. It's never happened since I've been here."

"It just seems really weird, that's all."

"My girl, if *weird* bothers you, then you've come to the wrong place."

Ruth didn't argue. As the shift wore on she forgot about the words of Sarah Cork. The shift ended and she went upstairs to relax and pray while the meatloaf that was to be her dinner baked in the oven.

As dusk began to darken outside her window, her curiosity returned. She wondered what the visitors would look like. Would they have the Innsmouth Look as well? Every so often she peeked out her window, but they weren't arriving by the back door.

Below the sound of the television from the nurse's lounge she heard muffled, deep voices. The visitors must be here already, she realized. She went to the cast-iron radiator and sat on the floor beside it, then put her ear to the pipe. The weather was still mild enough in the evenings that the furnace had not been turned on. The chill iron pipe against her ear channelled the voices from below, but she could not quite make out what they were saying. It was as though they spoke in some foreign language. She remembered the voices behind the Marsh Refinery. These were similar, but there were both male and female voices.

She wanted to sneak down the stairs and have a look at the visitors, but knew that if she were caught, it would mean dismissal. Nurse Cork would probably be watching for her. Instead, she contented herself with crossing the hall to the cafeteria, which was empty. Its windows overlooked the front of the building.

It was almost an hour before someone came out of the doors below the window where she sat. From the back it looked like an elderly woman. She was fat and walked with the aid of two white canes. Her long black dress trailed on the gravel of the walkway and she seemed to be wearing a hat with a veil, although Ruth could not be sure of this because the old woman kept her back turned. She must be crippled up with arthritis, Ruth thought as she watched the woman, who did not so much walk as hop by means of the two canes.

The overhead light snapped on.

"What are you doing in here?"

Sarah Cork stood in the doorway, her hand on the light switch. "I ran out of milk. I thought there might be some left over in the fridge."

"Was there?"

"No."

The little fat nurse studied her for several seconds.

"Go back to your rooms."

Ruth left the cafeteria without speaking another word and returned to her apartment. She had not actually violated any of Nurse Cork's instructions, but it was clear that Sarah knew why she had been sitting in the lunch room, and didn't like it.

4.

It was a little more than two weeks after Ruth started work at the Marsh Facility that Eunice came into her apartment in the wee hours of the morning and shook her on the shoulder. The nurses living there never bothered to lock their doors at night. She opened dry eyelids and squinted against the light from the bedside lamp that the other nurse had switched on.

"What do you want?"

"You've got to get up and get dressed, my girl. You're needed outside."

Something in the other woman's voice stopped the questions Ruth might have asked. She got dressed quickly while the other waited with her arms crossed, tapping her toe on the floor. They hurried downstairs and out the front door.

"Will you tell me what's going on?"

"Some of the patients got out. We need to round them up and bring them back."

"Got out? Isn't the outer door locked at night? How could they get out?"

"Some of them are brighter than they look," Eunice said grimly.

"Does this happen often?"

The big woman grabbed her arm and stopped her on the gravel path they were following through the trees. "Listen. Do you hear that?"

Ruth listened. The rhythmic sound of waves breaking on the sands of a beach reached her ears. Mingled with it was the murmur of many voices.

"If the wind is just right, it carries the sound of the waves into the Facility at night, when it's dead quiet. The patients hear them."

"Hear what? You mean the waves?"

"The waves draw them outside and down to the beach. That's where they'll be. Don't worry, the rest of us know what to do. This happens three or four times a year."

The nearly full moon made walking easy as they descended the winding path. The beach lay outside the claustrophobic bounds of Innsmouth Harbor. Waves ran in freely from the open ocean, turning to white foam as they tumbled across the broad crescent of sand.

Ruth paused at the top of the sand dune in horror. The scene was like something out of Dante. Dozens of patients who possessed the power of locomotion stood or knelt or rolled in the waves as they curled across the sand. The patients were all naked. Their hospital gowns and Johnny shirts lay scattered around them or floated on the water. The patients danced or flopped up and down in the water, some standing as deep as their chests, and chanted in a rhythmic but inarticulate way, as though calling out to the waves that rolled to greet them.

Several of the staff were already on the beach, trying to get the more severely disabled out of the water, but the patients resisted their efforts with aggressive determination. They grunted like animals and struck out with their fists, or bit the hands that touched them.

"Someone's going to drown if we don't get them out," Ruth said.

She and Eunice hurried down the sloping sand as more staff arrived.

They managed to drag the less violent out of the water a few at a time and led them back to the Facility in relays. Then they concentrated on the more difficult patients one by one, pulling them from the clinging waves as they fought and chanted their wordless chant. Some of the deformed men were enormously strong in the upper body. Ruth managed to avoid getting bitten, but a flailing fist caught her above the eye and made her see stars for a few moments.

"Are you all right?" Eunice demanded.

"It's nothing," Ruth said. "It's not the first time."

Eunice laughed and nodded. Those who cared for the mentally disabled or demented became accustomed to watching out for stray fists, but it was impossible to avoid them all. It was a hazard that went with the job.

"Be glad he missed your nose," Eunice said, wrestling the grunting, gulping man down with her thick arm around his neck. A male nurse helped her drag him out of the water.

When Ruth was helping another male nurse lift a patient from Ward Three into a wheel chair, she noticed a head with white hair bobbing in the waves some distance out from the beach, watching her. She called to Eunice.

"That man is going to drown unless someone goes in and gets him."

Eunice looked, then smiled. "That's Lucas Crowley. Don't worry about him. He's real good in the water."

The white-haired man turned lazily and swam further out with slow strokes of his arms. He swam as though he were swimming toward something, but there was nothing in front of him except waves. As Ruth watched in mounting alarm, unable to turn away, she saw a hand lift from one of those waves and beckon to the swimmer. Its unnaturally elongated fingers were webbed. She blinked and it was gone.

"Did you see that?"

"See what?" Eunice asked, turning from a woman she had just wrapped in a dry towel.

"There was something in the water. It looked like a hand."

The big nurse squinted and shook her head.

"I don't see anything but Lucas."

The white head began to bob up and down, then disappeared beneath the waves.

"He went under," Ruth said frantically. She could not swim, but even so she had to resist the insane urge to run into the water. "Someone, please, get him out."

The rest of the staff glanced at her but made no move to enter the sea. They seemed amused by her concern.

"Lucas will come out when he's good and ready. He's done this before," Eunice told her. "You just see that the others get dried off and back to their beds."

Ruth could not turn away. She stood staring out the sea, waiting for the swimmer's head to come up, but it never did.

"I'll pray for your soul, Lucas," she murmured. It was all she could do for him.

5.

The next morning when she came down to work, she was assigned to Ward Three for the first time. As she entered the ward, she saw Lucas Crowley sitting on one of the beds. He wore a kind of tent-like garment of white cotton that looked handmade. No store-bought article of clothing would have fitted over his squat, broad body. His shoulders were massive, but his legs were so short, they disappeared under his prominent belly. She recognized him by the shock of snow-white hair that covered his misshapen skull, which was elongated and flattened. His eyes projected from his head like ping-pong balls, but his nose was so flat it was almost absent, and the broad slash of his mouth had no lips.

He felt her gaze upon him and turned to look at her with a vacant expression. The flaps of skin on either side of his neck moved up and down.

"I thought you were drowned for sure, Lucas," she said to him.

He tilted back his grotesque head and made a gulping noise in his throat. After a while she realized it was a kind of laughter. He was laughing at her.

"I'm your new nurse," she said, controlling her annoyance. "My name's Ruth Bowers. I'll be taking care of you."

He raised his hand and flicked his long fingers in a dismissive gesture of contempt. There was a web of skin between them.

"Can you speak? Do you understand what I'm saying to you?"

He began to grunt and bob his head at her, glaring at her with his strange eyes, until at last she moved away from him to the next bed. Almost at once he went back to staring at the blank wall in front of him, like some monstrous caricature of the Buddha.

Ward Three was a difficult ward. All of the patients were severely deformed, and most of them were retarded as well. They couldn't use the toilet on their own, or wash themselves, or even feed themselves. A few, like Lucas, could move around on their deformed limbs. He could not walk, but he could hop. Fortunately for the nurses, he seldom left his bed.

As she bathed him and fed him day after day, she began to feel an irrational aversion. Her skin crawled when she was forced to roll him over to apply the ointment that prevented bed sores. Handling his bedpans was particularly disgusting.

She knew she should not feel this way, that it was both unprofessional and un-Christian of her, and she tried to be pleasant toward him when she attended to his needs, but the trollish creature seemed to sense how she really felt, and showed his dislike for her in subtle ways. He would mock her with his gulping laugh, and stare at her with an almost palpable malice in his frog-like eyes.

At night, Ruth knelt at the side of her bed and prayed for guidance. "What am I to do to help Lucas Crowley, O Lord?" she asked.

For several weeks God did not answer her. Then one night he laid his hand on her head, and she knew his will. It was to be the same blessing she had administered at Arkham Hospital. Lucas Crowley was to be the first who received it at the Marsh Care Facility. Her heart filled with pure joy. "Yes, Lord, I understand. Thy will be done."

She kissed the cross around her neck and went to bed content that once again she was to become God's instrument.

Because of his broadness, Lucas could not fit into a conventional shower stall. It was necessary to lower him into a special stainless-steel bathtub to bathe him, which was much wider and deeper than an ordinary tub. He seemed to enjoy the water, to judge by the mewling sounds he made in his throat. Ruth hated washing him. It forced her to put both her arms deep into the tub, which brought her face down until it almost touched his.

The day after her revelation in prayer, when she was lowering Lucas into the tub using the special electric hoist with its lifting harness, she deliberately tipped the machine into the tub. Lucas went under the water with the full weight of the heavy machine pressing down on him, and the harness around his body prevented him from working himself loose. To be certain, Ruth leaned her full weight on the tipped machine. This brought her over the tub, where she was able to watch Lucas drown. She remained on top of the lifting hoist for a full ten minutes. At the end of this period she studied the grotesque face under the water.

His eyes were still open, which was to be expected. They seemed to stare at her with hatred, but she knew this was only an illusion. He did not move. He was dead, and she had fulfilled the will of God to release his tortured soul from its prison of deformed flesh. Now he could know peace. She unbuckled the lifting harness from around his body and replaced the hoist in its usual upright position, then left the tub room with a happy heart. Someone else would find him in the tub and assume his death to be an accident.

She was always very clever when she liberated the souls of those who suffered. She made certain there were no witnesses, and no evidence that could be turned against her. Any accusations were circumstantial and easy to deny. Too many of them had accumulated at Arkham Hospital, forcing her to resign her job, but before she left she had managed to help dozens of suffering souls find peace. With the divine grace of Jesus resting on her head, she knew she would have equal success at Innsmouth. So many of these poor tormented monsters needed her blessing.

It was almost lunchtime when she left the tub room. She took her lunch break with a happy heart.

When she returned to Ward Three with the insulin injections needed by two of the patients, the first thing she saw was Lucas Crowley, sitting on his bed in his white tent of a gown, staring at the blank wall. The shock was so great, she dropped the plastic tray with the empty syringes.

"Clean up your mess, Nurse Bowers," Head Nurse Sarah Cork said tartly from behind her.

Ruth felt the blood leave her face. She turned and nodded, avoiding eye contact with the other woman. Several of the patients laughed mindlessly at her mishap, but Lucas did not even turn his head.

6.

Ruth's failed attempt to give Lucas Crowley peace with the Lord took place on a Friday. After her shift, she went to her little apartment and settled down for quiet night of Scripture study and prayer. Just after nine o'clock a rap sounded on her door.

"The Director wants to see you downstairs," Sarah Cork said to her when she opened the door.

"The Director?"

"The Director of the Facility. He wants to see you in Conference Room B."

Ruth stared at the head nurse with surprise. This was the first time the Director had ever been mentioned.

"You said we were never to go downstairs on visiting night."

"The Director wants to see you now. Immediately." Her voice held the snap of authority.

Ruth left her apartment and shut her door behind her.

"What do you suppose he wants?" she asked in a nervous voice.

The shorter woman stared up at her with bright eyes.

"I'm sure he'll tell you himself, when you talk to him."

"Are you coming with me?"

"I haven't been summoned."

"I hope no one's filed a complaint against me?"

Sarah stopped beside the open door to the nurse's lounge.

"Do you remember what I told you when I gave you this job?"

"What?"

"You don't get a second chance."

With this cryptic remark, she left Ruth in the hall and went into the lounge, from which emanated the laugh track of some television sitcom.

The conference rooms were at the end of the hall. She was able to reach them without passing the three wards. This was a relief. She had no wish to confront any members of the visiting families. She felt an instinctive aversion to them that was almost a phobia. Her palms began to sweat when she imagined meeting them.

She hesitated outside the conference room door, wiped her palms on the sides of her dress, and went in. The overhead pot lights were turned low on the dimmer and shed a reddish glow over the long conference table. All the chairs along both sides of the table were occupied. As they turned their faces to look at her, she gasped with surprise. All of them had the Innsmouth Look in its most advanced stages. The women wore broad hats with black lace veils that partially obscured their features, but the faces of the men were plainly visible. They stared at her with their protruding eyes. They were dressed in suits of an archaic cut that must have been tailor-fitted to their squat, broad bodies. The sides of their thick necks rippled.

The man at the head of the table stood on his short legs, leaning forward so that the weight of his massive torso was supported on his powerful arms. His hands were enormous, their long fingers webbed. He had no neck, and his elongated skull was hairless. His mouth was grotesquely broad, like the mouth of a frog. He wore a three-piece suit, with a gold watch chain across his striped vest.

"Come in, Nurse Bowers. Take a seat," he said in a voice both deep and wet.

She advanced timidly and sat on the edge of the chair at the foot of the table. There was a strange smell in the air, a kind of fishy odor. She resisted the impulse to wrinkle her nose in disgust.

"The town council has just been discussing your case."

Ruth realized these antique horrors must be the leaders of Innsmouth.

"Are you the Director?"

"Forgive me for not introducing myself. I am Jonah Pyke, the Director of the Marsh Care Facility."

"Why have you called me here?"

"Isn't that self-evident? You tried to murder one of our patients today."

"Nonsense. I did no such thing," she replied tartly.

He turned his head and said something in a gulping language she did not understand. A door opened behind him, and an orderly who also had the Innsmouth Look, though not to any advanced degree, wheeled in a metal table on which sat Lucas Crowley. The Director made gulping noises at him, and Lucas responded with similar wet sounds in his throat.

"My nephew tells me that you held his head under the water of the bathtub for ten minutes in an effort to drown him."

The men and women seated at the table laughed, as though Pyke had made some extremely funny joke.

"Lucas can't talk," Ruth said.

"There you are wrong, Nurse Bowers," Pyke told her. "He cannot form the words of English because his vocal apparatus has evolved beyond it, but he can speak very well in the language of the Deep Ones."

"I don't believe you," she sniffed. "This is a trick. You're trying to make me betray myself."

Lucas stared at her with his bulbous eyes, and she felt his mockery.

"It doesn't matter what you believe, Nurse Bowers. My nephew never lies. He may be handicapped, but he is perfectly capable of describing what you did to him."

"If I had held him under the water for ten minutes, he would be dead."

Again those seated at the table laughed, and Lucas joined in with his gulping.

"You can't drown a man with gills, Nurse Bowers," Pyke said.

Lucas leaned forward and caused the flaps of skin at the sides of his neck to expand and collapse rhythmically.

"You're all insane. I don't have to listen to any more of this."

She felt strong hands on her shoulders, forcing her back down into her chair. A male attendant had crept up behind her unseen.

"We've already come to our decision," Pyke said. "We can't allow you to continue to work here. Nor can we release you, now that you know so much about our town. You will have to remain as a ward of the Facility."

She stared at him, unable to believe that she had heard him correctly.

"You want to keep me here as a patient?"

"To make you more accepting of your new circumstances, a small operation will be performed on the frontal lobe of your brain. Don't worry, it's perfectly safe."

"A lobotomy," she said in a weak voice. "You're talking about a lobotomy."

"That's correct. I'm told that after you've had the operation you will be happy living at the Facility."

"You're insane." She looked around the table, and the room seemed to spin under her chair. "You're all insane."

"Naturally we will have to modify your body so that you will blend in with the other patients," Pyke told her.

Ruth didn't hear the rest of what he said. She was too busy screaming.

7.

She woke up lying in a bed in Ward Three, but she didn't recognize it. There was a white gauze bandage wrapped around her head and over her face. Her face felt as though it was on fire. She lifted her arms to touch the bandages and saw that similar bandages covered the ends of her wrists, which terminated in stumps. She pressed the stump of her right arm to her cheek, and it left blood on the bandage. This caused her no great distress. It seemed unimportant.

Across the ward, Lucas Crowley watched her from his Buddha posture. When he saw that she was awake, he squirmed off his bed and dropped to the floor on his long arms, then hopped across to the side of her bed.

For some reason Ruth could not explain, she felt a vague dread at his approach. She tried to say something, but only bleats came from her mouth. Her throat hurt almost as much as her face.

A shadow rose up on the side of the bed as Lucas lifted himself on his arms so that his broad, flat face hung over hers. She smelled a rank fishy odor and realized it was his breath. He stared down at her from only a few inches away with his frog-like eyes, the gill flaps on the sides of his neck opening and closing. Her anxiety increased, even though she could not have explained why she felt anxious. Her thoughts were so slow and dull. Nothing seemed to be working right in her head. She tried to cry out for help, but no sound came from her lips. Tears of frustration formed in the corners of her eyes.

Lucas opened his slit of a mouth. Extending his tongue, so much like the tongue of a bullfrog, he licked her tears.

The Lament Horror

1.

A young gentleman in a gray pinstriped suit jumped down from the step of the train to the rough planks of the rail depot platform and looked around with a doubtful expression. Apart from a pair of laborers installing clapboard siding on the front of the as-yet-unfinished building, the depot was deserted. The freshly painted sign above the entrance that read "Lament, Mass." at least assured him that he was in the right place.

Smoke from the funnel of the great black locomotive swirled around him on the fitful morning breeze and made him cough. He raised his hand to his mouth and saw with annoyance that his starched shirt cuff was marred with a dusting of soot.

Behind him, the elderly conductor said something that was drowned out by a sudden hiss of steam that billowed between the wheels of the engine. The gentleman found himself lost within a white cloud for a moment. Then the breeze carried it away.

"I said, I'll have your trunk set down on the platform, young sir," the conductor repeated in a rasping voice.

"That will be fine," the young man said.

The conductor scratched his gray beard in a calculating way and eyed his former passenger from his starched white collar to the spats on his shoes, then back up to the tapered silk hat on his head. He extended his hand.

Grunting, the young man dug into his pocket and gave him a silver dollar.

A boy of about twelve years of age squeezed past the conductor and jumped down to the platform. Two others of similar appearance and manner followed. They stood together unspeaking with eyes downcast. All had heads recently shaved of hair. Small bite marks were visible amid the stubble that had begun to regrow on the whiteness of their scalps. They wore drab gray shirts and trousers that had the look of a uniform, although they were unmarked, and scuffed shoes on their feet that had seen previous owners.

"Let me pass," ordered an amply proportioned woman who loomed in the doorway behind the conductor. She had the look of a widow in mourning, with her black crape dress and veil-draped black cap.

The conductor stepped down and turned to assist her. She ignored his hand, choosing to lower herself with difficulty by hanging onto the vertical iron rail at the side of the doorway.

These four were the only others in the single passenger car. The rest of the train was made up of a dozen empty boxes with tall sides that were open at the top. Throughout the journey from Uxbridge the young man had sat facing the woman and the three boys, and none of them had spoken a single word.

"Get my bags," she snapped.

The conductor scowled behind his bristling facial hair.

"What about the youngsters?"

"They're from the poor farm in Grafton, fool. They have no luggage."

"I know they're from the poor farm," the old man said evenly. "But sometimes the boys have little bundles with them tied up in rags."

"These boys don't."

Two uniformed negroes carried a heavy travel trunk down the steps and set it beside the door of the depot. Without looking at those who watched them, they returned to the train and in moments emerged with two carpet bags and a hat box. The woman ordered them to take these items into the depot and shooed the three silent boys in after them.

"Not the most sociable of women," the young man said with a wry smile.

The conductor shrugged. "That's Mrs. Sharp. She's one of those from the new Congregationalist church that meets on the Little Hill, over yonder." He waved his hand in a vague way westward beyond the depot. "None of them is much of a talker." Dislike was evident in his voice.

"What was she doing with the boys?"

"She bought them at auction from the poor farm in Grafton. There's boys and girls coming in all the time from different poorhouses across Worcester county."

"Does she represent some charitable institution?"

The conductor bent over laughing and slapped his leg. "Not an ounce of charity in her. The boys work in the mine and the girls work in the laundry. Josiah Harwood built a kind of barracks for them where they sleep, and she runs it. He gets them body and soul for three years, while the county pays for their food and clothes, and then they're free to go their own way, the ones he doesn't work to death."

The young man became conscious of a dull, rhythmic thump in the distance, like the slow beating of an enormous heart.

"What's that sound?"

The conductor squinted at him for a moment, then comprehension dawned across his face. "That's Old Mariah, the steam engine up on the Big Hill. You'll get used to the sound by and by."

He pointed to where the train tracks curved past the base of a hill of no pretentious elevation, although it was the tallest in the valley. On the crest stood a timber-frame building with a great spoked wheel and an enormous iron beam extending from its side. The wheel turned as the beam rose and fell. Each time it did so, a dull thud shook the air, like the footfall of a giant.

"Is that where the coal mine is?"

"Yes sir, up on the top of the Big Hill. The pit entrance is right next to Old Mariah, under that tripod."

"Why do you call it that?"

"That was her name when they shipped her across the Atlantic Ocean from Cornwall. Cornwall's in England, sir."

"Yes, I know where Cornwall is."

"They needed her to pump the water out of the mine. It started to flood when they dug down to the lower coal seam, you see. She's a grand old girl, is Old Mariah. They say she was built in 1817, and spent twenty years pumping out a tin mine in Cornwall before Mr. Harwood and his consortium had her took apart and shipped here."

"I'm surprised there's enough coal in the mine to make it worth the expense," the young man said with faint interest, gazing around at the darkly forested hills that rose on all sides of the valley.

"Coal is valuable," the conductor said. "You see, young sir, there isn't much of it to be had in Massachusetts, and the new railroads that are starting up everywhere are keen to get it, because it's so expensive to ship in from out of state."

The young man nodded with indifference. "There was supposed to be someone here to meet me."

"I'm sure someone will be along presently. Now if you will excuse me, we need to move the train and fill those empty boxes with coal."

He waved his hand at the engineer, who was leaning out of the window of the locomotive, watching them, then stepped up into the train. The brass whistle atop the boiler let out a long shriek, steam gushed across the platform, and the train lurched into motion with great gouts of jet-black smoke shooting up into the air from its funnel.

The young man watched it follow the curve of gleaming steel until it was beneath a long wooden chute that descended down the hillside from the mine. Another short blast from the whistle caused coal to rattle along the chute into one of the open coal cars.

2.

"Mr. Witherspoon?"

The young man turned. Approaching him across the planks from the depot entrance was a tall, slender man dressed entirely in black, who wore a broad-brimmed black hat with a domed crown.

"Mr. Henry Witherspoon?"

"I am, sir."

The other gave a slight inclination of his head. "My name is Reverend Redemption Feake. Forgive me for being late. I was delayed."

There was a kind of brightness in his dark eyes that Witherspoon found vaguely disquieting. He was thankful that Feake did not offer his hand. "I was just admiring your little valley."

Feake looked around with a smile. "It is a beautiful place in its way, isn't it? Not up to the standards of your native Boston, but the hills shelter us from storms and the trees provide lumber for our homes and fuel for our fires, or they did until recently. We use coal now, of course. The white water you see cascading down that distant slope is called Enoch Brook. It runs through the middle of the village. It's spring-fed and supplies all our water needs. Walk with me."

Witherspoon went with Feake through the unfinished depot and out the other side. The village of Lament consisted of several dozen houses and other structures arranged haphazardly on both sides of the brook. Two bridges spanned the serpentine length of this not inconsiderable watercourse, which was almost broad enough to deserve the name river. Both were made of rough-hewn timbers. All the buildings in the village were painted white. Beyond them, near the cascades, rose a low hill with a large structure on its crown. By its square bell tower he knew it must be a meeting house.

They descended the steps of the depot and followed the unpaved road that wound its way at the side of the brook through the village of Lament.

A woman in a white apron opened her door to look out as they passed. Witherspoon touched his finger to the brim of his hat and nodded at her with a smile. She stared at him for a moment, then stepped back into the house.

He noticed a curious decoration painted on a circular board above her door. It was a triangle inside a star with five points. He started to ask Feake about it, but the minister was striding along so briskly with his long legs, Witherspoon had to hasten to catch up.

They passed three men dressed in the same black garments worn by the minister. All had hats with wide brims on their heads. Their expressions were guarded. They nodded to Feake as they passed but did not speak. Witherspoon imagined that he could feel their gaze on the back of his neck. He resisted the urge to turn his head.

"Lament is growing rapidly," Feake said. "We now can boast of a livery stable, a grist mill, a blacksmith shop, a bakery, a laundry, and even a general store. And the schoolhouse, of course."

"Where am I to stay?"

"Do you see that large house across the brook? The one with the dormers that lies midway between the bridges? That is the rooming house of the widow Ephesia Bond. All those who come to live in the village from away board there. I've made arrangements for your trunk to be carried up and set within your room."

"I'm eager to see the schoolhouse where I am to teach."

"And so you shall, in due time, but first the head of our village council, Mr. Josiah Harwood, wishes to have a word with you."

They crossed over the nearer of the bridges.

"Harwood. He owns the mine, doesn't he?"

"The mine is owned by a consortium of investors, but Mr. Harwood is one of its principals. He put up the money for the exploratory excavation. Once it was determined there was coal in Lament, he had to turn investors away. Do you know that he raised over fifty thousand dollars in Boston?"

"That is a great deal of money."

"Indeed, but it's not just for the mine itself. It was necessary that a rail line be constructed to the Blackstone Canal to get the coal to market. The rumor is that in a few short years a railroad will run the full length of the Blackstone River Valley, all the way from Worcester to Providence."

"That will certainly be an improvement over the canal packet boat."

"Slow things, aren't they? I've heard that it takes a full day to travel from Providence to Uxbridge."

"That is correct. I came up on the packet from Providence and spent last evening in Uxbridge, before traveling by rail to Lament."

"A short year ago you would have had to travel from Uxbridge by wagon," Feake said. "The pace of progress is astonishing. It gives one heart for the future of mankind."

Witherspoon looked around at the soot-stained white facades of the houses. Everything had a grimy look. Even the new-washed laundry drying on the clotheslines did not appear to be absolutely clean.

Feake seemed to divine his thoughts. "The coal dust gets into everything, I'm afraid. But that is the price of progress, and after all, it is a small enough price to pay."

They passed a building with a congregational look to it. The shutters on its windows were closed.

"Is that your meeting house?" Witherspoon asked.

"That?" Feake laughed. "Dear me, no. It's true that was a meeting house at one time, but it has been abandoned. Not enough members in the church to keep it solvent, you see. The Baptist minister who maintained it was forced to move away with his family. No, my meeting house is that large building on the crest of the hill, just above the village." He pointed at the imposing structure Witherspoon had noted earlier. It, too, was white.

"I confess, I'm a bit surprised by the lack of variety."

"What's that? Oh, you mean the color. Well, white is the new trend, isn't it, even in Boston. It gives everything a classical Grecian appearance. We do endeavor to keep up with the latest trends."

Witherspoon laughed self-consciously. "It has a kind of sepulchral air to it, don't you think?"

Feake sniffed through his long nose. "I've never considered the matter. No, I don't think so."

"I didn't mean it as an insult," Witherspoon added quickly. "It's just that mausoleums and funeral crypts are so often white."

"They would be, wouldn't they, being made of marble."

Witherspoon realized he had unintentionally insulted the dignity of the village and chose not to speak in response to this mild rebuff.

Feake stopped walking in front of a two-story house with a gambrel roof that was surrounded by a wrought-iron fence.

"Here we are. This is the house of our village elder, Josiah Harwood. I'll just go with you to the front door and introduce you."

3.

Josiah Harwood was an intimidating presence in his early sixties who stood several inches above the average height. His round belly filled his waistcoat to bursting and stretched his gold watch chain, and his flowing white moustache merged with the white side whiskers on his cheeks. He wore a black suit and a curious little brimless black cap on his head that resembled a smoking cap.

The Reverend Feake made his introductions and backed his way out of the house with a series of bows, as though leaving the audience chamber of an Eastern potentate.

Harwood escorted Witherspoon into a large room with an ornate French writing desk, an enameled German stove that was set into the fireplace, and several wingback leather chairs. Shelves of books lined the walls.

"Well, sir, what do you think of our little community?" he demanded.

"It's quite … picturesque," Witherspoon said.

The older man chuckled at the term and opened a cedar box on the corner of his desk. "Cigar?"

Witherspoon noticed that his palms were covered with a fine powder that glittered like tiny diamonds when it caught the light.

"I don't smoke."

"A drink of brandy, then?"

"I'm sorry, but I don't drink."

"Very temperate of you. Your mother must be proud."

"My mother died three years ago."

"You have my condolences, sir."

"Thank you."

Witherspoon watched Harwood trim the end of the cigar with his penknife, slip off its paper band, and light it in the shade of an oil lamp that burned on his desk. Even with the lamp, it was dim in the office. The north-facing window let in scant light from the smoke-filled sky, and the walls were paneled in black walnut. From somewhere outside he heard the slow beat of Old Mariah's iron heart, and from the hallway the ticking of a grandfather clock.

"I keep this lamp burning to light my cigars," the older man told him.

He walked around the desk and took a padded chair opposite Witherspoon, crossing one leg over the other at the knee. Even seated he demanded attention. His eyes were a clear, pitiless blue. For a time they studied Witherspoon without blinking, while the smoke from the cigar enfolded Harwood's hoary head in a rising cloud.

"If you don't mind me asking, why did you take this job?"

Witherspoon shrugged. "I suppose I like to teach."

"But your father's a wealthy man, isn't that correct?"

"I suppose so, by some estimates."

"By any estimates, from what I've heard. And you attended Harvard, did you not?"

"Yes, I received my bachelor's degree at Harvard."

Harwood spread his hands in a display of bewilderment.

"Then why would you come to a backwater like this? It can't be for the money."

"No, sir, it is not about money."

"Then why?"

Witherspoon took a deep breath and let it out slowly, conscious of the smell of burning tobacco, which was not unpleasant.

"My father and I had a disagreement."

"Ah," said Harwood.

"He was determined that I should assume a position in his Boston bank. I was just as determined that I did not wish to become a banker. We had a parting of the ways."

"He disinherited you?"

168

"More or less. He is willing to overlook my rebellion against his authority if I come back to Boston and apologize to him."

"Which you have no intention of doing," Harwood said.

"That is correct, sir."

"Let me be plain, Mr. Witherspoon. I don't approve of gentlemen who pretend to be commoners. It's an affectation. They do it for a few weeks, a month perhaps, and when they've had enough of working life they go back to their polo ponies and croquet."

"I've never owned a polo pony, and I don't play croquet," Witherspoon said.

"What do you do for recreation, then?" the older man asked, blinking at him owlishly.

"I read. I hike through the countryside."

"Hiking. Admirable for the constitution." Harwood hesitated. "A word to the wise. Don't go hiking about after sunset. There are wolves in the hills, and they sometimes venture down into the valley."

"It was my understanding that wolves seldom come near human habitations," Witherspoon said in surprise.

"So they say, but don't believe it. My advice to you, sir, my strong advice, is that you stay inside after dark."

"I will consider what you've said."

Harwood puffed on his cigar. "Well, sir, I have my misgivings about you, but I can't deny you the position. The school board has appointed you over my head. They are concerned about the state of education in Lament."

"I understand you have only one teacher at present for almost a hundred pupils."

"At present that is correct. We did have a second teacher, a man from Providence named Jordan Capp, but he left the village one night without prior notice and has not been seen since."

Witherspoon smiled. "It would seem, then, that you are in dire need of my skills."

Harwood shrugged his heavy shoulders. "I won't fight the board of education on the matter of your appointment. You may have the position in a probationary capacity, and if you prove satisfactory, it will be made permanent. Though why a rich man's son would want to waste his time in such a manner is beyond my comprehension, sir."

They sat in silence for a time, Harwood smoking his cigar. Witherspoon tried to relax into the comfortable leather back of his chair, and wondered when it would be socially appropriate to get up and leave.

"Lament is my child, you know," Harwood said.

"Yes?"

"My wife died some years ago. We had no children. I have made this village my progeny. I'm determined that it shall prosper. The Boston men thought I was a fool when I spent my own money to drill exploratory holes, but I had the laugh on them. We found coal. Not just one seam, mind you, but two, one a hundred and fifty feet below the other. That changed their tune. You should have seen them come running to me, waving their money. Well, I took it and used it to buy a Cornish engine to dewater the mine, and to build a rail line to the canal. After years of toil and frustration Lament stands on the brink of prosperity. That is my legacy to this village. Once the coal begins to ship in large quantities, there will be no limit on our expansion. I tell you, young man, I have great plans for Lament, great plans."

"What you've accomplished is impressive, sir," Witherspoon said, not knowing what else to say.

The fire blazing in Harwood's blue eyes slowly faded. He was not looking at Witherspoon, but through the wall behind him at some distant vista of his own imagining.

"It was not without risk. I could never have done it without the support of Reverend Feake's church." His gaze flicked to Witherspoon. "What is your religion, sir?"

"My family are Baptists," Witherspoon said slowly, wondering what this sudden leap of subject portended.

"Have you ever considered becoming a Congregationalist?"

"No, I can't say that I ever have."

"You should, sir, you should. I'm sure Reverend Feake would be happy to instruct you in the finer points of church doctrine."

"Are there no Baptist churches in Lament?"

"There is only one church in Lament at present, the Church of the Morning Star."

Witherspoon considered the name. "A reference to the twenty-second chapter of Revelation, no doubt."

"You know your Scripture, sir," Harwood said with approval.

"I was instructed in the Bible at an early age by my father. Is the church Congregationalist?"

"It is rooted in Congregationalist practices, but it professes a unique doctrine that I'm sure will intrigue you."

Witherspoon pondered a response for a moment or two. He had no wish to offend Harwood's religious beliefs. He said, "I would be most grateful if Reverend Feake would allow me to attend a Sunday morning service, so that I may become better acquainted with his church."

"I'm confident he would be delighted to do so."

Harwood clamped his cigar between his teeth and stood up from his chair with surprising ease in spite of his bulk.

"Come with me. I will escort you to the schoolhouse myself and introduce you to your fellow teacher, Miss Whyte."

4.

Witherspoon discovered the schoolhouse to be a modest single-story clapboard structure with two large rooms. In front was a well with a pitched wooden roof over it and a crank for the bucket. Behind the school, on either side of a spreading chestnut tree, stood a pair of identical outhouses.

As they approached along the road he heard the sound of children's voices reciting in unison the seven-times multiplication table. They entered a narrow entrance hallway with a closed door on either side. The walls were lined with brass hooks for hanging coats, but in the present warm spring weather they were unoccupied except for a scattering of caps.

The sound of recitation ended, and the door on the left opened to emit a slender young woman with a bun of honey-gold hair and a spray of freckles across the bridge of her nose. She wore a conservative gray dress with white lace trim that complemented the misty gray of her eyes.

"The children heard you enter, Mr. Harwood," she said. Her voice was deeper in tone than that of most women, but pleasantly mellow.

"Young ears are sharp," Harwood said. "We lose so much as we age, don't we? Miss Whyte, allow me to introduce you to Henry Witherspoon, the replacement for the late Mr. Capp. Mr. Witherspoon, Miss Maud Whyte."

The young man and woman assured each other that they were delighted with the meeting.

The Lament Horror

"I will leave you together to plan your syllabus," Harwood said. "I'm sure Miss Whyte can introduce you to your pupils, fine young lads all of them. This room on your right, which is presently vacant, will become your classroom. Miss Whyte has had to carry the full workload since the departure of Mr. Capp, and has been forced to teach a mixed class of boys and girls. Now that you are here, you will receive the boys and she will return to teaching the girls. Isn't that right, Miss Whyte."

"Yes, of course, Mr. Harwood."

"Very well, I will leave you to become better acquainted. I'm sure you know your adopted trade, Mr. Witherspoon, and scarcely need my oversight."

"I'm sure I can manage, Mr. Harwood."

"Good. I'll leave you, then."

They watched through the open front door as he strode ponderously back along the road. Witherspoon turned to the woman and cleared his throat, wondering what to say.

"I expect you've had a hard time of it, teaching both classes by yourself."

She smiled shyly and shook her head.

"The children are really very good."

"Have you been teaching long?"

"Not long. I came to Lament last spring."

"You weren't born here?"

"Oh no. I was born in Lowell."

"You've come a long distance."

"Positions are hard to find, especially for a woman with no prior experience as a teacher and no college degree. I had to take what I could get."

They stood in the open doorway, listening to the thump of Old Mariah.

"It must have been a great shock when Mr. Capp disappeared."

A shadow passed across her face, but it was gone before he could define its nature.

"It was inexplicable. One day he was at the school, cheerful and enthusiastic, and the next he wasn't. No one knows how he even got out of the village, except that he didn't take the train. No horses were missing."

"A mystery," Witherspoon said.

"Indeed. The men searched the hills for two days but found no trace of him."

"I believe Mr. Harwood thinks he was eaten by wolves."

"Please don't laugh," she said seriously. "People have heard things moving around their houses at night."

"Do you believe it is wolves?"

"I don't know what to believe. No one has seen them."

A man and a woman walked past the school along the road, their arms linked. Both were dressed in black. The woman was veiled as though in mourning and the man wore the same kind of unstylish broad-brimmed hat Witherspoon had seen so often since his arrival. The man stared at him long and hard, then somewhat reluctantly nodded his head. Witherspoon nodded back at him.

"Why in heaven do so many people in this village wear black?"

Miss Whyte laughed at his tone.

"It is a bit startling at first, isn't it? I wondered the same thing when I arrived here. It's the Church of the Morning Star. They all wear black, along with those ugly hats and veils. You never see them with their heads uncovered. When they are inside their houses the men wear soft black caps and the women cover their hair with black kerchiefs."

"Do their children attend school?"

"No. They teach their children at home."

"They sound like some kind of cult."

"I believe they are mostly Congregationalists," she said with a short laugh.

"You're not wearing black."

"I'm Catholic. There is no priest in Lament so I keep my faith privately and confess myself to God. What of you, Mr. Witherspoon?"

"My father is a Baptist, as was my mother when she was alive, but I have little religious belief of my own."

"Are you an atheist?"

He smiled at her shocked tone. "No, just a man of uncertain faith."

"It would probably be wisest not to speak about it in Lament." She lowered her voice and glanced at the closed door of the classroom. "This is a very devout community. As Mr. Harwood observed, little ears are sharp and tales are carried out of school."

"I may convert," he said jokingly. "It would help me become one with the community."

"Please don't," she said with unexpected fervor, then smiled shyly. "I feel enough of an outsider as it is."

He laughed. "Well, I won't do it today. Are you going to introduce me to the children?"

"Yes, of course."

They opened the door of her classroom. Seated at long desks on benches were boys and girls who ranged in age from five or six to fourteen or fifteen. They looked up from their copy books at him with round eyes. The boys were seated on one side of the room, the girls on the other, with a narrow space between them. The room was crowded. He was surprised to note that the girls were much more numerous than the boys.

Nine of the girls wore the same plain dresses of sturdy cotton. These must be the girls who worked in the laundry, Witherspoon realized. Their drab clothing was in stark contrast to the embroidered and pleated dresses of the village girls.

Witherspoon quickly counted heads, and found that there were thirty-nine boys. Only four wore the gray shirts and trousers of the poorhouse.

"Class, this is Mr. Henry Witherspoon. He has come to replace Mr. Capp. From now on he will be teaching the boys. Say good morning, Mr. Witherspoon."

The response was ragged but sincere.

"Well, perhaps I should get started right away," he said to Miss Whyte. "Are there benches in the other room?"

"Yes. Everything is as Mr. Capp left it."

"Very well. All you boys, follow me across the hall. Bring your books and pencils."

He was dismayed at the condition of his classroom. It was apparent that Mr. Capp had not been a man of scrupulous habits. The floor was dusty, the glass in the windows caked with grime, and even the woodwork filthy with the accumulated dirt of countless brushing hands.

"Right, lads. First order of business. Who knows where to find a bar of soap and a scrub brush?"

The boys looked at each other. A smaller boy coughed into his hand and then raised it.

"I do, sir."

He wore the gray of the poorhouse and appeared to be around eight years of age, although his face looked older.

"Good lad. What's your name?"

"Timmy, sir. Timmy Sykes."

"Well, Master Sykes, off you go."

The boy needed no further urging, but darted from the classroom.

"The rest of you, open the windows to air out this room. Find a broom and some rags. I want the woodwork and desks washed and the floor swept. Wipe the fly specks off the window glass. Someone, pick up that trash in the corner." He clapped his hands. "Get busy, we have a lot of work to do."

While the boys began to bustle about, he went to the blackboard to erase a chalk drawing that had been left on it. The crudeness of the drawing suggested that it was the work of a child. He paused with the felt eraser in his hand, studying it, trying to determine what it represented.

There was an object he could not identify on a table, or it might have been on an altar of some sort. Stick figures surrounded it. Lines of chalk extended from the object to these figures. In front of the table a smaller figure lay on the ground. Instead of round circles for its eyes the artist had drawn small crosses.

He shook his head and smiled. The imagination of children knew no boundaries. He used the eraser to send the drawing into that oblivion where all drawings and writings of chalk ultimately reside.

5.

Mrs. Bond was a jovial, obese widow of around fifty years of age. Mercifully, she did not wear black crape or a veil. Witherspoon considered it a mercy. He had grown tired of looking at all the dour, silent figures in black who moved around Lament like brooding ghosts.

His room was small but tidy, the wardrobe adequate for his needs, the mattress well-padded and the quilt that covered it quite new. There was a washstand with a basin and pitcher of water, a small mirror on the wall above it, and a chamber pot under the bed. He found little reason to complain, particularly since the weekly charge was slight. His travel trunk had been duly deposited in a corner behind the door.

The evening meal around the common dining table was a boisterous affair with little ceremony. Accustomed as he was to dressing for dinner, and having servants wait at his elbow, he found it strange yet at the same time oddly refreshing to have that same elbow jostled as he reached for the china bowl of mashed potatoes.

"Pass it round, Mr. Witherspoon, pass it round," Mrs. Bond said from the head of the table.

He gave the bowl to a smiling bald man with a round face who sat on his left.

"Thanks," the man said. "My name's Matthew Poorish, by the way. You're the new teacher, right?"

"That's right."

"I thought so. You've got a bookish look about you. I'm the stationary engineer up at the mine. I keep Old Mariah's bob ticking down."

His accent was odd but Witherspoon could not place it.

"You're not from New England."

"Lord, no, I'm from Cornwall. I came across on the boat that brought the old girl to Providence. I've been looking after her most of my life."

Witherspoon's gaze wandered across the table to Miss Whyte, who caught his glance and smiled momentarily before continuing her conversation with a woman beside her.

"You're from Boston, I believe, Mr. Witherspoon," said a skinny man with wire-frame eyeglasses who sat on his right.

"Yes."

"It's gratifying to have another educated man in this village. I'm afraid few of the locals have read anything other than the Bible."

"The mine appears to have brought quite a few strangers to Lament."

"Oh, yes. The locals were mostly farmers, you see. They didn't know the first thing about digging a coal mine or building a railroad. I'm Samuel Taff, by the way. I'm the mining consultant."

"Harwood hired you to run the mine, I suppose."

"Well, I don't actually run it. That's the job of Bullum Bedford, that heavy-set man you see near the end of the table."

Witherspoon regarded the red-headed man, who sat eating his roast beef and potatoes with a scowling intensity. He did not raise his eyes at the sound of his name, which was singularly apt. His shoulders were massive and his neck uncommonly thick.

"Bull's the pit boss. He runs the mine. I consult on matters of a more technical nature, such as hydraulic influx and the design of the support framework."

"Hydraulic influx? Flooding, do you mean?"

"Yes. We have a serious inflow of water on the lower level. Ground water, you know. The water table is not far below the surface in this area. Fortunately, Mr. Poorish's Cornwall engine can handle it."

"She can handle it and a lot more, if it comes to that," Poorish said with his mouth full, chewing his beef as he spoke. "The old girl isn't even straining her boiler."

"The whole operation would be impossible without the engine," Taff said. "We use it not only to de-water the pit, but to move the men and raise the boxes of coal. The pit is vertical, you see. Most people have the idea in mind that a mine goes into the side of a hill on the horizontal, but that's usually not the case. Our mine runs straight down for fifty feet to the upper seam, and then down another hundred and fifty feet or so to the lower seam."

"You mean the access is vertical, but the two coal seams run laterally," Witherspoon said, trying to visualize the mine.

"That's correct," Taff said. "The upper seam is five feet thick, although it's starting to taper. The lower seam is only four feet, which is why we use boys to mine the coal on the lower level."

"Men can't stand upright, you see," Poorish said.

"The boys from the poorhouses," Witherspoon said.

Both men nodded.

"So that's why there are so few of them in school. They are working in the mine."

"Every boy works for his bread," Bedford said suddenly in a rough voice. "I make sure of that."

"Except for the boys who are too sick to swing a pick, or those who we learn have some infirmity that prevents them from doing a day's work," Taff said.

"The poorhouses try to send their cripples to us," Bedford said. "They hide their condition, and we have to discover it for ourselves when we set them to work. They won't take the boys back, neither. The village ends up feeding and housing the worthless little snipes."

"Mr. Harwood doesn't like that very much," Taff said with a sour little smile.

"No, he does not," Bedford affirmed.

"There's a boy in the school, a small boy named Sykes," Witherspoon said.

"I know that boy," Bedford said, chewing as he spoke. "Consumption.

He collapsed when we tried to work him. He won't live out the summer."

"You must allow me to take you on a tour of the mine, one day when you are at your leisure," Taff said.

"I'll show you around the old girl when you come up the hill," Poorish added.

"You're very proud of your engine," Witherspoon said with a smile.

"That's the truth and no mistake. I couldn't think more highly of Old Mariah if she was my own mother."

Witherspoon gazed around the table, and noticed for the first time than none of the diners wore black.

"Are there no members of the Morning Star in the house?"

"You mean those heathen crows who gather on the hill," said a skinny woman with a pinched face and an habitual pained expression.

This drew a bark of laughter from Bullum Bedford.

"That's Mrs. Hoffman, the woman who runs the laundry where the workhouse girls wash the clothes and bedding for the miners," Poorish murmured into Witherspoon's ear. "She was sweet on that teacher who disappeared."

"I'm a Baptist myself," Mrs. Bond said with a smile.

"I am a Congregationalist," Taff said. "I occasionally attend Sunday morning meetings on the hill, but I don't belong to the church. They have their own queer way of doing things that doesn't sit well with me."

One by one those at the table declared their faith. Both Taff and Bedford were Congregationalists, non-practicing. There were three Baptists in addition to Mrs. Bond and Witherspoon, one Episcopalian, and three Presbyterians. Mrs. Hoffman said she was a Unitarian, and Poorish admitted he was a Methodist. Miss Whyte did not speak.

"That's quite a diversity," Witherspoon said.

"The crows keep us here together so we won't mingle with their true believers and cause them to stray," Mrs. Hoffman said sourly.

"That's not true," Mrs. Bond admonished in a pleasant voice. "You know you are free to live anywhere you choose, Esmeralda."

"So you say," Mrs. Hoffman sniffed. "But just try to find a room for rent anywhere else. Just you try it, and you will learn soon enough that I speak the truth."

Mrs. Bond laughed, and the supper conversation passed to other topics.

6.

That Saturday afternoon, Witherspoon found himself idle and bored. The school was closed. All of the other residents of the boarding house were occupied in various ways. He might have sought out Maud Whyte and asked her to walk with him in the hills, but she was cleaning the house of a village woman who had just given birth and was still confined to bed. He decided to take Taff up on his offer to show him the coal mine. The mine operated six days a week, shutting down only on Sunday.

He put on his hiking garments, which were of a rough woollen weave designed for hard use, and followed the path up the slope of what was known locally as the Big Hill to the entrance of the Lament Coal Mine. As he drew nearer, the intermittent thud of Old Mariah began to dominate every other sound, even the rattle of coal in the chute and the grinding pound of the crusher. The steam engine was half in and half out of the three-story building that had been built around it, so that it seemed to be trying to break out of its confinement. A great iron beam that was longer than a rail locomotive rose and fell with an inexorable rhythm, and an enormous spoked iron wheel that was larger than the water wheel of the grist mill spun with bewildering speed.

Poorish noticed him through the open doorway and waved him over. The beaming little man's grease-stained face dripped with sweat. Witherspoon went into the building with him.

Through the soles of his feet he could feel the engine breathing its great gusty sighs of escaping steam. Poorish said something.

Witherspoon cupped his hand behind his ear. "What was that?"

"Come with me, and I'll show you what makes Old Mariah go," Poorish repeated more loudly.

Witherspoon let himself be led through the building on a tour of the steam engine. He saw where coal was shoveled into its firebox to keep the fire glowing. He saw the riveted brass boiler where the water was turned into steam, and the upright cylinder in which the single piston slid up and down. The cylinder was sheathed on the outside with vertical strips of hardwood held in place by metal bands, and was as broad as the thickest oak tree.

"What's that?" Witherspoon asked in idle curiosity. He was not particularly interested in the steam engine, but felt the obligation to be courteous to his fellow boarder.

Poorish looked up at the great iron beam as it rose and fell on its pivot. "That's what we call the bob."

"This whole iron beam that's going up and down?"

Poorish nodded. He led Witherspoon outside to where the extending beam rose and fell with the inexorable thrusts of the piston and the turning of the flywheel. It was noisier outside than inside because of the crusher. A shrieking came from some part of the machine.

"See those long vertical rods attached to the end of the bob?" Poorish said, pointing to two rods that hung from the beam and disappeared through holes in an iron plate that lay flat on the ground.

Witherspoon nodded.

"Those rods pump the water out of the lower seam of the mine. If you look over there you can see the pipe that discharges the water down the slope and into Enoch Brook."

"I'm surprised you can suck water up such a distance," Witherspoon said, looking from the sliding rods to the gush of the discharge pipe some thirty or forty yards away.

Poorish laughed. "You can't. Water won't draw up more than thirty-four feet, and the mine is much deeper than that."

"Then how on earth do you get the water to come up?"

Poorish pointed at the rods.

"At the other end of those rods is a pump that drives the water out of the mine. You can't draw it this high, but you can push it."

This was new information to Witherspoon. His school studies had concerned Latin, Greek, and English literature, as well as some history and philosophy. The practical aspects of well pumps had not formed part of the curriculum.

"What's that dreadful shrieking noise?" he shouted. "It sounds like a soul in torment."

"The bob needs grease," Poorish said. "Old Mariah isn't shy. When she needs to be greased she lets the whole world know about it. I'll get to it presently, but I want to show you something else."

He drew Witherspoon over to the edge of the open timber platform on which they stood and pointed up to the tripod that was built over the pit opening. A rope ran from a spindle at the engine to a pulley hanging from this tripod. A workman operated a lever and made the drum of the spindle turn and slowly wind in the rope.

"That's how we get the men up and down the shaft. This man engages the drum here, and moves these levers to raise or lower the cage. The coal is raised the same way. Are you going down into the mine?"

"I thought I might, if Mr. Taff has time to show me around."

"Then you'll ride on this rope. Don't worry, young gentleman, it's safe enough. The rope is almost new."

"I must see if I can locate Mr. Taff." The shrieking was getting on Witherspoon's nerves.

"He's in the pit," Poorish said. "You'll have to wait for him to come up, but I don't imagine he'll be very long. Look down there. Do you see those moving plates?"

Witherspoon admitted that he did see the thick iron plates that were opening and shutting in a rhythmic way in time to the beat of the engine's heart.

"That's what crushes the coal to a nice uniform size, after which it goes down the chute and into the rail cars that carry it to the canal."

"Very interesting, I'm sure," he said, unable to completely conceal a yawn behind his hand.

"All this is done with steam and a single piston going up and down. If that isn't a modern marvel, I don't know what is," Poorish said with evident pride.

"The march of science," Witherspoon said.

"What's that? I can't hear you. I better get that grease on the bob before Old Mariah takes it into her head to do something nasty. Look, up the hill, there's Mr. Taff coming out of the shaft now."

Witherspoon watched an iron cage emerge from the pit opening. Inside it were Taff and two other men. Taff opened a door in the side of the cage and they stepped out. Witherspoon turned to take his departure from Poorish, only to find that the little man had vanished into the building, no doubt in search of a pot of grease.

7.

"You're not by any chance subject to fits of nervousness in tight spaces?" Taff asked as he closed the door of the lift cage.

"Not to any morbid degree," Witherspoon said.

"That's just as well. Coal mines are not only gloomy places, they are confining."

The Lament Horror

The cage lurched and began a slow descent into the darkness. The candle burning in Taff's tin lantern was soon the main source of light, as the square of the shaft entrance above their heads became smaller and smaller. From below, Witherspoon heard the sound of picks and shovels, and male voices.

There was a smell in the mine, a kind of animal den smell of sweat and urine mingled with the scent of oil and burning tallow. It was cloying in the back of his throat and made him cough into his hand.

"You soon get used to it," Taff said with a wan smile. "The men and boys can't come to the surface to relieve themselves, so they go in buckets."

When they exited the iron cage at the upper level, Witherspoon was amazed at how low the roof was. It brushed his hair even when he stooped over and hunched his shoulders. The miners were all in the same posture as they dug away at the face of the coal seam with their picks and loaded the chunks of coal into iron boxes, which they pushed along the length of the mine on gleaming steel tracks. As they worked shoulder to shoulder, they joked and made crude remarks that caused Witherspoon's ears to burn. He was not accustomed to such talk, or for that matter, to such male company.

"Mind your tongues," Taff said loudly. "We've got a gentleman among us."

A few of the miners laughed, but they stopped their crude remarks, at least while Witherspoon was near enough to hear them.

"This coal is what they call anthracite," Taff told him as they watched the miners at work by the dim light of their lanterns, and by the naked candles fixed in their hats. "It's a hard coal all around—hard to mine, hard to ignite—but it burns cleanly and doesn't leave much ash."

"What's the lower level like?"

"I don't think you'll want to go down there, Mr. Witherspoon."

"That's where the boys work, isn't it?"

"That's right. It's very cramped quarters down there. Not enough room to stand up."

"Why don't you just cut away some of the rock above the coal seam and give yourselves more head room?"

"We could do that," Taff said with a smile. "We could give ourselves nice barrel-arched ceilings."

"Well, why don't you?" The faintly mocking tone of the other man was starting to annoy him.

"Well, you see, it costs to remove rock. The more rock you take out, the more it costs, until you reach a place where your coal mine isn't making any profit at all."

"So you just follow the seam, no matter how narrow it is?"

"That is the usual practice. If a seam narrows too much to be worked, the mine is closed. But you'd be surprised at the space a miner can work in when he knows his job."

Witherspoon was beginning to feel difficulty in breathing. It was as if a weight were pressing on his chest. He knew it was only in his mind and used his annoyance to shake it off.

"I'd like to see the lower level."

"Very well. I'll signal to have the cage lowered."

The descent to the lower coal seam was longer than the initial descent. The blackness all around enfolded them like a cloak of sable. Eventually they heard the sound of work below, and voices. They were not the deep voices of men, but the higher voices of children.

The cage bumped to a stop on the bottom and Taff swung the door wide. "Mind your head," he said sharply. "The roof is low here."

Witherspoon wondered if Taff's reluctance to descend to the lower seam was motivated only by the tightness of the space, or whether there was some other reason. He felt his way out of the cage and followed the mining consultant, who shuffled along with his back hunched and his legs bent, toward the flickers of light at the end of tunnel. In places the stone above was less than four feet from the stone below.

The sight that greeted Witherspoon's gaze as they came into the light made him cringe inwardly. A dozen or more boys ranging in age from five or six years up to the early teens crawled and crouched as they dug away at the black wall of coal. As the pieces fell from the face, they were shoveled into iron boxes with wheels that ran on steel tracks back to the vertical shaft. Some of the coal pieces were so large, they were loaded individually by boys who could barely lift them, and who were so covered with coal dust that the whiteness of their skin was nowhere evident. The only white was the whites of their eyes—even their teeth were stained black. Sometimes one or another paused to bend over with a racking cough. The rest paid no attention, but continued with their labor. When the fit passed, the boy afflicted merely spat out blackness from his mouth and joined them.

Sounds of picks could be heard from other tunnels of the mine, where boys presumably performed the same work.

Witherspoon stared at Taff in the light of his lantern.

"I never realized," he said. He tried to say more but words failed him.

"Boys turn into men quickly in a coal mine," Taff said, smiling faintly at the expression on his companion's face.

They made their way in crouched silence back toward the waiting cage. There was water in pools on low lying sections of the floor. It squished when Witherspoon hobbled through, and he felt its wetness on his feet inside his leather shoes.

"This whole level would flood in under an hour if we didn't keep pumping day and night," Taff said.

"What's down there?" Witherspoon asked, pointing to a side tunnel.

"Nothing. It's not being used."

"I'd like to take a look, if you don't mind."

"There's really nothing down there. It would be a waste of your time."

"Even so, since I'm here and I'm not likely to be here again, I'd like to see."

Taff made no further objection. Silently he waddled his way into the dark passage, and Witherspoon followed his grotesquely crouched, weaving silhouette. His legs were starting to burn from the strain of being ceaselessly bent over, and the small of his back ached. He wondered if he should have insisted on coming this way.

"There's the end of it," Taff said. "See, there's nothing." There was a slight tremor in his voice.

"What's that on the coal face?"

"That? Oh, that's just a kind of marker."

It was a triangle with a lidless eye inside it, painted on the coal with white paint. Lines of paint radiated around the triangle, so that it appeared to be shining with its own light. At least, that was the effect intended by the person who had painted it, but it was crudely done.

"What does it mark?" Witherspoon asked as he studied it.

"I don't know. I wasn't here when it was painted."

The younger man looked at him curiously. "You mean, you have no idea what it marks? Surely you were told about it by the miners?"

Taff laughed uneasily and glanced around. "They say something was found in the coal."

"Something? You mean an object?"

"I really couldn't say. It was probably a fossil. As you know, coal is formed from decayed plant material, and it's not unusual to find the imprint of ferns and even the trunks of trees."

"Is that what the miners say was found? A fossil?"

"You know how laborers are. They like to tell fanciful stories. I've never paid attention to them. It's all nonsense anyway."

"Why is this face not being mined?" Witherspoon asked.

"I don't know."

"You don't know why? But you're the mining consultant."

"Before I was hired, Mr. Harwood gave orders that mining should cease on this face. I have not felt that it is my place to ask why. I've always presumed that he wished to preserve the fossils embedded in the coal for later removal. Perhaps, when you next see him, you can put the question to him."

"I certain will. It's a very curious thing. This coal face is closer to the lift than the face where the boys are working."

"I'm sorry, I know nothing more about the matter. Now, we really must get back to the surface."

8.

Witherspoon stood in front of his desk with a yardstick in his hands and surveyed the faces of his pupils. The younger boys sat at the front benches, and the older ones behind them. Rearmost of all were the four poorhouse boys in their gray clothes. These had grown ragged around the cuffs and showed signs of crude mending with needle and thread, which had probably been carried out by the boys themselves, since they were segregated in the barracks from the girls who worked at the laundry. They sat huddled together, but some distance apart from the village lads, who by a common unspoken consent shied away from them.

The village boys wore what might be called their school clothes, which were at least clean if they were not well-tailored, but the poorhouse boys had no good clothes, only the rough cotton shirts and trousers they had worn since coming to Lament.

The clothing of the young miners who went up the hill every morning and came down at sunset, too exhausted to do anything but scrub the coal dust off their bodies, eat their evening meal and fall into their cots, was in no better condition. They must possess at least one change of garments to wear while the others were being washed, Witherspoon reasoned. He wondered what would happen when their gray uniforms rotted away? Surely at some point the Lament Mining Consortium would replace them?

None of the four in the classroom had traveled with him on the train from Uxbridge. They were earlier arrivals who had been reluctantly deemed unfit to labor in the mine. One who was ten years old had a lame leg and could walk only with the aid of a crutch. Another of some thirteen years suffered from a withered arm that he held curled against his chest. At some point during his early childhood, due to an injury, it had ceased to grow and was no larger than the arm of an infant. Another shook with a kind of palsy and had great difficulty talking.

The fourth poorhouse boy was little Timmy Sykes, the child with advanced consumption who had fetched the water on the day of his arrival. He sat with a rag in his hand, and periodically raised it to his mouth to cough into it. He was so thin, his cheekbones appeared ready to cut through the stretched parchment of his gaunt face.

By a curious caprice of fate, his lips were tinted a natural rose color and his hair was the purest gold Witherspoon had ever seen on a human head. It curled over his forehead and around his ears in an almost playful way. It was the face of an angel on a body that probably would draw its final breath before the summer ended. For some reason that Witherspoon could not conceive, the child was always smiling.

Over the past week Witherspoon had come to appreciate the enormity of the challenge that faced him. The boys had been poorly instructed by his predecessor, Jordan Capp. From what they told him, the incompetent Mr. Capp had attempted to pound his lessons home by applying a rod to their backsides. Only two of the older boys could read in a way that was not painful to hear, and their penmanship and spelling were both appalling. Few could recite the alphabet, and none could say the multiplication tables from beginning to end. During the previous week he had drilled them on these basics, and had made some progress, but this bright Monday morning his mind was occupied with another matter.

He used the yardstick to point at a chalk drawing on the blackboard. It was a star with five points. At its center there was a small triangle. It was similar to the design he saw above the front doors of several houses in the village.

"Who made this?"

The boys stared at him with wide eyes.

"Don't be afraid to answer, I'm not going to beat you. I just wish to know what it represents. Every morning for the past week it's been on the board. I've been erasing it without comment, because I assumed it was just a foolish lark, but I've noticed similar signs affixed to some of the houses and barns around Lament."

"Not on the houses of the crows," an older village boy named William Ford said with a hint of defiance in his voice. He was the son of a farmer who lived just outside the village. The boy had wide-set brown eyes, like those of an ox.

"Did you draw this, William?"

The boy shook his head.

"What do you know about it?"

"Nothing," the boy said, dropping his gaze.

In the lengthening silence, the thud of Old Mariah on the Big Hill could be plainly heard. Witherspoon became conscious of the smell of burning coal from the black plume of the steam engine, which seemed able to find its way into every building in Lament even with the windows and doors tightly closed.

"I'm waiting," Witherspoon said.

"It's for good luck, sir," Timmy Sykes blurted from the back of the room.

"What do you mean, Timmy?"

"It wards off the evil that walks by night," Ford said before the younger boy could speak.

Witherspoon regarded his pupils with amazement.

"Do you mean it's some kind of heathen hex mark?"

None of them answered. Ford met his gaze with a defiant glare.

"What is this evil that has everyone so afraid?"

"No one has seen it, unless the crows have, but they don't say much," Ford said.

"Crows? You mean the members of Reverend Feake's church?"

"We all call them crows in the village, on account of the black clothes they wear."

Witherspoon shook his head, smiling in spite of himself. He remembered Mrs. Hoffman's use of the term at dinner several days ago.

"Boys, you must know that this is only a foolish superstition. There's no evil walking abroad in the village at night."

"Tell that to Jeb Nicker's little sister," Ford said.

The boy who was named nodded solemnly.

"Tell that to my brother," Ford said. "Tell that to Mr. Capp who disappeared without leaving so much as a footprint in the mud."

"I don't understand, William."

"They all went missing, sir."

"So did boys from the barracks," Sykes said. "Four of them last month."

"They come in the night," Jeb Nicker added in a nervous voice that cracked as his Adam's apple bobbed up and down. "They steal you right out of your bed, and in the morning your mother finds it empty."

Ghostly fingers brushed along Witherspoon's spine and made him shiver. He frowned.

"It's just a fairy tale, boys. Open your copy books. We'll say no more about it."

He went to the blackboard and took up the chalk eraser, then hesitated, staring at the symbol on the board. Clenching his jaw, he drew the eraser over it with broad strokes until it could no longer be discerned.

9.

Harwood escorted Witherspoon into his study with a broad gesture and indicated a chair.

"Take a seat, Mr. Witherspoon, take a seat. Tell me how your work at the school is progressing. Is everything in order? If you need supplies, you have only to ask and I'll instruct a servant to get whatever you need."

Witherspoon sat and waited for the older man to take his seat before speaking.

"That's not the reason I wished to speak with you," he said.

"No?" Harwood frowned beneath his flowing white eyebrows. "Why have you come?"

"It's about the boys working in the mine."

"Those boys are not your concern, Mr. Witherspoon. Their food and clothing is paid for by the county. Their other needs are met by the Consortium."

"Are they being educated?"

"As I said, that is not a matter of your concern."

"My concern is for their future welfare. Today they are boys, but tomorrow they will be men, and men without education are ill-equipped to prosper in the world, given the rapid pace of progress."

"They are fed, housed, clothed, and instructed in a trade that will serve them well all the days of their lives."

"Trade? You mean coal mining?"

"Of course. The training these boy receive from the benevolence of the Consortium will allow them to seek work in any coal mining operation in America."

There was a certain logic in what Harwood said that made Witherspoon pause in thought. He had not looked at the matter in this light.

"Even so, is there not some way that the boys could attend school? Even if it were only a single day a week, they could be taught the rudiments of reading and writing."

Harwood shook his head. "That is impossible. I understand that a spirit of charity is your motive in proposing this, but it is completely out of the question."

"In heaven's name, why?"

Harwood stood and went to his sideboard, where he poured himself a whisky from a crystal decanter.

"Economics, plain and simple. Do you think the mine dug itself? Do you think the rail line laid itself? Do you think the Cornish engine just materialized out of thin air? They cost money, sir, a great deal of money. That money is tied up in Lament, and those who supplied it expect a fair return on their investment. The coal must continue to come out of the ground, sir. That is all there is to be said on the matter. If the flow of coal to the canal were to cease even for a brief time, confidence in the Consortium would be destroyed. Financing would be withdrawn. The entire enterprise would fall to ruin."

"But surely there must be some way—"

"You are a gentleman's son. I don't expect you to understand such matters. You've never done a real day's work in your entire life. This school teaching is a lark for you, and soon you will grow weary of it, get on the train and return to Boston. You and I both know this to be true. You must accept my word as a man of business when I tell you solemnly that the production from the mine cannot be interrupted, not even for one more day a week. If it were in my power, by God I'd make those boys work on Sunday as well, but some things cannot be helped. I have six days a week, and that is all I have, so I must make do with it."

Witherspoon realized that he would get nowhere by arguing the matter. The hoary face of the older man might as well have been cut in granite beneath the odd little felt cap he wore.

"Perhaps you might enlighten me regarding another matter that has come to my attention," he said.

"What is it?" Harwood made no attempt to keep the impatience from his voice.

"There is a rumor current among the children regarding an evil that walks at night and abducts them from their beds."

Harwood stared at him, then snorted laughter. "Are you serious?"

"I know it is nothing more than a fairy tale. What I wished to ask you is whether there have been disappearances in the village?"

The older man drained his whisky glass and shrugged his broad shoulders.

"No more than might be expected in any community. The boys from the poorhouses sometimes run away."

"They must not be aware of the inestimable blessing you confer on them by instructing them in the mining trade," Witherspoon said dryly.

Harwood did not smile. "I enjoy sarcasm as much as the next man, but not from those who are in my employ. What you are saying is arrant nonsense."

"Was the disappearance of Jordan Capp nonsense?"

The older man sighed heavily and set his empty glass down on the sideboard with enough force to make the decanter rattle on its silver tray.

"The man drank. He developed an irrational affection for Miss Whyte, an affection she rebuffed, and in his fit of despondency he left Lament during the dead of night. There, sir, you have the whole of the sordid tale of Jordan Capp, which I would not have divulged had you not pressed me."

There was nothing Witherspoon could think of to say in response to this revelation. He began to feel foolish for bringing up the children's tale.

A uniformed servant entered.

"What is it, Andrews?"

"The Reverend Feake wishes to speak to you, sir."

"I'm afraid I must terminate our conversation," Harwood said to Witherspoon, who rose from his chair. "I hope I've made clear that what you request is absolutely impossible."

"You have been very clear, sir. I will take my leave of you."

"Andrews will show you out. Admit the Reverend Feake when you have seen to Mr. Witherspoon, will you, Andrews?"

"Of course, sir."

Witherspoon encountered Feake in the entrance hall. The minister was in the act of removing his broad-brimmed black hat. Beneath it he wore the same brimless, soft felt cap that Harwood wore. The teacher wondered if all male members of his church wore the cap.

The minister's hands sparkled with tiny flecks that glittered like diamond dust in the light from the fan window over the front door.

"How are you getting on in Lament, Mr. Witherspoon?" he asked with a tight little smile.

"As well as may be expected."

"Excellent, I'm happy to hear it. I didn't see you at services Sunday last."

"No, I was so busy with preparations for my class that I didn't have time to attend services."

"That's understandable. Settling in and all that. Perhaps you will grace our meeting house with your presence this coming Sunday?"

"That is my intention."

"Good, good. We're always gladdened at heart to see new faces. I'll look forward to your attendance."

Witherspoon stepped from the house into the wan sunlight. The world had a washed-out look, like a faded watercolor. When the breeze blew the black plume from Old Mariah over the village, the sun had difficulty sending down its rays to the earth. The plume of smoke created a kind of twilight that might last for minutes or hours at a time.

On the crown of the Big Hill to the south, the bob and wheel of the Cornish engine and the tripod above the pit stood out in silhouette against the pallid sky. Toward the west, on the Little Hill, rose the imposing meeting house of the Church of the Morning Star with its square bell tower and white-pillared portico. Between these looming sentinels lay the village of Lament like a patient on his sickbed, or so it struck Witherspoon's momentary fancy. The ribbon of Enoch Brook traced its serpentine course between the houses, dividing the community in twain. Above the village it was a foaming line of silver, but below the village it became a turbid, dirty gray.

10.

Witherspoon was whistling to himself when he descended from his room to the parlor of the boarding house. It was early Sunday morning. For a change of pace, the sun was shining down warmly, and the birds sang in the branches of the chestnut tree outside his window. He was in good spirits. He had almost convinced himself that the plight of the workhouse boys was, after all, not his problem, and in any case not something within his power to change.

Maude Whyte was the only person present in the parlor. She sat next to a window, reading. When he entered, she closed her book and stood from her chair. Through the open window he heard the tolling of the meeting house bell.

"You're wearing your Sunday best," she said.

"Well, it is Sunday."

"But last week—"

"I was busy with class preparation."

"So you mean to go up the hill?"

"Going up the hill" was an ambivalent colloquialism in Lament. Witherspoon had learned that it could mean either going to the mine, or going to the meeting house of the Morning Star church.

"Yes, I'm going to the meeting house."

"You shouldn't. You're a Baptist."

He laughed as her odd urgency.

"I have an invitation from the Reverend Feake. It's not as though I'm a heathen, or a—" He stopped his tongue.

"Or a Catholic," she finished tartly. "It may surprise you to learn that the Reverend once invited me to his meeting house."

"Did you attend the service?"

"I most certainly did not."

She stood with her finger between the pages of her book, baring the way to the front door.

"Forgive me, Miss Whyte, but I really don't see why you should be concerned about so trivial a matter."

He started to step around her but she moved to block his passage.

"There is something not right about them," she said in a lowered voice.

"About whom?"

"The members of the church, of course. Reverend Feake. Josiah Harwood. All of them."

"Well, I admit they are an odd-looking congregation of the faithful, but I see no reason for alarm."

"Look at their heads," she whispered, glancing at the archway that led to the stair.

Heavy footsteps sounded on the treads. Bullum Bedford came into the parlor with his habitual scowl.

"Morning," he grunted, and moved directly to the table that held the most recent Boston newspapers.

"We'll speak again when I return," Witherspoon said to Miss Whyte in a casual tone.

"Yes, of course," she said lightly. "God go with you."

Witherspoon puzzled over this decidedly odd conversation as he followed the road that wound alongside Enoch Brook. On the crown of the Little Hill he could see the front doors of the meeting house opened wide in invitation. The rapid tolling of the bell in the tower became slow and regular, indicating that the service would soon begin. He wondered if Miss Whyte suffered from emotional instability. It was well known to physicians that hysteria was an affliction of the womb. Or was she superstitious enough to be made fearful by village rumors about the church?

He joined members of the church walking in the same direction along the road. They glanced at him with approval and nodded, but did not speak. There was nothing particularly odd about them, other than their uniformly black clothing. It was true, their eyes held an unusual brightness, but Witherspoon set that down to religious enthusiasm. He had seen a similar gleam in the eyes of the devout in Boston.

Their heads were covered, as was always the case. The men wore the same broad-brimmed black felt hats with rounded crowns. The women wore black caps from which descended veils of black lace.

Miss Whyte's words echoed in his mind. He peered narrowly at the heads of the men and women who walked in front of him and beside him, but saw nothing out of the ordinary. He even glanced over his shoulder at those behind him. All wore a similar solemn expressions on their pale faces. All had the same brightness in their eyes. The only oddity was the silence they maintained. None of them spoke so much as a word to him or to each other.

The Lament Horror

The Reverend Reformation Feake stood to one side of the open doors of the meeting house, his slender hands clasped in front of his waist. He nodded to the faithful as they passed between the pillars of the portico, and they returned his nod in silence. He caught Witherspoon's eye with a slight smile. The teacher returned it.

Inside the door, someone handed him a brimless black felt cap of the same kind Harwood had worn in his study. He looked around and saw that the men were removing their hats. All wore similar black caps beneath them. The caps were peaked slightly in the center. Feeling a little foolish, Witherspoon pulled on his own cap. He wondered if the practice of the men covering their heads to worship had been inspired by a similar custom of the Jews.

The interior of the meeting house was quite plain, as was to be expected. Congregationalists were notorious for their hatred of decorations in their places of worship. The only extravagance, if it might be so called, was the squat iron German stove near the front of the room, similar in style to the one he had seen in Harwood's study, but much larger. A metal chimney extended from it out through the wall. It was cold now but no doubt glowed red during the winter months.

He saw Harwood at the front of the long room, moving into the foremost pew, which he had purchased, probably for a considerable sum of money. The other leading citizens of Lament took their seats beside and immediately behind him. The more common folk sat toward the rear. Indeed, the yearly incomes of all the faithful could easily be estimated by where they sat in the rank of pews.

There was one unusual feature that caught his eye. In front of the pews stood a kind of lectern. It was approximately two feet square at the top, and rose from the floor to a height of around four feet. Draped over it was a green velvet cloth with a golden fringe and golden tassels at the corners. Upon the front of this was embroidered in gold thread a triangle, and within the triangle in silver thread a staring eye. Six silver rays radiated around the triangle. The design was quite similar to the marker painted on the coal face in the mine.

A bearded old man sat to one side of this lectern cradling the neck of a bass viol on his shoulder, a bow in his hand. In common parlance this instrument was known as a church bass. Evidently the congregation did not possess the funds to purchase a church organ, Witherspoon thought—or perhaps they did not wish to expend them on such a frivolous affectation.

The gathering settled into an expectant silence. From outside the walls of the meeting house Witherspoon heard the dull, regular thump of Old Mariah.

Reverend Feake took a stance behind the lectern. For the first time Witherspoon noticed that the green cloth draped over it glittered as though covered with diamond dust. It was the same glitter he had seen on the minister's hands, and on the hands of Josiah Harwood.

Reverend Feake opened the morning worship with an extemporaneous prayer.

"Thou who art high and great; most potent mover of the earth; who slept for a hundred million years but is now awakened; who anticipates with us the coming transformation of our flesh; whose all-seeing eye marks the least of transgressions; who rewards the faithful with promises of perfection; heed thou our prayer, we beseech thee; we who are less than dirt on the hem of thy robe; less than the pebbles beneath thy feet; guide us through our daily lives that we may dwell in the radiance of thy righteousness forever. Amen."

The congregation voiced the final word of the prayer. Stately chords from the bass viol echoed from the high ceiling, and Witherspoon rose with the rest to sing the first hymn. A chorus of voices filled the air. It was a hymn he knew well, and he lent his full voice enthusiastically to the swelling sound. As a boy he had always enjoyed singing in the meeting house.

> How wondrous great, how glorious bright,
> Must our Creator be,
> Who dwells amid the dazzling light
> Of vast infinity!

The service progressed in the usual way. Apart from the caps on the heads of the men, which were a definite oddity, he had seen nothing out of the commonplace, certainly nothing that should cause the villagers to fear this gathering. Yet as he looked around, he realized he was the only soul in the meeting house who was not a member of the church. He was the only outsider. He would have expected at least a sprinkling of other Baptists, since the Baptist meeting house was shuttered. It was curious, but it was not sinister.

Reverend Feake chose to deliver his sermon on the subject of

Lazarus resurrected from the dead. One portion in particular caught Witherspoon's attention.

"I say to you that we are all dead, although we think ourselves to be alive; and only when we believe ourselves to be dead shall we truly live. For we are vessels of corruption that begin to decay on the day of our birth, but in eternity we shall put on crystalline armor immune to the insults of time. As a mighty tree grows from the smallest of mustard seeds, so shall we grow into glory from the seeds that have been planted within us by the Shining God who guides our steps and measures our works."

It was an uncommon choice of imagery, but otherwise an unremarkable sermon. Witherspoon found himself yawning toward the end. He was glad when the final prayer had been uttered and the final hymn sung. Throughout his life the most joyous moment of any religious service had always been the moment of leaving the meeting house, and it was no different today. He paused on the steps to speak a word or two to Reverend Feake.

"A wonderful sermon," he said. "I found it most uplifting."

"I'm pleased it met with your approval," Feake said, smiling. "Perhaps you will become a regular member of our little church."

I would rather be beaten with axe handles, Witherspoon thought.

"We will see what the future holds," he said, matching Feake's smile with his own.

"Even the humble woodsman may find salvation in our Lord," Feake said.

Witherspoon's eyes widened in surprise at this choice of words, but before he could speak the minister had moved on to talk to another member of his congregation.

11.

Witherspoon managed to persuade Maud Whyte to walk with him up into the hills above Lament in the cool of the late afternoon. For a time they talked about inconsequential matters connected with the school, but as they were returning down the slope along the forest path, their conversation became more serious.

"We all guard our words when members of the church are nearby,"

Maud Whyte said. "I know it sounds foolish, but it's almost as though they can read our thoughts."

Witherspoon remembered the incident on the meeting house steps.

"Also, we never know who among the villagers is a spy for Harwood and Feake."

"Do they cast such a long shadow over Lament?"

"They do. Harwood considers Lament his personal possession, and Feake fulfills his every command."

"You speak as though it were a sinister relationship."

She paused her step to look at him with a solemn expression. "Not everyone in Lament was in favor of employing the poorhouse boys in the mine, but you will hear no objections raised today."

"They changed their minds?"

"They no longer express an opinion, those who are still living in the valley."

"You don't mean—?" He laughed uneasily.

"There have been disappearances. Not just the poorhouse boys, and not just Jordan Capp, may God rest his soul. He was a poor teacher, but he spoke up for the welfare of the boys before Harwood."

"Don't tell me you believe the children's tale of monsters that roam the streets at night and snatch them from their beds."

"No, of course not. But I have come to believe that some malevolent influence hangs over Lament like that black pall of smoke from Old Mariah. That's why I believe you should go back to Boston."

"I have nothing to return to," Witherspoon said. "My father has disowned me. He was quite clear on the matter. Unless I took up a position in his Boston bank, he would cut me from his will and stop my allowance. Well, the allowance was stopped, and I have no reason to believe that I am still among his heirs."

"Go back and humble yourself before your father. Take the position at the bank," she said fiercely. "There is danger for you here, I can feel it."

"If that were true, Miss Whyte, why do you stay?"

She shrugged her shoulders beneath her white blouse. "Who else is going to take care of the children? In any case, just like you, I have nothing to return to."

While Witherspoon listened in silence, she told her tale of sorrow, which was no different from similar tales told by countless young women all across New England. Only the details differed. Her father had died of heart failure years ago. Her mother had struggled to maintain the household, but at last crushed by a burden of debt she had taken her own life with a dose of laudanum, leaving her only daughter to make her solitary way through the world.

"I enjoy teaching. I truly believe it is my calling in this life, and these children are sorely in need of a guardian to watch over them."

"Then we will watch over them together, for I have no intention of going back to Boston."

They walked in silence for several minutes, enjoying the sunlight.

"Harwood said something to me that I found disturbing," Witherspoon murmured.

"What did he say?"

"It concerned your relationship with Mr. Capp."

"I had no relationship with Mr. Capp."

They halted and faced each other.

"If you'd rather not speak about the matter, I will respect your wishes."

"There is nothing to conceal in my past. What do you wish to know?"

"Harwood told me that Mr. Capp had developed an infatuation with you, and that it was your rebuff of his affections that caused him to depart so suddenly from Lament."

She blushed. Witherspoon could not help but admire the color that rose to her cheeks. It enhanced her beauty and at the same time made her appear vulnerable.

"It's true, Mr. Capp did profess feelings for me. I told him plainly that I did not reciprocate them, and that was the end of the matter."

"He wasn't distraught?"

"Not in the slightest. He laughed and agreed that we should remain just friends."

"So you don't believe your rejection of his affections could have caused him to leave Lament in the middle of the night without any of his possessions."

She thought for a moment, then shook her head. "He was not upset by my response. His behavior was unchanged for the rest of the day. I can't believe my denial had anything to do with his disappearance."

As they emerged from the forest and crossed a sloping meadow of ragged grass and wild flowers at the edge of the village, the whistle atop Old Mariah began to scream.

"Merciful heaven, no," Miss Whyte said, her hand to her mouth.

"What is it? What's going on?"

"There's been an accident at the mine."

12.

Four of the bigger poorhouse boys carried the injured boy to the schoolhouse on a stretcher of wood and canvas. They were all so caked with coal dust, it was difficult to tell where their skin stopped and their clothing began. The filthy shirt of the injured boy was soaked with blood that continued to flow out in spite of the rag he pressed to the side of his chest.

"Set him on my desk," Witherspoon said.

The boys laid the stretcher gentle down on the desk and dragged the desk under the windows for more light, while Samuel Taff and Bullum Bedford looked on with interest but no obvious concern.

"Someone best go fetch Mrs. Greer," Bedford said.

One of the boys volunteered and ran out of the room.

"Who is Mrs. Greer?" Witherspoon asked Miss Whyte.

"She's the midwife. We have no doctor in Lament."

"In God's name, what happened?" he asked Taff.

"Young Jack Meeker was where he shouldn't have been," Taff said with a shrug. "I can't count how many times I've warned the boys away from the western face, but some of them won't listen."

"Western face, what's that?"

"Do you remember the coal face with that white marker painted on it?"

An image of the white triangle with the eye inside it that he had seen painted on the coal flashed across his mind. He nodded.

"Somehow a loaded coal box fell on him and crushed his chest."

"It wasn't no coal box," one of the boys said.

"You shut your mouth, Jeb Reeve, when your betters are speaking," Bedford told him harshly.

"We all know what it was," the boy continued, staring at Bedford in defiance. "It was one of them things."

"What things?" Witherspoon asked.

"Them things that come out of the coal—"

A back-hand blow across the mouth delivered by Bedford cut off his words. The boy used his fingers to wipe blood from his split lip, glaring hatred at the mine boss, but held his tongue.

"The boy was mining coal where it's forbidden," Taff told Witherspoon.

"Why would he do that?"

"The coal is easier to break loose there, but it's a dangerous place. There have been other incidents."

"He was trying to make his quota the easy way, and now look what it got him," Bedford said, pointing at the bloody shirt.

A middle-aged woman of ample proportions bustled into the classroom with a little leather bag in her hand. She wore the black mourning dress that widows typically wore, but it was not the style of dress worn by women in the Church of the Morning Star.

"Where is he?" she demanded.

The boys parted to reveal the desk and its burden. She took one long look with her lips pursed.

"I'll need water and clean rags. Give me room to work."

"I'll draw a bucket from the well," one boy offered, and hurried out.

Everyone stepped away from the desk. By this time other villagers and miners had gathered, and the classroom was rapidly filling with the morbidly curious.

"There are too many people in here," Mrs. Greer said.

"You there, clear out," Bedford said, waving some of the gawkers from the room. He stood blocking the doorway to prevent their return.

The midwife gently drew aside the boy's trembling hand and peeled the blood-soaked rag from his chest. Witherspoon saw three parallel rents in his shirt. The slashes went deep into his flesh, so that bone was showing, and blood continued to well from them. Mrs. Greer pressed around the slashes gingerly with her fingertips, which made the boy groan, and probed his abdomen.

"His ribs are broken. Something else isn't right with his insides. I think maybe his spleen is ruptured."

"Will he live, do you think?" Taff asked with mild interest, peering down at the boy through the little round lenses of his spectacles.

She did not speak. The boy groaned again, and his eyes closed. She looked at Taff and solemnly shook her head.

"Let me pass, you fool, let me pass." Reverend Feake shouldered his way through the door, shoving Bedford aside. He approached the desk and stood looking down at the injured boy without expression.

Witherspoon noted how the others in the room drew away from Feake, as though unwilling to be close to him. He realized they were feeling the same indefinable repugnance that he had felt upon his first meeting with the minister. Mingled with it was an undercurrent of fear.

"There's nothing you can do, preacher," Mrs. Greer told him in a low voice. "Unless you want to say a prayer over him."

"Stand aside, woman," he said coldly.

He put his left hand on the top of the boy's head and laid his right palm over the gashes in his chest. Drawing a deep breath, he closed his eyes and bowed his head.

Witherspoon glanced at Miss Whyte. She raised her eyebrows.

"What's he doing?" Bedford asked. No one answered.

Witherspoon felt something. It lifted the tiny hairs on the backs of his hands and on the sides of his neck. It was a kind of prickling he had felt at times just before a thunderstorm.

"My Lord," Feake said. "I ask that you heal this boy so that he may continue to do your work."

At first nothing happened. Then the boy gasped and opened his eyes. His back arched and his entire body went rigid for several seconds before collapsing onto the stretcher. Reverend Feake removed his hands and stepped away. For just a moment Witherspoon thought he saw a light glowing at the crown of the boy's head beneath his filthy, disordered hair. Someone stepped in front of him, and the light, if it had ever existed, was gone.

The midwife approached and examined the boy in amazement, probing with her fingertips as before.

"I don't know how, but the bleeding has stopped," she said, looking at Feake with wide eyes. "He's stronger. I think he just may live."

"He will live," Feake said with assurance. "It is the will of our Lord."

"I'll have a bed made up for him at my house," she said. "You boys, pick up the stretcher and follow after me."

"Clear out of the hall," Bedford bellowed at the onlookers, who murmured in fearful amazement at what the minister had done.

Witherspoon and Feake stood together watching the removal of the stretcher.

"You have the gift of laying on hands," Witherspoon said.

"It's not my gift, it comes from our Lord. I am only his humble instrument."

"One of the boys said something strange before you arrived. He spoke of things in the mine, things that come out of the coal."

Feake turned to look at him, and the contempt was undisguised in his dark eyes.

"I know nothing of such superstitions."

"What do you know about the western coal face, the one with the marking painted on it?"

"It was gratifying to see you at morning service on Sunday last," Feake said with a slight smile at the corners of his lips. "I hope you will attend again this week."

Before Witherspoon could think of a response, he turned and left the classroom. Witherspoon found himself alone with Miss Whyte. For a time they busied themselves in returning the desk to its former position in front of the blackboard, and picking up the books and other items that had been knocked onto the floor.

"Reverend Feake knows more than he is willing to say," he murmured as they stood looking out the window at the procession that wound its way up the road and across the higher bridge to the midwife's house.

"Strange things are happening in Lament," she said. "The disappearances are only part of it. That is why you should leave."

"I've already told you, I'm not leaving."

"I think it would be safer for you if you left," she said, then smiled. "But I'm glad you've decided to stay."

"I need to talk to that boy who spoke of things from out of the coal. What was his name?"

"Jeb. Jeb Reeve, I believe it was."

"That was it. I need to ask young Reeve what he knows. Maybe he won't be afraid to talk to me, while he's still filled with anger about his friend's accident."

13.

Witherspoon made his way cautiously around the engine house, the thud of the steam piston loud in his ears. The moon was near full, but a cover of clouds obscured its light. He could just see its dull glow through the overcast that hid the stars. The winch and crusher were not running, but the sound of the engine pumping water was enough to hide his footfalls.

He was more concerned about being spotted by the solitary workman who kept the fires beneath the boiler stoked throughout the night. The man had not appeared outside, but he might feel the need to relieve himself.

Something hissed in the darkness. He stared hard and made out a small form.

"He's coming," a young voice whispered.

"Good work, Timmy. You go down to the barracks now and go to bed."

Sykes coughed softly. "I'll stay, if you don't mind, sir."

"Very well."

They waited, and heard approaching feet kick loose pebbles on the path.

"Mr. Witherspoon?" a voice whispered. "It's Jeb Reeve."

"This way, Jeb. Over here, behind the rocks."

The boy approached, feeling along the path with his feet.

"It's near as dark as the lower level with the lanterns out."

Witherspoon extended his hand and felt a shoulder. He patted it.

"Timmy's here with me," he said.

"A bit of a lark this is, right, Tim?" Reeve said.

"It is that," Sykes said cheerfully.

"The Bull would whip me if he knew I was up here."

"There's no need for him to know, Jeb. I just want to ask you a few questions."

"What about?"

"Jeb, you said something when Jack Meeker was carried into the school. Do you remember what it was?"

"I told the Bull what for."

"Yes, you did. But you said something about things that come out of the coal. What did you mean by that?"

"Just what I said. Everybody knows about them, but they're all afraid to talk. Some nights they crawl up out of the mine and take people."

"I was told this was only a fairy story."

"It's no story. It's real enough. I've seen one of them."

Witherspoon reached out in the darkness again and grasped the boy's arm. "Tell me what you saw."

There was a brief silence while Reeve chose his words.

"It was like an animal, all hunched over, but it walked on its back legs.

I only saw it for a moment, up on the ridge over there, against the stars. It was wicked quick. It was there and gone before I could blink twice. I got out of there fast, I can tell you."

"What were you doing out at night?"

Timmy Sykes giggled.

"There was a girl who worked in the laundry," Reeve said. "I knew her from back in the poorhouse at Worcester. I was going to meet her, but she never showed. I never saw her again. I think it took her."

"Why do you think they come out of the mine?"

"Because we hear them down there while we're eating our noon meal. They move around outside the light, but they won't come closer when there are a lot of us together. They back off if we throw bits of coal toward them, and when we try to shine the lanterns on them, somehow they're not there anymore."

Witherspoon considered what he needed to learn from the boy.

"Why aren't you mining the western face of the coal seam?"

"You have to ask Mr. Harwood about that. He's the one who made it out of bounds."

"What do you know about the symbol painted on the coal?"

"I don't know nothing about that. It was there when I first got sent here from Worcester."

"Do you know anything about what happened to the teacher who used to be here, a man named Jordan Capp?"

"Only what I heard. He took off in the night and left everything he owned in his room, even his pocket watch."

Witherspoon considered what the boy had told him.

"Is that all, sir? We need to get back to the barracks or we'll be missed and there'll be the devil to pay for it."

"That's all I need to ask for now, Jeb. I may want to talk to you again."

"Just tell Timmy where and when, and I'll try to get there."

"Good lad."

They were starting down the path to the village below when they heard a scrabbling from the crest of the hill.

"What's that?" Timmy whispered.

"Hush," Witherspoon said, laying his hand on the boy's head. "Look up by the pit."

They crouched behind the bough of a scrub pine that grew from between two large rocks and stared past the engine house at the tripod

204

that stood over the mouth of the mineshaft. The clouds were a sooty charcoal gray along the horizon. Against their backdrop moved something that was jet black. Witherspoon strained his eyes, his heart pounding. It was crawling its way up out of the pit. It moved in a way that was almost simian, but kept its massive head close to the ground like a dog seeking a scent. Between the thuds of the Cornwall engine they heard a kind of snuffing as it swung its long snout this way and that. Something glittered and winked like a single star on the top of its head as it caught the pale moon glow that filtered through the cloud cover.

"Look," Reeve whispered. "There's another one."

A second hulking figure crawled its way out of the pit and stood upright, sniffing the air. Behind it, a third emerged.

"We need to get out of here," Witherspoon breathed softly into the darkness. "No noise, boys, no noise at all."

They stole down the path like silent ghosts. Witherspoon paused now and then to glance behind, but he had lost sight of the creatures. They could be anywhere. His skin prickled between his shoulder blades as he followed the two boys.

When they reached the lower bridge over Enoch Brook, they stopped and looked behind them, but could see nothing through the darkness but vague shadow forms of trees and rocks.

"They must have gone down the other side of the hill, toward the meeting house," Jeb Reeve said.

Witherspoon looked up the brook at the crest of the Little Hill. He was surprised to see lights burning in the windows of the meeting house.

"They gather there at night sometimes," Reeve said.

"You boys get back to the barracks and get some sleep. Say nothing about this to anyone."

"Who would believe us?" Reeve said.

"I won't say anything, sir," Sykes promised.

"Good lads. Off you both go."

Witherspoon watched them until he could no longer follow them through the darkness, then made his way up the road to the boarding house and entered through the rear door, which was never locked to allow residents access to the outhouse. It was some time before he could fall asleep. He kept rising from bed to peer fearfully out his window. His room was on the second level of the house, but if those things could climb up a mineshaft, they would have little difficulty ascending the side of a building. He thought about closing his shutters, but what would that accomplish? They would be no barrier to such brutes.

He found himself shivering under his blankets, although the night was not cold, and prayed that those shadow-things had not caught his scent.

14.

Sleep and bright morning sunlight sent most of Witherspoon's night terrors fleeing into the shadows. He felt ashamed at the way he had cowered in his bed like a helpless child. Over breakfast, while the other boarders gossiped and laughed around him, he considered what needed to be done.

He could go to Harwood, tell him what he had seen up at the pit, and demand that he close the mine. It was not difficult to imagine what Harwood's reaction would be. He would not believe, or at least he would profess not to believe, and would remind Witherspoon how important the mine was to the economic prosperity of Lament, to say nothing of his own profit as an investor. There was no possibility that Harwood would listen to him.

What about the Reverend Feake, then? Witherspoon had no liking for the preacher, but perhaps he might listen when the lives of his congregation were at risk.

"You're very silent this morning," Miss Whyte said. She was seated beside him at the table. By silent accord Matthew Poorish had exchanged chairs with her some days ago.

"I'm sorry, I'm being rude. Tell me, Maud, have any of those who disappeared from Lament been members of the Morning Star church?"

She thought about it. "I really don't know. The question has never occurred to me, but now that you ask it, I confess I cannot remember anyone from the church going missing."

She caught Mrs. Bond's plump arm as she was passing with a platter of fried bacon to set on the table, and repeated his question to the landlady. Mrs. Bond stopped and looked at the ceiling with her lips compressed, then shook her head.

"I can't think of anyone from the church. It's been mostly poorhouse boys and girls. Then there was Mr. Capp. And several of the village children have vanished, but none of them was part of Reverend Feake's congregation, I don't believe."

She put the question to the table, but no one seated there could think of a single missing person who had been among Feake's flock.

"It is curious, to be sure," Poorish said. "Funny that I've never noticed it before."

"Nothing curious about it," Bedford said as he picked bacon bits from between his teeth with his fingernail. "The poorhouse boys ran because they didn't want to work. The village children got lost in the woods and were taken by wolves."

"Why would Mr. Capp leave so suddenly?" Miss Whyte asked.

Bedford leered at her. "Maybe he was frustrated and went looking for a woman with blood in her veins instead of well water."

She blushed at his insinuation, and Witherspoon felt his own color rising to his face. It was driven not by shame, but by anger.

"I'll thank you to keep a civil tongue, Mr. Bedford," he said.

Bedford stared at him, then burst into laughter. He continued to eat his bacon strips, chuckling to himself.

"Are you finished with your breakfast, Miss Whyte?" Witherspoon asked.

"I believe I am," she said.

They rose together and left the dining room with Bedford still chuckling behind them.

"That man has no breeding," Witherspoon fumed as they walked along the road toward the schoolhouse.

"Pay him no mind," she said. "When you live in a common house, as we do, you must take the bad with the good."

The sun was rising above the forested hills to the east. It shone beneath the black plume from Old Mariah and cast its warmth upon Witherspoon's cheek. In the brightness of the morning, the soot-stained white facades of Lament looked tawdry and dull. There was nothing to suggest that anything out of the ordinary lurked behind them.

"What made you ask such an odd question?" Miss Whyte said.

"I'll tell you about it when we reach the schoolhouse."

They always tried to arrive at least an hour before school commenced so that they could prepare for the lessons they intended to teach and write what was needed on the blackboards. As usual, when they reached the little building, it was empty. They went into Witherspoon's room and sat on one of the benches.

The Lament Horror

The odd symbol of the triangle in the pentagram was drawn on the blackboard in white chalk. It was always there when he entered the room in the morning. Witherspoon had never tried to catch the person who drew it because he considered it such a minor matter, but today he wondered if he should lie in wait some night. Would the superstitious lad who drew the symbol be able to offer any useful information about the mystery of disappearances, or the black things from the mine? Probably not, he decided.

"You have something to tell me," Miss Whyte said.

"I want to confide in someone, but I don't know that it is fair to burden you with this information, which will only frighten you if you take it seriously."

"Why wouldn't I take it seriously?"

"It is so strange, I scarcely know whether to believe it myself."

"Tell me anyway. Information is never a burden to me."

In as matter a fact manner as possible, he related what he had heard and seen the previous night atop the Big Hill. She listened with a serious expression, not speaking. He feared she would scoff when he finished, but her expression did not change.

"What you say you've seen is strange, but it does accord with the stories the children tell each other."

He felt a great relief that she did not disbelieve him.

"It would account for why the villagers keep so close to their houses after dark," she continued. "They always seem fearful about something, but they will never tell me what they fear. I've always assumed it must be Reverend Feake and his congregation with their silent manner and intimidating mode of dress."

"That symbol on the blackboard," he said, pointing. "It was drawn for the same reason the villagers put similar signs over the doors of their houses and barns. It's intended to ward off the evil."

"Superstition," she said.

"Yes, I agree, but it indicates how fearful they are, and after what I glimpsed last night, I do not believe their fear is ungrounded."

"The mine must be shut down. A hunt must be made by armed men to find and kill these creatures."

"Harwood would never believe me. Harwood would rather cut off his own right arm than close the mine."

She nodded reluctantly. "You're right, of course. What we need is some irrefutable proof that we can show to Harwood, or to state authorities in Boston if need be."

"In view of what we know, perhaps you should reconsider leaving Lament," he said.

"Are you leaving?"

"No." He smiled. "I'm not a brave man, but I'm curious. There is something happening here, and I could never rest without learning what it's about."

15.

The corpulent midwife was sweeping off her front veranda with a broom when Witherspoon opened the gate in the little picket fence that surrounded her front yard. She had on the same mourning dress she had worn in the school house three days earlier, but a soot-stained apron was tied around its waist. She straightened and leaned on the broom, watching him approach with narrowed eyes.

"A good afternoon to you, Mrs. Greer," he said cheerfully.

"I suppose so," she said, looking up at the sky. "Or would be if it weren't for the dust."

Witherspoon looked up. The plume from Old Mariah was blowing directly over Lament, diming the sun to a red ball in a dirty yellow sky.

"It can be hard to keep anything clean," he agreed.

"Hard?" She grunted. "It's impossible. When I hang my washing out, it's white. When I take it in, it's gray."

"You could always use the laundry."

"Spend my money on work I can do myself? Not likely. What do you want?"

"I'm sorry to bother you. I came to see how Jack Meeker, the boy who was injured in the mine accident, is getting along."

"He's gone."

"Gone? Where?"

"I'm not the boy's keeper, Mr. Witherspoon. He got up and left sometime last night."

"But he was seriously injured, wasn't he?"

"He was. Whatever the preacher did healed him. He ate a big supper and was chattering away like a jay-bird when I put him to bed last night.

This morning he was gone without so much as a thank-you."

"A miracle," Witherspoon said.

"Maybe. Maybe not. Miracles come from God."

"I'm not sure what you mean."

"I've got something on the stove that needs tending. Good day."

Without waiting for his response, she went into the house and closed the door behind her. Above the door was the familiar circled pentagram with the triangle at its center.

He walked slowly back to the boarding house, wondering how it was possible for a boy with broken ribs and a ruptured spleen to get up and walk away only three days after his injury. Could Reverend Feake have indeed worked some kind of miracle? He didn't believe in the laying on of hands, but it was hard to discount the evidence. The boy had walked away—or had he been carried?

Little Timmy Sykes was waiting for him on the front step of Mrs. Bond's.

"I found out what you wanted to know, sir," the boy said.

Witherspoon glanced around to make sure no one was near enough to overhear.

"Jeb says a girl at the laundry told him the church is going to have another meeting at midnight tonight."

"Is he sure about this?"

"The girl knows someone who works in Harwood's house. She overheard Harwood talking to Feake about it."

Witherspoon patted the boy on the head.

"Good work, Timmy."

"I'd like to come with you tonight, sir. I could keep watch for you—"

The boy's expression suddenly changed. He snatched a rag from his pocket with a practiced motion and bent over, coughing hard into it. When he took his mouth away Witherspoon saw flecks of blood on the rag.

"You go back to the barracks and do your homework," Witherspoon said in a kindly tone.

Dejected, the boy turned and walked slowly away with his head hanging down.

"Poor little beggar," Witherspoon muttered to himself.

Miss Whyte opened the screen door and came down the steps with a handbag in her hands.

"It's tonight," he said in a low voice.

"I wish you wouldn't go, Henry."

"I have to know what's happening in Lament. Somehow it's all bound up with Feake and his sect."

"There's danger. What about those things you saw?"

"If they were coming for me they would have come by now."

"At least promise me something."

"Of course, Maud. Anything you wish."

She glanced up and down the street, then stepped close to him. Opening her handbag, she took something from it and pressed it against his chest. He reached up and felt cold metal.

"It was my father's. Promise me you will take it with you tonight."

Witherspoon saw that he was holding a small revolver. He slid it into his trouser pocket.

"Very well," he said with a smile. "I have little use for guns, but I'll carry it to please you."

"Don't hesitate to use it," she said, meeting his eyes.

"I doubt there's any real danger," he told her, but he did not believe it. "All I intend to do is look in on the meeting. Maybe I can peel back another layer from this onion of mystery."

"Don't joke. Be on your guard at all times. You may laugh, but I have a feeling about this, and it tells me you are in great danger."

"Woman's intuition."

"That's right. I've learned not to disregard it. Don't trust anyone. There are spies always listening."

"What are you two doves cooing about?" Samuel Taff asked from the doorway.

Miss Whyte blushed and stepped away from Witherspoon.

"Really, Mr. Taff."

He stepped onto the porch with a cynical little smile playing at the corners of his mouth.

"Don't mind me. I find it refreshing. Young lovers and all that."

"We were talking about the school curriculum," Witherspoon said stiffly.

"Of course you were." Taff eyed the bulge in the teacher's trouser pocket through his spectacles. "I didn't mean to interrupt. I'm just going up to the pit. Enjoy yourselves."

They watched him until he crossed the lower bridge over Enoch

Brook and passed behind a house.

"I don't trust him," she said in a low voice.

"Taff's all right," Witherspoon said. "He's just a bit cynical about life. He told me that after receiving his degree from Cambridge he traveled across Europe. The trip jaded his sensibilities in some way. I suppose he got involved in gambling and various other vices."

"I don't trust any of them. Only you."

He put his hand on her arm. "After tonight I may have a better idea of what we're facing. We can decide whether to confront Harwood or simply pack our bags and leave Lament."

"Do you mean, together?"

He nodded. She reached up and covered his hand with her fingers. They regarded each other without speaking, both conscious of the many eyes that must be upon them.

16.

The grandfather clock in the hallway downstairs was chiming eleven when Witherspoon rose from his bed and began to put his clothes on. He chose his hiking gear because the wool was dark in color.

For a full minute he stood with Miss Whyte's revolver in his hand, debating with himself whether to take it or leave it behind. Finally he slid it into his pocket.

The boarding house was asleep. Everyone in it had to rise early for work, so they usually went to bed around ten. He knew he would be exhausted teaching tomorrow's class, but that could not be helped.

Letting himself out the back door, he crept behind the houses, avoiding those with dogs, then made his way along the brook toward the Little Hill. Every few steps he paused to listen with his breath stopped. Since seeing those things climb out of the pit, he had not been able to go out at night without nervousness. The rest of the village must have felt the same way, because there was seldom anyone about after sunset.

The windows of the meeting house were still dark. They peered down at him in what he imagined was disapproval as he climbed the grassy side of the hill in a crouch, keeping to the tall bushes where he could to avoid being seen, should anyone be inside and looking out. The moon cast silver over the leaves as they fluttered in the wind, making a constant rustle that concealed the sound of his approach.

There was no cover on the crown of the hill. He crossed the mowed lawn that surrounded the meeting house and pressed himself into the shadow of its side. Looking down the way he had come, he saw lanterns on the road and realized he had only minutes to conceal himself.

He tried the small door at the rear of the building and found it unlocked. No sound came from the other side as he eased up the iron latch and entered. The interior was in absolute darkness. He drew a match from his pocket and struck it on the wall, then cupped his hand around the flame to conceal most of its glow.

He was in a utility room of some kind. In one corner stood a wooden bucket with a mop in it beside a worn corn broom. Hymn books were stacked on a shelf. There was a wooden bin filled with coal for the German stove in the front room that would not be needed until autumn chilled the air. The church bass he had seen played during the service he attended inclined against a wall.

The double doors rattled open at the front of the meeting house and he heard voices. He blew out the match and dropped it, then felt in his pocket for the revolver. What he was doing had made sense at the boarding house, but it now struck him as reckless in the extreme, and he began to wish he were still in his bed. He did not know what danger threatened, or even if there was any danger at all, but the unknowing only intensified his apprehension.

Light spilled through cracks between the planks in the wall and around the door that led to the main room of the meeting house, as those who had entered lit the candles in their tall stands. He put his eye close to one of the wider cracks.

He found himself looking down the center aisle from behind the lectern. The Reverend Redemption Feake stood before it with his back to Witherspoon, wearing his black suit and the brimless black cap that Witherspoon thought of as his indoor hat. He faced the throng of men and women who were taking their seats in the pews. Harwood was among them and assumed his usual place at the front. Witherspoon recognized the dour features of Mrs. Sharp, who oversaw the barracks of the poorhouse boys. He began to count the covered heads, and estimated that there must be at least three score of them, which was less than half of the regular Sunday congregation. The murmur of voices gradually ceased.

"We are gathered here tonight for a solemn purpose," Feake said, his voice loud in the sudden stillness. "A new worshipper joins our congregation. Tonight he meets the Shining God for the first time. It is the moment of sacred mystery that defines our church. You have all experienced it. I have experienced it. And now he will know the glory that we know, the glory that we carry within us always. Bare your heads in reverence."

He reached up and took off his cap. The men in the pews did the same and the women removed their caps and veils. In the candlelight something glittered on the tops of their heads with prismatic colors, like the pieces of cut glass hanging from a chandelier when struck by sunlight. At first Witherspoon assumed it must be a kind of tiara worn by all the members of the sect, but as he studied the glittering crystals, the suspicion grew upon him that they were in some way attached to the skulls beneath the hair. He remember the flash of light he had seen between Feake's fingers as the minister laid his hand on the head of the boy injured in the mine accident.

Even as this thought passed through his mind, that same boy approached from the shadows at the back of the long room. He wore the black suit that was the uniform of the church and held a felt cap between his hands. No crystal glittered on his head.

"Approach the altar, Jack Meeker," Reverend Feake said in solemn tones. There was absolute silence in the meeting house.

The boy walked nervously forward and stopped a few paces from the lectern, which Witherspoon realized was not a lectern at all, but some sort of blasphemous altar. Feake reached into the bottom portion of the altar under its green velvet cover and took out a square box with a hinged lid. It was of no great size, about twelve inches in all dimensions, and made of some dark wood that caught the light and gleamed.

Feake set the box on top of the altar. The boy stared at it the way a rat stares at a snake.

"Are you ready to meet the God of this world?" Feake asked.

"You saved my life," the boy said. "I'm ready to do what you want me to."

"Brave lad. The Shining God gives special favor to those who join his church without coercion."

"I said I was ready." The boy shifted uneasily from one foot to the other.

Feake undid the latch on the cover of the box and opened it toward the boy. The upraised lid concealed its contents from Witherspoon, but a multicolored light shone forth across the face of the boy and across the upturned faces of the seated congregation, who released a collective sigh of wonder.

"Come forward and touch your God, Jack Meeker. There must be physical contact before he can transfer his glory into your body."

The boy hesitated, looked around as though considering escape, then squared his shoulders and stepped close to the altar. He reached out his right hand and laid it on whatever thing was in the box. Immediately his face was illuminated from within with dancing colors. He began to tremble.

"What you feel now was felt by every one of those within this room," Feake said. "It is the glory of the Lord extending its roots through your flesh. There is some pain, but do not be afraid. The pain will pass once the glory has pressed its way out through the top of your skull."

The boy began to wail in agony but seemed unable to draw back his hand. Witherspoon heard a crunch, like the breaking of a chicken bone, and something moved on top of the boy's head. It pressed its way upward through his hair until it projected more than an inch, a shining pyramid of blood-stained crystal. After a time his teeth ceased to chatter and his body stopped shaking. He drew his hand away from the box and the light went out from his face, but continued to gleam on the top of his head.

"I understand," he said in a voice filled with wonder and delight. "I hear him speaking to me, telling me not to be afraid, promising me future gifts for faithful service."

"Say hallelujah, friends," Feake said, raising his arms into the air. "Another soul has been saved in the service of our Lord."

A chorus of hallelujahs went up from the congregation.

"Take your seat among us, Jack Meeker. You are one of us now."

The boy sat at the end of a pew and was patted on the back by those behind to him.

Feake raised his hands again, and the room fell silent.

"As you know, my friends, when the God illuminates one of us, power flows out of him and that power must be replenished. Mr. Bedford, let the servitors of the God bring in the sacrifice."

A man stepped out of the shadows at the back of the room, and Witherspoon saw that it was the mine boss, Bullum Bedford. His head was uncovered, but no crystal projected from his closely cropped red hair.

Bedford went to the doors and opened them. What entered from the outer darkness struck Witherspoon rigid with horror.

There were two of the things he had seen against the horizon at the pit. The candlelight revealed them in all their hellish detail, but so alien were their forms, his mind refused to make sense of them in their totality. He could only glimpse different parts of their bodies for a moment as they moved, now a leg, now a shoulder, now a tooth-filled mouth. The rest was a blur of shadows.

They were figures from nightmare, shining like oil in the rainbow radiance that spilled from the altar. Although they walked upright, their legs bent the way a dog's hind leg bends and were impossibly long. A halo of serpentine tentacles writhed around their enormous heads, by turns concealing and revealing their elongated snouts that were vaguely like the snout of a dog.

Between them they carried a naked form that he recognized as Alex Kingsley, the little crippled poorhouse boy in his class who walked with the aid of a crutch. The boy was not bound or gagged, but trembled as with an ague.

They brought the boy before the altar. He shook his head and tried to speak, but all that came from his mouth was a kind of gurgling.

"Don't be frightened, boy," Feake said in a kindly voice. "This is the greatest moment in your life. The honor has fallen to you to replenish the life-force of the God of Ages who has existed upon this world from its early beginnings.

"Long before the creation of mankind, when great saurian monsters walked the jungles of the earth and battled each other with tooth and claw, our God fell from the heavens like a blazing star and began his dominion over all living things, taking life from some and giving life to others at his pleasure.

"A great cataclysm cast him deep into the abyss, and there he lay for more than a hundred million years until Brother Harwood discovered him embedded in the coal seam." Harwood nodded and smiled at the boy from his pew at the mention of his name as Feake continued. "He was the first to worship the Shining God in our age, but soon the entire world will know his glory. Rejoice that you have been chosen from all the rest of your kind to feed his hunger."

Witherspoon knew that if ever there was a moment for him to burst forth from his hiding place and save the boy, now was that moment. But he could not move, not even so much as to cock the hammer of the revolver in his hand, a weapon that seemed laughably inadequate against the black things who carried the child between them.

In that moment of clarity Witherspoon realized that he was a coward, that he had always been a coward, and always would be a coward. The awareness left a bitter taste in his mouth. He wanted to sacrifice himself in some heroic, hopeless gesture, but his body would not obey him. It trembled and shook but otherwise would not move.

"Bring him forward," Feake said.

The creatures lifted the boy toward the open box. Feake came around and took the boy's right arm. He extended his hand into the box, then released his arm. A convulsion caused Kingsley's back to bend like a bow. White flecks of foam flew from his open mouth. He began to make a high-pitched keening noise that rose to an ear-piercing scream. Smoke curled up from his naked limbs, and suddenly he shriveled in upon himself, so that where there had been a living child, there was now only a smoking, blackened husk, its eyes burned from its head, tendrils of smoke rising from its ears and gaping mouth.

Whatever held Witherspoon immobile suddenly released him, and he jerked sideways into the church bass, which fell with a booming of its strings that was like some great resonant drumbeat.

He did not linger, but bolted out the rear door of the meeting house and ran down the hill to the village, heedless of what was in front and around him, conscious only of what might be following. All higher mental functions had vanished from his brain. He had only one thought—where was the third creature?

It was when he reached the silent boarding house that he realized he still held the revolver in his hand. He slid it into his pocket and crept quietly into the back hall and up the stairs to his room, then undressed and crawled into bed. He lay there shaking with terror, unable to think, cold in spite of the blankets held close in both fists under his chin.

When the hall clock downstairs struck one, he began to breathe more evenly and to relax his stiff muscles, although a tight knot remained in his abdomen. There was a sick feeling in his stomach. He rolled on his side, and realized that he was bone weary. His eyes began to close.

A footstep sounded in the hall. His eyelids flew up but he did not move. He heard the familiar creak of his door opening, and the soft groan of a floorboard. In the moonlight that shone through the parted curtains at the window, he saw a man's legs approach along the side of his bed.

The revolver was still in the pocket of his trousers, which were draped over the back of a chair too far from his bed to reach. The moonlight gleamed on the naked blade of a knife. He could not have moved or spoken even had he wished. The same paralysis that had gripped him in the meeting house took command once again. A shadow fell across his face as the intruder leaned nearer. Through the slits beneath his lowered eyelids he recognized Bullum Bedford.

Bedford continued to study him for what seemed an eternity. Then the big man straightened and left the room as quietly as he had entered it, shutting the door after him with a soft click.

17.

Witherspoon awoke at his usual time with one thought in his mind—to get away from Lament as quickly as possible.

He splashed his face in the enameled basin with water from the porcelain pitcher that Mrs. Bond refreshed daily, shaved himself with his straight razor in the tiny square wall mirror, dressed in his best suit, then put everything else into his travel trunk. Even if he could not take the trunk with him when he left, he reasoned, he could always send for it later. The revolver he slipped into his trouser pocket.

When he went downstairs for breakfast, he avoided meeting Bullum Bedford's speculative gaze and sat reading a Boston newspaper in the parlor until called to the table. Miss Whyte had not yet come down from her room. At Witherspoon's urging, Mrs. Bond sent the girl who helped her clean the house to see if the teacher had overslept. The girl reported that Miss Whyte's room was empty.

Witherspoon ate his breakfast without appetite, a sick feeling curdling the scrambled eggs and fried ham inside his stomach. It was possible Miss Whyte had stepped out earlier that morning to do some task and had not yet returned to the boarding house, but as the minutes passed his concern grew.

Returning upstairs, he slipped quietly into her room for a quick look around. Her bed was unmade, as though she had just risen from it. Her dresses appeared to be still on the rack in her wardrobe, and her travel trunk was sitting at the foot of the bed. He examined the water in the pitcher on her washstand. It had not been used.

He walked to the schoolhouse alone, conscious of the black-hatted Congregationalists who nodded to him as he passed. He thought he detected a kind of slyness in their gleaming eyes, but it may have been only his imagination. Did they all know what went on in the meeting house at night? If they had all been initiated into the sect they must know, he reasoned. They were murderers, or at the least complicit in murders.

One by one the students gathered in the school yard. When the hour came to admit them to the school, Miss Whyte had still not appeared. He gathered both girls and boys into his classroom and taught them together, scarcely aware of what he was saying. His mind was divided between concern for Miss Whyte and desire to leave Lament behind.

He thought about walking directly from the school to the rail depot, getting on the train that was presently loading coal, riding it to Uxbridge and from there taking the packet boat down the Blackstone River Canal to Providence, where he could book passage on a ship to Boston.

Only his concern for Miss Whyte held him in Lament. In spite of the terror that gripped his heart, he could not bring himself to abandon her, if indeed she was still alive. She had disappeared in exactly the same way as Jordan Capp, and Capp had not been seen since. Witherspoon had a good idea of what had become of him. The Shining God needed sacrifices. Unless he did something the same might happen to Miss Whyte, assuming it had not already happened.

He forced his unwilling legs to carry him along the road toward the meeting house. It would have been prudent to wait until after nightfall so that his movements would be concealed by darkness, but when Witherspoon considered it he realized that he simply did not have the courage to approach the Little Hill at night, not with those three things roaming about.

He decided he could always make some excuse for being at the meeting house should Reverend Feake appear and demand an explanation. He would tell Feake that he was interested in joining the church.

The front doors opened when he tried them. The main room of the meeting house was empty. He smelled the melted beeswax from the candles of the previous night. They had not yet been renewed in their stands. Wax crusted the sides of the stubs.

For a time he stood listening, but heard no sound. He returned to the doors and opened one side to peer through the crack between them down the hill at the village. A man and a woman were walking along the road, but they were too far away to recognize their faces. Realizing that he might not have much time, he closed the doors and went cautiously along the aisle toward the altar at the front of the big room.

Here, his courage almost failed him again, but he forced himself to feel for the wooden box in the base of the altar. It was surprisingly heavy as he set it on top of the green cover, and its polished sides were warm to the touch.

Standing in front of the altar as far away from the box as possible, he reached out and undid the latch with his thumb and forefinger, than quickly flipped open the lid.

Even in daylight, the changing array of colors that radiated against his face was dazzling. Squinting against it, he leaned nearer. Inside was a single multicolored tetrahedral crystal that almost filled the box. It was like a miniature pyramid. The colors shone out of its transparent depths, as though projected through it from some other realm.

Witherspoon reached out to touch it. He did this automatically, and only managed to stop himself at the last instant, just before his fingers brushed its shining side. Blinking in alarm, he stepped away from the altar. Something had taken momentary control over his arm. There was a kind of tension or pressure in the air that raised the hairs on the back of his hand.

"Don't be afraid. Touch it."

Reverend Feake emerged from the storage room where Witherspoon had hidden the previous night, a shadow of a smile on his thin lips.

"Forgive my little subterfuge. I saw you approach along the road and decided to surprise you."

Witherspoon drew the revolver and cocked it, then pointed it at Feake, who did not appear alarmed.

"You were there when I healed the boy. Do you really think that can hurt me?"

"What have you done with Maud Whyte?"

"She's perfectly safe, I assure you."

"Where are you keeping her? Tell me, or by God I will shoot."

"You must do as you think best, but she will be with us presently if you have the patience to wait a few moments."

"Very well, we'll wait," Witherspoon said, looking around the room.

"But stay where you are."

"I'm perfectly content here."

He gestured at the box with his gun. "What is that thing?"

"The Shining God of this world, who was lost for aeons but who has returned to take up his kingdom."

"The star fallen from heaven," Witherspoon said with sudden insight. "It's not a reference to Revelation, but to Isaiah."

"How art thou fallen from heaven, O Lucifer, son of the morning!" Feake recited with an expression of rapture.

"What were those black creatures that I saw last night? Demons?"

"Some might call them demons. They are servitors of the Shining God. They dwell in his realm beneath the earth, but come when he summons them."

"Your God has another name in Revelation. Wormwood."

"You have a quick apprehension, Mr. Witherspoon. I do hope you will join our congregation voluntarily. The bond is so much stronger and more intimate when it is entered into of your own free will."

"What are those things on your heads?"

Feake reached up and removed his felt cap. The crystal projecting from his hair had the same tetrahedral shape as the larger crystal in the box.

"This is how the God talks to us. It allows us to draw upon his strength, as you saw me do when I healed Jack Meeker."

"It uses the crystals to control you."

"There's no compulsion involved, I assure you. Once you feel the presence of the Shining God, you will never wish to be parted from him."

The front doors of the meeting house opened behind Witherspoon, but he did not turn his head.

"I told you she was not harmed," Feake said, and gestured toward the doors. "See for yourself."

Witherspoon stepped to the side and half-turned, keeping the gun trained on Feake. At the end of the aisle stood Bullum Bedford and Miss Whyte. She wore the black dress, black hat and veil of the church.

"Miss Whyte is one of us now. We would never harm one of our own."

"What did you do to her?" Witherspoon felt his dry throat strain with the words.

"As I told you, we did nothing. The Shining God accepted her as his adoring servant."

"Maud, get out of here," he croaked, feeling a sickness rise within him. "Run. I'll keep them covered with the revolver. Quick, run away."

She approached slowly along the aisle and took off her cap and veil. Her blond hair was not done up on her head but hung long to her shoulders. From the top of her skull projected the point of a shining crystal. Her face was tranquil, her eyes unnaturally bright. She smiled at him.

"Why would I run? Everything I could ever have wished for in my life is right here."

"You've been possessed. That thing in the box is controlling your mind."

"No, Henry, you're wrong. I want this. It's true that I was frightened when Mr. Bedford brought me here last night, after you ran away, but once I touched the God my mind became clear, and my terror vanished. I realize now that it was only an illusion, a shadow that the light of the God dispelled from my mind. Henry, you must join us. It feels so wonderful to be released from all doubt and fear."

"They are killing people, Maud. These lunatics are sacrificing human beings to this ... this ... thing."

"The sacrifices are necessary," she said. "The God hungers and must be fed."

"You might as well join us, Mr. Witherspoon," Feake said. "Soon, everyone in Lament will worship the Shining God. We keep a few men who are loyal to us, such as Mr. Bedford here, separate from the church to act as our agents in dealings with the greater world, but in time the God will spread his crystalline seeds across the state, then across the nation, and finally around the world."

"How is that possible? It's only a single crystal," Witherspoon said numbly. Miss Whyte's words had shaken him.

"Your thinking is limited by your flesh," Feake said. "The Shining God has no need for procreation."

He reached deep into the box and brought out a handful of tiny crystals that glittered like diamond dust. Witherspoon realized that he had seen the residue from such crystals before on Feake's hands, and on the hands of Josiah Harwood.

"Each of these grains has the power to transform a human being and make him a part of our congregation. It requires only a single touch. When we have enough of them, we will mingle them in among the pieces of coal that are loaded into the train. Anyone who handles the coal thereafter will become one of us. The coal is being shipped far and wide across Massachusetts, and beyond."

"If that's true, what are you waiting for?" Witherspoon demanded.

"The production of the seed crystals requires life-force in the form of sacrifices. But we are nearly ready to begin their distribution."

"You're all insane."

Without warning, Witherspoon pointed the revolver at the shimmering crystal in the box and began to fire. He emptied the cylinder and heard the hammer click on spent chambers. Slowly, he lowered the smoking muzzle. The crystal was unharmed.

"The God spent a hundred million years locked in the coal seam before Mr. Harwood freed it. If that enormous heat and pressure could not do it harm, did you really imagine that it could be destroyed by a few bullets?"

Witherspoon looked at the revolver, then at Miss Whyte. She stepped toward him and took the weapon out of his lax fingers.

"Tie him up and put him into the storage room," Feake told Bedford, who grunted and took hold of the teacher roughly, pulling his arms behind his back. "Mr. Witherspoon has great hostility in his heart toward the God. I think we must forsake the intention of making him a member of our congregation. However, his life-force is strong, and he will make an excellent sacrifice at tonight's service."

18.

Witherspoon had no way to estimate the passage of hours. Bedford had tied his wrists and ankles together with slender hemp rope, and then run a length between the two bindings and pulled it taut, so that his back was arched and he could barely move as he lay on his side. His mouth was gagged with a dirty rag that tasted of paint thinner. It made him want to vomit, but with a supreme effort of will he managed to keep his stomach under control. At first his hands hurt a little, then they hurt a lot. After a while longer he lost the feeling in his fingers. It was as if they didn't exist.

He heard sounds in the front room of the meeting house and thought Reverend Feake and Bullum Bedford had returned, but when the inner door opened it was little Timmy Sykes who stared down at him wide-eyed in the rectangle of light that shone through the doorway.

Witherspoon grunted and jerked his head toward his feet. Eventually the boy understood. He searched around the storage room and found a knife. The blade was rusty and dull, but it was sharp enough to saw through the rope that bound the teacher's hands.

Witherspoon lifted his hands to his face and saw that they were swollen with an unnatural purple color. He still could not feel them. When he tried to tear the gag away from his mouth, they would not obey him.

The boy slid the knife under the gag and gently sawed outward until the rag fell away. Witherspoon spat out the piece that had been balled up in his mouth.

"Cut my feet free," he gasped.

While Sykes worked on his feet, he shook his hands and slapped them together. For a while they were like blocks of wood. Then a fuzzy sensation began to return to his fingers.

"I saw you go up the hill," the boy said. "When you didn't come out, I was afraid they'd killed you, but I couldn't come up to see until all of them left. The Bull stayed a long time."

"They were going to kill me, tonight at midnight." He flexed his swollen fingers. They felt weak but they moved. Pins and needles were starting to prick his fingertips.

"We have to get out of here before they come back," Sykes said. "It's almost dark."

The boy helped him to his feet.

"There's something I have to do first," Witherspoon said.

He explained to the boy about the crystal in the box under the alter, and how it was controlling Jack Meeker, Maud Whyte, and the rest, and the way Alex Kingsley had been sacrificed.

"Those black things we saw up at the pit are its servants. God only knows what hellish realm they climbed up from."

"Couldn't we just run away, sir? I'm scared."

Witherspoon forced a smile. "I'm scared, too, Timmy, but if we run and then try to tell others what's happening in Lament, they will never believe us. Harwood and Feake are planning to spread the evil on the coal. We can't let that happen."

"What can we do, sir?" He pulled from his pocket the rag that served him for a handkerchief and coughed into it.

Until that moment Witherspoon had no idea what he would do, but he said without hesitating, "They need the crystal. If we steal the crystal they won't be able to sacrifice anybody or spread the evil. I'll take it to Boston and show it to the scientists at Harvard University. I know people there. They'll believe what I have to say when they see it."

The pins and needles in his hands were excruciatingly painful, but he could feel his fingers once again and bend them.

They crept into the main room. Fear was in Witherspoon's heart that Feake had removed the crystal from the meeting house, but when he pulled aside the covering over the altar and reached into the bottom part, he felt the box. He lifted it awkwardly. Its weight assured him that the crystal rested inside it. His hands were still so weak, he almost dropped the box.

"Let me carry it, sir," the boy said.

Reluctantly, he passed the box to the boy.

"Don't drop it, and whatever you do, don't open it."

They left the meeting house by the rear door. Darkness had almost fallen. There was still an orange glow in the sky to the west, but the sun had been down for some time. It was that gathering twilight in which everything turns the same uniform gray.

"Where will we go, sir?"

"I don't know, Timmy. Do you think anyone in Lament will hide us?"

The boy solemnly shook his head. "They're all too scared of the crows."

"I think you're right," Witherspoon agreed.

"We could run into the woods," Timmy suggested.

"Without a light? We'd be tripping over rocks and bumping into trees. We wouldn't get very far. And even if we could steal a lantern, they would see it and hunt us down."

"What are we going to do?"

"Let's go across the brook and wait over by the rail depot. Maybe in the morning when the train comes, we can hide on it and get to Uxbridge."

As they were wading across the brook where it cascaded over a ledge of rock, a blood-chilling howl sounded behind them. It was something like the howl of a wolf. A second howl from down in the village sounded in answer.

"It's those black things," Witherspoon said. "Somehow they know we took the crystal. They're hunting us."

The Lament Horror

A third howl came from the direction of the rail depot. The things were on three sides.

"We can't go down there. We'll have to go over the Big Hill," he told the boy.

They ran as quickly as the dim light would allow up the grassy slope of the hill toward the pit.

"Maybe we can hide down in the mine," the boy said, panting for want of breath.

"No, we'd be trapped down there. Anyway, there's no way to get down without riding the cage."

The howls were closer. They had converged behind them, and seemed to be driving them toward the mine. Somehow the things were smelling their trail like a pack of bloodhounds. Witherspoon realized that he and the boy could never outrun them in the gathering darkness. They needed a place they could fortify.

There was only one such place: Old Mariah. Someone would be in the engine house. The mine pumps were kept running day and night to prevent the mine from filling with water, and a man had to stoke the furnace with coal to keep up steam pressure in the boiler.

He wondered if the door would be stout enough to withstand the strength of those three hellish creatures? Stout or not, it was their only hope.

The things were close behind when they pounded up the steps of the engine house. Above the slow thump of the piston and the groaning of the beam, he could hear behind them the quick footfalls of their hunters and the pants of their breath.

He slammed the door shut. Mercifully, it had an iron bolt on the inside. He slid it home just as the things reached the platform. The planks groaned under their weight.

"What are you two doing here?" An elderly man with rolled-up shirtsleeves scowled at them from beside the machinery of the engine. His arms and face were covered with streaks of coal dust and grease.

When the answer didn't come, he set his oilcan onto the floor and advanced menacingly toward them. "You're not supposed to be in here. Nobody is allowed in here after dark."

"Listen," Witherspoon said, raising his hand. "Do you hear that?"

"Hear what?"

"Outside the door. Listen."

Something massive rubbed its shoulder against the planks of the door. There was a snuffling sound. Then the door flexed inward against its hinges and bolt with a wooden groan.

"Is it a bear?" the workman asked.

"It's no bear, and there are three of them," Witherspoon said. "I don't know how much you know about what goes on in Lament, but you must have heard stories about what comes up out of the mine at night."

The workman's flushed, sweating face turned pale beneath its overlay of grease and coal, and his eyes widened.

"If they get in, they won't discriminate. They will kill all three of us, as surely as the sun rises," Witherspoon told him.

Something banged hard against the planks of the door, sending dust and bits of loose wood showering down.

"Sweet Jesus, what are we going to do?" the workman asked.

"Have you got anything we can use to reinforce this door? An iron bar we can prop under the crosspiece, maybe?"

"I've got a crowbar," the man said.

"Well, get it, and be quick."

In moments he returned with a heavy iron bar about six feet long that was bent slightly and tapered at one end. They wedged it at an angle under one of the lateral planks that held the door together.

"Is there any other way in here?"

The workman scratched his balding head. "Not unless they can squeeze past the flywheel or the bob."

Witherspoon went with him and inspected the openings. There was no more than nine or ten inches of space on either side of the enormous spoked flywheel, and less than that on either side of the great iron beam where it extended through the front of the building. Any creature foolish enough to try to squeeze past these moving masses of metal would surely be crushed.

As they were looking at the darkness through these openings, the glow from the lantern the old man carried reflected from two redly gleaming disks, and Witherspoon realized that one of the things was peering at them through the gap. The crystal on top of its head glittered. It howled, and Witherspoon moved quickly to catch the workman as his knees gave way beneath him.

"I always thought they were just stories," the workman said. "I never wanted to believe they were true."

"Believe it. Have they ever been seen in daylight?"

The man shook his head.

"Maybe if we can hold out until morning, they will go away."

"Do you think so?" The workman grasped his arm so tightly, it was painful.

"It's our only hope."

He did not add that others would almost certainly come before morning who were just as deadly as the three black things outside.

He noticed a massive iron shaft extending out the side of the building through a small trap door that fitted around the shaft without touching it. The square opening was no more than two feet across and the round shaft filled the center of it. Witherspoon judged there was not enough space between the frame and the shaft to admit the servitors, not even enough for him to squirm through. However, it might be just wide enough for the body of a small boy.

"Where does this go?" He pointed at the shaft.

"It drives the crusher. It's not engaged. We turn it off at night."

It was a faint hope, but if they waited Reverend Feake and his congregation were sure to come, even if the monsters did not succeed in breaking the door down. He had to keep the crystal away from them until he could get it to Boston. He motioned for the boy to come over.

"Timmy, do you think you can fit between the wall and that iron shaft?"

The boy went over and peered at the gap. "I believe I can, sir."

"Good lad. I'm going to distract the creatures by hammering on the front door. When you hear them all outside the front, I want you to crawl through the hole with the box and run as fast as you can into the woods. Can you do that?"

To his great credit, the boy did not hesitate. He immediately nodded.

Witherspoon swallowed with difficulty. He knew he was probably sending the lad to his death, but he also knew that both of them, and probably the workman, would die if they remained trapped in the engine house.

"Stay hidden in the woods until daylight, then come back and try to get on the train without anybody seeing you. If I don't reach you in the morning, take the box to the sheriff at Uxbridge and tell him that it must go to the university in Boston." He dug into his pocket. "Here's all the money I have. You may need it."

228

"I don't want to leave you, sir." There were tears in the boy's eyes.

"Wait until you hear them all gathered at the front," Witherspoon repeated.

"There's something I need to tell you, sir," the boy said.

"There's no time, Timmy."

"It was me who drew the sign on the blackboard. You're not angry at me, are you, sir?"

"No, Timmy," Witherspoon said in a gentle voice. "I know you did it to protect us all."

He looked around and found a heavy brass wrench as long as his forearm. It would make a formidable weapon, but he knew it would not be enough against the rippling muscles of the black horrors outside. He began to bang it against the door.

"What are you doing?" the workman said in dismay.

"I'm gaining their attention," Witherspoon said. "Help me."

The man stood for a moment, then took a smaller wrench from his back pocket and began to bang on the door also.

A howl went up from the other side of the stout planks. It was answered by another just beside it. A third howl came from the side of the building. The creatures continued to sing in chorus.

"I think it's working," Witherspoon said. "Off you go, Timmy."

The boy needed no urging. He set the box down beside the shaft and lifted the trap door, then grabbed up the box and pushed it into the space between the frame and the shaft. Watching from the door, Witherspoon felt a moment of nausea when the box appeared to jam, but the boy worked it through, then squirmed his slender body after it. For a few seconds he became stuck, but at last managed to work his hips through the hole and vanished outside. He could not have done it had the consumption not wasted his body away to almost nothing.

"Keep banging," he told the terrified workman.

Crossing to the opening, he knelt and peered out through the gap. The silver light of a newly risen moon showed the boy making his way carefully along the ridge beside the shaft.

"Did he get away?" the workman asked from the front door.

A black shape darted from the shadows and grabbed the boy. With a howl of glee it ripped his small body into two pieces and threw them down into the coal crusher below. It picked up the box almost delicately in its enormous taloned hands, which were covered with the boy's blood.

Witherspoon realized he had sent an innocent child to his death. All hope left his heart.

The black thing fumbled with the box as its bloody hands slipped on the polished sides. The box flipped from its grasp and fell into the crusher. The creature howled in dismay and leaped in after it. Witherspoon jumped to his feet, ran to the workman and grabbed him by his shoulders. "Start the crusher."

"What? Why would you want to do that?"

"Just do it, man, if you value your own life!"

The workman hurried over to the bank of long levers that extended up from the floor. He grasped two of them, and pulled them downward. With a deep groan that made the entire engine house shudder, the shaft began to turn.

Outside, the massive jaws of the crusher began to work open and shut with a sound like thunder.

"Dear Jesus, let it be in time," Witherspoon said.

The shaft hesitated, turned a bit, then stopped. The thunder of the crusher ceased. From all around him he heard a deep groaning of tortured iron. He realized the massive flywheel had ceased to turn and the bob has stopped rising and falling.

"What's happening?" he hollered to the workman.

The man's face was frozen in horror as he stared at the gauges of the steam engine. Witherspoon had to repeat himself.

"The crusher's jammed. I didn't think there was anything hard enough to jam it. The engine's trying to turn the shaft but it won't turn."

The groaning of iron became more tormented. From somewhere there was a scream of escaping steam. The workman pulled on the levers he had used to activate the crusher but they would not move.

"She won't take much more of this," the man said. "I've got to vent the steam."

As he ran toward a large valve that projected from an insulated pipe, Witherspoon struck him in the back of the head with the brass wrench. The old workman dropped like a sack of potatoes and lay without moving.

Abruptly, the crusher shaft jerked around a half turn. Something exploded outside the engine house, and almost at the same instant, the boiler of the steam engine split and vented all its steam with a thunderous roar.

Witherspoon would surely have been killed had he not stood on the opposite side of the boiler and some distance away from it, behind a heavy set of gears. These shielded him from the explosion. The concussion knocked him unconscious.

19.

When Witherspoon came around, the first thing he noticed apart from the ringing in his ears was the silence. The great piston no longer rose and fell in its cylinder, the flywheel had ceased to turn, and the bob that drove the mine pump stood motionless.

He pulled himself to his feet and saw that the workman's chest had been caved in by the blast. He went to the door and listened, but heard nothing. For a few minutes he waited. Then, with a fatalistic shrug, he kicked the crowbar aside and drew open the iron bolt.

The three black creatures were gone. From the platform he saw lights winking on in the windows of houses all over Lament. The explosion had awakened the entire village. They would be up the hill soon.

He went quickly around to the crusher and examined it in the moonlight. The smears across its iron jaws looked black, but he knew they were red. He climbed down and peered into the mouth of the machine and all around it. The jaws, at least three inches thick, were bent outward as though by some massive dynamite charge. Nothing remained of the boy's body or that of the creature. Of the shining crystal tetrahedron there was also no trace, nor could he find any of the tiny crystalline seeds.

The first person he met as he descended the path was Reverend Feake.

"What happened, man?" Feake demanded. He was disoriented, his eyes wild, his hair disordered. There was no covering on his head, and Witherspoon saw that the crystal that had extended from his skull had vanished. He recognized another member of the congregation with his head bare, and he also bore no crystal.

"Your Shining God is dead," Witherspoon told him.

"Dead?" Feake stared at him with incomprehension. "How is that possible?"

"Old Mariah killed him."

Josiah Harwood hurried up the path, puffing from the unaccustomed exertion. Bullum Bedford was at his side.

"The mine will flood," he said. "We're all ruined. There's no way to pump out the water without the Cornish engine. We won't be able to show a profit. Our investors will desert us."

Witherspoon started past the babbling old man. Bedford blocked his way. Witherspoon pulled out the rusty knife he had carried out of the meeting house and showed its blade in the moonlight. An expression of uncertainty came over Bedford's broad face.

"Let him pass," Harwood said in a weary voice. "It doesn't matter now. Nothing matters. We're ruined."

Matthew Poorish came running up the path, his bald head bobbing like a toadstool in the moonlight. Lines of silver tears streamed down his cheeks. "She's done for sure," he wailed. "I heard her boiler split. I know that sound. She's dead and done."

He might as well have been mourning the death of his only child. He rushed by the teacher without even noticing him.

When Witherspoon crossed Enoch Brook by the lower bridge, he saw Miss Whyte standing in front of the boarding house. She waited for him to walk up the road. She had on her night dress and a knitted shawl. Her long blond hair hung down over her shoulders. Witherspoon was relieved to see that no crystal projected from the top of her head.

"Are you—" he stopped, unable to find the words.

"I'm free," she said. "It fell off and turned to black smoke."

"How much do you remember?"

A shudder ran through her entire body. "Everything."

He took her into his arms. She rested her head on his shoulder.

"We'll leave Lament tomorrow," he said. "We'll get married in Boston."

"What if your father doesn't approve?"

"He will, once he comes to know you."

She stared past him at the line of villagers who climbed frantically along the path up the Big Hill to view the wreckage of the Cornish engine.

"Is it really over?"

He related the events in the engine house.

"The coal crusher shattered the crystal, but it broke Old Mariah. The mine is flooding, and Harwood and his consortium won't be able to find enough capital to buy another steam engine. If there's anything still in the coal seam, it will be submerged under more than a hundred feet of water."

"Will that be enough?"

"It will have to be enough," he said, and heard the doubt in his own voice.

He wondered if the three black servitors of the Shining God had been destroyed along with the crystal. How deep had been their sense of loyalty? Would they seek to find him, and would they be able to smell out his trail in Boston? Suddenly he longed for the light of morning, so that they could be away from this accursed place forever.

"It's over," he said, and when she did not speak he repeated with more emphasis, "It's over at last."

From somewhere in the forest behind the Big Hill they heard an eerie howl.

The Wall of Asshur-sin

1.

A fitful gust of wind cast a wraith of sand through the open window of the Land Rover. Fine grains salted the sweating neck of Eric Tenisan. By turns the wind obscured and revealed the horizon, playing with his expectations like a mischievous child. The Bedouins called this remote part of Yemen the Land of Lost Souls. It was a fanciful way to describe so bleak and empty a waste, yet strangely evocative.

He glanced at the profile of his beautiful young wife, Sheila. No matter how hot the sun, she never perspired. Her gaze was fixed on a tiny red spider that clung for life at the lower corner of the windscreen. The spider had been with them since they turned off the paved highway. She had said little for the past hundred miles. With a habitual gesture, he fingered the irregular edge of the gold medallion that hung around his neck on a chain through the hole at its center. The medallion had been with him for so many years, he was barely aware of doing it.

"Most of the dust is being stirred up from the road. We'll leave it behind soon."

The spider flew away. Released from her meditation, she smiled acknowledgement and turned to watch the cyclopean stones flash past her window. The desert was piled with massive rounded boulders that projected up through the sands like the bald skulls of buried giants. Long black hair at the side of her face veiled her features. As he so often had over the brief months of their courtship, he wondered what might be on her mind.

The steering wheel lurched and he caught it in time to guide the car across the surface of a huge rock. It was white and gently domed, like the shell of some vast lunar egg. He remembered it as though he had seen it yesterday, even though it had been over fifty years—but who is so empty of romance that he ever forgets the road that leads to Asshur-sin?

The last time he crossed this dome of rock, he had been a wide-eyed seventeen-year-old mounted awkwardly on the back of a camel, doing his best to pretend that he knew how to ride so that his father's Arab diggers would not laugh at him behind their hands. The road had not existed. It was his first experience as the paid member of a field expedition, and he could barely contain his excitement. Through the shimmering heat of memory he saw the sweat-stained white shirt and gray hair of his father, the great Norwegian archaeologist Olaf Tenisan, who rode his white Arabian horse with familiar ease across the treacherous dome of stone.

The sand from the open roadway hissed annoyance at the escaping vehicle, and then they were lost among the flowing boulders and sensuous rills where the wind wept in dizzy eddies. He leaned forward to gaze up through the tinted edge of the windscreen at the sun. It was just past noon.

2.

"Darling, are you absolutely sure you want to walk the Wall?" he had asked her a week ago in the darkness of their Cairo hotel room.

They had just finished making love, and lay in the bed side by side with a single crisp cotton sheet drawn up to their hips, surrounded by a gauzy veil of mosquito netting. The ancient air conditioner beneath the window was unequal to the task of countering the night heat. Rather than listen to it banging away in futility, he had turned it off and opened the window wide to the breeze from the Nile.

When she said nothing, he spoke again. "The climb alone is almost a kilometer, and it's over three across the top in the hot sun, to say nothing of the descent down the ramps and the hike back to the truck."

"Of course I want to climb the Wall, Eric. I'm looking forward to it."

Her tone was subdued, almost indifferent, a curious contrast to the enthusiasm with which she had begged him to make this irrational trek back into his past as part of their honeymoon adventure. He should be accustomed to her moods, he told himself. She changed like the sea. It

The Wall of Asshur-sin

was her unpredictable nature that had first attracted him—that, and her strikingly original beauty.

"Who was that man who spoke to you at dinner?"

"I didn't speak to anyone."

"That dark man with the odd symbol tattooed on the back of his hand."

"I don't remember. Let me sleep, darling, I'm completely exhausted."

The tip of her cigarette glowed once, then she ground it out in the ashtray on her bedside table and turned her back to him in darkness.

He lay on his left shoulder and vainly sought to distinguish her outline while he listened to the slow beat of his own heart.

What business had a man in his late sixties to take a young bride less than half his age? Months ago, when he first saw Sheila staring up at him with rapt attention during one of his public lectures at Cambridge, his routine had been comfortable and predictable. He had long since reconciled himself to a solitary and sexless life. An elderly housekeeper fed his tropical fish and took in his mail while he was away from his residence at the university on lecture tours.

What more did an aging professor of archaeology need? If asked at that time, he could have confidently stated where he would be and what he would be doing on any day in the coming year. Yet here he was, only a few months later, lying in a hotel room in Egypt with this strange and beautiful woman at his side.

Even today, he had no idea what it was about his manner or interests that attracted her. True, he was a respected authority in his field, though not nearly so renowned as his father. No one could hope to fill Olaf Tenisan's boots. But his father was dead, and that made him arguably the world's leading authority on Asshur-sin and its artifacts. Yet these were scarcely qualities to attract the love or stir the desires of a worldly woman such as Sheila Marsh. She had her own more-than-adequate source of income, so it was not his money she was after. He had eventually convinced himself that she must truly love him, and had begun to love her in return.

3.

The mammoth rocks of the Land of Lost Souls formed a natural road that declined at a slight but noticeable angle. He downshifted, and the Rover's engine whined as it slowed the vehicle on a steeper-than-normal slope. For a dozen kilometers the way twisted like a dying snake, the weaving stone buttresses that rose abruptly on either side concealing the path to come and the path behind. He attempted no more conversation, but forced himself to be aware of the landscape around him—of the bit of green high in a stony fissure on his left; of the gray lizard atop a boulder that ate the withered corpse of one of its cousins with quick motions of its almost human-like hands. In the midst of life there is death, but here there was far more death than life.

In spite of his resolve, his mind slipped into memory.

"Are you happy?" he had asked her on the train platform the day of their arrival in Yemen.

She had brushed strands of wind-blown hair away from her large, ice-blue eyes and gazed up at him with the serious yet enigmatic expression that had become so familiar. "Deliriously so. From the window of the train I watched a little girl with a great clay water pot balanced on her head. At each step it swayed back and forth, threatening to fall, and the girl kept raising her hand as if to steady it, but never once did her fingers actually touch the pot. She was walking east, so I knew it was a good omen."

It was the kind of thing she said from time to time. He had come to expect such cryptic remarks, and no longer tired his brain trying to decipher their meaning.

She turned from him to handle their baggage. With mingled feelings of love and possessiveness in his heart, he watched her stride across the train platform to argue with the almost somnambulant porter. Once again he found himself marveling at her indifference to the heat. Her conservative gray travel suit retained its crease from the morning. He had never seen her perspire, even though her pallid skin, so white that it was almost blue beneath the blazing Arabian sun, always looked slightly moist. This was just an illusion, but at times it disturbed him. Her complexion reminded him of the ivory underbelly of a frog, and the impression was not lessened by her large and oddly prominent eyes.

She had confided early in their relationship that her entire family was cold-blooded by nature. "I'm descended from a long line of Yankee traders who made their living upon the southern oceans of the world. There is more salt water than blood in my veins."

Once, in a teasing way, he had called her his undine lover. She had stared into his eyes for so many moments he was certain he must have offended her, but then she smiled and kissed his cheek.

"My Nordic troll, so big and clumsy and awkward," she had murmured seductively into his ear.

4.

His pulse quickened with expectation. The stony ground became more level and the shrouding cliffs on either side of the road parted like a theater curtain. Alive to Sheila's reaction to her first glimpse of the Wall, he drove onto the crest of the lookout and turned off the Rover's engine.

The Wall towered on the far side of the valley, its sheer size making it seem nearer than it was. This was the first time he had viewed it stripped clean of its ancient veil of rubble, and it was even more impressive than he remembered. Surely she must feel a similar emotion, gazing at the greatest wonder of the world, from the vantage where he had first seen it, seated on the back of a camel in his awkward youth. But she remained silent.

He cast his wide gray eyes across five decades of time, and still further back, across untold millennia to the very childhood of man. The same potent blend of humility and wonder he had felt as a teenager returned into his heart. He had not felt it for many years.

The Wall of Asshur-sin, wall of walls that rendered China's defense less than a hedgerow. Fifty years ago it was deemed a miracle. A local Bedouin had detected something unnaturally precise in a range of coastal mountains and informed his shaykh. After monumental excavations supervised by the elder Tenisan, the wall at last had revealed itself to the admiring eyes of the worshipful. Poets, mystics and scientists made pilgrimages from the far corners of the world to stand at its base and marvel. But that was half a century ago, and the world, ever preoccupied with the concerns and novelties of the present moment, had turned its gaze elsewhere.

It spanned the gap between the western mountains of the valley like a stone Samson, twisting perspective with its impossible bulk. Eric stretched his mind yet still could not contain its edges—nearly a kilometer tall and three kilometers across, what meaning had such dimensions? For untold ages the Wall had stood, defending the lost civilization of this desert valley against that most jealous mistress of the world, the sea.

"Magnificent," he said from the depths of his heart. "I wanted you to see it first as I saw it. We'll continue down now."

He restarted the engine and released the parking brake.

5.

He wondered if she was thinking of Johnny Azotha, the man with the dark eyes and shining black hair they had met in Egypt. Surely it was no more than his morbid fancy that the man had followed them from Cairo? A coincidence that he should arrive in Yemen at the same time, nothing more. While dining at the English Club in Sana'a, it had been natural that she should seek out his table, since his was the sole familiar face.

"Your wife tells me you go to see Asshur-sin," the dark man greeted him when he returned to the table with her package of cigarettes. He spoke English well, with a trace of the British accent he had acquired as a student at Oxford.

Eric frowned, thinking they sat too close.

"Most tourists are not keen enough to endure the journey now that the Wall has lost its newness," the man continued. "But I suppose it has a special significance for you, Doctor Tenisan. You were one of the first, weren't you?"

"I was part of the initial exploratory dig. My father headed the expedition."

"Ah, yes, the great Olaf Tenisan. You must be so proud to be his son."

She had been unusually expansive that night, doing her best to draw him out of himself in spite of his bad mood. "I had to plead with him to bring me, Johnny, he was like a mule." She mimicked his Norwegian accent. "You won't like it, Sheila. All that horrible dust."

They both laughed. Eric found himself toying with the medallion at his throat. He inched the chain that suspended it around his neck through its central hole. It was a habitual response to frustration.

The Wall of Asshur-sin

The Arab pointed at it. "That is a curious trinket. Where did you buy it?"

Eric resisted the irrational urge to hide the spiral design behind his hand. The medallion was shaped like a wheel with curved spokes and an open hub. "I found it, actually, when I was seventeen. At the Wall."

It was a subject he did not like to talk about. Sheila would not relent, and for her sake he told the dark man the story.

"The second night of the dig I was restless with excitement. I couldn't sleep. There was a full moon that night, bright as day, so I got up and walked from where the tents were pitched in the plaza of the ancient city ruins. I climbed— that is, I must have climbed—the ramps to the top. The diggers found me there the next morning at the middle of the causeway. I was clutching this medallion in my fist."

Unconsciously he closed his fingers around it until his knuckles grew white.

"He was completely traumatized," Sheila finished for him. "Couldn't even speak for three weeks. No one could pry that medallion from his hand. They say he screamed like a banshee whenever anyone tried to take it away, so finally his father strung a chain through that hole in its center and hung it around his neck just to get him to go to sleep. He has no memory of picking it up. He was flown to a hospital in Cairo and has never once returned to the Wall."

While his wife talked, Eric found himself staring at the tattoo on the back of the dark man's left hand. It stirred something buried deep under the layers of his psyche. The blue design depicted a creature that vaguely resembled an octopus. A shudder of revulsion swept through his body. He forced his gaze away.

"I have been there, you know, several times." The dark man shrugged. "I don't think so much of it. Only stones piled on stones, after all."

"And the ocean behind, does that impress you?" he asked coolly.

"Ah, the ocean. I have a theory. When this Asshur-sin, whoever he was, built his wall, there was no ocean. And then later the waters rose up until"—he spread his tanned hands—"there you are."

He remembered disputing this falsehood under the other's mocking stare. She had smiled the shadow of a smile, catching the flavor of the dark man's irreverence.

6.

The drive across the valley floor took on a nightmare quality for Eric. Always it seemed the Wall could get no larger, yet always it grew upward until at last its black face blocked half the sky. The effect was strange, a pressing on the chest and a shortness of breath, as if the Wall itself were squeezing out the stuff of life. He climbed dizzily from the Land Rover onto the packed brown sand, holding its roof for balance, his eyes irresistibly drawn to the summit.

The Wall was not perfectly vertical, though it appeared so when standing near its base. The blocks that formed it were made of black rock not indigenous to this part of Yemen, but the quarry for the Wall had never been located. The general presumption was that the stones had been brought from some distant land across the sea by barge. Each regular block was forty meters long and twelve meters high, but the foundation blocks at the base were even larger.

Eric had never seen most of these stones with his own eyes. Half a century ago they had been obscured by a titanic slope of sand and rubble that ascended nearly to the top of the Wall. Yet nothing in his life was more familiar. He had studied thousands of photographs and films of the stones over the course of his archaeological researches.

Stepless ramps ascended either side of the Wall in diminishing zigzag diagonals to the top. In keeping with its monstrous proportions, each ramp was four meters wide, as though designed for a race of giants. When uncovered from beneath the debris fifty years ago, a debate had raged as to their purpose. They were unsuited for dragging large objects to the top due to the tight bends where the ramps met, and were in any case too narrow to accommodate the stones of the Wall itself, yet their architecture was wastefully extravagant, when narrow and steeper flights of steps would have served to provide ascent.

The waves a thousand meters above me, he thought, his mind numb. *And through the stones where I stand, black ooze and things that have never seen the sun.* This nameless hidden valley was the lowest land elevation in the world—more than twice as far beneath sea level as the previous record holder, the Dead Sea. If the Wall were ever to collapse …

He shuddered and took his wife's arm, guiding her to the very foot of the edifice where the inscription had been unearthed from beneath uncounted tons of till. Cut into the side of one of the massive foundation blocks was an unpretentious recess not more than two meters deep. It appeared to be a later addition to the architecture, added long after the building of the Wall itself, although its date remained unresolved. An open sarcophagus of the same native white stone they had driven across on their approach to the valley rested within the recess. Neither the lid of the sarcophagus nor any trace of its contents had ever been found. It lay upon an oblong dais of black Wall-stone, part of the great foundation block itself, that raised it to within arm's length of the ceiling of the recess. Steps were cut into the sides of this dais as though to allow access to the open stone vessel, or from it.

Eric entered the recess and led his wife behind the elevated sarcophagus. The glare of the desert sun, reflected from the distant white mountains, shone into the cavity and highlighted the shadows of cuneiform characters that were deeply carved into the ceiling above the sarcophagus. Although he had studied reproductions of these letters on countless occasions, this was the first time he had seen them with his naked eyes. He felt a sense of awe tighten his throat.

"What does it say?" his wife asked in a casual tone, yet he detected suppressed interest in her words. Her large ice-blue eyes shone as she stared upward at the letters with an expression almost of reverence.

"It's written in an ancient Sumerian proto-dialect," he said, unconsciously adopting his professorial lecturing voice. "This is the only example that has ever been found, so all translations are conjectural. But I believe it to be some kind of warning."

"A warning? How exciting."

She took his hand into hers, and he felt the coolness of her palm. Her slender fingers were never warm. He pointed to each character in turn as he read the primary inscription aloud. "*Asshur-sin, king*—or perhaps *high priest,* or *herald,* it's not clear which—*keeps this Wall for*—or perhaps *against*—*the awakening of the Deep One. Beware his Emissaries.*"

He pointed at one of the characters that had been damaged and was largely obscured. "I take that to stand for the Wall itself, from the context of the text, although it is obviously illegible."

"It has been chiseled away," she said.

The confident tone in her voice caused Eric to glance at her. She stared at the damaged symbol almost with resentment.

"Possibly. Or it may have been chipped when the sarcophagus was placed on its dais."

"Come on." She pulled him by the hand back into the open. "Let's climb it."

He followed with his eyes the set of ramps that ran up the left side. "It's too far."

The words caught in his throat. Suddenly he was a boy, running through the moonlit darkness from something that trilled and rustled over the sand behind his pounding heels. How many times had he awakened in his bed, drenched in sweat, with the memory of the same nightmare? He could almost see his pursuers in the corner of his vision when he turned his mind toward them, but at the last instant they always faded back into the darkness and left him shivering.

"I'm sure it looks worse than it really is," she said lightly, pulling on his hand.

"You go—I'll stay in the Rover."

"Eric, I need you to come with me."

He looked into her face, saw the determination there. The terror that had visited him five decades ago while he lay on top of the wall in the moonlight with his eyes squeezed tightly shut, hugging his knees to his chest, returned. With more violence than he intended, he tore his hand away. She stalked across the sand toward the lowermost ramp without a backward glance, leaving him to follow or not.

7.

As they climbed, the floor of the valley widened beneath them. He caught up with her and kept her to the inside of the inclines, supporting her alternately with his left and then his right arm as the direction of the ramps reversed at each landing. They stopped often to rest, when the ache in their legs became too demanding to ignore. The shadows of afternoon lengthened across the valley. Many years ago he had climbed the Great Pyramid. This was harder.

Imperceptibly, the nature of the valley altered as they mounted ever higher. Details merged and larger shapes defined themselves. What appeared from the ground to be chaotic piles of stones revealed themselves as the decayed foundations of the nameless city, tucked into the eastern end of the valley between looming mountains. Excavations had revealed roads wider than normal, and a curious lack of steps. Eric had done his doctoral thesis on the city. Gazing down upon it like some god on Olympus, he knew every structure, every alleyway. But of the inhabitants, no trace had ever been unearthed, not even their place of burial. The prevailing theory was that they had burned their dead, though where they had found fuel for these funeral pyres in the barren desert remained unclear.

"We're almost there," he puffed, badly out of breath. "Two more ramps to the top."

"I can smell the ocean."

The resonance in her deep voice startled him. He stole a glance at her face—it was radiant. Her prominent eyes shone with that curious icy-blue glow that made her so different from other women. Though his linen shirt was drenched with sweat, her pale cheeks were cool and she seemed unwearied.

He heard the muted rumble of the sea as it rhythmically broke itself against the immovable stones. It had done so without pause for uncounted thousands of years. Each rolling wave made the ramp tremble beneath his feet, as if from distant thunder.

"Now you must see," he said somewhat incoherently as they mounted the last incline and the sea breeze touched their faces. "It's the oddest feeling, standing with a vast empty space on one side and the horizonless ocean on the other. As if the world were flat and you stood balanced on its edge."

He had no conscious memory of the view, yet somewhere deep within him he saw it lit with moonlight. They walked like insects across the twelve-meter wide span known as the causeway to the edge of the ocean and gazed down on moving blue water that was so close, its broken spray caught in their hair and salted their lips. The rumble, as each successive wave struck the flat stones, made speech difficult.

Sheila approached the seaward side and stood with the toes of her hiking boots extended off its edge. She spread her arms wide and stared at the western horizon in exultation.

"*Kthulhu p'tang ma'zathu agulu'ka,*" she intoned in a voice that rose above the thunder of the breakers.

Eric drew her gently back from the edge.

"What was that you recited?"

She shook her head, still staring out to sea. "A line from a song my mother used to sing to me. Just nonsense words."

They turned north and began to walk the Wall. It curved toward the ocean like the bow of the early moon, defying the pressure of the waves. He experienced a few moments of vertigo. The floor of the valley was so far away. Suddenly he seemed to be striding along the razor edge of the infinite with the great ocean on one side poised to overwhelm the world on the other. Nothing held back the cataclysm save this tissue-thin structure of black stone.

"Show me where you found your medallion," she suddenly demanded as they approached the midpoint of the wall.

Eric looked in front and behind him, trying to reawaken the long buried memory of that night. Nothing appeared familiar. He did not even remember finding the golden disk, only running with it clutched in his hand through the moonlight, with those sliding menacing things following close behind. But that might be no more than a bad dream.

"I don't remember—"

She took his arms in her hands and turned him roughly toward her, then stared into his face with solemn intensity.

"It's important, Eric. Think. Where did you find the medallion?"

He realized he was sweating profusely, so much so that drops of perspiration ran down his face and fell from his nose and chin. An image flashed in his mind of something disgusting and horrible. It had a cluster of writhing tentacles at its top. Then it was gone, taking even the memory of the image with it. He grasped at the medallion and held it tight in his fist.

8.

A shout made them turn to the north end of the Wall. A man in a red shirt and white canvas pants approached along the causeway with rapid steps. He waved, and even at that distance Eric recognized the toothy smile of Johnny Azotha. His confusion turned to annoyance. His wife grabbed his hand and pulled him along. Fifteen minutes later the three met breathlessly.

"Johnny, what are you doing here?" Sheila demanded with delight.

"I felt like some exercise, and I knew you two were coming today, so I decided to join you."

Was it his imagination, or did a glance pass between his wife and the dark man? Eric felt the irrational urge to hurl Azotha over the nearest edge. Instead he forced a polite smile.

The Arab took out a white silk handkerchief and mopped his face. "Quite a climb. At least there's a breeze from the ocean."

The three turned and stared out to sea at the unbroken horizon through intermittent curtains of white foam cast up by the rhythmic breaking of the waves.

"I was trying to persuade Eric to tell me where he found the medallion around his neck."

"Where did you find it, Doctor Tenisan?" Azotha asked. "I would be interested to hear the story."

Eric shook his head and turned away from the sea to gaze at the distant mountains across the valley.

"Did you find it on the top? Was it near the center?"

"I don't remember."

Sheila hugged his arm possessively between hers. "You must remember something, darling."

"No."

"Perhaps if we retraced your steps," Azotha mused. "Where were you before you climbed the Wall?"

"Enough!" Eric jerked his arm free from his wife's grasp and glared at the dark man.

Azotha smiled apologetically and spread his hands, then tucked his handkerchief into his vest pocket. Sheila folded her arms and walked toward the sea-edge of the Wall, her back stiff. There was an awkward silence.

Eric turned back to the mountains. His heart raced and the blood thundered in his ears, but not from anger. Suddenly he did remember. As clearly as though reflected in a mirror, he saw himself amid the ruins of the nameless city that sprawled across the eastern elevation of the valley.

He stood in its oddly shaped plaza, gazing down the valley at the moonlit Wall. Before him, at the center of the plaza, rose an octagonal block of black Wall-stone two meters across and a meter in height. As he examined it with the eye of memory, he realized that it had served as some sort of pedestal for a statue—the center of the block was worn by the removal and replacement of some heavy stone object over a span of many centuries. It was curious that in the five decades he had studied

Asshur-sin and the nameless city he had never before considered the true function of this stone block.

The moonlight shone strangely on the black stone. It cast into stark relief a circular ring of eight protrusions on its surface. Eric had examined images of the stone a number of times over the years, and was sure these bumps were not visible in the photographs. Yet under the light of the full moon they were undeniable. He watched his younger self walk around the block counterclockwise as though moving in a trance, pressing each knob of stone as he passed it. As the final knob descended into the body of the stone, it rumbled softly. A square panel grew out from its eastern side. Eric recognized it as a drawer. He watched himself reach into it and take out the gold medallion, then place the medallion in the center of the octagonal pedestal and orientate it in some way to the moon.

A feeling of awful dread clutched his heart. He closed his eyes and wiped his hand down his face. His sweat felt cold on his palm.

"It really is too bad you won't tell me where you found the talisman, Doctor Tenisan," Azotha was saying behind him. "It would have been so much easier."

Eric turned and saw the dark man with his arm around Sheila's throat. A black automatic pistol rested loosely in his other hand, pointed at his wife's temple.

"Johnny, what are you doing?" Sheila began to struggle, her look of shock giving way to one of terror.

He cursed her in Arabic and tightened his grip on her throat. "Be still, unless you want your brain splattered at his feet."

"What are you doing?" Eric repeated with incomprehension. He took a step toward them. The warning in the Arab's dark eyes made him hesitate.

"Listen to me, Doctor Tenisan. Unless you tell me where you found the talisman that hangs around your neck, I will shoot your lovely wife through the head. Do you understand?"

Eric could do nothing but stare.

Azotha pressed the barrel of the automatic into Sheila's hair just above her ear and put his finger gently on the trigger.

In a numb voice Eric began to describe his childhood memory. Azotha questioned him on the details and made him describe the knobs on the octagonal pedestal several times.

"I know this black stone," he said. "You have done the right thing, Dr. Tenisan. Now give me the talisman. Throw it to me."

"Yes, of course, only don't injure my wife."

He undid the chain around his neck and slid the medallion off it, then let the chain fall to the stone beside his shoe. He threw the gold disk in a careful underhand motion to Azotha, who caught it without loosening his grip on the woman.

"If you wanted to steal the medallion, why didn't you just tell me? It's not worth the safety of my wife."

An expression of anger clouded Azotha's features.

"Do you think me a common thief? I could have taken the talisman from you in Cairo. The talisman is useless without the knowledge of where you got it. My family searched for its hiding place for centuries, and you, a foolish child, stumble across it one night by some wild stroke of luck and use it for jewelry."

The contempt in Azotha's voice was palpable. As he talked, he relaxed his grip on Sheila's throat. She straightened, her face no longer afraid, but strangely calm.

"You cannot begin to comprehend the power I hold in my hand. My family is descended from the race that built that city below us. They worshipped a god of the ocean deeps that came from a distant star. They built their city at the base of this great thing we are standing on, what you call a wall. But it is not a wall, it is a portal, and this is its key."

"You expect me to believe that you are descended from the people of Asshur-sin?"

"Asshur-sin was not of my people. He was the king who conquered this valley, overthrew its city, and had thousands of tons of stone and sand piled up against this portal to prevent it ever being opened again. He thought he had slain all my race, but a few survived. They managed to drug his food, and after he was laid to rest in his white sepulcher, they came in the night and carried off his still-living body and committed abominable rites over it to ensure that he would walk the pathways of hell for eternity. And so he walks in hell to this day."

Eric paid little attention to the fantasy of this insane Arab. He watched his wife. Her eyes smoldered with a suppressed excitement that was almost exultation.

"Sheila, come over here," he murmured. "Stand behind me."

She laughed, her voice pitiless. "I told you my New England ancestors were sea traders. They had many dealings with barbarous tribes in foreign lands. In the South Pacific they made a bargain with a race of islanders who worshipped a god of the sea, and in return the sea yielded up its treasures to them, making them wealthy and powerful."

"Sheila, what are you saying?"

She slid her arm around Azotha's waist. "Isn't that obvious, you old fool? Johnny and I worship the same gods."

Azotha raised the automatic and shot Eric in the head.

9.

When Eric regained consciousness, it was night. He lay with his left cheek in a pool of his own dried blood. It looked black under the silvery rays of the full moon. He pushed himself into a sitting posture and gingerly felt his scalp with his fingers. The bullet had entered the skin above his left eye at the hairline and had run around the surface of his skull to exit from the back of his head. His entire head throbbed with pain.

Faintly, above the rhythmic thunder of the waves, he caught the sound of voices chanting in an unknown language. It was a man and a woman— Azotha and Sheila. The walls of the valley acted as a natural amphitheater, and the desert air was incredibly still, enabling the sounds to travel to the top of the Wall. Or was it a portal, as Azotha had so confidently claimed? Could a true history be conveyed through the generations of a single family for so many centuries? Eric dismissed the notion. Azotha was mad, and so apparently was his own wife. Yet something stirred in his subconscious, impelling him to stand and stumble toward the nearer of the two ramps, the one in the north by which Azotha had ascended.

As he made his way down the reticulated ramp, his mind began to clear, and his steps became more sure. The cool night air revived him. The chanting continued, rising and falling in intensity.

Eric became aware of a change in the stones beneath his shoes. They began to ripple as though under the influence of a small earthquake. A faint humming, so deep that it was almost below the level of human hearing, raised the hairs along the back of his neck. It was as if the stones were responding to the chant with a song of their own. And beneath all this there was a lower vibration, a series of booms with long intervals of silence between, like the slow, deliberate footfalls of a giant.

The Wall of Asshur-sin

He left the bottom of the ramp and ran across the desert sand to where the Rover was parked. Not far from it sat Azotha's rented car, partially concealed behind a decaying wall of one of the outlying city ruins.

Eric stopped, an internal battle of wills raging within him. He knew that the wise course would be to jump into the Rover and drive away from the valley before Azotha or Sheila could move to stop him. They had tried to murder him once and would not hesitate to try again. He started slowly toward the Rover. An invisible force descended on his limbs and held him still. An intelligence of great power spoke within him below the level of words, but intuitively he understood. He must stop the Arab and his wife from finishing the ritual.

He remembered this silent voice. It had spoken to him five decades ago, when he had run from the city and climbed the Wall with the medallion clutched in his fist. He had been powerless to disobey. He felt the same acquiescence within his soul that he had experienced then. It was not a surrender but an acknowledgement of a higher wisdom and a superior will.

As he began to jog across the uneven sands and loose stones of the desert, his eyes downcast to guard against a stumble, the chanting abruptly ceased. There was silence except for his gasping breath and the dull, slow booms that seemed to emanate from the depths of the earth. Then the voices of Azotha and Sheila began to cry out in unison a single repeated barbarous word of evocation. Eric recognized it as one of the words his wife had uttered earlier.

"*Kthulhu, Kthulhu, Kthulhu …*"

He stopped and stood bent in half with his elbows resting on his knees as he struggled to regain his breath. At sixty-seven, he was too old for moonlit sprints across the desert. He spat the taste of blood from his mouth and straightened. An instinct caused him to turn around, and the sight that met his gaze made him quail inwardly.

The lower two-thirds of the Wall had become transparent. In the center of this glassy expanse turned a vast spiral wheel of radiating energy that was a sickly green in color. It was not the spiral wheel of force that horrified him, but what lay beyond. By the penetrating light of the moon he could see through the stones of the Wall and into the dark waters on the other side. Shadow shapes moved through that water, large shapes. Their outlines did not resemble anything Eric had ever seen. Deeper still, beyond these restless shadows, something vast and hideous approached

250

on slow serpentine limbs. As it dragged itself forward, it emitted a dull boom each time its bulk settled to the sea floor.

How Eric could see such things in the darkness, how he could distinguish the shape of the approaching horror through countless meters of water, he made no attempt to understand. In some way he knew that what he saw was true, that his eyes were being assisted to penetrate the distance and gloom of the ocean depths, and more than this, that what he saw was not merely present in the deeps of the sea but also existed on some plane of reality that had been merged with the earthly plane by the chanted words. Azotha and his wife truly were insane, for they intended to open the Wall wide enough to allow that lumbering thing to enter this world.

The shouted evocation abruptly ceased. For a few seconds there was silence, then screams split the night. They came from human throats, but so great was the terror of those who made them that they sounded like the cries of pain-maddened beasts. The screams multiplied on the night breeze and ascended in pitch.

Eric began to run toward the nameless city, careless of where he put his feet. It was impossible to believe that such cries could continue for more than moments, but they went on and on. He thought of the face of his wife and felt sick. One of the voices was hers. The other sounded like that of Azotha, but was so shrill it might have been the screams of a young girl.

Long before he reached the outskirts of the ruins the screaming stopped. He approached the stones with cautious steps, struggling to catch his breath. The walls of the ruined structures came no higher than his waist in this portion of the city. He was able to look across the irregular rectangles of foundation stones that had once defined the houses of the ancient race of the valley. The ruins were utterly deserted. Conscious that Azotha might be crouching behind any corner waiting to put a bullet in his heart, Eric made his way down the broad central street toward the plaza of the black stone.

The plaza stood empty. He swept his gaze past two low shadows near the base of the pedestal stone, seeking any sign of his wife. As he crept toward the stone, alert for the lurking Azotha, the shadows defined themselves, and he recognized the bodies of human beings. Each naked corpse was completely covered in blood. No, he corrected himself, they were not covered in blood, but made of blood, along with glistening organs and exposed bones. Both bodies had been stripped of their skins. The wet blood appeared black in the moonlight.

10.

Eric put one hand on the octagonal stone to steady himself as he stared down at the female body. Just in time he turned his head, and vomited sour liquid over the plaza. The booms from behind the gate continued to increase in force. His mind numb, he allowed the sounds to draw his gaze. The green spiral had not diminished with the cessation of the chant. If anything, it was larger and revolved with greater urgency. Through its translucent rays he saw the shadow outline of the vast thing more clearly. It was closer to the Wall. *Not the Wall,* he corrected himself, *the portal.* The opened portal.

A gleam of gold caught his eye. The wheel of his medallion rested in the center of the pedestal stone, exactly as he remembered seeing it in his boyhood memory. It was even oriented to the moon in the same way. He fumbled to pick it up. It adhered to the stone as though magnetized. When at last he pried it loose with his fingernails, a blue spark crackled between the medallion and the pedestal. At the same moment a trilling cry arose from deeper in the ruins of the city on the eastern side of the plaza. The walls were higher there, blocking his view, but the cry had not been human.

As though in response, from beyond the swirling portal issued a subsonic rumble that Eric felt in his chest rather than heard with his ears. The sheer fury of the sound compelled his attention, and he saw the spiral eye on the transparent stones begin to close. In the dozen seconds he stood mesmerized by the sight, it dimmed and shrank.

Behind him the trilling he had heard earlier was repeated. A second trilling arose from another part of the ruins, followed by a strange sifting and grinding noise, as though heavy cables were being dragged along a beach.

Eric became aware of his danger. He bent his head and ranged back and forth across the plaza, searching for Azotha's automatic. Eventually he found it, some dozen meters from the corpse of the Arab. The hammer was cocked, with a round in the chamber and the safety catch off. Why had Azotha not fired to defend himself and Sheila from their attacker? The image of the terror of his nightmares returned to him with photographic clarity. At the last the dark man's courage had failed him. Or maybe he refused to fire upon the emissaries of his god. The sandy grinding did not cease, but drew relentlessly closer. It came from two places in the depths of the ancient city. He peered into the ruins and saw a shadow pass over the stones of a crumbling house wall, but the thing that made it was still obscured.

Eric did not wait to have his terror confirmed. With the gun in his right hand and the medallion clutched in his left, he ran wildly down the valley toward the Rover. The full moon hung in the west above the Wall and lit his way, but in spite of this advantage Eric was soon forced to slow his pace to little more than a fast walk. The race up the incline of the valley floor to the city had left him utterly exhausted. His head throbbed and his eyes blurred, so that he found it difficult to keep his balance. The trilling sounded behind his left shoulder, and was answered from somewhere further back to the right. The sifting noise did not get nearer, but neither did it fall behind. In the still night air it was impossible to tell the distance that separated him from his closest pursuer.

He risked a glance over his shoulder. The strength sapped from his legs and collapsed him to his hands and knees on the hard stones. It was not just the horror of the following things, but their familiarity. They were the nightmares of his youth, returned to haunt him, as they had haunted his sleep all the days of his adult life. Every night he ran from them, and every morning he blocked them from his memory.

A ring of short, thick tentacles around its base provided the creature with locomotion across the desert. It was from these that the grinding and sifting emanated. From its apex writhed longer and more slender members that reminded Eric of a cluster of vipers with their tails tied together. Some of the snake-like appendages had black barbs on their ends resembling the curved, black legs of insects. These dripped with fluid that was flung off from them as they writhed, so that it scattered through the moonlight like milky pearls. Along the lengths of these upper tentacles were reddish-black hooks that resembled curved thorns. It was not difficult to imagine what had stripped the clothing and skin from the living bodies of his wife and the dark man.

Just beneath the serpentine crown of the creature were three black eyes, equally spaced around the circumference of its body. As it rocked from side to side over the loose stones, the trailing eyes came alternately into view for an instant, but it was the central orb that held Eric's attention. It glared at the fallen man with an unmistakable malice. The second monster was like the first. It had remained further back and ranged to the right, as though seeking to block his escape should he choose to flee along the road and up the pass between the mountains.

He pushed himself to his feet without realizing that he had fallen. The gun was gone, lost amid the shadows, but the medallion remained in his closed fist. In the seconds it took him to get up, the nearest of the creatures closed almost half the distance that separated it from its prey. He turned and ran on. The nightmare repeated itself. Simultaneously, he was a terrified seventeen-year old and an old man grieving for his lost innocence. With some part of his mind he realized the spiral vortex of the dimensional portal had vanished. The transparency of the black stones also began to fade. The bright circle of the moon kissed the top of the great barrier and slipped into the waters beyond as he ran beneath the black shadow of the Wall.

He rounded the rear bumper of the Rover and jerked the driver-side door open. Even as he reached for the key in the lock, some instinct warned him that it would not be there. He fumbled over the steering column and then across the floor mats. He remembered leaving the key inserted. It had to be there. In the moonless shadow, the noise of the approaching horror was deafening. He could not see it, but he could feel its nearness. The truth struck him at the same instant he rolled from the driver's seat and ran toward the dark bulk of the other vehicle. Azotha had removed the key, probably at the time of his arrival, to ensure that he would not drive away while Azotha was still climbing the ramps.

The car was unlocked, but no key rested in its steering column. He felt along the dash and over the passenger seat, then turned down the sun visors, praying that a spare might be tucked behind them. He cursed. The keys for both vehicles must be in the plaza of the ruined city, lying amid the fragments of clothing that surrounded the skinless bodies of his wife and her accomplice. As he spun out of the car, a metallic rasp indicated that the thing following so close behind had slid one of its barbed tentacles over the metal of the Rover's body. It sounded remarkably similar to fingernails dragged across a blackboard by a malicious child.

For an instant Eric considered trying to slip past the monster in the darkness of the lunar shadow, and making his way back toward the pass that was the only egress from the valley. But the trilling of the second creature came from directly between where he stood and the way to safety. He did not even consider that this might be an accident. These things could not have known about the keys, but they had no intention of allowing their human prey to outflank them. In any case, he had little reason to suppose that the nearer of the beings was blinded by the darkness.

A barbed tentacle lashed out and struck the opened door of Azotha's car with a harsh clang, not more than three paces from where Eric stood. The immediacy of his danger galvanized him. He ran in the opposite direction, toward the base of the northern ramp. His eyes had become accustomed to the almost total darkness in the Wall's shadow, so he was able to keep his feet and stay ahead of the pursuing nightmare. He thought of casting the medallion onto the ground behind him, but some guiding awareness not his own made him keep it tightly pressed in his left fist. Again came the uncanny feeling of déjà vu, the certainty that he had experienced an identical impulse to cast the medallion aside, and received the same directive not to do so, on the night of its discovery five decades ago.

He was able to climb the first in the series of ramps only by putting his hands against his knees and pressing down with each step. His legs trembled and burned. Each weighed as much as the stones he climbed. At one point he managed to laugh bitterly when he realized why the Wall was ascended by inclines rather than stairs. It had not been constructed for human feet, but for the stubby ambulatory tentacles of the monsters. Had he come to this realization in the security of his university flat, surrounded by his books and papers, it would have been the crowning achievement of his career, but now it merely mocked his ignorance.

He had researched the valley of Asshur-sin for five decades and had learned nothing of importance. All the while he had kept some of the answers suppressed just beyond his reach in his own memories. His young wife had known more about the Wall than he had learned in all his years of research. So had Johnny Azotha. With agonizing clarity he realized what a fool he had been.

The trilling only two ramps below him was answered by an identical trill that echoed from the rocky slope on the opposite side of the Wall. The other creature had moved quickly to cut off his escape. There would be no chance to cross the causeway and descend by the southern ramps. It was exactly as it had been on that night, so long ago, when he had fled similar beings. How had he escaped that night? Eric racked his memory as he fought his way up the endless reticulated incline, but the final part of that night of terror remained as hidden as the face of the moon.

Three deaths awaited him at the top, should he retain enough strength in his legs to reach it. One lay on the hard stones at the base of the Wall so far below. The other was wrapped in the chill, choking waves of the ocean. The third hung on the barbs and hooks of the tentacles of the dread guardians of this passage to the underworld. Three ways of death, and perhaps a single way of salvation, if only he could remember.

11.

After what seemed more than a lifetime, he crawled on his hands and knees from the final ramp to the level stones of the causeway. It was almost more than he could bear to force his bruised and bloody knees to straighten and hold him erect. How long he had crawled, he did not remember, but it could not have been more than a few of the ramps or the creature would have caught him. It was close behind. The moon had just set below the horizon of the ocean in the west. An eerie phosphorescence illuminated the waves as they struck the side of the Wall. The stars had begun to pale overhead, indicating that morning was not far away. He wasted a moment to glance at the eastern mountains and saw the rose-gray tint of approaching dawn.

Hope surged in his heart. At last he remembered the final minutes of that night, so long ago. Swaying, he staggered on stiff legs from the horror that tipped itself upright onto the top of the causeway, so close behind. If only he could stay in front of it, he had a chance of survival. But the thing moved faster on a level surface than it had on the sloping ramps, and faster still across the smooth stones than on the rocky valley floor. It seemed to sense his thoughts, for it increased its speed. Had he stumbled, he would never have risen again. The smooth stones that speeded the hellish thing behind were his own blessing. He was able to drag his nerveless feet across their surface without catching his toes or heels. Somehow he managed to keep his balance.

As he neared the center he heard an exultant trilling in front of him. The other creature had finished its ascent and now barred his path. He continued to shuffle toward it. There was nowhere else to go. As it approached, he had more opportunity than he wished to examine its writhing, hooked appendages and leathery body. He dared not look away for fear of losing his balance and sprawling on his face. The thing behind was very close. He heard the barbs of its tentacles click against the stone just behind his heels.

Finally, there was nowhere else to run. Eric turned and stared defiance into the lidless black central eye of the monster that followed. A strange peace descended into his body, as though a cooling cloak of silk had been draped across his skin. Fear left him. He felt a sense of recognition for the horror that closed swiftly upon him with its barbed ropes lashing the air. He saw it, not with his own eyes, but with the eyes of an older and wiser soul that had in some inexplicable way merged with his own. The monster abruptly stopped and appeared indecisive. Eric knew that by some psychic faculty it had perceived the same presence within him.

It was this possessing presence, not Eric, that passed the medallion into his right hand and threw it far out over the waves. It vanished from view against the paling stars while in the air, but as it struck the water it cast up a small splash of luminous white.

Eric experienced a rush of liberation. A debt had been paid. An obligation had been fulfilled. Calmly he turned to face the nearer of the tentacled things and awaited his own death.

Even as the creature glared malignantly and thrust itself forward for the killing lash, a ray of the rising sun struck its tortuous crown. At once its leathery body became transparent, just as the stones of the gate had become transparent under the moonlight. It writhed in a frenzy of frustration and threw itself forward on its stubby squamous legs. Eric closed his eyes. He felt a tingling on his skin. He opened his eyelids with surprise, then turned. The monster had passed completely through his body, as though it were no more than a projection of light.

The two creatures came together and stopped. They seemed to converse. Eric heard their trilling voices, but strangely remote as though they came from many miles away. Under the strengthening rays of the sun their bodies faded and became as clear as glass, and within a few moments more, they vanished.

Eric blinked at the sun. He was too numb to feel emotion, but he knew the ordeal had ended. The things had disappeared into whatever dimension of reality had spawned them, the same way they had faded into nothingness on the morning of that night so many decades ago.

The Wall of Asshur-sin

The destiny of his life, so long postponed, was at last fulfilled. Later there would be time to reflect on the meaning of what had taken place, time to grieve for the death of his wife and to ponder her hidden purposes, time to piece together the bits of information he had gleaned from his own memories and from Azotha's words, but for the present he merely enjoyed the sunrise.

Behind him, a sinuous rope of gray flesh as thick as his waist rose silently from the waves. It wrapped around him in a gentle coil, as though embracing a lover, and with a smooth arc slipped beneath the surface of the sea. Where it passed, the stones were empty. Ripples spread from the place of its descent, but soon the waves erased this brief memorial.

The Colonids

1.

It's not what you want, it's not what I want, it's what the studio wants," Armory Moreau said, waving his glass for emphasis. Some of the rum in it slopped over the broad lip and dripped on the black leather couch.

Jack Stainton glanced across the living room at his wife. Angelu quirked the corner of her mouth and shook her head almost imperceptibly. He breathed out slowly, controlling his temper.

"Armory, it damn well *is* about what I want. My name is going on this script. My reputation's on the line."

"No, it isn't about you!" Moreau snapped. "We need backing. That means getting a major studio on our side, and the only studio interested in this project is Lakeview. If they say to make the lead role female, that's what we're going to do."

His frown made the lower half of his round and somewhat corpulent face jowly, like that of a truculent English bulldog. A network of purple veins decorated his bulbous nose, and his dark gray eyes were bloodshot from too much alcohol. Stainton could not remember seeing the movie producer in any other condition.

"Changing the sex of the protagonist will change the entire dynamic of the plot. It won't be the same story, Armory."

"Look, Jack, I know you're an artist, but the studio doesn't give a fuck. Without their money nobody is ever going to see this picture. It won't matter what you write because no one will ever see it."

A compact young woman with short brown hair glanced across from the other sofa with a disapproving pout. "Daddy, don't browbeat Jack.

We're guests in his house, for Christ's sake. Show some class."

The young black man seated beside her said nothing but looked uncomfortable.

"Cleo's right, Armory," Angelu said with a smile. "This is a social gathering. You and Jack can lock horns tomorrow."

"Business," Moreau grumbled sourly, rattling the ice cubes in his empty glass. "What else have I got except business? Since Ellen left me last month I haven't even had sex."

"You're too old for sex anyway," his daughter said. She extended her hand toward Angelu, who pressed her palm flat and peered down at it intently.

Moreau snorted and pushed himself up from the couch.

"Need a refill, Armory?" Stainton asked, half-rising from his chair.

Moreau waved him back down. "I'll get it, Jack. What about you and your man, cupcake? Want a drink?"

"Rum? Eeck! Don't joke, Daddy. But I wouldn't mind getting high."

"We've got some grass," Angelu said, still examining the girl's palm.

"Not for me, thanks," the black man said. He looked apologetically at the girl. "I've got a game next week and I don't want to test positive."

"Payton Hill, you are such a fence picket," Cleo said.

"What position do you play?" Stainton asked.

"Running back."

"Just don't give my daughter any coke," Moreau muttered. "I'm still paying the medical bill to fix her nose from last year."

"What wet blankets you men are," the girl said, sticking her tongue out the corner of her mouth at her father. He paid no attention. She turned back to Angelu. "Can you really see the future in my palm?"

"Of course. The lines tell all," the slim blond woman said. She glanced at her husband, who rolled his eyes.

"Bollocks," Moreau said, returning with a full glass.

"How can you make horror movies and not believe in the occult?" his daughter demanded.

"Ask Jack. He writes the damned things. Do you believe in the occult, Jack?"

Stainton shrugged at the older man. "Until I hooked up with Angelu, I would have said no, but she's shown me some freaky shit, Armory."

"Like what?" Cleo demanded.

He thought for a moment.

"Like the time we did this séance around a heavy wooden table, and the damned thing lifted straight off the floor and stuck against the ceiling. Remember, hon?"

The blond woman nodded, her eyes on the girl's hand. "There was some serious ectoplasmic energy in the aether that night."

She started to read the girl's palm. Stainton tuned the voices on the other side of the living room out.

"So how's the house, Armory?" he asked the older man.

"Couldn't be better," Moreau said as he settled himself on the couch. "Pierre and Marie did a great job taking care of the place over the winter. He told me the wind took off some siding, but his brother-in-law helped him put it back on."

"We get some wicked winds on this side of the Island," Stainton agreed.

"I still have to get him to say everything twice before I can understand him," Moreau laughed.

"You grew up in France. Canadian French shouldn't be too hard."

"It's the fucking accent. It's so thick, it's like a whole other language. Anyway, it's been a lot of years since I was last in France."

"I'm glad it's working out," Stainton said. "I have to admit, I had my doubts when you asked me to sell you a piece of my land for you to build a summer house on."

"I had an ulterior motive," Moreau said. "When I'm here I can ride herd on you and make sure you make the script changes we need. It's not so easy putting the thumbscrews on you over the Internet."

"You were lucky to get the Arseneaus. A lot of the French around Chéticamp way don't much like English-speakers like us moving in. They've been living on this coast of Cape Breton for generations and they figure they own it, every rock and tree, no matter what land title deeds might say."

"As long as they can put up with me for a couple of months in the summer, that's all I ask," Moreau said. "I'll tell you, Jack, it's a relief to get out of Los Angeles. The bullshit I have to deal with there would drive you insane."

"I know," Stainton agreed. "Why do you think I live here and send my work in over the Net? I couldn't take California. Neither of us could. We had to get out."

"Well, you got just about as far out as you could get without crossing an ocean," Moreau joked. "We're on the ass end of nowhere."

"Great, isn't it?"

"It sure is."

"Gentlemen, put down your drinks," Angelu said grandly. "It's time to look at the circle."

Cleo clapped her hands like a pre-schooler. "The Indian circle! I've been dying to see it for weeks."

"You told her about the circle?" Stainton asked his wife, standing up.

"We text," she said.

"What is this Indian circle?" Moreau asked.

"The correct term is indigenous people," Angelu told him. "Nobody says Indian anymore."

"Fuck correctness."

"It's a stone circle that Angelu uncovered in our woodlot while she was clearing away deadfalls and brush."

"It's old," she said, excitement lighting the depths of her blue eyes. "I've done some discreet research."

"Why discreet?" Peyton asked.

"We don't want anyone from the government snooping around, telling us what we can do with our own property," Stainton explained to him. "We're keeping quiet about this circle."

"In fact," Angelu said, "you three are the only other people in the world who know about it."

"Angelu thinks it's a Stone Age site," her husband said.

"That's really, really old, Daddy," Cleo said. "Older than the Indian tribe that lives on the Island."

"It wasn't built by the Mi'kMaq?" Stainton asked his wife in surprise.

She shook her head. "Not according to my research. It's unlike anything they build. It's really old, Jack. I can feel energies coming out of the ground when I meditate inside the stones."

"Here we go again," Moreau said as he lit a cigar and puffed vigorously on the end.

"Daddy, do you have to smoke those things?"

"Do I complain when you and your friends stink up the house with those enormous doobies? No, I do not. Kindly let me smoke my cigars in peace, little girl."

They left the rambling old white farm house that Stainton and his wife had renovated over the past several years through the back door, and walked slowly across the lawn and under the trees. Angelu had made the woods near the house into a kind of park. The afternoon sun was warm where it found its way between the branches overhead, and the song of birds was all around them.

"This is really nice," Cleo murmured.

"This is just a start," Angelu told her. "Give me a couple more years and it will be really nice."

"My wife, the woodsman," Stainton said to Moreau.

"At least one of you knows how to make cuts."

As they progressed deeper into the woods, it became denser and more difficult to walk through. There were deadfalls leaning over and lying across the forest floor, supported by their naked branches. Every autumn, the wind storms did their damage. Not more than a thousand feet ahead lay the edge of the parcel of land he had sold Moreau, Stainton thought, but no one would ever know it climbing through these brooding spruce trees. He breathed deeply the scent of spruce gum. It wasn't the pleasant aromatic scent of pine, but it wasn't a bad smell once you got used to it.

They came upon a small clearing, and stood speechless. Within the grassy patch an irregular circle of boulders pressed their rounded heads above the moss and sod, but it was not at these rocks that they stared.

"What the fuck?" Stainton said under his breath.

In the center of the circle stood the skeleton of a large animal. It was like a museum exhibit, or a sculpture. Every white bone was perfectly articulated. They gleamed in the sunlight. Stainton studied them in disbelief, and realized that they were probably the bones of a deer. They had not been in the circle the day before.

2.

After a time, Moreau took the cigar from the corner of his mouth. "Is this some kind of gag?"

Stainton looked at his wife, who stared back at him, wide-eyed.

"It's the skeleton of an animal," Payton said.

"What's holding it up?" Cleo asked.

That was a good question, Stainton thought. The bones were slender and delicate. He slowly walked around it. He could see no wires, no traces of epoxy or other adhesives. The bones should not have been standing together in that way. They seemed to glow with a kind of inner light that was more than just the brightness of the sunlight on their snowy surfaces. He extended his hand.

"Don't," his wife said.

He looked at her with surprise. There was fear in her voice.

"Why not?"

"Just don't."

Moreau grinned and turned to stare up at the surrounding treetops. "I don't know how you managed this, Jack, but it's a good gag. Where are the cameras? In the trees, right? You've got them well hidden."

"This isn't a gag, Armory."

"Come on, you set this up. This is some kind of practical joke. Did Spielberg put you up to this? The little cocksucker told me he was going to get me after I painted his Maserati pink last year."

"It's not a joke," Stainton said with more force than he intended. He deliberately lowered his voice. "I don't know how this got here. I don't know what it is."

"It's a skeleton," Payton said again.

"Well thank you, Captain Obvious," Cleo said.

"There's some kind of aura around it," Angelu said. With great care she extended her hands toward the bones, but did not touch them. "I can feel it vibrating. It's very powerful."

"Oh, shit, you people are something else."

Moreau slapped at the skeleton. Stainton expected the delicately-balanced bones to fly apart, but they did something completely unexpected. They turned to a fine white powder. It fell to the grass and lay there, looking like chalk dust. Moreau snatched back his chubby fingers and shook them.

"I got a shock," he said.

"What do you mean? Like an electrical shock?" Stainton asked.

"What the fuck other kind of shock is there? Yeah, like electricity."

Payton poked at the pile of white dust with the toe of his tennis shoe.

"Whatever the aura was, it's gone now. I don't feel anything," said Angelu.

"You really don't know how this got here?" Cleo asked her. The blond woman shook her head.

"It wasn't here yesterday. I didn't come out to the circle this morning."

"So somebody put it here this morning, as a gag," Moreau said.

"It doesn't make any sense, Armory. Nobody knew you were going to visit the house today. Nobody has any reason to play tricks on me or Angelu. For that matter, nobody even knows this circle exists but us."

"Maybe it's the Frenchmen from town," Moreau said. "Maybe Pierre found out about the circle and they set this up."

"How?" Angelu demanded. "You saw the bones. How could anyone make them stick together like that? And how could anyone make them crumble to dust?"

"Maybe they weren't bones," Payton suggested. "Maybe they just looked like bones."

"That's it!" Moreau said. "They weren't bones. They were a prop. Some of Spielberg's people rigged this up. Damn, I'm going to get that little weasel when I get back to Los Angeles. He probably filmed the whole thing."

He turned in a circle and raised his arms. "Spielberg! I'm gonna get you back, you son of a bitch."

Cleo crouched and picked up some of the powder. She rubbed it between her fingers and let it sift back to the grass. "Anyway, since we're here, we might as well see the circle."

Angelu looked at her husband. He shrugged.

"There isn't much to see in the circle itself," she said to the girl. "There are thirteen stones, all of them almost completely buried. Only the domes of their tops stick up above the grass. The circle isn't really a circle—it's an ellipse."

"Ellipse? What does that mean?" Cleo asked.

"It means it has two foci … two focal points," Payton said. "A circle has only one focus, but an ellipse has two." He looked at the others and shrugged. "Geometry."

"Which means?"

"Damned if I know."

"Anyway," Angelu continued, "there are no carvings of any kind that I could find on the stones. There's nothing in the center of the circle—at least, there was nothing until today—but I haven't dug into the sod to see if anything is buried under the surface."

"Why not?" Cleo asked.

"I didn't want to disturb it. It's been this way for thousands of years."

"You mean you didn't do anything yesterday that was out of the ordinary?" Stainton asked.

"I don't—oh, I see what you're getting at. No, I don't think so. Nothing except a small cleansing ritual."

"What's that?" Cleo asked.

"It's just a ritual to banish discordant vibrations and bring a place into harmony. There's really nothing to it. You walk three times around with salt, water and incense. I do the ritual all the time to cleanse places where I meditate."

"You've been meditating in the circle?" Stainton asked.

His wife nodded.

"Every day for the past couple of weeks."

"It might be best not to do that anymore."

"Okay."

"Why do you say that?" Cleo asked.

"Just a feeling."

Stainton looked around at the shadows between the trees. Whatever had just happened, it wasn't a practical joke. Of that much he was certain. Nobody knew about the circle, and even if they had known, it would have meant nothing to them. In any case, it would have been impossible for even a professional team of special effects artists to set up the skeleton in a few hours, without leaving a single trace. No one had seen any strange faces in the area, or he would have heard about it—gossip traveled faster than light in rural communities.

"A hell of a trick," Moreau muttered to himself around his cigar. "Well, cupcake, I guess we better get back to the house."

"I'll drive, Daddy," Cleo said. "You're plastered."

"Why do you drive over here?" Angelu asked Moreau. "You do know that your house is only a few hundred yards through the trees in that direction?"

He looked at the trees and shook his head. "Easier to drive."

They walked with their guests out of the woods and waited in their driveway until Moreau's Mercedes disappeared around the bend in the gravel road.

"They'll be in their own driveway in less than a minute," Stainton said.

"Maybe it's just as well. I'm not sure I want them popping through the trees without warning."

"Armory can be quite an ordeal once he gets rolling," he agreed.

"What did you think of Cleo's beau?"

"He seems like a nice enough kid."

"Are you going to change the script?"

"Hell, no. Lakeview can go fuck itself."

"Armory may fire you and hire another writer."

Stainton chuckled and put his arm around her shoulders.

"He can't. It's my story. I retained control in the contract."

They walked back toward the front door.

"He is going to be so pissed off at you."

"It won't be the first time."

"So what do you think it was?"

He stopped. In spite of the sunlight on his golf shirt, he felt a sudden chill, and shivered.

"I don't know, but it felt ... wrong, somehow."

"I felt it, too. Like some kind of violation."

He nodded without speaking. *That was it. A violation. But a violation of what?*

3.

The persistent ringing of the telephone woke Stainton early the next morning. They didn't use cell phones, but relied on an ancient wired phone in the kitchen. His wife was a heavier sleeper than he was, and did not wake up.

"Jack? You have to get over here right away."

"Armory? What's wrong? Is somebody hurt?"

"No, no, it's nothing like that. Look, you just have to see this for yourself. Get over here as fast as you can."

"Okay, take it easy. I'll get dressed and cut through the woods. See you in five minutes."

"When you come out through the trees, be careful where you step."

"What? What the hell are you talking about?"

The dial tone of the phone rang in his ear. He hung up the receiver.

When he emerged from under the trees onto Moreau's rolling back lawn, at first he didn't see any problem. The morning air was still chilly, and he was glad he had taken time to slip into a turtleneck sweater. Unlike the producer, he had no layer of fat for insulation. *Armory must be getting the D.T.s,* he thought. Well, no one in Hollywood would say they were premature.

The Colonids

Moreau came around a clump of ornamental cedar trees and waved him over anxiously. Stainton trotted across the lawn, which was still wet with dew, so that his feet left a track behind him.

"What the hell is the emergency, Armory?"

"Just look. I can't describe it; you need to look for yourself."

They rounded the trees and stopped. Stainton just stood and stared, saying nothing.

Where the back lawn should have been there was an enormous crater in the ground. It looked around ten feet deep and about thirty feet across. On the other side of this hole, the two house servants, Pierre Arseneau and his wife Marie, stood looking at him. Beside them was Payton Hill, wearing only pyjama bottoms and bedroom slippers, his muscular torso bare to the breeze. He hugged himself and shivered. Cleo stood barefoot inside the crater in a pair of pink silk pyjamas. An aluminum ladder leaned from the lip of the depression to its concave bottom.

"Are you crazy? Get out of there, cupcake."

"It's not dangerous, Daddy," she said with scorn. "You get so excited over nothing."

The crater did not appear to have been formed by a sudden impact, but neither did it look excavated. There were no signs of earth-moving machinery on the grass or on the muddy sides of the hole, which was roughly hemispherical in shape. No, not quite, he corrected himself. The hole was slightly longer than it was wide.

All this, however, was beside the point. In the air above the middle of the hole floated two rocks. They were the size of pumpkins and they floated at roughly the same height as the lawn. This put them just out of Cleo's reach, although the girl jumped repeatedly in an effort to touch them.

"If you don't come out of there now, you are grounded forever," her father said.

"You can't ground me. I'm nineteen."

Stainton cleared his throat. "It might be better for you to do what your father says, at least until we know what's going on here."

She pouted, but allowed Payton to help her up the ladder.

"Are they real rocks?" Stainton asked doubtfully, as he stared at the floating boulders. They slowly rotated in the air, no more than three feet apart from each other.

"They look real," Payton said.

His face had a kind of ashy-gray hue. Stainton realized the young man was in shock. Cleo, on the other hand, seemed to be having a great time. She pried small pebbles out of the grass at the edge of the hole and threw them at the floating boulders. They ticked as they bounced off, but otherwise caused no effect.

"Are they magnetic?" Moreau asked.

"How should I know?" Stainton said.

"Stop being a little brat, Cleo."

She threw the pebbles down in disgust and folded her arms over her chest.

"Mister Moreau," Pierre said in his heavy French accent.

"What is it, Pierre?"

"Do you want me to phone for the police?"

Moreau looked down at the hole, then at the floating boulders. "What can the police do? No, we won't contact the police until we know what's going on."

Pierre nodded. After a while, he and his wife returned inside the house to prepare breakfast. The other three continued to stand at the edge of the pit, watching the slowly revolving rocks in fascination.

"No ordinary magnetic field is strong enough to support those rocks," Peyton finally said. "Even if there is some iron ore inside them, it would take magnetic coils that are enormous."

"Maybe the rocks are hollow." Moreau giggled. "Maybe they are filled with helium."

"It sounds more as though you're filled with helium," Stainton told him.

The older man glared at him. "You're the writer. You're supposed to know things."

Without replying, Stainton went into the woods and got a long branch from a fallen tree. He broke off all the twigs so that he had a gently curved pole some seven feet long. Standing on the edge of the pit, he leaned forward to nudge one of the boulders with the tip of the branch. It was not long enough. He cursed under his breath, then began to descend into the hole on the ladder. At the top, the sides were steep—almost vertical. He managed to get both hands and one knee covered with damp mud before he found himself standing on the incline at the side of the pit.

"Don't get under them," Moreau said.

The Colonids

"I have no fucking intention of getting under them, Armory," Stainton said.

He advanced deeper into the crater. The air seemed to have the same sort of hum that had surrounded the deer skeleton in the circle of stones. Was it his imagination, or did a very faint halo of blue light flicker on the surface of each floating boulder?

He extended the branch upwards and touched one of the rocks. A jolt of electricity ran through his arm and down both legs. At the same instant, the two boulders dropped to the mud at the bottom of the pit with a single dull thud.

"Fuck," Moreau said.

"Pull me out, Armory."

It was Payton who did most of the pulling. Stainton stood beating the mud from the knee of his jeans.

When Moreau spoke again, his voice was quiet. "What the fuck is going on, Jack?"

"I have no idea, Armory."

"Is Cleo in danger? Should I take her and get away from here?"

"I don't know, Armory."

"You're not much fucking use."

Stainton thought for a moment, then nodded. "You're right."

"I don't like this, Jack. It feels strange. Weird, you know what I mean? It's just not right. This shit shouldn't happen."

"What happened to your Spielberg theory?"

"Not even Spielberg could pull this off."

Stainton regarded the two rounded boulders in the bottom of the hole. They were approximately the same size and shape as the thirteen stones that composed the circle in the woods.

"At least there's one thing," he said.

"What?"

"At least there's no danger. Nothing bad has happened. Nobody has been hurt."

Moreau thought for a moment. "Yeah, you're right. At least there's that." His bloodshot eyes widened. "Shit."

"What?"

"I have to record this. I have to get my camera." He turned and ran for the back door of the house.

"A producer who does his own cinematography is like a murderer

270

who defends himself in a court of law," Stainton murmured to Payton.

The black man said nothing.

4.

Pierre brought folding chairs out to the edge of the pit for them to sit on. By this time, Moreau had induced Stainton to wake his wife. She stood in the middle of the hole. Moreau leaned over the edge with his video camera in his hand.

"I wish you would put on something more colorful," he grumbled. "Maybe a red shawl, or a blue scarf, or something."

Angelu shrugged and spread her arms. "What you see is what you get."

She wore a pair of cut-off, badly tattered jeans and a white blouse that was tied around her waist. Her blond hair was done up in the back.

"You look fine, honey," her husband told her.

"Can I go down into the hole with her?" Cleo asked.

"No, you can't," Moreau snapped. "And if you talk while I'm recording, I will kill you."

"Ready anytime you are, C. B.," Angelu said.

"And, we're rolling," Moreau murmured.

The blond woman closed her eyes and turned in a slow circle, her arms held slightly away from her sides.

"There's an awareness here—not in the hole, but close. It's looking for something."

"What is it looking for?" Moreau asked.

Angelu's blue eyes opened. She stared at her husband.

"Us. It's looking for us. It's as if it's blind and it's feeling around for us with its hands. It has so many hands."

"When you say an awareness, what exactly do you mean?" Moreau asked. He knelt in the grass and zoomed the lens of the camera on her face.

"It's really strange. It's not like any spiritual entity I've ever encountered before. It's one consciousness but at the same time it's divided into many separate entities that are all united on some level. I can't really explain it."

"It's one, but it's also many?"

She nodded, a frown on her brow. "Yeah. I know I'm not making sense but this is totally alien to me."

"Is it aware of you?" Moreau asked.

The Colonids

She closed her eyes and concentrated. "In a way. It knows I exist, but it can't find me. It's like I'm hiding in the dark, and it's feeling around for me with its hands—except they're not really hands, more like energy conduits."

"Ask it what it wants with us."

"It's hungry. It needs mental energy to extend itself through something—I'm getting layers. It's like a worm that eats through the pages of a book, only those pages are different dimensions, and it isn't one worm, it's a thousand worms all connected on some level."

Her eyes widened. "Oh shit. Pull me out of here."

"What's wrong?" Stainton asked.

"Shut up, Jack. I'm still rolling."

"Fuck you, Armory."

He hurried to the edge of the crater and helped his wife up the ladder. She was trembling.

"What did you see?" he murmured into her ear as he held her.

She pushed away from him and stared around at them all. "We can't tell anyone else about this."

"Why not?" Moreau asked. He continued to record her.

"That's how it finds us. It becomes aware of our existence when we think about it—about what it does, I mean. When we think about the traces of its presence in our world."

"But none of us knew it existed before yesterday," Stainton reminded her.

"That was a fluke, Jack. A one in a billion chance. But once we became aware of its existence, it became aware of us."

"What does it want with us?" Cleo asked, forgetting her father's threat.

"I already told you, it's hungry."

"It wants to eat us?" Cleo laughed nervously. "That's crazy."

"Not our bodies. It doesn't give two shits about our bodies. It wants our minds."

"It told you this?" Stainton asked.

"No. I don't even know if it's really intelligent. I just sensed it."

"So everything you've told us is just your intuition," Moreau murmured.

She glared at him. "Yes, Armory, it's all just my woman's intuition. Make of it what you will. But we can't tell anyone else about this, or it will spread. It wants us to talk about it. It wants to spread as widely as possible through all the dimensions of space. It wants to fill everything with itself."

"It's like a mind cancer," Cleo said.

"That's it," Angelu agreed.

"Except it's not in our minds, it's in our backyards," Stainton said.

"No, Jack, what we see here is only the result of its passage through our reality. It's in our minds. We all got infected with it when we looked at that deer skeleton."

"What does it have to do with the stone circle?" Moreau asked from behind his camera.

"I don't know, Armory. Maybe nothing. Maybe it was just coincidence."

"I don't buy that," Payton said.

It was the first time he'd spoken since Moreau began to record them. They waited for him to go on.

"Look at the shape of the pit. It looks like a circle but it isn't. It's half of a three-dimensional ellipse. Those boulders were floating where its two focal points would be."

"The stone circle is an ellipse, too," Cleo said.

"Exactly."

"That's too much of a coincidence," Stainton agreed.

"You have to destroy that video recording, Armory," Angelu told him.

"Are you crazy? This is documentary gold."

She stepped forward and wrenched the camera out of his hands. Ignoring his protests, she turned it off.

"Haven't you listened to anything I said? This thing can spread through human awareness of it. We can't let anyone else know about it. Not ever."

"Give me back my camera."

He jerked it away from her before she could move out of his reach. "All we have are your psychic impressions, Angie. I know Jack has faith in your abilities, but seriously? Do you expect the rest of us to run our lives according to your intuition?"

"No," she said coldly. "I guess not."

"I'll tell you what—I don't want anyone else to find out about this until I do some research. We'll hold off saying anything about it for a while. I'll swear Pierre and Marie to secrecy. How's that?"

"If that's what you're going to do, I guess it will have to be good enough."

Stainton knew his wife's moods and realized that she was seriously pissed off. He went over and put an arm around her shoulder. "We'll talk more about it and decide what we have to do."

"There was one other thing," she said. "I don't know if it's important, but I got an impression, a word, a name of some kind."

"Name for what?" Moreau asked.

"For it, whatever it is."

They all waited in silence.

"Colonids."

"What does that mean? Jack, did you ever hear that word before?"

Stainton shook his head.

"How could it have a name, if it's so alien?" Cleo asked her.

"It doesn't. That's just the word that came into my head when I wondered what it was. I don't even know what it means. Maybe it means nothing."

"This is some real spooky Charles Fort shit we've got going on here," Peyton said.

No one disagreed.

5.

It was the following afternoon when Stainton found the worm tracks in the woods. That's what he called them in his own mind, because he didn't know what else to call them. Each of the shallow trenches bent and curved for ten or fifteen feet. They were around three feet in diameter, and they were everywhere throughout the woods. Dozens of them. They weren't dug out of the ground. It was as though the ground had suddenly ceased to exist. Large rocks were sheared off cleanly, flush with the sides of the tracks.

"I think these are the channels left in our reality by the colonids," Angelu said when he showed her the tracks.

"What happens to the dirt?"

"How the hell should I know? I'm just the psychic, remember? All I get are impressions."

"Armory didn't mean anything by that intuition remark," he told her soothingly. "It's just his way. He has as much tact as a bull in a china shop."

"I want you to talk to him when he isn't drunk, and get him to erase that video."

"Catching Armory when he isn't drunk may not be easy."

"I'm more worried about Pierre and Marie. How are we going to make them keep quiet about what they've seen?"

"Are you sure it's so important?"

"Jack, the strongest impression I got was the need to make sure no one else ever knows about this thing, or things, whatever the fuck it is. The more people that know about it, the easier it will be for it to come through."

"I guess we could all just commit suicide."

His wife didn't say anything.

"I was joking."

"I'm going to bury the stone circle. I don't want anyone else to ever find it."

"I'll help you," he said quietly.

It took a couple of hours of pick and shovel work to cover up all the stones so that it would not be obvious that they existed, once the grass grew in on top of them. Midway through, Stainton took off his shirt. His upper body gleamed with sweat and streaks of dirt. He had one of those skinny, wiry bodies that is a lot stronger than it looks. Frowning at his soiled golf shirt, he used it like a towel to wipe himself dry.

"I'm going to grab a quick shower, then walk over to Armory's place and talk to him."

She nodded and brushed a damp strand of hair away from her forehead with the back of her wrist. Her beautiful face had a haunted look. She laid a hand on his arm. "Jack, be careful. It isn't over."

He walked through the woods, as before, taking care not to step in one of the worm channels. They seemed to be everywhere. He wondered why he never saw one being formed, but only came across them after they were made? Just another unanswered question to add to the list.

There were more channels in Armory's back lawn, and something else. Here and there, thick white stalks grew up from the grass, their tops expanded in the form of grooved disks. They resembled mushrooms. There were small ones no more than a foot tall, and big ones five or six feet in height, with tops that spread three feet across. The more he looked at them, the more he thought they looked like some strange form of nouveau sculpture. The circular grooves in their tops were deep enough to fit his hand into in places.

He touched the top of one of the disks, and instantly had an impression

275

of an angry Moreau, yelling at his daughter to hurry up and get dressed. It came in a flash on all sensory channels. For just an instant he was Moreau, feeling his emotions, seeing Cleo through his eyes.

Looking at his hand, he rubbed the tips of his fingers together. No electrical shock this time. Nothing fell to dust. Nothing collapsed. Experimentally, he touched another grooved disk, and snatched his hand back, embarrassed. It was Payton, making love to Cleo. He actually felt her pressed against his skin, and felt the black man's arousal thrusting within her.

These were some kind of recordings, he realized. Mindscapes. The circular grooves on the tops of the disks were like the grooves in a phonograph record.

He wondered if Armory had already experimented with touching them? What was it about the human species that made it impossible to resist reaching out and poking anything strange? It was almost a reflex. Maybe if they had never touched the deer skeleton in the stone circle, none of this would have happened. Had the video camera any connection with these disks? It was a recording device just as they were.

He opened the back door of the house and walked in. No one kept their doors locked in this part of the island. "Armory, are you around?"

The house seemed strangely silent. He stood in the back hallway and listened. There wasn't so much as a footfall or the murmur of a voice. With a growing sense of unease, he began to walk through the rooms, calling the names of those who lived here. When he finished the downstairs, he was sure the house was empty, but he checked the upstairs just to be certain. He wandered out the front door, and saw that Armory's Mercedes and Pierre's old Volvo were in their usual parking spots on the gravel turning circle.

He felt numb. *Maybe they all got picked up by somebody and taken for a drive,* he told himself, but he didn't believe it for a second. Pierre and Marie would never both have left the house while the others were out.

Moving without haste, he walked back through the house and into the backyard. As he passed the mushroom disks, he looked at them with new insight. They were what remained of Armory, his daughter, her boyfriend, and the two servants. They weren't mindscapes, they were brain farts thrown off by the colonids in the process of devouring his friends. Mind shit. That's what they were.

When he was at the edge of the lawn, he stopped and returned to

276

the house. He found the video camera in Armory's downstairs study and erased the memory card, then broke it between his thumbs to be sure.

6.

"The colonids are going to come after us," Angelu said.

"I know that," Stainton murmured.

"Maybe we should make a run for it."

He shook his head. "If they follow us, we'll just spread the infection. We're isolated here. It's better that we stay where we are."

"Like a quarantine."

"You got it."

They sat in the living room of their old farmhouse, drinking white wine. He was in his favorite chair, and she lay half-sprawled on the black leather couch. Outside, night had fallen, but neither of them bothered to get up to turn on the electric lights or close the drapes. The rising harvest moon cast enough light through the windows to allow them to see each other in black and white.

"Something got Armory and Cleo and the others," she said, staring morosely into her wine glass.

"Whatever it was, it didn't look like a threat, or they would have run in the other direction."

"Maybe they did run."

He set his glass down decisively on the coffee table. "I'm going to do some acid."

His wife looked at him silently for several seconds. "Is this really the best time for tripping?"

"Maybe not, but we need a weapon. We need a new perspective. We need something."

Angelu didn't raise any other objection. Stainton didn't take LSD often, but he claimed that when he did take it, the drug opened his mind and made him a better writer.

"Do you want me to join you?"

"No. Too dangerous. I want you clear-headed and objective."

She got up and found the little roll of stamps under the tobacco can that held their stash of weed. He took one and put it on his tongue. Then he sat down to finish his wine. Neither spoke.

The Colonids

"Nothing's happening," he said after what seemed like a long while. "Maybe the active compound broke down from age. Those tabs are pretty old."

"The sparrows in the chimney chase the fireflies," she said.

He looked at her and noticed that her head had been replaced by a giant toadstool with red specks all over its upper surface. The air inside the living room glowed with a pale blue radiance. It was like a thin fog.

Three heavy thuds came on the front door. It sounded like someone hammering the door with their fist. He stood up.

"Someone's at the door."

"No one's at the door," the toadstool said.

The journey across the living room floor took several years.

"Don't open the door, Jack."

"Someone's at the door," he repeated.

"Whatever you do, don't invite them into the house. They can't come into the house unless you invite them."

He opened the front door, and found himself looking at another door. It floated in the air, a rectangle of soft blue light. It was featureless and had no thickness, but it almost filled the doorframe. He started to reach out his hand to rap on the floating blue door with his knuckles, but hesitated.

"Remember what happened to Alice," his wife said behind him.

Before he could knock on the blue rectangle, it opened. A man wearing the upper half of a dark business suit and an English bowler hat drifted into the living room, forcing Stainton to take a step backward.

The man had no eyes. Where his legs should have been, a thick white stalk, like the stalk of some species of fungus, extended through the blue rectangle and supported him, so that he never actually touched the floor. He did, however, have a cluster of penises, long and white and drooping down in front, sprouting from a tuft of rank black hair that resembled bear fur.

The half-man in the bowler hat opened its mouth. A stream of screeching words came forth, like a weak radio frequency that was almost drowned out by static.

"*Unger, unger, ungrier, ungrier, ungrier, grueler, ruler, growler, howler, fowler, lower, layer, under, under, hinder, finder, hounder, ever, ever, ever.*"

"It's someone trying to sell us something," Stainton told his wife.

"Wheels within wheels, Jack. Don't get run over."

"Sorry, bud, we don't want any."

He started to shut the door. A mass of fine white tendrils, each no thicker than a strand of spaghetti, erupted from the thing's mouth, which emitted a howling noise that was like an air-raid siren. They kept coming and coming, until they almost completely filled up the space in the living room, yet they never actually touched Stainton.

"Jack, take the book," his toadstool-headed wife shouted behind him. Her voice sounded dim, as though smothered beneath the weaving threads.

He turned and instinctively caught a hardcover book she threw at him through the mass of waving threads, which moved aside to allow the book to pass. It was not a book he remembered owning. The cover was elaborately-tooled black leather.

"There's no time to read," he said. "I can never find time to read."

"You don't read it, you eat it."

Suddenly, he knew what to do with the book. He opened it near the middle. Bright, iridescent colors exploded outward from the exposed pages. He held it up in front of his chest with the pages facing outward, and advanced on the man-thing.

It seemed to wilt in the multicolored light from the book. With bewildering quickness, the mass of white threads filling the air of the living room withdrew themselves back into its head, and its mouth snapped shut. It cringed and shrank backwards through the blue rectangle.

Stainton did not hesitate. He turned the book in his hands and snapped it shut over the edge of the rectangle, so that the rectangle was trapped between its pages.

"The book's too small," he said.

"Make the book bigger," his wife suggested behind him.

He tried to visualize the book enlarging in his hands. "Can't," he said with frustration.

"Then make the blue door smaller."

This worked. When he concentrated his mind and visualized the rectangle of light shrinking, it became smaller and smaller, until at last it disappeared between the pages of the black book.

His wife approached him from behind. He turned and saw that she had regained her head. She carried the wicker sewing basket they used to sew on buttons and mend tears in their clothes.

"Bind it, Jack."

Without needing a prompt, he took from the basket a length of thin red ribbon and tied it three times around the book to keep it shut, then knotted it with nine knots.

"Ding-dong, the witch is dead," he said.

7.

The next day, after he came down from the acid and caught a few hours of sleep, he examined the book. It was not, as he had assumed, a Bible. It was a how-to book on home plumbing maintenance. He had tied the book closed, not with red ribbon as he thought, but with red button thread.

"The content of the book doesn't matter," Angelu said, watching him from the sofa. "It's the structure of a book itself."

"How do you mean?"

"Think about it, Jack. What is a book, other than a kind of doorway? You open the cover and enter the world of the book by reading it. You trapped a doorway within a doorway, and locked it shut with nine knots. Nine is a mystical number. There are nine worlds in Norse mythology."

He set the book down carefully on the coffee table. "It's a good thing you knew to throw me that book last night. What was it, psychic intuition?"

"I didn't throw you the book."

"What? Yes you did."

"Unh-uh. You grabbed up the book yourself, when you started talking about a salesman at the door."

"What exactly did you see?"

"Not much. When you got up and opened the door, I saw a kind of glow but it may just have been the moonlight."

"If you didn't see anything, how did you know what I was doing with the book?"

She shrugged and grinned. "I had all morning to think about it, while you were asleep. You didn't marry a dummy, darling."

He went over and bent down to kiss her on the lips, then sat beside her. They both regarded the book.

"What do we do with it?" he asked.

"I say we bury it in the middle of the stone circle."

That afternoon, Stainton dug a hole in the middle of the ring of stones they had earlier covered with dirt. He put the sealed book inside a zip-lock plastic freezer bag, and then inside his aluminum attaché case.

"We don't want the threads rotting off the book before we're both dead from old age," he explained to his wife.

He patted down the earth with the back of his shovel and stepped back. He and his wife looked at each other, then back to the ground. It was like standing over a fresh grave. Once the grass grew over the dirt, there would be nothing to show that it had ever been disturbed.

"Eventually the trees will grow over it," he told her.

"Good," she said with some bitterness in her voice. "I never should have exposed those stones."

He dropped the shovel and gave her a hug and a kiss. "Don't beat yourself up. How were you to know?"

"I'm supposed to be psychic, remember?"

The work was done, but still they lingered under the trees.

"Is it over, Jack? Is it really over?"

"It's over," he told her with conviction.

The conviction lasted until he turned on his computer to surf the Internet, and saw Moreau's video clip of the crater on YouTube, with more than half a million views.

The Thing on the Island

1.

"**D**o you really think it's another Oak Island?"

Jimmy slapped a mosquito on his sweating neck and flashed a grin over his shoulder at Shawna MacLeod. "Something's buried there. We won't know what it's worth until we dig it up."

"Pray it isn't another Oak Island," Skeeter said behind the young woman. "Nothing ever came out of the Money Pit but broken dreams and bitter tears."

"Bitter tears," Jimmy repeated with a chuckle. "Listen to the English Lit major."

Skeeter's girlfriend, Pam, slapped him playfully on the back of his bare arm. "Don't be a cynic. It might be pirate gold. Pirates and privateers operated all up and down the Nova Scotian coast."

"It might be a lot of things," Skeeter said. "I won't believe it until I see it."

They had left Skeeter's Jeep Wrangler behind three hours ago, at the head of the fire road, and still had another full hour of hiking along the narrow trail through the hot, breathless spruce forest of northern Cape Breton before they would reach the shore of John Dee Lake. The early autumn days had been uncommonly warm, and deer flies, black flies, and mosquitoes tormented them to madness. Even a liberal application of Muskol to their bare arms and legs would not keep them away. The men carried the tents, and the women most of the other supplies. All had sleeping bags rolled and tied to the tops of their heavy packs.

Jimmy Dolan was a local Glace Bay boy, and Skeeter Smith lived in Sydney, but both women had come to the Island from away to attend

Cape Breton University. Shawna MacLeod had grown up on a farm near Antigonish, just across the Strait of Canso on the Nova Scotia mainland, and Pam Beaudreau was a native of Bathurst, New Brunswick. Physically, they were very different. Shawna was tall and blond, while Pam was small and dark-haired. They had become best friends as freshmen, and had met the local men the previous semester while taking a credit course in historical conservation methods. The young women lived in adjacent dorm rooms at Harriss Hall, and the four spent most of their free time together.

"How do you think a lake in the middle of the Cape Breton Highlands got named after a sixteenth-century English astrologer?" Pam mused.

"Don't know, don't care," Jimmy said. "I just want the treasure."

"It was probably named after another John Dee," Shawna suggested.

"I doubt it," Skeeter told her. "It's not a very common name."

"So who was this John Dee anyway?" Jimmy asked.

They all looked at Shawna. She was majoring in history.

"Don't look at me. None of my courses covered him."

"He was an Elizabethan alchemist who used a crystal ball to talk to angels," Skeeter said. "He was tight with Queen Elizabeth, and sometimes acted as her espionage agent when he traveled across Europe."

"You mean like a spy?" Jimmy asked.

"That's it."

"Pam called him an astrologer," Shawna said.

"He was both. Back then, any scholar worth his salt tried to learn the sum total of human knowledge. Dee was a typical Renaissance man. He studied mathematics, cartography, history, astrology, astronomy, alchemy, medicine, you name it."

"How do you know so much about him, Mr. Smarty Pants?" Pam asked brightly.

He grinned back at her. "How do you think? I did a search on the Internet."

"I doubt what's buried on the island has anything to do with the name of the lake," Jimmy said.

"What made you swim out to the island in the first place?"

"I don't know, Skeet. I had some free time. I decided to take a swim to cool down. The other guys in the crew were off doing something in the woods. Maybe I was curious to see what was on the island."

During the summer, Jimmy had joined a university research team taking soil samples in the Highlands to measure the effects of acid rain. It was a way to earn some money and get a full science credit at the same time.

"The trees on the island are stunted, but grow real thick in places. I don't know why I kept going, but I pushed through them and worked my way to the center. It was like something drew me deeper in."

The other three listened in silence. This was not the first time they had heard the story, but it held a fascination for them.

"I couldn't see the lake. I couldn't even see much sky until the trees opened out into a clearing, where only grass grew. At first I didn't notice anything. I sat down on a flat slab of stone that was covered with grass and lichen to rest, and then realized that somebody must have put the stone there. I started digging around in the grass with a stick. There are three slabs laid side by side, each around a yard square and three or four inches thick. All of them were split and squared with hammers, wedges, and old-fashioned stone drills. They've got to be at least a hundred years old, maybe a lot older. I tried to move one but I wasn't strong enough to do it by myself, so I swam off the island and joined back up with the sampling team."

"Why didn't you say anything to them about the stones?" Pam asked him.

Jimmy laughed scornfully. "Are you crazy? There's got to be something buried underneath them. If I had said just one word about it, the Canadian government would have taken over and I'd be lucky to get a thank-you letter. Whatever's under there, I want it all."

"You want a quarter of it," Skeeter corrected.

"Sure, sure, that's what I meant."

"What if it's just a grave? Maybe some early explorer's expedition lost a member of their party and buried him on the island."

Jimmy shook his head. "Think about it, Skeet. If someone died, would they take the extra effort to bury him on an island in the middle of a lake? Would they cut three huge rock slabs to cover the grave? It doesn't make sense. Whatever's under there has to be something valuable to make whoever buried it go through all that trouble."

"We've been through all this," Skeeter said wearily. "All this talk gets us nowhere. We agreed to help you move the slabs for a share in whatever we find under them, and we agreed not to tell the government about it. There's no use speculating about what it is. If anything's there, we'll dig it up and see."

"Not if it's as deep as the treasure on Oak Island," Shawna said.

"I don't believe there is any treasure on Oak Island, or they would have found it long ago," Skeeter told her.

"This isn't Oak Island, this is my island, and there's something buried on it. I can feel it."

Skeeter glanced back at Pam, who just rolled her hazel eyes. Ever since swearing them to secrecy and telling them about the island, Jimmy had been getting increasingly obsessive about it. He was glad they were finally going to resolve the mystery, so that Jimmy would come back to his usual happy, careless self. He didn't expect to find anything of value under the slabs.

2.

By the time they reached John Dee Lake, it was late afternoon. They were so tired, they were on the point of collapse, but Jimmy wouldn't let them rest. He made them gather windfalls from the forest, and used his hatchet to limb them and cut them to six-foot lengths, then lashed them together over cross poles with some climbing rope to make a raft. They piled all their camping gear on the raft and added their boots and most of their clothes.

The lake water was ice cold in spite of the warm sunlight that played over its rippling surface. They swam two on each side of the raft with a hand on it to steady it. The large, tree-covered island that dominated the center of the lake was not far enough away to make the swim an ordeal. The water refreshed them and gave them a respite from the flies.

"I'm going to get leeches, I know I'm going to get leeches," Shawna moaned as they reached the muddy shore and pulled the raft through the tall grasses that grew there.

"There aren't any leeches," Jimmy told her.

"If there aren't any leeches, what's that on the back of your leg?" Pam said.

"Shit, shit, shit, get it off, get it off!"

Skeeter used a disposable lighter to burn the leech until it curled up and dropped off his friend's calf. Nobody else had them. They unloaded the raft while waiting for the sun to dry their bodies, then put back on their short pants, boots, and short-sleeved shirts. Slinging the packs over their shoulders, they made their way into the dense spruce trees, following Jimmy, who took the lead.

"Remember, whatever we find, we don't report it to the government," he said. "I'm putting my trust in you guys."

"We already agreed to that," Skeeter told him.

"Just making sure you all understand. If the government knows what we're doing, they might fine us or even arrest us. We keep this to ourselves."

The other three murmured assent.

The plan was to set up the two tents in the clearing and spend the night on the island. They came out of the trees suddenly. The clearing occupied a crest that contained only grasses and a few scattered shrubs. Near its center, the sod was disturbed by rough digging.

"Nobody's been here," Jimmy said with an exhalation of relief. "It's just the way I left it." He threw off his pack and hurried over to the disturbed area.

"Shouldn't we set up the tents first, Jim?" Skeeter suggested.

"We can do that later. I need to see what's under these stones."

The slabs were of a local gray stone and just as Jimmy had described them. Most of their surface was covered with earth and grass—he had only had enough time to uncover their corners and some of their edges. Skeeter got a folding camp shovel from his pack and began to dig around the slabs. It was one of those shovels where you could lock the blade at an angle and use it as a pick. Jimmy clawed at the tall grass with his hands, pulling the sod away in patches.

"Use your shovel, stupid. You're going to break your fingernails."

Jimmy stared at him for a second. "You're right."

He got his own shovel from his pack, and the two men dug while the women stood with their arms folded and watched. In fifteen minutes they had the slabs uncovered and all the edges exposed.

"Let's get them lifted," Jimmy said, his blue eyes wide and shining.

"Wait," Pam told him. "There are some marks on the middle slab."

She fell to her knees and brushed the loose earth away from the top of the stone. It was damp, and some of it stuck to the uneven surface. She took one of the shovels and used it to scrape the dirt off.

"It's some kind of writing," Shawna offered.

"I told you it might be a grave," Skeeter said.

They all crowded their heads above the slab and began to read silently to themselves.

"It's English, I think," Pam said.

Jimmy formed the words slowly aloud.

"*Break not this ground, or ye be damned. Iohn Dee.*"

"That's 'John', not 'Ion'," Skeeter corrected. "In older English writing, they used the I for a J."

They all sat back and stared at the inscription.

"Do you think maybe it's just a joke?" Shawna asked nervously.

"John Dee," Pam breathed. "Could it really be *the* John Dee?"

"If it is, these slabs have been here for four hundred years."

"Fuck it." Jimmy stood up. "I don't care what it says, I'm going to see what's under it."

The women used the points of the shovels to pry up the central slab while the men gripped it by its corners and tipped it on its edge. They let it fall over onto the grass with a dull thud. They did the same for the other two slabs. It was surprisingly easy with four people working together.

"Now we dig," Jimmy said. He grabbed a shovel and started jamming the blade into the hard-packed earth.

"Only one of us can dig at a time," Skeeter told him. "I'm going to start setting up the tents."

"I'll help you," Pam offered.

Jimmy gave no answer. He continued feverishly prying and scraping at the hard ground, which was packed with small stones. It gave way to the shovel reluctantly. Shawna took up the other shovel and used it to push the dirt out of the way of the hole as her boyfriend piled it up on the side opposite the slabs.

"I'll be glad when this is over with," Pam murmured to Skeeter, out of the hearing of the others.

"I know what you mean."

"I thought it would be fun to hike to the lake, but Jimmy's too intense. It's like he's a little crazy."

"Once we see what's down there, if anything, it will be all over."

"You don't think there's a treasure?"

"Why would there be? In the middle of the Highlands? Talk about crazy."

By the time they had the tents put up and the sleeping bags unrolled inside them, Jimmy was in the hole up to his knees. He streamed with sweat and his shirt and shorts were soaked. His black hair lay matted flat against his forehead.

"You should take a rest," Skeeter said.

Jimmy threw the shovel at his feet. "I will. Your turn now, buddy. Earn your share."

He climbed out of the hole and went to his pack, got out his canteen, and drank long and deep.

Skeeter looked at Pam and shrugged. He dug until his hands were red and blistered and his back ached. Just as he was ready to quit, the point of the shovel struck something with a hollow thud. It was not the sound of steel against a rock. He began to tap all around the spot, feeling out the shape of whatever was buried there.

"What is it, what did you find?"

Jimmy jumped into the hole and pushed him out of the way. Grabbing the shovel from Skeeter's hands, he began to feverishly dig and scrape.

"Ease up," Pam said. "Whatever it is, you're going to break it."

This struck home. Jimmy began to probe the soil with greater care. "It's some kind of a box," he said, bent over. "I think it's made of lead."

3.

The others couldn't see into the bottom of the hole. Their own shadows blocked the light. After cursing for ten minutes, Jimmy pulled out a dull metal box about a foot long and half that in width. He set it carefully on the grass beside the hole.

"It does look like lead," Skeeter told him.

"That's what I said."

"How does it open?" Shawna asked.

Jimmy turned the box over. Something rattled faintly inside it. There did not seem to be any seam or hinge. The top was soldered into place.

"We'll have to cut it open," he said. "Get my bowie knife out of my pack."

Shawna ran to get the knife and gave it to him. He set the point in the top of the box near one corner and began to hit the butt end of the knife with the heel of his palm. The lead was not thick. The sharp steel blade cut through it like a can opener. He peeled the top away and felt inside the box. With a frown, he drew forth a rolled sheet that was held tight by a copper band, like a napkin ring.

"That looks like parchment," Skeeter said.

Jimmy slipped off the band and unrolled the sheet. It was yellowed but not brittle. He stared at it for a long time, an unreadable expression on his face. Then he started to laugh.

Pam reached down and snatched the parchment out of his hand. She and Skeeter bent their heads together over it, and Skeeter read what was written there.

"*It flies by night. It feeds on blood. Keep it from the light of the moon. I. D.*"

"What does that mean?" Shawna asked.

"It means we're fucked," Jimmy said, still laughing. "There's no gold. There's nothing but this fucking piece of paper."

"But what does it mean?"

"Who gives a shit what it means. Didn't you hear what I said? No treasure."

He started to climb out of the hole, a look of disgust on his face.

"Maybe you just didn't dig deep enough," Pam suggested.

Jimmy froze in place, half in the hole and half out of it.

"Holy shit, that's it. This was just another stupid warning to scare people away. We've got to go deeper."

"That's what they said at Oak Island," Skeeter murmured.

Jimmy didn't hear him. He was already digging furiously at the bottom of the hole, which was now deep enough to hide him from view when he bent over with the short folding camp shovel.

Skeeter put the parchment and its copper ring back into the lead box and pushed the lid shut over them.

"I'm going to build a campfire. Let me know if he finds anything."

He was just finished gathering wood from windfalls for the fire when Jimmy's excited shouts drew him back to the hole.

"This is it, buddy, this is it," the other man told him.

"What did you find?"

He leaned over the hole, and moved sideways so as not to block the light. Something smooth gleamed, reflecting the late afternoon sky.

"It's glass, or maybe crystal. Help me dig around it so we can lift it out."

They soon realized that the object was quite large. They took turns widening the hole until they were able to expose its ends and sides. It was cylindrical in overall shape, with what looked like beaten silver trim at each end. The silver had turned coal-black from all the years in the ground, but did not seem badly corroded.

"This thing is huge," Jimmy grunted as he tried to pry up one end without success. The tightly packed earth held it firmly in place in the bottom of the hole, which by now resembled an open grave.

"I'll have to dig some ledges to put my feet on. Get the rest of the climbing rope. I'll see if I can pass it under one of the ends. Then we can pull it up together."

Skeeter brought back the nylon rope. It was thin but very strong. By this time, the woman had grown bored watching them dig and had begun to prepare the evening meal over the open fire. The sun hung just above the stunted trees in the west, a great orange ball that illuminated the undersides of the clouds with gold.

Jimmy looped the rope under one end of the crystal cylinder and climbed out with both ends. He handed one to Skeeter and positioned himself on the opposite side of the hole.

"We pull together, nice and easy. Give the dirt a chance to let go."

They pulled until their fingers got tired. Then they tied the rope ends around the handles of the shovels and tried again.

"It's coming!" Jimmy said.

"Dinner's ready," Shawna called across the clearing. "It's going to get cold."

Skeeter became aware for the first time of the savory scent of beef stew in the air, intriguingly mingled with the smell of wood smoke.

"About time; I'm starving."

"Will you just forget your stomach and pull?"

They put their backs into it. A brittle cracking sound came from the hole. The rope slackened and flipped out.

"You broke it," Jimmy said with disgust.

"I broke it?"

"I told you to pull easy."

"I pulled the same as you."

Jumping into the hole, Jimmy began to lift out shards of glass.

"There's something else down here," he said with sudden excitement. "It must have been inside the glass container."

He disappeared in the hole for several minutes. Skeeter glanced over with longing at the pot suspended above the camp fire on a tripod of sticks. His stomach grumbled with discontent.

"Help me get it out."

He knelt on one knee, taking care to avoid the broken glass, and reached into the hole. Jimmy passed one end of something large into his hands that felt hard and dry and leathery. It looked like an old gnarled and twisted tree stump that had been blackened all over in a fire. It was not very heavy. They lifted it out of the hole and laid it on the stone slabs.

"What the fuck is it?" Skeeter said.

He ran his gaze up and down the thing, unable to make anything of it, other than that it was some five feet in length and a foot or so thick.

Jimmy pointed at one end. "Is that a face?"

The moment he said it, Skeeter saw it too. It looked like the wizened face of a little old man with sunken cheeks and closed eyes. Once he recognized the face, it became easy to pick out other features. He saw where its arms were close to its sides, its hands folded across its groin, its legs and feet pressed tightly together. The whole body was naked and as black as tar. It looked dried out and all shriveled up.

The women came over and stood gazing down at the creature with expressions of disgust. Skeeter couldn't quite bring himself to think of it as a man. It was human-like, but it wasn't quite human in its proportions. Its arms were too long, its legs too short, for its height.

"Maybe it's some kind of mummified monkey," he said.

"Are those wings?" Shawna asked, pointing at the bony shoulders of the figure.

Now that Skeeter studied them, the shoulders did appear to be wrapped in some kind of dried, membranous wings, like the wings of a bat. They extended all the way down the sides to its feet. He picked out other details. The folded hands of the thing had long fingernails that were almost like talons, and there was something peeking out between its heels that resembled the tip of a tail.

"It's like the Jersey Devil," he mused.

"What's that?" Shawna asked.

"It's a mythical monster, like Bigfoot. Stories of its sightings in the Pine Barrens of New Jersey go back to the start of the eighteen hundreds. Legend says it was the cursed thirteenth child of a woman named Mother Leeds, and that when it was born it was human, but that it changed into a monster. It was described as about five feet tall, with the wings of a bat."

"Trippy," Shawna said.

"Whatever the fuck it is, we're taking it back to Sydney in the Wrangler," Jimmy told them.

"We can't just leave it sitting out all night," Pam said. "The dew might spoil it, and what if it rains?"

"She's right," Skeeter agreed.

"You could put it in my sleeping bag and zip it up. I can sleep in Jimmy's bag with him," Shawna said.

"That's what we'll do," Jimmy said. "This thing may be valuable, we don't want it to spoil."

"We'll throw a ground sheet over the sleeping bag to keep it dry," Pam said.

Not long after that, they sat around the campfire enjoying their beef stew and speculated with excitement what the mummified black creature could possibly be as darkness fell and the full moon rose above the trees. A dozen steps away, the thing lay on the upturned stone slabs inside a forest-green sleeping bag, with a blue plastic ground sheet draped over it that was held down against the wind by four heavy rocks. Nothing had changed when they put the fire out and crawled into their tents to sleep.

4.

"I can't find Jimmy."

Skeeter put his hand up to block the light from the open flap of his tent and saw Shawna kneeling half in and half out. Her usually placid face bore a look of barely controlled panic.

"What's happening?" Pam asked in a sleepy voice. She unzipped the side of her sleeping bag and sat up, rubbing her eyes.

"Jimmy's gone," Shawna said, trying to control the fear in her voice. "I looked all over the island. There's no trace of him."

"Calm down," Skeeter told her as he tried to blink the sleep out of his own eyes. He glanced at his wristwatch. It was early morning. The sky through the opening in the tent was not even blue yet, and the sun was still below the horizon. "When did you last see Jim?"

"Last night. He got out of the sleeping bag and took a flashlight. He said he was going out to pee. I didn't think anything about it and just went back to sleep."

"Take it easy, Shawna; we'll look for him," Pam said.

They dressed quickly and made a careful search of the island. It did not take long.

"He's just gone," Shawna said. "He must have gone back to the Wrangler."

"There's something else," Skeeter told the women. "Come over here."

They followed him to the hole. The blue ground-cover sheet lay in a crumpled mass to one side, and the sleeping bag gaped open and empty.

"He took the mummy with him," Shawna said.

"He wants it all for himself," Pam suggested. "You know how possessive he was of his treasure, as he called it. He had no intention of sharing it with us."

Skeeter stood looking at the sleeping bag, a puzzled expression on his face. He shook his head. "That doesn't make sense. How could he carry the mummy by himself all the way back to the Wrangler? And did you notice the raft? It's still on the island. How could he swim across the lake with the mummy? Did he balance it on top of his head?"

"Don't make jokes," Shawna told him. "Jimmy's missing."

Pam turned and looked at the trees that surrounded the clearing. "Do you think maybe he drowned in the lake?"

"Why would he go swimming at night?" Shawna said. "That's crazy."

Skeeter bent and picked up the bright-yellow plastic flashlight that lay on the grass beside the sleeping bag.

"That's my flashlight," Shawna said.

Skeeter handed it to her. She tried it, but the battery was dead.

"It was left switched on," Skeeter told them.

He studied the open sleeping bag. The lead box was still there beside it. They had put it under a corner of the ground cover to keep the dew out of it.

"What it looks like to me is that Jimmy came out to take another look at the mummy and unzipped the sleeping bag."

"Then what happened?" Shawna demanded.

He said nothing.

"Then what happened?"

"He doesn't know," Pam said, more forcefully than she intended. "How is Skeeter supposed to know what happened?"

"But how can they both be just gone?" Shawna spread her hands in disbelief. "He must have taken the mummy back to the Wrangler. It's the only explanation."

The Thing on the Island

Skeeter looked up at the pale, pre-dawn sky, then at Pam, who met his eyes. Both knew what the other was thinking, but neither voiced it aloud.

"You're right, Shawna, that must be what he did," Skeeter told her. "He probably thinks he's playing a practical joke on us. I bet he's waiting for us back at the Wrangler."

There was no reason for them to stay on the island. They made an early breakfast and started to pack up the tents. Skeeter put the parchment scroll into a ziplock plastic bag and left the lead box where it was. It had no markings on it, so he saw no purpose in lugging the heavy, awkward thing down the trail. They made one more quick search of the island, just to make sure they hadn't missed anything under the trees where the brush was thickest, but they found nothing.

As before, they piled their packs onto the raft and took off most of their clothes and their boots before lowering themselves reluctantly into the icy water. Now that the sun was up, the temperature of the air had risen rapidly. It promised to be another sweltering day.

They pushed the raft away from the muddy bank, Pam in front of Skeeter on one side and Shawna alone on the other. None of them felt inclined to make conversation. They swam in silence, eager to get out on the far bank.

Skeeter heard a splash from the other side of the raft.

"What was that?" Pam asked, turning her head to look at him.

He shook his head to indicate that he had no idea, and worked his way to the end of the raft and around the other side.

Shawna was gone.

"Shawna's gone under the water," he shouted.

Taking a deep breath, he pushed away from the raft and plunged his head under the surface with his eyes wide open, looking for some trace of Shawna's long blond hair. The water was not as clear as he would have expected from such an isolated lake, but he could see a dozen or so feet through it. He began to swim downward. The lake was not deep. In seconds he touched the muddy bottom and felt across it. His hands stirred up more mud and made it impossible to see further than the length of his arms.

Something touched his side. He jerked in terror, then realized it was Pam. She put her face close to his, with bubbles escaping in a thin stream from her nose, and pointed upward. He nodded and let himself float upward to the surface, where he gulped the warm air and looked all around to see if Shawna was floating on the water. There was nothing.

Pam's dark hair broke the surface, and she gasped as she drew a breath.

"I couldn't find her," she said, her eyes wide with terror.

"She has to be down there," he said, trying to make his voice controlled, even though his heart hammered inside his ribs. "Let's take another look for her. You go that way and I'll search this side."

They searched under the water for half an hour, until they had to stop from exhaustion. So much mud had been stirred up, it was impossible to see anything. They were searching by touch alone. Numerous times they encountered each other, but never the blond woman.

"We'll have to call the police when we get back to where there's a cell signal."

"She's dead, isn't she?" Pam asked in a small voice.

Skeeter hesitated, then nodded seriously at her. "She has to be dead. There's no way she could go anywhere except under the water, and she never came up."

Tears welled into Pam's soft hazel eyes. She brushed them away with the back of her wet hand.

"Let's get the raft across and climb out of this fucking lake before we freeze," he said.

They dragged the raft partway onto the bank and got dressed.

"What do we do with Shawna's things?" she asked.

"I'll leave my tent, and take her personal things in my pack."

She stood looking back across the water at the island. There was no breeze, and the forest was dead silent. "I wish we'd never come here."

"So do I," he muttered as he closed his pack and slung it onto his shoulders.

"Do you think Jimmy is waiting at the Wrangler?"

"We won't know until we get there."

5.

They walked along the trail slowly, Skeeter in front. Both were exhausted, not just from the effort of searching the lake, but from sheer emotional fatigue.

"Suppose that thing was a Jersey Devil," Pam said.

Skeeter didn't turn his head. "If it was, it's a long way from home."

The Thing on the Island

"But suppose there's more than one of them. Suppose John Dee buried it here to keep it from getting loose and flying back to England."

"Don't talk like that. You're going to scare yourself."

"If he carried it all that way across the Atlantic Ocean, sealed up in that glass cylinder, it must be really dangerous, right? I mean, he would never do that unless it was too dangerous to bury it in England, or even in Europe."

"We don't know anything about it, Pam. Somebody might have mocked it up from mummified animal parts and put it here as some kind of joke."

"Those stone slabs were old, Skeeter."

"So it was an old joke. It makes more sense than calling it the Jersey Devil."

"I think we should hurry," she said with sudden intensity. "We're taking too long to reach the Jeep. I don't like these woods."

"Calm down. You're spooking yourself. I've seen others do it. If you let your imagination get the better of you, we're screwed."

"You're not brave, you're just in denial," she snapped at him.

Yes, I am, he thought to himself, *and I'm going to stay in denial until we're out of this fucking forest.* But he didn't say this aloud.

They had done about an hour of the four-hour hike when a dark shadow passed over their heads. Pam looked up and screamed.

"Did you see it? Did you see it?"

"See what?"

Skeeter scanned the sky that was visible between the treetops on either side of the trail. It was bright and blue and empty. Not even a cloud.

Pam grabbed his hands in hers and gripped his fingers with surprising strength, staring into his eyes.

"It was the Devil," she said.

"You're letting your imagination run away with you. It was just a bird."

"We have to get out of here now. It killed Jimmy and Shawna, and now it's coming for us."

She turned and started to run down the trail.

"Pam, stop. Pam, don't run like that. Goddamnit, Pam, don't run."

She had already disappeared from view behind some trees. Cursing through his gritted teeth, he started to run after her. She was having a panic attack. If he didn't stop her, she might run right into a tree.

The ground cover was so thick and tall, he couldn't see where he was putting his feet. He stepped into a gap between two large rocks and fell hard to the side. Before he struck the ground he heard a sickening crack and felt a kind of electrical shock of pain lance up his left leg.

He lay on the ground, not daring to move. Whenever he tried to shift his body, the pain washed over him and almost knocked him out. At last he summoned enough determination to push himself to a sitting position and used both hands to lift his foot from the hole between the rocks.

His ankle was broken. There was no possible doubt about that. His foot hung limp at an impossible angle, and blood dripped out his hiking boot.

"Shit," he said, then he screamed it as loudly as he could.

Should he take off the boot, or was it better to leave it on? He decided he didn't want to try to pull it off over his heel. The pain was almost impossible to bear when he did nothing at all, and didn't even touch his foot. He doubted he would be able to pull off the boot without passing out.

It was about twenty minutes later that Pam appeared, returning along the trail. When she saw him on the ground, she let out an involuntary cry and ran over to him.

"You came back," he said with a forced smile.

"What happened to your foot?"

He told her how he had broken his ankle.

"It was my fault. I shouldn't have run like that."

"It wasn't your fault, Pam."

He looked at her with admiration. It must have taken all the courage she possessed to come back along the trail. She kept glancing over her shoulders and up at the sky. She was still terrified.

"Can you walk on it?"

"Not the way it is now. No way."

She began to unlace his boot. He winced but pressed his lips together to keep from screaming.

"I need to see how bad it is," she said in apology.

After loosening the laces as much as possible, she carefully worked the boot over his heel. This time he could not keep the scream inside. His vision got dark for a few seconds. She pulled the boot off his toes and edged down his sock, which was soaked in blood.

"Jesus, Skeeter, there's a bone sticking through."

"Just what I needed to know."

"I have to stop the bleeding."

They had not brought a first-aid kit with them. She ripped up her spare shirt into strips and used them to bind his ankle tightly.

"Maybe if I make a brace, you'll be able to walk on it."

He didn't object. Privately, he was convinced that he wasn't going to be doing any walking any time soon. She was gone for a while. He closed his eyes, and when he opened them, he found her tying four sticks to his ankle, two on each side, with the rest of her shirt. *At least it looks straight,* he thought. Every time her fingers touched his skin, the pain was like that of a toothache, lancing up his leg, only much worse. It was the worst pain he had ever felt.

"I've got some extra-strength Tylenol in my pack. You better take three or four."

He didn't argue. He must have passed out for a few minutes, because when he opened his eyes, she was wiping his sweat-covered face with a towel. She took three pills from the little bottle and put them into his mouth, then held her canteen to his lips so that he could fill his mouth with water. He swallowed the pills.

The sky looked different. There were puffy white clouds in it. *They came over fast,* he thought.

"We'll wait for the pills to work before you try to stand up," she said.

"How long do you think we should wait?"

She shrugged. "Maybe an hour."

He glanced at his watch. His eyes widened. It was late afternoon. "Was I unconscious?"

"Some of the time. You went in and out."

"I don't remember."

"It doesn't matter."

He gripped her hand and held it. "Listen, Pam, you have to go down the trail and get help."

"I'm not going to leave you again, Skeeter."

"It's not about that. We have to be practical. Even if I can stand up and hobble, I won't be able to move very fast. We had three hours of hiking ahead of us when I fell. It would take me at least six hours to do the trail with this broken ankle, and I'm going to be honest with you, I don't even think I can stand on it."

Tears formed in her eyes and ran down her cheeks. "What do you want me to do?"

"Just hike down the trail to the Wrangler. You know Jim always keeps a spare key under the floor mat. Drive to where you can get a cell signal and call the police. It's the only way. I'll be fine here. I'll probably sleep the whole time."

She hesitated, but the logic of their predicament was impossible to deny. The trail was very little used. It might be weeks before any other human being hiked along it. He couldn't walk on such a badly broken ankle. There was only one conclusion.

"I have to go," she said, and he nodded. "But I don't want to leave you."

"I'll be fine," he said, trying to make his voice cheerful and upbeat.

She glanced fearfully around at the trees. "What if that thing comes back?"

"It was a bird, Pam," he said firmly. "It was just the shadow of a bird."

She stared into his eyes without speaking for a time.

"I'll leave my water along with yours, and my pain pills. Don't take too many of them at once."

He smiled crookedly. "They don't do any good anyway."

She did her best to make him comfortable and covered him with a plastic ground sheet. He was shivering all through his body from shock.

"I'll be back as soon as I can," she said, standing up and looking down at him.

"I know you will, hon. Take it easy on the trail. Watch where you step. Don't run."

She vanished from view between the trees.

6.

I've got to hurry, hurry, hurry, she thought as she followed the narrow path through the dense undergrowth. In places it widened out and became almost a track, but in other places it all but vanished from view. She wished she had paid more attention to the trail markers on the hike to the lake. With Jimmy and Skeeter to guide her, she had not imagined it would be necessary.

Twice she wandered off the trail into the trees, and it took her precious minutes to find the trail once again. She glanced at her wristwatch. After five. It was early fall, but the days were already getting short. She realized she had to hurry, or she would not reach the Wrangler before it got dark.

At least there will be a full moon again tonight, she thought. *Skeet will be able to see around him, even if his flashlight fails.* She didn't have a flashlight in her pack. How could she have imagined that she might ever need one? Every so often, she glanced back over her shoulder. She tried to keep from peering into the shadows between the trees on either side of the trail. They were mesmerizing and tended to draw her attention, and she needed to stay aware of how she placed her feet. It would be fatal if she managed to hurt herself the way Skeet had done. If only she hadn't run, he would never have fallen trying to catch up to her.

Something cracked in the woods to her left. She stopped and tried to see into the maze of hanging evergreen boughs and dark trunks. Taking a breath, she held it and listened. There was another crack of a breaking stick.

It could be an animal, she thought. *Maybe a moose or a bear.* Under ordinary circumstances, this possibility would have frightened her, but today she found it strangely comforting. A moose was sane and normal. It was a threat she understood. Skeeter had not seen what she had seen when she looked up at the shadow sailing over them.

She started to walk faster, while trying to make as little noise as possible. The Wrangler seemed so far away. Somehow, she never doubted for an instant that it would be there, waiting for her. Jimmy had not carried the mummy off the island. Just the opposite had happened when he opened the sleeping bag under the moonlight to gloat over his treasure. What had the warning parchment from John Dee said? "Keep it from the light of the moon." That was it. Maybe it was the Jersey Devil and maybe it wasn't, but it was something just as evil.

Another crack of a broken twig came through the trees, this time from directly in front of her, on the trail. She stopped, frozen into place by terror, unable even to move her feet for fear of making a noise. Another crack, and a crackle of dry brush as something pressed its body between the bushes. She wished she could somehow make herself invisible. She wished she were somewhere else, anywhere else that was not these woods.

Through the trees she saw a black hand, long talons extending from the ends of its widespread fingers, push aside a spruce branch. Something snapped inside her. She ran off the trail to her right side with no regard to her own safety. The beating branches cut at her face but she ignored the pain. Several times she stumbled and almost fell, but she kept running. It was the only way to hold the scream that was in her throat from bursting forth.

She finally stopped running when she could not run any more. Her throat was raw from gasping for air, and she tasted blood in her mouth. Her side ached. All her clothes were soaked with sweat. Somehow she had managed to keep her pack on her back. She stood for a long time, surrounded by dense trees, while her heartbeat slowed and her breathing returned to normal.

Glancing at her watch, she experienced a pang of pure horror. It was almost sunset. She had to get back on the trail—it was her only way out of this forest. Which way was it? Has she run in a straight line? She began to retrace her path as best she could, but the trees looked completely different when seen from the opposite side. She had not had enough presence of mind to memorize any landmarks. Her flight was a jumbled blur in her memory.

She wondered if her footsteps were taking her closer to that creature, that monster, that thing, whatever it was. Even so, she had no other course to follow. If she kept away from the trail, she would become hopelessly lost, and Skeeter would never get the help he needed. She didn't know much about medicine, but she knew it wouldn't take many hours before his ankle got infected, with the bone sticking out like that. How long could he last if no help came? A few days at best.

I'm already lost, she thought. *I don't know where the trail is. I'm lost.*

When the sun sank, and the sky turned from blue to black, and the full moon rose, she was still pushing her way between the unyielding trees. The little green needles made her hands red, and the spruce gum stuck to everything—her clothes, her skin, her hair. She had been bitten so many times by mosquitoes, she no longer paid any attention to them. Blood streamed from the edges of her exposed ears where the blackflies had taken little pieces of her flesh. She had not had a drink of water since the morning, and her throat felt dry and sore.

Above the trees she heard the beating of wings. She stopped, too weary and emotionally numb to run. A shadow passed in front of the moon, a large black shape that flew swiftly through the air. She heard a thud on the ground. Something rolled a short distance and came to rest against her foot.

The Thing on the Island

When nothing more happened in the night sky, she looked down. It was round and large. She turned it with the toe of her boot. The bloody face of Skeeter stared up at her with dead eyes. His head had not been severed cleanly but had been torn from his shoulders.

She dropped to her knees and touched his cheek. The blood was sticky on her fingertips. Lifting her face, she screamed and screamed and screamed, until, finally, it came back.

Womb of Evil

1.

The black Mercedes ground its way up the steep grade of the narrow mountain road in low gear. The road was terrible, but the big old sedan had evidently been built with these conditions in mind and was able to handle the potholes and washouts, some of which had not been completely filled in since the last rainy season.

Father Theodore Ranier peered out his side window and trembled at what he saw. On his side of the car, the mountain fell away straight down for hundreds of feet. The scrub trees on its slope would do nothing to stop the plunge of the car, should the driver make a mistake. He worked a finger inside his clerical collar and pulled it away from his plump, sweating neck.

The army colonel seated beside him on the soft leather of the rear seat chuckled.

"Don't worry, Father, my driver knows what he is doing."

The priest glanced at the officer and saw a wire-thin man of no great height with an equally thin moustache on his upper lip and large dark eyes that were almost womanly.

"This entire assignment is absurd, Colonel Martinez," he said in a quarrelsome tone. "I shouldn't even be here."

The colonel shrugged and pursed his lips. "We share something in common."

"Yes, what is that?" Ranier asked. He winced as the car went over a boulder and lurched to the edge before the driver guided it back into the road.

"We are both soldiers. I am a soldier of the state, and you are a soldier of the Church. We go where we are ordered to go and we have no say in the matter."

"On that you are correct," Ranier agreed. "I tried to tell my superiors at the Vatican that it was a foolish extravagance to send me all the way to Peru, when it was perfectly obvious that the matter could be resolved by the local bishop, but they insisted I fly here to make a report."

"I, too, will have to type up a report when this affair is concluded," Martinez said sadly. "I hate paperwork."

"At least it won't take us very long to conclude the matter. I already know what I will find at the monastery."

"It is a strange place," Martinez said. "We hear stories about it, down in the city, but it's hard to know what is fact and what is only superstition."

"I can give you a few facts. The Hieronymite monastery of Santa Maria is one of the oldest monasteries in South America. It was founded in 1549."

"I didn't know it was so old."

"It was originally established to give the priests who came with the conquistadors a place of retreat and holy reflection."

"What does this, how did you say it, 'Hieronymite' mean?"

Ranier tried to keep the contempt out of his expression. This man was stupid, like most military men. "The Hieronymites are the followers of the example of Saint Jerome, who was a hermit. They are devoted to prayer and solitude."

"The monks keep to themselves," Martinez agreed. "They seldom venture outside the wall of the monastery compound."

"The thing is, the Hieronymites as a religious order are moribund," the priest said. He noticed the lack of comprehension on the officer's face. "They hardly exist anymore. There are a handful of nunneries in Spain and one monastery, but even that is a modern revival."

"Is that why the Vatican wants to shut Santa Maria down?"

Ranier felt his ears pop and chewed the air. The sounds of the car changed and became louder. The road had carried them to a considerable elevation. He peeked past his right shoulder and felt vertigo. There was nothing beyond the window but empty air. The car's tires must be right on the edge.

"The monastery is beset by superstitious and decadent practices. The information we've received claims that the monks have taken native women to live with them and bear them children. Some of these children are said to be congenitally deformed due to incestuous unions. It is even said that the monks venerate some kind of ancient pagan idol. I assure you, Colonel, if any of these reports are accurate, my visit is just a formality. I've been given the authority by my superiors to close the monastery down."

"Why have my men and I been assigned to accompany you? Do you expect resistance?"

"I've been told by the Bishop that it is almost certain. The Hieronymites have been allowed to do as they please for so long, they are like a world unto themselves."

"Well, don't worry." Martinez slapped the pistol in its holster at his side. "We can handle any resistance a few unarmed monks are likely to give."

Ranier looked behind through the rear window of the car at the canvas-covered army truck that followed close behind them, lurching from side to side on its stiff springs. He almost pitied the soldiers in the back. They must be terrified.

"I doubt your men will even be needed. The Bishop insisted they be sent with me for my protection, and I didn't argue with him."

"I'm delighted that I was assigned to protect you," the colonel said. "It makes a welcome change from chasing bandits through these hills."

The priest cranked down his window and breathed the air. Now that they were so high in the Sierra, it was cooler but still dry. Its clarity invigorated him. He had never breathed such clean air.

"Look over there, Father," the colonel said, pointing out Ranier's open window. "Across the valley."

Ranier squinted and found the building by following with his eyes the thin, winding line of the road on the mountain slope.

"Is that the monastery?"

"That's Santa Maria."

It was a reddish rectangle broken by numerous small windows on its upper levels, and roofed with a steep pitch of red tiles. Even in the distance it gave the impression of size. It was located near the crest of a low mountain. High walls extended out on either side of the imposing facade and ran backwards behind it, no doubt enclosing the monks' garden and livestock. To the left of the wall, a small cluster of huts were visible.

"Ugly, isn't it?" Martinez said. "Like a big red face frowning down the mountain."

Ranier looked again, and had to admit to himself that the building did have a forbidding aspect.

They stopped so that the soldiers could remove a large boulder that had tumbled down from somewhere above and lodged itself in the middle of the road. It took all the efforts of the six men to roll the massive chunk of stone over the edge of the cliff. Ranier leaned over the edge and enjoyed with the rest the pleasure of watching it rebound down the slope, smashing trees out of its path as though they were matchsticks.

That could be the car, he thought. One slip of the driver's hands on the steering wheel, and it would follow the rock down the mountain with him tumbling around inside it. He forced the image from his mind. In a couple of days he would be back in Rome, enjoying Renate's gentle embrace. He reminded himself to buy her a little present at the airport gift shop before leaving Peru.

2.

It was the middle of the afternoon by the time they arrived at the monastery. In front of its sheer front was a small area for turning and parking vehicles. The soldiers jumped down from the truck and began to unload their gear without being told.

Ranier climbed from the car on stiff knees and wandered to the edge. The view across the mountains was inspiring, but also terrifying. Not so much as a low wall divided the parking lot from a sheer drop of a thousand feet. It was a relief to turn and walk away from it.

The monastery presented a grim facade of red bricks unbroken by windows on its lower level. There was only a plain oak door not much larger than the door to a house, and this too was windowless. On the left side of the building, a gate in the wall led to the enclosed grounds behind it. A scattering of peasant huts hugged the exterior side of the wall, but at present they appeared empty.

Ranier approached the door with Martinez and hammered on its planks three separate times, but it was not until Martinez had one of his soldiers apply the butt end of his rifle to the door that it finally creaked open on its iron hinges.

Ranier pushed impatiently past the young monk in his archaic brown and white robes, the traditional habit of the Order of Saint Jerome. "I am

Father Theodore Ranier, special investigator from the Vatican. No doubt you received the letter that was sent advising your abbot of my coming."

The young monk stared at him. Ranier studied his face more closely. He had the standard physiognomy of the Peruvian Indians—a short and stocky body, dark copper skin, and an enormous hawk-like nose—but there was something about the cast of his facial features that was not quite right. His eyes were smaller than normal and slightly slanted. They continued to stare at the priest dully, and Ranier noticed a line of drool at the corner of his partially open mouth.

"This boy is retarded," Martinez said, continuing into the large entrance hall. His soldiers followed with their weapons and canvas sacks of gear.

The floor of the hall was red brick, its ceiling high above their heads paneled hardwood. Windows on the second and third levels let ample daylight into the hall. A staircase of dark carved wood ran up on the right side to a landing, and continued from this upward to serve the higher two levels. Here and there, the heads of monks gazed down over the banisters, silent and impassive. Ranier noticed that all of them were of a strongly Indian cast, and many had the same congenital facial deformities as the young monk who had opened the door. They were the unmistakable signs of severe inbreeding.

A gray-haired monk came down the stairs, moving with nimble steps in spite of his obvious weight of years.

"You must be Father Theodore Ranier," he said with a curious accent to his Spanish. "I've been expecting you."

The priest stepped forward. "Am I addressing the Abbot of Santa Maria?"

"My religious name has always been enough for me," the old man said. "Call me Brother Matthew."

"Well, Brother Matthew, I would like to have a few words with you in private, if I may."

"Of course, come with me to my sitting room. You must be thirsty after your long drive up the mountains." He glanced at the colonel. "Would your friend care to join us?"

Martinez looked at Ranier, and the priest shook his head.

"Thank you, Brother Matthew, but I need to supervise my men. Another time."

Ranier followed the old abbot out of the entrance hall and into a modest room with several chairs and a sofa. On the walls hung woven mats with creatures from native myths on them. He recognized the winged serpent and the thunder bird. There were no religious scenes, and no crucifix.

Brother Matthew went to a sideboard and poured brandy from a crystal decanter into bell-shaped glasses.

"I can't express how delighted I am that the Vatican heeded my request and sent you here."

Ranier regarded him with surprise as he accepted his brandy. "It was your request that brought me here?"

"I can't imagine how it could have been anything else."

"Why did you ask that I be sent?"

The abbot sat heavily in the chair opposite. Once he stopped moving, he looked tired. "Because the Vatican wishes to close my monastery, and that can never be permitted."

Ranier sipped his brandy and paused to appreciate it. "I have been given the authority to close Santa Maria. You should be aware of this."

"Thank you for telling me. I will be equally candid with you. I cannot and will not allow you to close this monastery."

Ranier raised his eyebrows and swirled his brandy in his glass. "You really have no say in the matter, Brother Matthew. It is my decision to make, and I will make it without coercion from you or anyone else. I have the authority of the Holy See and I have been given the army to enforce my decision."

"So I observed. But even so, you cannot abolish this institution. The work we do here is too important."

Ranier smiled blandly at him. "I was under the impression that the followers of Saint Jerome did nothing but pray."

"Here in this place we have one other duty."

"And what would that be?"

The old man finished his brandy and pushed himself out of his chair. "It is better if I show you. Follow me."

3.

They went back into the entrance hall and followed it to the rear of the great building, where there was an exterior door. A monk opened this for them. They passed out to a field at the back of the building that was completely enclosed by a high brick wall. The dark crowns of the surrounding mountains frowned down disapprovingly over the top of this barrier. At the end of the enclosure were vegetable gardens and pens for goats. But what drew Ranier's eye was the stone structure that occupied the center of the grounds.

"Is that a pyramid?" he asked in surprise.

"It is," the old man said.

They walked slowly toward it. The gray stone blocks that composed it were weathered with centuries but intact. It was of no great size but it was beautifully carved with animal heads and decorative friezes.

"Is it Aztec?" the priest asked.

"No, it is much older than that."

"What on earth is it doing in the middle of the monastery grounds?" He remembered the rumor that the Hieronymites worshipped some stone idol.

"Our high wall prevents others from entering it."

"It has an interior?"

"Come and see."

As they drew near, Ranier realized that what he had first taken for a shadow across a hollow in the side of the pyramid was an open doorway. The projecting carved head of a wolf on one side and the head of a panther on the other glared at him with malevolent hatred. The stone eyes seemed to follow him as he entered under the cooling shadow and passed through the portal. The stone slab beneath his shoes sloped downward. Somewhere ahead in the darkness, light flickered. They continued into an open chamber that was illuminated by two flaming lamps set in the rock on either side of the rough entrance to a cave.

"The pyramid was built over the mouth of this cave," he said.

The abbot nodded, watching him.

"Why?"

"For the same reason my holy order built the wall around the pyramid five centuries ago."

He took one of the oil lamps from its niche and bent his head to enter the cave. After several seconds, Ranier followed him.

The floor of the cave sloped downward. Its walls were of rough natural stone, but in places crude tools had been used to widen the passage or level its floor. After descending what seemed to Ranier to be at least several hundred feet, the tunnel widened into a chamber. It was featureless save for a false doorway that had been carved into the wall opposite the tunnel.

Ranier went forward to study it. The stone carving was amazing in its precision. It almost appeared that the stone had been cut by some mechanical drilling tool, so sharp were its edges and corners. The doorway extended into the stone about four feet and terminated on a black wall. It was rectangular in shape, not quite tall enough to stand in. Around the frame of this doorway wound the carved body of a large snake, which the priest assumed must be an anaconda. The Piura Region of Peru where the monastery was located was not far removed from the headwaters of the Amazon River.

"Why have you shown me this?" Ranier asked impatiently. "There's nothing in here."

"There's nothing here ... now," Brother Matthew said.

"Are you implying that the doorway is not always empty?"

"I state it outright, and by doing so I break the most sacred vow of my order, which has never been broken in five centuries."

Ranier looked around the empty cave, then back at the false doorway. "Do you mean people bring things and put them in the doorway?"

"Not people, no. Not people."

In spite of himself the priest felt a shiver run along his spine. The obtuseness of the abbot was beginning to vex him.

"Tell me what you wish to tell me."

The old man pulled himself up to his full height and met the priest's gaze. "At certain times of the year, which can be predicted astronomically, certain ... objects appear in this doorway."

"When you say appear, you mean—"

"No one brings them. They simply appear. They have been doing so for thousands of years, long before the monastery of Santa Maria was founded on this site, long before even than the pyramid was built over this cave."

The old man was insane, Ranier thought. He and his entire inbred order of monks worshipped a pagan shrine. The Vatican should never have waited so long to close this monastery.

"I have native blood in my veins," the abbot said. "So do my fellow monks. For uncounted centuries my tribe has watched over this cavern, and waited for the gifts to appear."

"Will you show me some of these gifts?" Ranier asked to humor his fantasy.

"That is not possible."

"Why not?"

"Because we destroy them as soon as they appear. We have always destroyed them, since before the Spanish came or the Aztecs ruled this land."

"Why do you destroy the things that appear?"

The old man's face hardened. "They are evil. My people call this cave *Xicotil-papajo,* the Womb of Hell."

Ranier almost found himself persuaded by the old man's measured tone of voice. In a place as eerie as the cave it was possible to believe almost anything. "What kind of things come through the portal?"

Brother Matthew blinked several times in recollection. "Once it was a red scorpion, about this long." He held his hands eight or nine inches apart. "It killed a young monk before we were able to kill it. On another occasion it was a bottle of clear liquid. We discovered it to be an acid that would eat through stone or flesh with equal ease. Yet another time it was a kind of music box that made those who listened to it stone deaf. Brother James smashed it to a thousand fragments, but to this day he cannot hear."

Ranier shook his head in amazement. Such a bizarre mythology could only sustain itself in complete isolation from the greater world. All the monks must share this collective delusion. Perhaps pernicious objects were even smuggled into the cave from time to time to sustain the myth. He had read about this kind of thing. The taboo of the gifts was used as a way to bind the monks to the monastery. Without it the place would probably have fallen to decay decades ago.

"May I see what's left of these gifts after you destroy them?"

The abbot shook his head. "We burn them to ashes. If they will not burn we hammer them to dust."

Of course. There would be no evidence to disprove the mythology or sow doubt among the true believers. He decided to see how far this protection of the myth extended.

"Why haven't your monks simply sealed up the entrance to the cave?"

"We tried several times. The cave opens itself. It will not stay sealed."

And again, the shared delusion protects itself from logical exegesis, the priest thought. A psychologist could write a paper on this.

"How do you suppose the cave chooses what gift to bring forth?"

"That is a mystery of God." The abbot hesitated. "Sometimes I think it must make what is in the minds of the brothers as they sleep, but how it determines which thought to make real, I don't know. And they are always things of nightmare, never good things."

"Is there any way I could observe the arrival of one of these gifts?"

The old man's face lit up and he nodded vigorously. "Yes, yes, that is why I was so pleased by your arrival. You came on the eve of a greater gift."

"Greater gift?"

"The cave spawns little gifts often, every few weeks or sometimes every few days, but the greater gifts only come at infrequent intervals. It has been years since the last greater gift."

"What exactly makes them greater?"

The abbot shrugged. "The gifts are bigger, heavier, more complicated."

Ranier smiled. No doubt the abbot and his monks had some ritual and grand illusion planned for him that was designed to change his mind about closing down the monastery. Well, he was in no great rush. Let them put on their stage performance. It would make no difference to his final judgment, which he had already made in his own mind. This place was an abomination. It had to be shut down.

4.

"I just got off the radio," Colonel Martinez told Ranier, talking as he chewed a piece of tough flat bread he had just torn from its loaf. "The road is out. A rock fall buried about a hundred feet. I was told it will take several days to clear it."

"So we're trapped here," Ranier said.

"For a few days."

They sat side by side at the long dining table in the dining hall of the monastery, enjoying the evening meal of roast goat, potatoes and flat bread with butter and cheese. The food was plain but the red wine was fair. The colonel drank freely of it.

"Your men were going to stay overnight at the monastery in any case," the priest said. "What difference does a day or two make?"

"That is what I say," the colonel agreed.

A young woman in a long brown and white robe, with a hood drawn over her head, poured more wine into his goblet and silently moved away.

"Have you noticed how many young women are in this place?" Martinez said, lowering his voice.

Ranier nodded, looking around the dining hall. There were almost as many women present as men. They served the men seated at the table without speaking or smiling and withdrew themselves quickly. There was a marked resemblance between the faces of the women and the faces of the monks.

"Are they nuns?" the colonel asked.

The priest shook his head. "There are no nuns here. Heaven alone can say exactly what purpose these women fulfill."

Martinez laughed through his nose. "I think I know one purpose they serve. There are children in the huts just outside the monastery walls, and they all look a little bit like the monks."

Ranier had been thinking the same thing. How else was a remote mountain monastery to replenish its monks over a span of centuries? The rumors that had caused him to be dispatched from Rome were evidently true.

One girl in particular caught his eye. She was prettier than the rest, about nine years old. She reminded him of his own dear Renate, who waited for him back in Rome. How he missed her sweet kisses. That was the hardest part of these missions of discovery to remote locations. His penis twitched between his thighs. As though sensing his thoughts, the girl blushed and hurried away back toward the kitchen.

"At least my men won't be cold in bed," the colonel joked. "There are many women here."

Women did not interest Ranier, but there were also many young girls. He wondered if it would be possible to induce one of them into his room that night. A few silver coins or some trinket should be enough, if only he could find a girl of the right age. The younger ones were so timid.

When the girl returned to fill his cup, he caught her wrist and stretched his neck to bring his lips close to her ear. "If you come to my room later, I will have a gift for you."

She blushed and seemed on the brink of tears. He released her when it appeared she intended to cry out and she hurried away with her head bowed. A few of the elder monks at the table cast him dark looks.

"Don't worry, my friend," Martinez said. "You will find another girl who is more reasonable."

The colonel was wrong. His winks and smiles and quiet hints were futile. In the end he was forced to retire alone to the small room and the narrow cot that had been provided for him. After he blew out the lamp, he continued to hear through the darkness the harsh laughter of the soldiers, and occasionally the protests or shrieks of women. The soldiers had been more fortunate. But then, their tastes were not so refined as his own.

When he fell asleep, he dreamed he was back in his apartment in Rome. He lay in his bed on his back, and little Renate straddled him, laughing. They were both naked. Renate's mother, who was also his housekeeper, stood beside the bed and held the little girl so that she did not fall off his thighs. It was such a blessing to have an understanding mother. It opened so many more possibilities that otherwise would have remained closed.

He was on the edge of orgasm when he awoke from the dream. He groaned and slowly relaxed his back, which was bent in a curve. Sweat covered his chest and face. As his desire slowly subsided, he lay listening to the silence. The monastery was quiet now. The soldiers had finished with the women.

Sleep eventually came again, this time without dreams.

5.

"You and the colonel are the first men not of our tribe to see the coming forth of a gift," Brother Matthew told Ranier in a low voice.

The cave was crowded. In addition to the abbot, himself, and Martinez, there were four monks present. All four were armed with machetes or hammers. They stood together, two on either side of the false doorway, silent and intense in their concentration.

The abbot took out a well-worn silver pocket watch and consulted it closely before snapping its cover shut and returning it to its pocket in his white and brown robes. He told the four younger monks to ready themselves. They stood sweating in the flickering lamplight, bodies as rigid as statues, eyes fixed on the false doorway in the rock.

"It will come any time now," Brother Matthew murmured to Ranier.

They waited in silence for several more minutes. Colonel Martinez paced restlessly back and forth.

"Are we to wait all afternoon?" he said sullenly, a scowl on his thin face. He still suffered the effects of the wine he had drunk the previous evening.

"It comes," the abbot said. "Look, it comes."

Ranier narrowed his eyes. The guttering lamp flames made it hard to be certain, but it did appear as though the space inside the doorway had darkened. He could no longer see the back of the niche, and wondered if it were possible that the back wall was moveable. That would explain how the sudden appearances the abbot had talked about might be contrived. They would indeed appear miraculous to the credulous monks.

There came from the doorway a pulse that was not wind and not sound but something else that could be felt as it passed over the body. It made Ranier feel dizzy and nauseated for several seconds.

"It comes, be ready," Brother Matthew said to the monks.

Suddenly, there was something crouched inside the false doorway. The shadow obscured its details, but it was almost as large as a man. It moved, and one of the young monks uttered the name of Jesus.

"Strike now," the abbot cried.

"Halt." There was an edge of military command in Colonel Martinez's harsh voice that froze the monks.

He stepped forward. In his left hand he held a flashlight and in his right hand, his automatic pistol. He aimed the flashlight and turned it on. Its beam illuminated a naked young girl who crouched in the hollow of the false doorway. She blinked against the brightness. Her eyes were a startling blue.

"The first man who raises a weapon against this child will die by my hand," Martinez said.

"You don't know what you are doing," Brother Matthew cried. "It must be killed."

He rushed forward, but the colonel swept him backward and off his feet with a blow from his left arm. The beam of the flashlight danced over the walls and ceiling of the cave. Ranier saw one of the monks raise his machete and move toward the doorway.

The blast of the automatic was deafening in the confined space of the cave. It left Ranier's ears ringing. The air filled with the sharp tang of gunpowder. The monk let the machete fall and staggered back, holding his ribs with his hand. When the beam of the flashlight settled on him, Ranier saw red seeping between his fingers.

"I have bullets for all of you," Martinez said.

The remaining monks backed away from the girl in confusion. One helped the old man back to his feet.

"Go and get her," Martinez told Ranier. "I will cover you with my gun."

The priest went forward cautiously. The girl had not moved from the doorway. She glanced around nervously. Her skin was almost white, and her long hair a reddish-blond. She was slender and pretty. He wondered where the monks could have found such a girl? No doubt the wily old abbot had selected her to play the part of the gift because of her unusual appearance. The back of the doorway must have a moveable panel. Had the monks really intended to kill the girl? It would have been murder. More likely they would have simulated killing her, then carried away her body before the deception was discovered. The bold action of Colonel Martinez had derailed their dramatic presentation.

He put his hand on the girl's bare arm. Her skin felt cool to his touch but she was not shivering. Gently, he pulled her out of the doorway. The monks all shrank away from her in terror, even the old abbot. Ranier put his arm around her shoulders and drew her close. "Don't be frightened, my child. No one will harm you," he murmured into her ear.

"They tried to commit murder," Martinez said. "It's a criminal matter now."

"I think it would be best if you had your men round up all the monks and place them under guard in a secure location," Ranier said. "If they are not confined, I'm worried they might try to kill this girl."

"Would they really be so foolish?"

"The mythology of their monastery demands it. Remember, Colonel, this is their entire world. They don't know anything else."

Martinez nodded agreement. The gunshot had drawn two of his men into the cave. He told them to take the monks into custody, and to gather the other monks into one of the ground-floor rooms.

"That was quite a trick," he told Ranier, who was murmuring gently to the girl. "Did you see how it was done?"

"False back in the doorway. It has to be that."

Martinez went to the doorway and felt around inside it. He thumped against its back with his clenched fist. "It feels like solid rock to me."

"It was a very convincing illusion."

"What do you want me to do with the girl?"

"Leave her with me. I'll see that she gets something to eat and some clothes to wear. I want to question her."

Martinez laughed through his nose. "Of course you do. I'll leave her to you."

Am I really so transparent? Ranier wondered. Or was it merely that a man such as Martinez thought the worst about everyone he met?

6.

The soldiers tried to gather up all the monks, but when they learned what had taken place in the cave, unreasoning terror possessed them. Half of them managed to escape through the front door of the monastery before the soldiers could stop them. Several were shot and wounded, but they were carried away by the other monks. In the end Martinez was only able to put about two dozen of the sullen men into confinement in a storeroom off the kitchen. Among them were Brother Matthew and three of the young monks who had been in the cave. The monk shot in the side by the Colonel died shortly after being put into the room, so Martinez ordered him taken away and wrapped in blankets, then placed into the relative coolness of the pyramid.

"When the road is repaired, I'll take the abbot and the other three who were in the cave back to the city for trial," Martinez told Ranier.

"I'm going to tell the Bishop to drive everyone out of the monastery and seal up the door. It should have been done long ago. There is nothing Christian in these walls."

Ranier tried to induce the women who remained in the monastery to find the girl something to wear and to eat, but they shrank away when they saw her, eyes wide with terror, and would not approach. He gave up the effort and managed to find a woman's robe in one of the rooms on the fourth floor, where most of the women slept. When the girl was no longer naked, he led her down the flights of stairs and back to the kitchen, and gave her some bread to chew and goat's milk to drink. She fingered the bread and smelled the milk, but she did not put either into her mouth.

"Why won't you talk to me?" he asked her in a gentle voice across the kitchen table. They were alone in the kitchen.

She looked at him with guileless blue eyes.

"We know you played a trick on us. Were you paid to do it? I will pay you more money if you tell me how the trick was worked."

She sat looking at him. Her bone structure was surprisingly delicate. High cheekbones accentuated by her thinness gave her a regal appearance. The line of her jaw, the straight bridge of her nose, the shape of her ears, all spoke of European heritage, yet at the same time there was something otherworldly and alien about her. It intrigued and aroused him.

"You and I are going to become very close friends," he said.

He reached across the table and stroked her hand with his fingertips. She did not pull her hand away. Indeed, she made no reaction of any kind, nor did her expression change. He wondered if there might be something wrong with her brain, or if she had been traumatized by the monks. Not that it really mattered—it was not her brain that most interested him.

Tonight he would keep her with him in his room, for safety. If she behaved well, he might make inquiries to determine whether there was some way he could take her with him back to Italy. The Bishop could probably help in such a matter. Renate would love to have a little friend to play with.

Colonel Martinez made no comment when Rainer told him he intended to keep the girl in his room during the night. He merely laughed through his nose in that sniggering way of his.

Alone in his room with her, he removed her clothing and admired every inch of her body as she stood passively before the lamp. There seemed little doubt that something was wrong with her brain. She had not tried to speak a single word, nor had her expression changed. It worried him that she would not eat or drink, but that was a condition which would probably cure itself when she became hungry and thirsty enough.

"It's time to go to bed, little one," he murmured.

Rolling down the bedcovers, he led her to the cot and induced her to lie on it. Then he quickly undressed, his penis erect and bobbing with engorged blood. He slid into the other side of the bed. It was so narrow they were forced to lie together to avoid falling off it.

The girl did not withdraw her slender body from his, but neither did she turn toward him. She merely lay there like a corpse. He caressed her with his hand and kissed her on the cheek and lips and nipples. She did nothing at all. It was like trying to seduce a department-store manikin. He thought about raping her, but that was not his style. He preferred a gentle seduction, at least in the beginning. His erection gradually shrank away to nothingness. At last he admitted defeat and turned out the lamp, then slid into the bed beside her. In spite of all the time he had lain close against her side, her body was still chilly to his touch.

"We'll talk about this tomorrow," he murmured into her ear. "Go to sleep, little one, and don't be afraid."

7.

He awoke from a nightmare with screams echoing in his ears, and lay listening to the silence in the darkness. The dream had involved the monks in some way, and Colonel Martinez, but try as he would, he could not remember its details and it slipped from his mind as he thought about it.

With a start of surprise, he realized he was alone in the narrow bed. The night was so dark, he could see nothing in the room. "Little one, are you here?"

There was no response.

He could not let her wander the monastery by herself. If one of the monks got free, he would surely try to kill her. He pushed himself reluctantly from the warmth of the bed and found his lighter in the pocket of his trousers, then used it to light the oil lamp. Pulling on his boxer shorts, he took the lamp into the corridor.

He went first to the archaic bathroom at the end of the hall, which worked by means of a cistern the monks filled with buckets, and when he found it empty, he began to examine the rooms one after another. They were all deserted.

As he descended the stairs to the ground level, he almost dropped the lamp. Its glow revealed a long streak of red along the wall, as though someone had dragged a bloody hand there.

He made his way through the entrance hall, the red bricks of the floor gritty and rough against the bare soles of his feet. To his surprise, the door of the storeroom that was serving as a temporary jail stood open. Cautiously, he extended the lamp into the room. It was deserted.

"Colonel Martinez," he said, and then called the name more loudly.

Martinez must have taken the monks outside the monastery for greater safekeeping, Ranier decided. They were probably in one of the huts beside the wall. But where was the girl?

When he left the storeroom, he again nearly dropped the lamp. There she was, standing in the entrance hall, waiting for him. She was still as naked as Eve. As the lamplight played over her slender, immature body, her limbs glistened with perspiration. The night air did not feel that warm to Ranier. He wondered why she was sweating so profusely. When he hesitated, she raised her hand and beckoned for him to follow.

This was enough for him. The minor mystery of what had become of the monks and the soldiers could wait for a solution. Inside his boxers his penis rose uncomfortably, until he used his hand to shift it so that it was inclined upward instead of downward. He resisted the urge to squeeze it. This strange, ethereal girl had awakened a powerful desire within him. One way or another it must be satisfied before the night ended. If he let the girl get away with her virginity intact he could never live with himself.

"I'm coming, little bird," he murmured, humming a song in his throat.

She waited for him on the top of the second-level landing, then as he neared the top of the stairs, she turned and made her way back to his room, gliding on her bare feet as soundlessly as a ghost.

When he reached his open doorway, he saw that she was standing beside the bed. He approached her with slow care, as though afraid she might take flight if he made a sudden gesture. Setting the lamp on the night table, he stood close to her, gazing down into her amazing blue eyes, which appeared purple in the indirect light from the lamp.

"You are such a beautiful little girl," he murmured.

She put her fingers over his lips to stop him from speaking, and he tasted something strange. He realized it was her sweat. Her entire body gleamed with perspiration. She wiped the palms of her hands over her breasts, so small and immature, then down over the sides of her slender hips. Raising them to his face, she began to brush his forehead and cheeks and nose lightly with her fingers. The odor of her sweat was not unpleasant. He parted his lips and licked her fingers, then laughed.

For the first time, she smiled at him. She drew off his boxer shorts and pulled him toward the bed, then pressed him gently down onto his back. Ranier did not try to resist. He was exactly where he wanted to be. His head felt light and dizzy, and he found that it was difficult to focus his eyes on the girl's face as she sat on the side of the bed and leaned over him. It was hard to move. His arms felt like lead weights, and his eyelids wanted to close so that he had to fight to keep them open. It was almost as though he had been drugged.

An electric thrill of fear ran along his nerves down to his fingers and toes. With more determination, he tried to sit up on the bed but discovered that he could no longer move. It was all he could do to keep his eyes open. His breathing became slow and heavy.

She leaned over him and continued to rub her fingertips over his face, neck and chest for several minutes. Satisfied, she brought her face closer to his. Ranier thought she was going to kiss him, but she opened her lips.

From her open mouth poured forth a torrent of large red ants. There were so many of them, they looked like a gush of clotted blood. They covered the priest's naked chest and began to bite his flesh. He realized that they were eating him alive. The drug in the girl's sweat had not dulled his ability to feel pain. He tried to scream but his face was slack. Nothing would work. In the silence of the night he heard the mouth parts of the ants chewing, chewing, chewing their way under his skin.

The girl smiled at him for a second time. She leaned down and this time she did kiss him on the lips. Something forced his jaw open. He felt a moving, twisting stream flow from her mouth into his mouth and down his throat, like a snake. It coiled itself in his stomach, and then he felt it begin to eat him from the inside. It was the red ants, thousands of them, crawling over each other inside his stomach, seeking for something to bite and chew and devour. They were still in his throat and mouth, biting, and now he felt them forcing their way into his intestines, working their way through this convoluted organ until his entire lower belly was filled with fiery agony.

Gently, with the utmost tenderness, the girl stretched herself across his body, pressing herself along his chest and legs with the chewing insects between them. She found his hands and laced her fingers with his lax fingers.

A gunshot broke the silence like a clap of thunder. The side of the girl's head exploded into a bloody mass and she slid sideways off him and fell from the bed to the floor. Ranier heard her strike the floorboards even though he could not turn his head. It was hard to see because the ants kept crawling across his eyeballs.

Something moved into his field of view. He focused his eyes with effort and saw that it was Colonel Martinez. His uniform was torn and he bled from hundreds of small wounds all over his body. Even his cheeks were bleeding. Ranier saw that one of his eyes was missing. There was only a bloody socket where it had been. He felt the ants biting at his own eyes.

"You poor bastard," Martinez said, staring at the priest's groin. The pity in his voice was mingled with revulsion. He pointed his gun at Ranier's forehead.

The priest tried to nod, but he could not make his head move. *Good-bye, Renate,* he thought. *I will miss you, little flower.*

As the ants began, one by one, to find their way out his anus, Martinez pulled the trigger.

The Organ of Chaos

1.

Sergeant Emma Lowe stood in her stirrups and surveyed the town that lay spread across the floor of the green river valley below. Her dust-covered face was made of lean, hard planes and the slits of her gray eyes were like polished steel. She sat back in her saddle and unclenched her jaw.

"I don't like the look of it."

Corporal Lamar Millar tried not to laugh, but some of it escaped through his nose in what sounded like a snort.

"What's so funny?"

"You always say the same thing, Sarge, every new town we come to."

"Yeah? Well, this time I mean it. It's too orderly. I've got a bad feeling."

"Orderly's good," Millar said. "It means all the Level Nines and Eights are dead."

Lowe didn't answer. She sat studying the town for another minute or so.

"Let's get this over with," she murmured. Flicking her reins, she urged her horse forward with her heels. They descended the broken remnant of a road through the weeds. Here and there, bits of asphalt were still visible.

Across the shattered land that had once been called America most of the road surfaces were gone, but the road beds beneath them were still the best way to get from one place to another. It always surprised Millar to see how much of the infrastructure remained after the passage of eighty-three years. Most of the buildings in this town they were riding into had been built before the Craze, and they were still standing. Granted, some colorful alterations had been made. He squinted at the roof of the nearest house that caught the sun with dazzling panels of blue and green and red, and finally realized that the roof was covered with old automobile hoods. They had been used like giant shingles. He smiled and shook his head at the crazy ingenuity of it. The madders were not unresourceful.

Lowe reined her horse to a stop in front of the house with the car-hood roof, which was some distance outside the town. An old woman in a dirty purple dress sat in a chair on the front porch. At first glance Millar thought she had no legs. Then he realized they were folded up under her dress, like the legs of a toad. No normal human being could hold her legs that way. She must be a deviant, probably born right after the Craze, to judge by her age. Her gray hair hung long and rank to her shoulders, and her fat cheeks around her mouth were streaked with something that resembled axle grease, but was probably just dirt that had been there for a long time.

"What's the name of this town?" Lowe demanded in her habitual military tone of command. Millar wondered if she was even aware of using it.

The old woman spat without turning her head. The gobbet cleared the lower step and landed in the weeds.

"Used to be called Summervale," she said in a surprisingly clear voice. "Lately the fools have taken to calling it Purgatory."

Lowe glanced at Millar. The name suggested religious fanaticism. They had been encountering more and more of that since entering into the region once known as Pennsylvania.

"Who's the leader of the town?" Lowe demanded.

"There's no leaders here, you smart-mouthed bitch."

"There's always a leader. Who runs things? Who gives the orders?"

The old woman shrugged and twisted her broad mouth. "Lately, the Preacher been telling people what to do. But we got no leaders."

"Does this preacher have a name?"

"He calls himself Judas."

"Fine. Where do we find the Reverend Judas?"

The old woman threw back her head and cackled.

"Where do you think you'd find a preacher, bitch?"

A kind of grunting noise came from inside the house through the screen door, which was patched all over its sagging surface with random bits of thread and wire.

"What's that?" Lowe asked.

324

"Expect that's my pig. She got a bad stomach."

Lowe looked at Millar. "Anything you want to ask?"

He quirked a grin. "You're joking, right, Sarge?"

As they started to ride away, the old woman jerked her hands from under her arms and spread her fingers.

"Shit, look at that," Millar said, working his reins to bring his startled horse under control.

Her fingernails were six or eight inches long, and coal black. They had not grown crooked the way long fingernails sometimes do, but were gently curved and resembled the talons of a bird of prey.

"You're going to die," the old woman shouted. "Both you little gun-toting pissants are going to die."

She began to babble and roll her bloodshot eyes at the sky while waving her taloned hands in a geometric pattern that almost looked ritualistic.

"Fucking deviants creep me out," Millar muttered.

"You and me both, kid," Lowe said.

The scene as they entered the town looked normal enough, on the surface. That was often how it looked. They had been through enough towns since leaving New Chicago not to be deceived by initial appearances. As they continued down the dusty main street, cracks in the facade began to appear. A woman wandered naked, talking to herself. A child whose head was twice as large as it should have been, and the wrong shape, pushed himself along in a rusting red wagon using two sticks. Where his legs should have been, there were only short pink appendages that resembled flippers. In the mouth of an alley lay the rotting and fly-infested corpse of a man. Someone had stolen his shoes, and both his feet had been gnawed off, probably by animals, but no one had cared enough to move the body.

"Looks pretty typical to me," Millar said under his breath.

"Just wait for it. I've got a bad feeling."

"You've always got a bad feeling."

He occupied himself by checking the rooftops for snipers. It was not likely there were any in a town such as this. Even so, it paid not to take anything for granted. He could get his rifle from its sling on his back to his shoulder in under a second, but he did need that second.

More than eight decades after the Craze, the scarred land had settled into a kind of normalcy. Almost all the Level Nines and Level Eights were dead. They were the uncontrollables, and were too violent to survive for long. There were still a few high-functioning Level Sevens around, but among the new generation being born there did not seem to be anything higher than a Level Six. This gave hope that whatever had caused the Craze was slowly wearing off, or at least diminishing.

The Craze had hit hard. Almost overnight, ninety-nine percent of the world's human population had gone insane. The affliction was not uniform. It ranged from the raving, homicidal insanity of the Level Nines to the mild delusions of the Level Ones. It is possible the world might have found a way to adapt to it, given a little time, but the nuclear warheads had fallen only three days after the Craze. They wiped out three-quarters of the population of what had once been the United States of America within a few minutes. Millions more died of radiation poisoning or starvation over the ensuing months, while the madness continued to rage unchecked.

The few who were sane and those whose insanity was mild enough to control most of the time began to coordinate and rebuild. It was discovered that children born after the Craze were often deformed in strange ways, but whether this was caused by the Craze or the radiation, no one claimed to know. The term "deviant" was adopted for those who were born different, and because so few normal human beings remained, they were accepted. Most of the population settled in small farming or fishing communities, as their forefathers had done centuries ago.

Technology was gone, no more than a dim memory in the minds of the elders. But slowly the Level Zeros, or norms as they were called, came together from all across the land that had been America in the city known as New Chicago, and began the patient, difficult task of rebuilding civilization. They sent out scouts to assess the conditions and count the inhabitants of the towns and villages that were scattered all across the crater-scarred landscape.

Lowe and Millar were one such scouting party, and they were a long way from New Chicago.

2.

The church was easy to find. It was near the center of town. At some point in its recent history a decision had been made to paint it black from its foundation stones to the tip of its shingled spire. Millar remembered spotting the spire from the hill, but had not realized that it belonged to a church. Black was not a common color for churches, even in these strange times.

On the side of the church beside the front doors, where a cross had probably hung at one time, was affixed a large triangular shard of broken glass. It was big enough and thick enough that it had probably come from the shattered plate-glass window of a store. It was painted black on its underside, so that it presented a shiny black mirror to the world.

"Whatever they're worshipping, I don't think it's Jesus," Millar murmured under his breath as they climbed the steps.

The double doors were heavy oak, but they were not locked. Just as they pulled the doors open, a wave of sound washed over them. It was loud and unlike anything Millar had ever heard—metallic and discordant, but strangely blended in a way that was almost musical.

Lowe said something. Her voice was drowned out by the extended chords of sound. The pitch was so deep it made Millar's teeth vibrate and his chest shake.

"What?" he shouted.

The wall of sound momentarily ceased.

"I said, choir practice," Lowe shouted back.

He grinned his lopsided grin. It had taken him almost a year to realize that Lowe had a sense of humor. It was a kind of wit so dry and so understated, it usually passed right over the heads of most who heard it. Millar had come to enjoy it.

The interior of the church gave demonstrable proof that there was a thin line between genius and madness. Above the ranks of oak pews stretched a complex spiderweb of steel wires and cables of varying lengths and thicknesses. They crossed and interlinked and converged on a space above the eastern end, where a stage had been built in place of the altar. About a dozen men and women sat on the rafters or stood on top of ladders among the wires, holding hammers and things that resembled the bows of bass fiddles.

A tall, slender man stood on the stage, robed completely in black like a Jesuit priest. He raised his arms. The others began to draw their bows over the wires, or tap them with their hammers. The church filled with discordant noise that was a mingled humming, clanging, and metallic shrieking.

327

The Organ of Chaos

Millar noticed that each wire was connected at its end to a hammered disk of steel or brass. The disks were dished or bowl-shaped, and surrounded the space above the stage. Some of them were no larger than dinner plates, while others were six feet or more in diameter. He realized they must serve as sounding boards to amplify the vibrations of the wires. It was these metal disks that generated the noise, or music, whichever it was.

The preacher saw them and made a motion with his hands that cut the sound off. Everyone stared down at them in silence. The disapproval was so thick, Millar could almost feel it beating against his skin. Or maybe that was the residual effect of the sounds of the wires. It was only then that he noticed another glittering shard of black glass high in the air above the stage. Like the one on the front of the building, it was in the shape of an elongated triangle. It almost resembled the blade of a gigantic black dagger, and gave off a sense of menace as it twisted slowly from its support wire.

"What do you want?" the preacher demanded.

"We're looking for the Reverend Judas," Lowe said.

"You found him. What do you want?"

Even his hair and eyes are black, Millar thought. But not his skin. His face was as pale as a corpse.

"We're from New Chicago."

"Never heard of it."

"We've been sent here by the provisional government of New Chicago to take a census of all the communities in this region," Lowe explained patiently. "We just need to ask you a few questions about your town, and we'll be on our way."

He stared at her with an unreadable expression on his long face.

"You have a most unusual voice. Are you a singer?"

"I don't sing, no," Lowe said. "If you would give us an hour of your time—"

"Are those the uniforms of the provisional government?" There was irony in the preacher's voice.

"These are the uniforms of the Free Army of the United Territories," Lowe told him coldly.

Millar found himself squaring his shoulders and standing straighter. They were both proud of the gray uniforms they wore, and the principles of discipline and honor they represented.

"You're soldiers. I judged as much by the weapons you carry on your backs. We allow no guns in Purgatory. We have no use for your kind here."

He turned his back on them and walked away across the stage. Lowe came forward into the middle of the church, and Millar followed, his eyes darting around cautiously. They were too exposed. He felt it as a tightness in his gut.

"You can't dismiss us that easily. We have a job to do," Lowe said.

Judas did not turn. He raised his right hand, made a fist, and pulled it down sharply.

"Sarge, look out," Millar shouted. He started to unsling his rifle from his shoulder.

Lowe turned with a scowl of annoyance still on her face. He saw one of the hammers glance off the side of her head and she went down like a sack of rags. Something flashed past his nose. Something else hit him hard in the hip. His skull rang like a bell and a brightness exploded in summer lightning at the back of his eyes.

3.

When Millar regained consciousness, the first thing he saw was Lowe bending over him. The short brown hair at the side of her head was matted with dried blood. He reached up to touch it without thinking.

"Lie still," she said gently. "You took a nasty hit to the back of the head."

He realized he was lying on the narrow lower cot of a steel bunk bed bolted to a wall of concrete blocks. The bare springs of the upper bunk were four feet above his face. He felt the crown of his head gingerly. There was a bump on his scalp the size of a hen's egg.

"Where are we?"

Lowe looked around. "If I had to guess, I'd say the town jail."

He lifted his head from the thin mattress—there was no pillow—and winced as his pounding headache began to thud more insistently inside his skull. His eyes did not want to focus, but past the toes of his boots he saw flat steel bars that were painted an ugly green.

"How long have we been here?"

"I've been awake for about two hours. They took my watch, so I can't tell you how long we were unconscious. They took everything."

"I should have been more cautious," he said, remembering the hammers in the hands of the men and women sitting on the church rafters and balanced on the tops of the ladders.

"We walked into it, all right," she agreed.

"Why did they attack us?"

"Why do the madders do anything?"

It was one of the stock questions shouted at new recruits by drill sergeants. He answered in the usual way. "Because they're all insane, Sarge."

"It's my fault," Lowe said. "I should have approached the church more cautiously. It's obvious that it's the center of the religious cult we've encountered in the last two towns. The cult is growing."

"The cult of the black triangle," he murmured. She raised an eyebrow and he shrugged. "That's what I call it, anyway."

"The preacher in the last town wouldn't talk to us, and the one in the town before that was so crazy, he didn't make any sense."

"He kept yelling about the convergence of dissonance and the transcendent sublimation of the primal chords," Millar said. "It didn't make any sense at the time, but I guess that's what we heard in the church."

"Music seems to be an important part of the cult dogma."

"I wouldn't call it music," Millar said.

"We should have stayed longer in the last town and tried to learn more about this cult. I've got a feeling it's important."

He raised his head again and looked through the bars of their cell. There was no movement in the corridor beyond, which was illuminated by two flickering oil lamps in brackets on the wall.

"What do you think they'll do to us?"

She shrugged. "Maybe they just want to talk to us to make sure we're not a threat to them."

He knew her well enough to know she didn't believe her own words. "Do you think this preacher Judas is a madder?"

"Probably a Level Seven. But he has it well under control."

He lay back on the pillow. "Shit, Sarge, we are so screwed."

The planes of her face betrayed no emotion.

"Stay alert, soldier. Stay ready. When your chance comes, grab it. Get the fuck out of here and make your way back to New Chicago. The

President needs to know what's going on in this region."

"We're both going back," he said.

"Maybe," she murmured. "Just remember what I told you."

It was an hour or so later when they heard a metal door somewhere at the end of the corridor clang open, and approaching footsteps echo on the concrete floor. The Reverend Judas came into view, followed by two scowling men who wore drab black clothing. Both men had facial deformities. A growth of some kind drooped down from the forehead of one of them, partially covering his left eye. The other had a harelip.

Lowe stood to confront them through the bars. Millar tried to stand beside her, but had to sit back down on the bunk with his head between his hands.

"Let us out of here," Lowe demanded.

"In good time," Judas said quietly.

"You have no right to hold us. We did nothing."

"You profaned a holy place with your weapons."

"The church doors were unlocked. How were we to know we were forbidden to enter?"

He cocked his head to the side as she spoke, and seemed to be listening to something no one else could hear. There was a faint smile on his lips.

"If you continue to detain us there will be repercussions from New Chicago."

"Why did you ride into Purgatory?"

"I told you: we are conducting a census for the provisional government."

"Were you sent here to spy on my church?"

"We didn't even know your church existed until we saw it."

"You're lying," he snapped. "There are churches of the faith in Regret and Sorrow."

Those were the names of the last two towns they had surveyed. Like Purgatory, they had recently been renamed.

"How did you know we passed through those towns?" Lowe asked.

Judas put a hand behind his ear and cocked his head, striking a theatrical pose.

"The voices of the winds whisper secrets down the wires. You can hide nothing from me, woman. I see your filthy soul cowering inside your prison of flesh."

"You've got a short-wave radio, don't you?" Lowe said. "You knew in advance we were coming."

"All things are known to the heralds of chaos," he said in a ringing preacher's voice.

"Is that what you worship? Chaos?"

"What else is real in the world?" He spread his arms. "All this that you see, these walls, this floor, these bars, are illusions created within your mind to imprison you. The mind of man is limited and flawed. It can create nothing but falsehoods. Only chaos is beyond conception by the mind of man, and only the inconceivable is real in its perfection."

"What are the black triangles? Do you worship them?"

He reached into his pocket and drew forth a gold cross on a fine gold chain. He held it up for her to see. Millar realized it was the gold cross Lowe always wore around her neck.

"This is a symbol of your pale and craven king of the dead. Do you worship it?"

"No. The cross represents the resurrection of the Son of Man."

He tucked the cross back into his pocket. "The shards of darkness represent the angles of chaos who come to cleanse the world of sin."

"*Angles?* Do you mean angels?"

"Enough," he said, his black eyes flashing. "You shall not question our faith again."

He turned to the silent men who stood behind him. "Take her for interrogation."

Millar stood from the bunk and tried to put himself in front of Lowe, but the dizziness in his head sent him to his knees on the concrete floor before the deviants even reached him. They pushed him aside and took Lowe by the arms. She did not resist.

"Remember what I told you," she said to Millar as she was pulled out of the cell.

He stumbled to his feet and managed to reach the door just as it was slammed shut.

Judas turned a key in the door's lock, sliding its bolt into place.

"We'll question you when you're feeling better, son," he said in a voice that was almost fatherly.

"If you hurt her, I'll blow your brains out, you crazy son of a bitch."

Millar lunged through the bars for the preacher's throat, but the other man slid back so adroitly that only one of Millar's fingers hooked in the pocket of his robe. The pocket tore and Judas knocked his hand away with a flash of annoyance.

"Don't be in such a rush, son," he said. "Your time will come, I promise you."

He left the corridor. The slam of the iron door behind him had a note of finality.

In the fluttering lamplight, Millar saw something gleam on the floor. He knelt and reached through the bars to pick it up, then sat holding it on his palm so that the light reflected from its polished gold. He had often seen Lowe's cross hanging around her neck, but this was the first time he had touched it. He brushed its smooth surface with the tip of his finger.

4.

The interrogation room was not far away, not nearly far enough away, from the cell where Millar lay with his arm across his eyes and his teeth clenched, listening to Lowe's screams. There was no way to judge the passage of time, but the screams must have gone on for hours. After a while, he realized they had stopped, and sat up on the side of the bunk, tense and alert. His headache was not so bad now, and he was able to focus his eyes. If they gave him a chance, he knew he was going to take it.

They never gave him a chance. Three men robed in black entered, but Judas was not among them. Two held an unconscious Lowe between them. The third opened the door with a key, then trained a revolver on Millar while the others threw Lowe into the cell. They locked the door and left.

He half-pulled and half-lifted the unconscious Lowe onto the bunk, then listened anxiously for her heartbeat with his ear pressed against her small, firm left breast. Her heart was strong and regular.

Her face was bruised, her nose broken. They had beaten her with their fists and burned her with looked like a heated steel rod, to judge by the ugly red sear marks. His concern shifted to her hands, which were wrapped in clumsily applied windings of gauze soaked with dried blood.

Millar held one hand between his, wondered if he should leave the gauze in place or try to re-wrap it more tightly. In the end, he carefully peeled the gauze strip away layer by sticking layer. When he reached the end, he sat staring in horror.

They had cut off her fingers, all of them, along with her thumb, and then seared the bleeding stumps with the hot iron rod to cauterize the wounds so that she would not die from blood loss.

He felt tears of frustration well into his eyes, and angrily blinked them away. He looked at her other hand, afraid to even touch it, but in the end he unwrapped it. Both hands were the same.

The single mercy allowed by fate was that Lowe did not regain consciousness before he finished binding up both hands with the filthy, clotted gauze. When she did come around, her gray eyes snapped open and she screamed. He caught her flailing arms, trying not to touch her hands, and pressed them to her sides. Her whole body shivered and shook as though with a fever, but he knew it was pain that made her tremble.

He stared fiercely into her eyes until she focused on his face, then let go of her arms. She made an involuntary noise in her throat and shuddered, but otherwise lay still. He drew from his pocket the gold cross and held it where she could see it. She blinked and nodded. He raised her head with one hand and looped the chain around her neck. She tried to reach her own hand up to touch the cross, but he gently pressed her arm back down. He tucked the cross into her shirt so that it lay concealed between her breasts. Neither of them said anything. Eventually, she drifted into a sleep of exhaustion.

She was still asleep when they came again. Millar stood defiantly as they opened the cell door. Again, Reverend Judas was not with them.

"I'm ready, you bastards," he said. "Take me and do your worst."

They pushed him roughly aside and dragged Lowe off the bed. She woke and stared around with wild eyes that met Millar's gaze for only an instant. Millar went insane and attacked them. While one of them held Lowe, the other two beat him to the floor of the cell with hardwood clubs and left him there. He heard the doors clang shut behind them.

He had not had any water to drink for more than twenty-four hours, and his head injury had left him weak in the legs, but he managed to push himself to his feet. He stood leaning against the wall, listening with his head cocked and his mouth open to quiet his own breaths, in order to catch the slightest sound from outside the cell. When her screams began, he pressed his palms against his ears and screamed along with her, but it did no good. He could still hear her.

Eventually the screaming stopped. He sat on the edge of the bunk with his head between his hands and waited for them to bring her back, emotions rushing through him that ranged from scarlet rage to black despair. A man came into the corridor and replenished the reservoirs of the two oil lamps that provided the light. He would not speak to Millar, who cursed him in the way only a soldier can curse.

Millar wondered if the madders and the deviants were just going to leave him in the cell to die of thirst. That was the thing about crazy people—you couldn't predict what they would do, because their motives made no sense. Religious fanatics were always irrational, but these people had been crazy before they found whatever it was they prayed to.

In a way, he wanted them to kill him. It would end his anguish over his inability to help Lowe. The only reason he was on the survey was to protect her, to watch her back, and he had failed her. He had failed his training. He should have known better than to walk into that church without a rifle in his hands. He should have known better than to stand in the aisle under all those madders when he could feel their hatred beating down on them.

At some point, he fell asleep from sheer exhaustion. It was a dreamless sleep. He wasn't even aware of closing his eyes or sprawling sideways across the thin, hard mattress on the bunk. It might have been day or night. He had no way to know.

The clank of the door at the end of the corridor woke him in an instant. Before he even realized it he was standing beside the bunks, watching for Lowe. Reverend Judas came into view, followed by the man with the harelip, who held a revolver in his hand. They stopped in front of the green bars of the cell and the man directed the muzzle of the gun at Millar's chest.

"They tell me you had a nice long sleep," Judas said in a soothing tone.

"Where is Sergeant Lowe?"

"Don't worry about her, son. We're taking good care of her."

"She's still alive?"

"Naturally she's alive. We have no intention of killing her."

"Why do you keep torturing her?"

Judas pursed his lips and shook his head in sadness. "It was hard, but it had to be done. Her mind and body needed to be conditioned for the work she must do."

"What are you talking about? What work?"

"You should feel very proud, son. Your sergeant has been chosen to take part in the coming forth of the angles of chaos."

Millar blinked in confusion. "I don't know what you're talking about."

The Organ of Chaos

"Sergeant Lowe has been chosen by the Unbodied Kings to sing the litany in the ritual of the coming forth by night of the angles of chaos."

"Did she agree to this voluntarily?"

"She is reconciled to her task."

"Reconciled," Millar repeated, trying to control his anger.

"It's a great honor, son. Neither you nor the Sergeant can realize how greatly you have both been blessed. You did not come to Purgatory by chance. You were led here by exalted intelligences to fulfil your parts in the coming forth of their servants into our universe."

Millar knew better than to try to make sense out of the ramblings of a madder.

"I'd like to see Sergeant Lowe."

Reverend Judas chuckled. The man beside him with the gun did not even smile.

"Why else do you think we're here?"

"You mean, you'll take me to her?"

"Of course. I want you to see for yourself the wonder that your coming to our town has enabled. You are the fulfillment of prophecy."

"Take me to her now," Millar demanded.

"Soon. I need to ask you a few questions before we go."

"What do you want to know?"

"Is it true that you are what is known as a Level Zero?"

"Who told you that?"

"Sergeant Lowe."

"Yes, it's true."

"You were born completely sane? No madness at all?"

"I'm sane."

Judas nodded and looked satisfied. "We can use your blood. We have very few sanes in Purgatory."

"What do you mean, use my blood? Are you going to kill me?"

"Perish the thought, boy. No, we need you alive to sire children on our women. We need to breed more sanes, or Level Zeros as you call them, to help carry forward the great work we have been entrusted with by the Unbodied Kings."

"Who are these kings? Are they your gods?"

Judas rolled his black eyes upward and seemed to consider.

"I don't think you would call them gods. No, I don't believe that is the word you would choose."

Millar tried to swallow his impatience but his dry throat would not allow it.

"When are you going to take me to Sergeant Lowe?"

"We'll go now," Judas said brightly. He unlocked the door of the cell.

Millar came out slowly, calculating in his mind what he needed to do to disarm the man with the gun and to kill Judas.

"Please don't do anything violent," Judas said. "Karl will shoot you."

Millar looked at Karl. The silent man's eyes did not waver from his face. They were professional eyes. At some point Karl had done some kind of police work or soldiering. *Probably as a mercenary*, Millar thought. There were always petty wars breaking out between the territories.

"Let me take you to see Sergeant Lowe," Judas said, turning his back on Millar. He led the way out of the corridor.

5.

It was dark outside the jailhouse, and raining. A strong gust of wind drove large raindrops against the side of his face like pellets of hail. Opening his mouth, he caught some of them on his tongue. They helped relieve the dryness. He realized that the jailhouse was just across the muddy street from the church. Judas did not pause or turn, but led him up the church steps and through one side of the double doors, which a man held open against the wind.

The church was illuminated by numerous candles and overflowed with townspeople. They all wore black clothing of various kinds. Their mood was solemn, with an undercurrent of excitement. Millar sensed their expectation. Some of them could not contain themselves. They waved their hands in the air or made grunting noises or rocked back and forth in their seats. The church had a rank animal smell that reminded him of wet horses.

The air above the rows of pews was a three-dimensional spider's web of wires and cables of different lengths, all terminating in the centers of curved metal dishes that focused down on the stage. Men and women sat on the cross beams or atop ladders with bows and hammers in their hands. Millar wondered if they were the same group that had pelted him with hammers. All their faces looked the same to him—solemn, fanatical, expectant. Many were deformed.

The Organ of Chaos

Every now and then someone would gently tap a wire with his hammer, as though testing its pitch. The air was filled with a metallic hum made up of mingled discordant notes.

Above the stage, within the space defined by the encircling metal dishes, the large black shard of plate glass twisted slowly on its support wire, catching the flickering glow of the candles and sweeping their reflections around the church. The golden light danced across the metal sounding disks and over the wide eyes of the congregation.

The stage was not empty. In the center rested a plain wooden chair without arms or padding. His gaze was drawn to something strange that sat on the stage beside it. It was rounded, about the size of a big pumpkin, and made of hammered brass that gleamed yellow in the candlelight. Something that resembled clusters of brass bells stuck out from both its sides, but they were pointing away from the pews and Millar couldn't see them clearly enough to guess what they were.

As Reverend Judas walked up the center aisle, a low moan of delight arose from the congregation. The murmur of over four hundred voices mingled with the subdued pinging and thrumming of the wires. The man called Karl nudged Millar up the aisle with his gun, then stopped him at the front row of pews and pushed him into an empty seat on the left side. He sat beside Millar on the end of the pew, the gun in his hand pointed at Millar's ribs.

Judas turned toward Millar with a satisfied smile on his lips.

"Watch and learn, son. This is your new faith." He leaned closer. "I caution you not to do anything disruptive. The townspeople would tear you into pieces with their teeth and their bare hands."

Millar looked around. The glow of fanaticism in the faces of the men and woman left no doubt that the preacher spoke the truth. The congregation was so wound up with emotion, it was all they could do to remain in their seats. Some were bouncing up and down and clapping as they stared in rapture at Judas.

The preacher mounted the steps to the stage and stood in front of the chair. He raised his palms for silence. The murmur of voices swelled, and then slowly diminished to nothing. Even the wires and metal disks above their heads were still. Millar heard the rain beating in wind-driven sheets against the windows of the church.

"We were born from the mud," Judas declaimed in ringing tones.

A murmur of agreement from the pews.

"We were formed in corruption and in darkness."

Another murmur.

"We were shaped with the filth of the earth."

Karl murmured with a slight lisp, "Yes, we were." It was the first time Millar had heard him speak. His eyes shone as he stared up at Judas.

"We were brought forth from the maelstrom of chaos at the center of the universe, and framed in chords of disharmony to be imperfect, that we might better serve those who made us."

"Unbodied Kings," someone shouted from the back.

Millar looked around the church, wondering how much more of this madder ranting he would be forced to endure before he was taken to Sergeant Lowe.

Judas raised his hand for silence.

"We, their lesser servants, have but one purpose, and when it is fulfilled we shall be permitted to return to the blissful oblivion of the chaotic vortex, where we will forget the torment of our earthly lives. For we are in hell, my brothers and sisters. We have always been in hell, and the only paradise is annihilation."

He pointed suddenly into the crowd. "What is our sole purpose on this earth?"

Millar turned his head. The woman Judas pointed at was struck dumb and began to stammer. Someone near her said "angles."

"To free the angles of the Kings," the woman managed to say.

"Correct, sister. Our sole purpose is to open the way for the greater servants of the Unbodied Kings, who will prepare this world for their return. The angles will cleanse this globe with their cold black fire. I have seen it in the visions the Kings sent to me while I wandered this world, unknown and unwanted. They will boil the oceans and level the mountains to the plains. They will burn the forests and dry up the rivers. They will turn the air itself into a deadly mist. When at last the world is purified, the Unbodied Kings will rule here again, as they did countless ages before they shaped us from the filth of the earth to serve them. And then, what of us, my brothers and sisters? What of us?"

He spread his hands and cocked his head, waiting for an answer.

"True death," someone shouted, and the words were repeated, "true death, true death, true death."

"There is no oblivion in common death, for we return again and again on the wheel of rebirth. Each of us has died and been reborn into this same hell for millions of years. There is no escape from our torment, except by the mercy of the angles, for their cold black fire gives true death, and final return to the vortex of chaos from which we were drawn forth in primordial aeons."

Murmurs of agreement arose from the congregation, who nodded their heads and rocked back and forth.

"It was for this purpose that the Unbodied Kings sent us the Craze. The blessing of madness enabled us to hear their words spoken inside our heads, to see the visions they sent to us in our sleep, and to know our place in the order of things."

Millar listened more intently. No one knew the cause of the Craze. It had come from nowhere. Scientists had speculated that it was caused by some invisible gas or dust cloud through which the solar system was passing in its revolution around the galactic core, but no measuring device or test had ever been able to detect such a gas. Was it possible that the Craze had been sent deliberately?

"This church was once a place of worship for the false god of suffering and resurrection, the craven pretender who hung his head and turned his cheek. Men came here to worship and rejoice in their eternal bondage on the wheel of rebirth. But we have transformed it into a temple of devotion to the Unbodied Kings and the shadow angles of liberation. The Kings spoke to us in our dreams and sent us visions, and we built what they commanded us, their faithful servants of corrupt flesh, to build for them."

He raised his arms and looked up at the web of wires and shining disks above his head. "It is finished. The final instrument of liberation has been prepared. Tonight, we herald the coming forth of the angles of chaos with their sacred chords and measures."

He turned to a man who stood at the foot of the stage. "Bring in the instrument."

The man left through a side door, and in a few minutes came back with two black-robed townswomen, who led a naked woman between them toward the stage. Her slender body gleamed with rainwater. It was only when Millar saw the gauze bandages around her hands that he realized it was Lowe. The bastards had shaved off all her hair, even the hair on her pubes and eyebrows. She wore wireframe eyeglasses with round lenses that were the same shiny black glass as the triangular shard that hung suspended above the stage. The light of the candles reflected in their mirror disks.

He started to stand up without thinking, but the men on either side of him were ready. They seized his arms and held him down. He struggled against them for a while, then went limp when he realized there was no way he could drag Lowe out of the church on his own. There were too many madders between him and the doors.

Judas stood to one side of the stage as Lowe was led up beside him. He gestured at the chair. The women in black guided the unresisting Lowe toward it, then pressed her into its seat. They tied her ankles to the front legs but left her arms free.

Lowe seemed to be in some kind of trance. Maybe she's drugged, Millar thought. He hoped so. At least that would be a kind of mercy. He started to call her name, then hesitated. What good would it do?

"Connect the instrument," Judas ordered.

At first Millar could not make out what they were doing. Half a dozen men began to move around the stage on stepladders, gathering in their hands fine wires that dangled from the metal sounding disks and drawing them together toward the chair. It was only when they began to tie fishhooks on their ends that he realized their intention. He jumped to his feet before his captors could grab him.

"Stop this," he shouted, staring around the church. "You're all insane. Stop what you're doing."

The congregation murmured its anger, but Lowe did not even turn her head at the sound of his voice. He struggled to break free from the men who grabbed his arms and pulled him back. They were too strong.

Judas frowned down at him from the edge of the stage and pointed his finger like some brooding prophet of judgement.

"You will be silent. Bind his mouth."

The men who held him had the cloth bindings to gag him in their pockets. He tried to resist, but Karl hit him with the revolver on the side of the head, and the strength left his arms and legs. In seconds they had his mouth tightly bound.

He sat and watched in horror as the fishhooks were inserted through various parts of Lowe's naked body, and the wires attached to them drawn taut so that the hooks pulled at her pale flesh and the metal disks above her vibrated. They put the hooks through her breasts, her sides, her abdomen and lower belly, even through her labia, so that the whole front of her torso was a mass of spreading, gleaming wires.

Reverend Judas stood behind the chair and gently removed her dark glasses. If there had not been a gag in his mouth, Millar would have vomited from the sheer horror of what he saw. They had pricked out her eyes and left only raw, empty sockets. Lowe was completely blind. For the first time, he noticed a small streak of dried blood that had run down from her ear. He wondered if they had also pricked out her eardrums to make her deaf.

Two of the workmen inserted hooks into her eye sockets and drew the wires taut. Small whimpers of pain came from behind Lowe's clenched jaw.

Judas picked up the gleaming brass sphere from the stage. He turned it around in his hands and slowly lowered it over Lowe's head. Millar realized it was some kind of bizarre faceless helmet. It completely enclosed Lowe's head and shoulders, and fitted over the back of the chair so that when it was fastened into place Lowe was held there. Slots in the front accommodated the wires that extended from her eye sockets but there were no openings for her eyes or her mouth. The things on the sides of the helmet that Millar had mistaken for bells were actually the bell-ends of brass trumpets. Three of them curled around on each side of the helmet, like the curling horns of a ram, spreading and extending forward.

"Call forth the angles of darkness," Judas commanded in triumph.

The church filled with a sound unlike anything Millar had ever heard. It shook his entire body. The cacophony in the church on their arrival in Purgatory was as nothing compared with this solid wall of clashing, thrumming, metallic dissonance. It did not remain constant, but rose and fell in pitch as bowed and hammered chords of sound merged and crashed into each other like storm waves breaking against a rocky cliff.

And then, something else began that rose above the sounds of the wires. It was a deep lowing of distress, like the bellowing of a bull caught in quicksand and struggling to free itself, but many times louder. It came from the bells of the trumpets on either side of the brass helmet around Lowe's head.

6.

Tears streamed down Millar's cheeks as the river of dissonance flowed through his flesh and along his nerves and made his chest vibrate. All he could think about was that he should be the one on that stage, not Lowe. It was his duty to protect her. If he could not do that, why was he even alive?

The lowing of the horns on the sides of the brass helmet was horrifying, but there was a kind of weird and savage beauty as it mingled with the shrieking, banging wires and the ringing of the metal sounding disks. In some way the acoustics of the helmet lowered the pitch of Lowe's shrieks of agony, while at the same time magnifying their volume. As she screamed, she flailed with her arms at the wires radiating from her body, and the pain as she struck the wires with her mangled hands redoubled the force of her screams.

Millar wondered if he would still be able to hear when the horrifying juggernaut of noise finally ceased, or if his eardrums would burst and bleed under the assault.

Judas raised his arm and pointed upward. He spoke, but his words were lost in the clashing chords.

Millar looked up with the rest of the congregation, and saw that something was happening to the air around the black shard of glass, which shimmered and danced as the waves of sound struck it. The air thickened and grew dark. It was not like smoke, but more like a kind of shadow that danced to the discordant symphony of chaos. As he watched, the cloud expanded and darkened so that it was hard to see the glass shard within it.

Something moved inside the shadow. He narrowed his eyes, trying to see it in the uncertain light. It turned and shifted its shape from moment to moment, but it was three-sided, like the shard of glass. The length of its sides constantly shortened and lengthened as it changed. One moment it appeared to have depth, but a moment later it seemed flat. As the great sounding disks vibrated their wall of noise at it, the moving, morphing triangle detached itself from the glass shard and drifted forward above the heads of the congregation. From its ever-changing edges, fine tendrils of darkness extended themselves out in all directions. Everyone in the church stared at it with rapture, including the men on either side of Millar.

They made a critical mistake, he thought calmly. *They gagged my mouth, but they left my arms and legs free.*

With one smooth movement he reached to Karl's belly and pulled the revolver from his belt. The world seemed to slow down around him and go silent. Continuing the motion, he shot first the man on his left, then Karl, but he did not even hear the gunshots. He stood up, staring at Judas on the stage. Their eyes locked. Somehow Millar knew that Judas knew what he was thinking.

I have three obvious targets of opportunity, Millar thought in that instant, with cold logic, *but there is only time for a single aimed shot at one of them before the congregation pulls me down from behind. I can shoot Judas and maybe end his religion. Or I can shoot Emma and end her suffering. Or I can shoot myself and ensure that these bastards will never be able to torture me.*

Judas looked into his eyes, and smiled, because he knew Millar had chosen a fourth way, and that was to spin around and kill those lunging to grab at him from behind, then make a break for the side door and freedom. There was no escape from Purgatory. Millar saw it in the preacher's black eyes.

So Millar chose a fifth way. He raised the gun and shot the hanging shard of black glass. It split into half a dozen large pieces that rained down on the stage. When it broke, the floating blackness vanished. One piece of glass embedded itself in the top of the Reverend Judas's head. Another fell sideways like a giant knife and cut through the wires attached to Lowe's torso before shattering into a thousand tiny fragments. The shrieking, groaning discordance of sounds stopped.

Judas staggered in a circle on the stage, batting at the air in front of him. Blood poured from his scalp over his face. The congregation sat in shocked silence, too stunned to move.

"I see them! I see them!" Judas screamed. "They're everywhere!"

He stumbled off the edge of the stage.

Millar leaped up past his twitching corpse and ran to Lowe. For a few precious seconds he fumbled with the straps that held the brass helmet in place over the back of the chair before he was able to rip it free.

He stepped back and raised the hand that held the gun across his mouth in an instinctive gesture of loathing. In some inexplicable way the strange music of the wires had deformed her head and enlarged it into a bulbous mass of wrinkled, pink flesh that bore no resemblance to anything he had ever seen, or even imagined in his nightmares.

The congregation of lunatics began to recover their wits. Confusion turned to hatred. Hammers rained down on the stage from above. One hit him in the small of the back, but he ignored it. The black-garbed men and women clambered over the backs of the pews toward the stage in their eagerness to reach him, their faces twisted with fanatical rage, and their screams and bellows and barks were like a chorus of damned souls.

He laid his hand on Lowe's naked shoulder. A shock flashed along his nerves. Somehow, he felt her altered mind running along the pathways inside his brain. Her thoughts were inhumanly powerful, magnified in some way by her ordeal. Without any question or doubt, he knew what she wanted. He pressed the muzzle of the revolver against the bloated pinkness and pulled the trigger.

A hammer glanced from the side of his head and sheared off his ear, making his skull ring like a bell. He ignored the pain as he placed the barrel of the gun into his mouth. Murderous hands grabbed his legs and ankles from all sides. Before they reached his arm he pulled the trigger again.

Forbidden Passage

1.

Uncle Willard was uncommonly talkative in the coach as he escorted me from his brownstone mansion to the pier on the East River from which my ship was to depart. I entertained myself with the fancy that he was feeling a trace of guilt over his treatment of me, but of course that was absurd.

"You must make a good first impression, Alice. There is no substitute for a first impression. Lord Curlew is a man of position in London society. If you are to enter his household as the governess of his daughter, both your behavior and your reputation must remain beyond the least reproach."

"Yes, Uncle."

In his black suit and tall beaver hat, he looked as though he were going to a funeral. I admit that I was not much more cheerful in my drab gray satin dress. It had been chosen for me, like every other aspect of my life. I would have picked something brighter, but Uncle liked to dress me in gray and black. He sometimes called me his little sparrow.

"This is a wonderful opportunity for you. Were it not for the fact that I attended Eaton with Lord Curlew, it would never have been possible to place you in so prominent a house in Belgravia. You should be grateful."

"I am grateful, Uncle, for all that you have done for me since the deaths of my parents."

He took a pinch of snuff from his engraved silver box, placed it on the back of his liver-spotted hand and sniffed it into his head, then rubbed the wet end of his nose with his fingers.

"Indeed you should be, girl. I raised you as a lady of standing in society and gave you the benefit of the finest tutors. They taught you how to speak, how to walk, how to sit at table. You can tinkle on the pianoforte and recite French verse with the best of them. You've always had your own lady's maid. Of course you cannot sustain this pose now that you have attained your maturity, being both penniless and an orphan, but what you have learned will serve you well when you arrive in London."

I sat listening with half an ear as we were drawn along the cobblestones of Broadway in the direction of the Battery. Most of my attention was on the well-dressed pedestrians and smart carriages that passed us in the opposite direction. In spite of the tragedy eight years ago that had brought me from my native Boston to this city, I had come to love New York. My heart ached with the thought that I should probably never see it again.

"Foremost in your mind must always be the need to find yourself a husband. This is your time, girl. You are not plain of face and you carry yourself well. There will be foolish young men willing to sacrifice wealth and position for a young woman who makes a pretty ornament on their arm. Do not delay your choice. In a few years the bloom will be off the rose and your prospects will dwindle. I say this not to be cruel, but only to advise you as to the truth of the matter."

"Of course you do, Uncle."

When Uncle Willard inherited my father's wealth, it was with the proviso that he raise me as a lady until my eighteenth year. It had surprised me to learn that my father left me no provision of my own in his will, but so my Uncle and his solicitor both solemnly informed me. With a forthrightness that was characteristic of his nature, on the day of my eighteenth birthday Uncle said that he could not afford to keep me about the house, and that I must seek employment and make my own way in the world. How could I be anything other than grateful when he found me a position as governess in London? Although I did wonder from time to time why there were no similar employments to be had in New York, or even in Boston.

The coachman turned the horses left and we made our way along the dark canyon of Wall Street toward the East River. The imposing stone buildings cast shadows across the road that were surprisingly cool on my face through the open window. The cherry blossoms were in bloom elsewhere in the city, but the last vestiges of winter chill had not quite been overcome by the lengthening days.

347

Forbidden Passage

We turned right onto South Street, which ran along the waterfront. It was a part of the city I had not seen before, a clashing crescendo of sights and colors and sounds that assaulted my senses. There were shipping offices, warehouses, and cheap eating-houses catering to the lowest class. Little nautical shops dotted the boardwalk, selling various instruments that were displayed in their windows or outside under striped awnings. As they flashed past, I was able to identify rusting anchors, a ship's wheel, what I thought must be a brass compass, and countless coils of tar-stained rope and rolled canvas. The scent of salt mingled with that of fish was like some barbarous incense from a strange land. The cobblestones thundered beneath the wheels of great wagons piled high with barrels and bales.

"Shut the window, girl."

I slid up the glass to mute the noise of commerce, and put my cheek against it in an effort to see up the street behind the coach.

"Should we not be further up the river?"

"What do you mean?"

"The newspaper says the Black Ball Line departs from Piers 25 and 26."

"What of it?"

I turned to look at his plump face. "You know that I expressed a wish that my passage should be on one of the Black Ball packets, because of the good report my friend, Ellen, gave me regarding their service."

"You are not booked upon a Black Ball packet."

This blunt statement hurt my feelings somewhat. Only a week before, Uncle Willard had assured me he would accede to my wish and put me on a Black Ball packet.

"Upon what line have you booked me?"

"Not on any line, as such."

My expression of dismay annoyed him.

"Do you know how much first-class passage on a Black Ball packet costs?"

"One hundred and twenty dollars. Or one hundred and forty, with unlimited wine privileges."

"You do know. That is a great deal of money, my girl, and money is not to be wasted."

"Have you booked me intermediate class?" He said nothing. A shiver of horror passed through my heart. "Not steerage? Uncle, say you haven't booked me in steerage?"

"Don't be absurd. In any case, there are no steerage bookings on this ship, and all accommodations are first-class. So you will have an entire stateroom to yourself all the way to England."

I did not inquire as to the cost. It was certainly less than the standard second-class fare of the major trans-Atlantic shipping lines.

"The ship is called the *Caledonia*. You will be pleased to hear that it was formerly a regular packet in the Black Ball Line, so you are giving up nothing in the way of comfort. Two years ago it collided with another ship in the English Channel and sustained damage. After its repair it was sold and became a transient vessel."

"A tramp, you mean."

"That is a vulgar word. Do not use it again."

The waterfront was a wall of towering ships, their naked masts rising up like a forest of leafless trees in winter. What is a sailing ship without her sails, but a bony reminder of death? There were hundreds of them, most of them engaged in the packet trade. New York was the major port of departure for the entire eastern seaboard. The stone piers swarmed with humanity of every station, either arriving or departing, all of them united in their hurry to be somewhere else.

The coach drew to a stop, and I leaned across to see through Uncle's window the ship tied up against the pier. The sight gave me heart. The *Caledonia* was still painted in the colors of the Black Ball Line—black hull with dark green trim along her rails, her longboats green. A slight difference in the shade of black paint betrayed where the collision had occurred. It must have left a hole not far behind her bow. In other respects she seemed a seaworthy vessel, at least to my untrained eyes.

"I won't get out. Robert will place your trunk on the dockside. We will say our goodbyes now, before we become emotional."

"Goodbye, Uncle. Thank you for all you have done for me."

He took my hand and squeezed my fingers. I was glad I was wearing gloves, although even their dark leather could not hide the stains of snuff.

"You must write to me once you are settled in Lord Curlew's house."

"Of course, Uncle."

"No sentiment, now; I hate sentiment. Out you go, girl."

The coachman, Robert, carried my sturdy wooden travel trunk to the side of the pier and I stood beside it, watching the coach diminish and vanish amid the chaos of South Street. Never had I felt so alone, or so vulnerable. Even on the night word came to the house in Boston that both my parents had drowned in a boating accident, there had been the familiar faces of servants all around to comfort me. Now I stood amid a throng of strangers. Most were seamen engaged in loading cargo onto the ship, or carrying the trunks of the passengers up the gangway on their shoulders.

The breeze that blew from the East River made me hug myself, and I realized that I was shivering, not with cold but with nervous expectation. What did the future hold for a woman of eighteen years with no family, no wealth, no husband, and no prospects?

2.

For a time I watched a large wooden crate being lifted in a rope net from the pier and swung over the middle part of the ship, then lowered with difficulty down through the hatchway. It must have been very heavy because it caused the steam crane to buck and strain, to the great alarm of the men who guided the crate with ropes. There was much harsh shouting and running about. A man wearing a long black cloak, who did not appear to be one of the crew, shouted the loudest and waved his silver-headed cane at the sailors. He used several terms that made me blush to the ears.

"Excuse me, Miss. May I be of assistance?"

He was tall and slender, dressed in a navy blue peacoat, the collar of which was turned up against the breeze. His dark hair contrasted strikingly with his pale blue eyes, and the slight natural redness in his lips stood forth in a provocative way against his clean-shaven cheeks.

I tucked behind my ear a strand of brown hair that had blown free from the bun at the back of my head.

"What makes you believe I need assistance?"

He blinked at my pert tone of voice, which I at once regretted.

"Well, I saw you standing here alone beside your trunk, and surmised that you were a passenger aboard my ship. Forgive me, let me introduce myself. My name is Jack Brawney."

I looked at him with less suspicion. "You refer to the *Caledonia* as your ship—are you her captain?"

He laughed.

"No, only the first mate, I'm afraid. But I have enough authority to find a man to carry your trunk on board and get you settled in your stateroom, Miss …?"

"Alice West. Yes, Mr. Brawney, you surmised rightly. I am taking passage on your ship to Liverpool."

I offered him my hand. He took it for an instant and inclined his head.

"Let me help you aboard. We sail shortly."

He caught the eye of a harried, sweating seaman and motioned him over. "Carry this young woman's trunk into stateroom—what number have you booked?"

"Twelve, I believe." My uncle had mentioned it in passing as we were leaving the house.

He gave me his arm and escorted me up the gangway, which swayed and bobbed alarmingly beneath my feet, then down a short flight of steps to the deck of the ship. The cabins in the bow and stern were elevated so that the decks above them were even with the ship rail, but the center deck was lower—so much so that the sides of the ship almost prevented me from seeing out. It was a bit like standing in a giant wooden bathtub filled with every manner of obstruction, from coils of rope to folded piles of canvas.

On either side of the ship a green longboat hung inverted to shed the rain. In the little pens constructed in the spaces beneath them huddled livestock. I realized they were there to provide fresh eggs, milk and meat for the dining tables. They did not look any happier than I felt, but pressed together with their heads down and made sounds of misery.

I realized that the ship was moving in a subtle way, even tied up at the pier. We are accustomed to the earth remaining forever motionless beneath our feet, but a ship is never fixed in place. The hemp ropes creaked as they strained in their blocks, and the sides of the ship cracked as they flexed.

The crew continued to load cargo into the open hatchway.

"Watch your step, woman; men are working here," snapped an ill-favored little gnome of a man with broad shoulders. A red scar ran across his face from his left eye to his right cheek, cutting through the bridge of his snub nose.

"You watch your tone, Mr. McGee," Brawney said with authority in his voice. "This woman is a first-class passenger."

The short man's expression changed from irritation to fawning apology. He touched his fingers to his cap.

"My apologies, Miss. I thought you was one of the—" He stopped, glanced at Brawney, and cleared his throat. "I thought you was seeing off one of the crewmen."

We made our way with care toward the stern of the ship, stepping over boxes of unsecured cargo that littered the deck.

"Who was that dreadful man?"

"Don't worry about him. He's Leaner McGee, the second mate of the Caledonia. You won't have any interaction with him in future. His job is to keep the crew from slacking at their work or fighting amongst themselves."

"Is he what's called the 'bucko' mate?"

He regarded me with appreciation. "Yes, he's the 'bucko' who keeps the men in line. I'm surprised you know the term."

"I've been reading up on the trans-Atlantic packets since finding out that I was being sent to England."

"This ship hasn't been a packet for two years, but the way things are run is not very different. Common seamen are a rough breed who like to drink and fight. They need a firm hand to keep them honest."

I paused to survey the men who stood over the open hold, throwing down bales of raw wool. Many of them had scraps of colorful cloth tied around their heads and dirty white skirts around their hips, but were otherwise naked.

"Your crewmen appear to be Orientals."

"About half of them are Lascars."

"I'm not familiar with that term."

"Natives of the South Pacific islands. But don't worry, they are as skilled at sailing this ship as any New Englander."

From the shadowed depths of the hold came a blood-chilling screech. It was so primal, it caused every man to stand motionless for several seconds.

"What in the world was that?"

"One of Mr. Walther's beasts, I would imagine." He frowned. "We are transporting a menagerie to the London Zoo. They've taken up most of the steerage and part of the hold."

"You look displeased."

"Transporting wild beasts is always a burden. They require so much careful handling."

Opening a companionway, he ushered me into a long room with two tables running down its center. Seated on benches at the tables were some of my fellow passengers. They glanced at me briefly as I entered, but were preoccupied with the last-minute hurry of departure. Between the tables, in the middle of the room, a copper cistern stood in a framework of heavy timber. I saw that a tap was set in its base, from which a young man with an enormous blond moustache was drawing off a cup of water. He noticed my attention and winked at me.

On either side of the room were rows of identical doors with numbers above them. They lacked windows, but their upper portions were fitted with wooden louvers. Ample light shone down from pyramid-shaped glass skylights that were set at intervals in the deck above our heads.

"This is the saloon where first-class passengers socialize and take their meals. Let me show you to your stateroom."

Brawney led me down one side to the door marked *12* and opened it. The stateroom was a tiny thing that held two bunks affixed to a wall, one above the other. The lower bed had been made up with sheets and blankets and had a pillow in a white slipcase. Affixed to the opposite wall I saw a small commode that held on its top a matching porcelain pitcher and wash basin. The top had a raised lip all around its edge to prevent these things from sliding off it. Opening its little door, I saw within a chamber pot. Beside the commode was a small chest of drawers, also built into the wall.

"How do you like your accommodations?"

I raised my hand, and found that I could touch the beam overhead. This was a novelty, accustomed as I was to the spacious floors and towering ceilings of my uncle's mansion. "It's rather dark in here."

"There are no portholes, I'm afraid, but light comes in from the saloon through the louvers in the door, and at night you are equipped with a whale-oil lamp and candles, should you wish to read."

The man carrying my trunk set it down at the end of the room with a bang of relief and stood wiping his forehead on the back of his hand. Brawney motioned him out.

"I must leave you at present, Miss West. The ship is about to sail and my duties require me on deck. But I'm sure we will have many occasions to converse over the coming weeks."

"How long do you expect the passage to take, Mr. Brawney?"

He smiled at my simplicity. "The North Atlantic can be fickle in any season, and the winds blow as they will. I would expect our crossing to take approximately three weeks, but it could well be several days less than that. If we were to run into bad weather, it might add more than a week."

He excused himself and left me to unpack my trunk into the drawers and wash my face in the basin. After that, I am sorry to say that I sobbed into my hands like a little girl whose toy has been snatched away. For perhaps ten minutes I let myself feel miserable. Then I brushed the tears from my cheeks and went out to become acquainted with the other passengers in the saloon.

3.

The terrors began on the third day. I was lying on my bed in my stateroom, recovering from a minor bout of seasickness, when a knock sounded on my door.

"Who is there?"

"It's Kathy Sullivan."

The door was barely parted before she rushed in to embrace me. I felt the thudding of her heart beneath her ample bosom and gently disengaged myself. Her broad face was the color of unbaked bread dough.

"What on earth is the matter?"

"Haven't you heard?"

"Heard what? I was asleep on my bed."

"A member of the crew has disappeared."

My stomach was still unsettled. I took a slice of ginger root from a saucer on the commode and put it into my mouth.

"You're upset. Come and sit down and tell me all about it."

I drew her to the bed and we sat side by side.

"He was noticed missing when the crew gathered for their noon meal. They are still searching the ship for him, but the general belief is that he has gone overboard."

"That's terrible."

"They say Mr. Brawney wanted to turn the ship around and search the water, but Captain Haire denied his request, and instead ordered that every inch of the ship be searched in case the man is hiding."

"Why would he hide?"

"That's the thing, my dear. They say he has no enemies among the crew. There is no reason for him to conceal himself. But the Captain will have his way."

I washed my face in the basin to banish the sleep from my eyes, and we went into the saloon. Mrs. Sullivan's two girls, five-year-old Jane and her big sister, Betty, who was two years older, sat on the red sofa at the end of the room, in the care of Madame Helena Volkovsky, a Russian spiritualist in her sixties who was engaged in what she called her world tour.

Madame Volkovsky was a jovial woman of ample bosom who liked to wrap herself in feathers. She habitually wore a feather boa around her broad shoulders, and had a number of striking hats that bristled with peacock feathers. Whenever I talked with her, after she left I invariably found a feather or two in her place, as if they were her calling cards.

"How are my little ones behaving?" Mrs. Sullivan asked, bending to stare into the brown eyes of the solemn girls, who both sucked their thumbs.

"Like little angels," Madame Volkovsky said in her strong Russian accent. "I love to take care of them. I could eat them both up for dinner."

She put her arms around the girls and made growling noises in her throat. The girls giggled and squirmed from her embrace to hide behind the black skirts of their mother. Mrs. Sullivan was still in mourning over the death of her husband. It was his death that had caused her to return to England, to live with her family in the Lake District. So she had informed me while we were exchanging confidences.

It amazed me how much personal information could be gleaned about complete strangers, if one found oneself shut up with them for days on end. Conversation is necessary for happiness, and having little else to do, we passengers talked amongst ourselves. Since we would probably never see each other again when the ship docked in Liverpool, there seemed little reason to be secretive. I had already told the two women about my unhappy circumstances, and in turn they had confided much of their troubled lives to my keeping.

I looked around the saloon. Most of the other passengers were here, their faces solemn. I wondered if they had been ordered to stay here during the search to keep them out of the way?

Leon Ives, whom everyone called Lefty, sat at a table, fiddling with his deck of playing cards. He was the young blond-haired man who had winked at me upon my first entry into the saloon. His accent was Western, which made me think of him as a cowboy. He always seemed to have cards in his hands, and was quite adept at manipulating them. The beam of sunlight that shone down through the skylight above his head caught the engraved face of the gold ring on his little finger as he expertly cut the deck with one hand, folded it together, and cut it again.

I did not like him and avoided his company. He was vulgar of speech and his clothing, although expensive when new, had seen better days. The cuffs of his shirts were frayed and the soles of his shoes cracked. A small tear in his jacket had been crudely repaired with needle and thread. This led me to suspect that he had fallen on hard times. When asked why he was travelling to England, all he would say was that he intended to try his luck in Europe. There was a rumor that he was fleeing gambling debts in California but he would say nothing on this topic. He flashed a gold-capped tooth beneath his blond moustache as I passed.

Further along the table sat the two most flamboyant of my fellow travelers, a muscular, bearded German named Hans Walther, and the stage impresario Orlando Whittier. In spite of their differences they always seemed to have their heads together; thick as thieves, as the saying goes.

Walther was the owner of the menagerie. When not in the saloon, he spent most of his time tending to the animals in steerage. This was a level of the ship beneath the cabins of the passengers and crew, but above the hold where most of the cargo was kept. While the *Caledonia* had served as a regular packet on the Black Ball Line, steerage had been filled with hundreds of poor people making their way from England to America, but now that the ship sailed as a tramp, the steerage level was used for cargo.

His well-combed and waxed black beard was so thick and dark, it almost looked false, but it matched the blackness of his eyes. He always wore a fierce look that was half-snarl, but I don't believe he was even aware of it. Over the years of tending dangerous beasts he had taken on a beast-like expression himself.

In sharp contrast to Walther's lean, hard body and dark complexion, Orlando Whittier was fat and pink, with long red hair and a full red moustache that connected to mutton-chops on his cheeks. He was about twenty years older than Walther, but seemed the younger of the two, so filled was he with animation and enthusiasm. When he talked, his voice boomed out from his barrel chest, and his hands slashed the air to emphasize what he was saying. This was the man who had shaken his silver-headed cane at the Lascars on the day of our departure.

He told us that he was sailing to England to take over management of a new wax museum that was to compete with the establishment of Madame Tussaud, who, he informed us, had just leased the upper floor of the Baker Street Bazaar for her popular exhibits. He claimed that his museum would not only have wax figures of famed and infamous individuals, but would be filled with authentic curiosities and horrors that he had gathered from around the world.

"I heard one of the Lascars say the missing man saw something in the hold that made him run screaming," Whittier said to Walther as I passed.

"You savvy their language?" Walther asked.

"I know a bit of Lascar."

"Maybe the man saw my mountain lion. That cat's a mean one."

"The crew knows about your beasts. Why would that send him running?"

I continued to the copper cistern, where I drew off a glass of water. The two Catholic priests seated on the other side of the table in their long black robes, Father Patrick and Father John, nodded to me and invited me to sit opposite them. Both had glasses of wine. A wine bottle stood between them, almost empty. For a modest sum in excess of the passage fee, passengers could have as much wine as they could drink. The elder priest liked his wine.

"We were just talking about this bad business," Father Patrick said in his Irish brogue. "The steward told us they are going to search our staterooms. Can you believe that? The indignity of it."

"They have to make a thorough search of the ship," Father John told the older man. His accent was English, and slightly slurred.

"Thorough is thorough, right enough, but why would any of us hide a sailor in our stateroom?"

"Maybe one of the passengers killed him," I suggested.

Father Patrick stared at me for a second, then shook his head. "Don't be morbid, Alice. You'll give yourself the vapors."

Lefty Ives came to the cistern with a glass in his hand that was half-filled with what looked to me like whisky and turned the tap to dribble some water into it.

"If you kill a man aboard ship, you throw him overboard. Everyone knows that."

"We don't know that he's dead, and if he is dead it was probably an accident," Father Patrick said.

"The poor man must have gone out of his head," Father John added.

Ives sat on the bench next to me, straddling it so that he faced me directly. I did not look at him.

"Would you like to play a game of cards to pass the time, Miss West?"

"I don't play poker, Mr. Ives."

"I'll play any game you can name. What about whist?"

"You play whist?" Father Patrick said. "I've played a little whist in my time."

"Splendid. We can put a small bet on the outcome to make the game more interesting."

"Well, as to that, I don't know," Father Patrick said.

"Men of God do not gamble," Father John told him, scowling.

"That's a pity," Ives said. He turned back to me. "You and I can play for pennies."

The door of the saloon opened and the chief steward, Elijah Smalls, bustled in, followed by the second mate, Leaner McGee, and one of the American crewmen.

"Nothing to be concerned about, good people," Smalls said, wringing his delicate white hands together, which were so much like the hands of a woman. "Stay calm, and everything will be done orderly. The Captain wishes a search made of all the staterooms in case the missing person is hiding in one of them."

A general groan of displeasure arose from the passengers. The door to number seven opened and the Fieldings came out. They were an elderly couple who seldom sat in the saloon. Both were white-haired. The husband supported his wife by the arm to help her walk.

"If any of our possessions are missing after the search, I shall take it directly to the Captain," Fielding said in a shrill voice.

"We're not thieves," McGee told him.

He pointed his man toward one side of the saloon and took the cabins on the opposite side, going through them methodically. There was nowhere a man could hide, so the search took only a few minutes.

"Can you tell us anything about what's going on?" Ives asked McGee as he was leaving the saloon.

The second mate glared at him. The scar across his face was bright red.

"A crewman is missing. We're searching for him. He hasn't been found."

"But why did he run screaming out of the hold?" Whittier asked.

"I know nothing about that."

"The Lascars say he saw something down there."

McGee grinned at Whittier. "You'll keep away from them savages if you know what's good for you."

"Do you mean they are dangerous?" Father Patrick asked in alarm.

"They ain't civilized the way we are. They don't think the way we think, or act the way we act. That's all I'm saying."

4.

The menagerie in steerage became a daily entertainment for many of the passengers. We were given full run of the ship, except for the hold. Only select members of the crew and Walther's hired man, Tim Edwards, descended into its dank depths.

In the mornings when Tim fed the animals in steerage, we would watch and laugh at their antics. The comedians of the menagerie were the racoons, whose comic expressions and dexterous little fingers always evoked laughter. They were quite particular with their food, turning it over and over to remove the least bit of straw or dirt before delicately biting into it.

The cages were mounted on the sleeping platforms that had formerly served the needs of whole families of penniless immigrants. Both sides of the ship were lined with these small platforms, one above the other, so that the only standing space for the steerage passengers was the open floor between them. There were no skylights to provide daylight. The rays of the sun came down the open hatchway, but it was sealed during bad weather to keep the water out. It was wretched enough that these poor animals were kept in such primitive conditions, but the thought that pregnant women and small children had endured the same abuse almost made me ill.

The mountain lion was not kept in steerage, but in the hold along with the other more dangerous beasts, such as the grizzly bear and the timber wolves, so we had no chance to observe it. Every now and then its savage screech would sound up from the darkness, like the cry of some demon in hell. The hatch was kept open to allow fresh air to circulate throughout the hold, and disperse the methane generated by the manure of the creatures.

Forbidden Passage

It was the second day after the disappearance of the crewman. I had descended to steerage looking for Mrs. Sullivan. She usually took her girls to watch the animals being fed. Not finding them there, I lingered near the open hatchway that led down into the hold. A curious kind of rhythmic sing-song came from the darkness. It sounded like the soft chanting of human voices. I leaned lower.

Strong hands gripped my elbows and drew me firmly backward. I whirled in annoyance, only to meet Mr. Brawney's concerned blue eyes.

"I beg of you to be more careful, Miss West. A fall into the hold could well prove fatal."

My annoyance became amusement. "I have fallen further than that and survived to tell of it."

"Indeed? What were the circumstances?"

"When I was ten, my cat escaped out my bedroom window onto a part of the roof. I crawled out to get her back. As I reached for her, she jumped past me into the bedroom, but the leap startled me and I fell to the ground."

"Were you badly hurt?"

"I suffered a concussion that resulted in fluid building up inside my skull. A surgeon had to cut a hole in my head with a chisel to relieve the pressure. He put a small metal plate over the hole to protect my brain until my skull grew closed. Here, you can feel it beneath my scalp."

Taking his hand, I placed his fingers over the place where the metal plate resided and he felt the slight bump it made.

"Thank heaven for the skill of your surgeon."

My expression became more solemn in recollection. "That was the same summer my parents died."

I found myself telling Mr. Brawney my life history. He listened with compassionate interest.

"It seems strange that your father would exclude you from his will."

"As it did to me, but I was assured of it by the solicitor who oversaw the division of his estate. My uncle received all of it, apart from a few provisions for the servants."

"I can think of no reason for such unkindness," he said, shaking his head. "Unless ..."

He turned his head quickly, but not before I glimpsed his expression.

"I have had the same thought myself, Mr. Brawney. Please, don't distress yourself over it. I grant that it might explain my father's omission, but he never behaved toward me with other than the utmost loving kindness. The universal opinion among the servants was that I had been born with my mother's hair and my father's eyes."

"My apology, Miss West. The thought would never have even arisen in my mind were it not for your exclusion from your father's will."

I was about to respond when I realized the chanting had stopped in the hold. Leaning forward, I cocked my head.

"They've stopped."

"Who has stopped what?"

"The chanting in the hold. Whoever was doing it has stopped."

A grim expression hardened the line of his jaw. "Your ears are better than mine. Had I heard them at it I would have stopped them at once."

"Has it happened before?"

He nodded. "Some of the Lascars have taken to creeping down here when they should be working. They sit cross-legged and chant in some barbaric tongue that I've never heard before. It's not a language they use amongst themselves."

A Lascar emerged from the darkness of the open hatch, followed by two others. He looked at Brawney, but instead of fear there was a kind of dreamy indifference in his dark eyes. The others were the same. Brawney ordered them to get back to their work, and they nodded in submission as they passed him.

"Maybe it's some kind of rite in their native religion?" I said quietly as they ascended the stairs to the deck.

"If it is, this is the first I've seen of it."

"They almost seemed to be walking in their sleep."

"Mr. McGee's strong right arm and knotted hemp will wake them up quick enough."

"Does Captain Haire know about this?"

He shook his head with a smile. "This isn't the sort of thing a second mate bothers his captain with. The Captain's only duties are to take a daily reading of the sun to ensure that we remain on course, and to give the sailing orders for the day. Unless there's an emergency, Captain Haire usually stays in his cabin."

I sensed there was something else he was not telling me.

"Since I came on board this ship I've only seen Captain Haire once."

"He has problems with his health," Brawney said evasively.

"What sort of problems?" I pressed.

He hesitated, and seemed to come to a mental determination.

"This is in confidence, do you understand?"

I nodded.

"The truth of the matter is, our Captain has pains in his joints that never leave him. To alleviate his suffering he takes opium. He was a good man in his day, one of the very best, but I fear his best days are behind him."

"I see. So he remains in his cabin—"

"And smokes his pipe. Sometimes he takes too much."

"You've been doing his work for him," I said with sudden realization. "You've been concealing his addiction from the crew."

"Captain Haire can still do his job when his wits are about him," he said in a defensive tone. "When he smokes too much of the black tar, I check over the log to make sure it is accurate, and correct what needs to be corrected."

"Your loyalty to your captain is admirable, but surely this cannot go on."

"No. I am in debate with myself whether to seek another ship when we land in Liverpool."

"I am sure you will have no difficulty finding another ship."

"You speak of something about which you know nothing," he said, his tone growing cold.

"I did not mean to be forward."

"We all have shadows in our past, Miss West. If Captain Haire is at fault, I am no less at fault than he, in my own fashion."

With that, he bade me good-day and left the steerage.

While I was pondering his words, Ives approached me. As usual, he was half-drunk. "Such a changeable nature our Mr. Brawney has. One minute all smiles and winks, and the next ..."

The anger that rose within me was too swift to control.

"Were you eavesdropping on our private conversation, sir?"

"I must have been," he said with a smile.

"That is not the behavior of a gentleman."

"I never claimed to be a gentleman, Alice."

"I have not given you permission to address me by my first name."

"What are such pointless formalities, when we are alone together? You may call me Leon, if you wish—I don't suppose you will call me Lefty, as my friends do."

"What I call you, sir, is impudent and rude. Kindly let me pass."

He continued to block my way for several seconds, then at last stepped aside and allowed me to ascend to the open deck.

5.

When the strange malaise began, I cannot be certain. It crept across the ship like a shadow, affecting passengers and crew alike. At some point during the second week of my passage I noticed that several of my fellow travelers were unresponsive when spoken to, and bore a vague, dreaming expression on their faces. If pressed, they would answer direct remarks with a few mumbled words, after which they instantly sank back into their passive state. They seemed to listen to some silent voice and wait for some hidden sign.

Mrs. Sullivan came to me and drew me into her stateroom, where her daughters sat side by side on the lower bunk. They were holding hands, and both had a faint half-smile on their lips.

"Look at them, Alice. Something is not right about them. Neither will talk to me unless I shake her by the shoulders. Are they sick?"

I went to the girls and bent to stare into their eyes. The open stateroom door admitted ample light. Their pupils were enlarged into black pools that almost covered the brown of their eyes. Neither seemed to see me, even though they looked directly at me. I shook the older girl, Betty, gently by the shoulder.

"Betty, do you know who I am?"

Her attention focused weakly on my face. "You're Alice West."

"What's wrong, Betty? Are you sick?"

"No."

"Why do you and Jane just sit on the bed?"

"I don't know."

Their mother wrung her hands. "They don't play with their dolls. They don't even want to go and see the animals. It's not natural, Alice."

I told her that I had observed the same condition among several members of the ship's crew. They went about their daily tasks as though sleepwalking, and never spoke unless spoken to.

"What's happening, Alice? Is it some disease, do you think? Maybe something they caught from those animals in steerage?"

Forbidden Passage

I tried to comfort her, but in the end what could I say? I had no more notion of what caused the strange listlessness of the girls than their mother. I left her and returned to the saloon.

Madame Volkovsky was laying out a pattern of cards on the table. This had attracted Leon Ives, who had a fascination for everything to do with cards. He stood leaning over her with his foot upon the bench and his elbow on his knee. I sat on the opposite side of the Russian woman.

The cards were unlike any I had seen before. They were covered with colorful images.

"What strange cards."

"Madame says they are the Tarot," Ives remarked.

I ignored him.

"What are you doing, Madame?"

She smiled at me with bright intelligence. "I ask the cards to tell me what is happening on this ship. The cards speak to me."

I lowered my voice. "Do you mean, the sickness that has afflicted some of the passengers?"

"It's not a sickness, Miss West," Ives said. I noted that he also muted his voice. "It's more like a fit of some kind, or a mania."

I could not continue ignoring him. I nodded toward the other end of the saloon. "The older priest has it. So do the Fieldings, I believe, although they are so elderly it is difficult to be sure."

He nodded agreement, his eyes directed at where the old couple sat together, staring at nothing. "And it's not only the morose condition, it's the headaches and the nightmares."

"I know nothing of headaches."

"Don't tell me you haven't been getting them?"

I shook my head.

"No bad dreams, either?"

"What kind of dreams?"

He shrugged and looked away, as though embarrassed to speak of it. "I don't know exactly. Horrible things. Dark immensities that lurk on the edge of vision, drawing ever closer. A kind of screaming in the blackness, like a troop of damned souls crying out to be forgiven." He paused and laughed. "Then there's the voice."

"What kind of voice?"

"I don't know how to describe it, exactly. It is a voice without words. It tells me to do things, but because it has no words I don't remember what

I'm supposed to do when I wake up." He laughed. "It's quite frustrating, in an insane sort of way."

"Has anyone else had these dreams?"

"At least a few that I've talked with."

"Not the same dreams, surely. How would that be possible?"

"No, not exactly the same, but quite similar in tone. There's always a black gulf with some horrific thing in it that draws ever nearer."

"I have had these nightmares," Madame Volkovsky murmured as she studied the cards.

"And the headaches?" I asked.

"Yes, I get headaches. But then, I have always suffered from headaches."

"There is something more," Ives said in a conspiratorial tone. "The chanting that comes from the hold. You've heard it?"

I nodded.

"Well, it's getting louder. And there's something more yet. You know that sailor who disappeared last week?"

"What of him?"

"Others have vanished from the ship. I heard Brawney talking to McGee."

A kind of chill went through my body. "How many?"

"From what I could gather, at least several."

"There has been no announcement of disappearances."

"Don't you see? They are hiding it from us. They are afraid to tell us."

"The cards speak," Madame murmured under her breath. Her eyes were closed to narrow slits and her head inclined forward on her double chin.

"What do they say?" Ives asked.

"I see something. It is as ancient as the mountains where it lay hidden and forgotten for so many ages, before the ground sank beneath the sea and then rose up again as islands. There is a dark concentration of malignancy around it, like a black cloud, a kind of hatred for all living things, even for life itself. At present it lies coiled up tightly, like the string around a ball, but it pulses with darkness."

Looking at the pattern of upturned cards, I could see nothing but enigmatic figures.

"How does this bode for the future?" I asked.

She sat in silence for several moments, then opened her eyes. "There is nothing more I can tell you."

Forbidden Passage

Gathering her cards, she turned them over and shuffled them back into the deck.

The impresario, Orlando Whittier, brought his glass of wine toward us and sat down on the opposite side of the table. He regarded the three of us with his intense gray gaze. "I have something to tell you," he said, his powerful voice no more than a low rumble.

None of us responded. He was not well liked among the passengers, because he tended to dominate conversations and impose his social and political views on others. Most of the passengers avoided him. The exception was Hans Walther, who treated the showman like a beloved older brother. Walther was not in the saloon at present. He was probably tending to his animals.

"It is my belief," he continued, "that we are no longer on our correct course."

"That's crazy," Ives said.

"No. I have been watching the sun. In my opinion, the ship is sailing ever further to the north."

"Sometimes the ship sails more northerly, and sometimes more southerly, depending on the way the wind blows," I told him. "Perhaps you are mistaken."

"No," he said firmly. "I have been watching the sun. We are going more north than east."

"Why would the Captain sail north?" Ives asked in an amused tone.

"I do not know why we are sailing north, only that we are doing so."

"I'll ask Mr. Brawney about it the next time I see him," I said to reassure him. He was becoming quite agitated.

"He is in on it," Whittier said. "They are all in on it. They must be."

"Old man, I think you need to drink a whiskey and relax," Ives said.

Whittier stood up. "Pah! You are useless. You don't even see what is happening all around you."

He retreated to the far end of the saloon to sit by himself.

"Show people are a little crazy," Ives said with a smile.

"Even so, I wonder if what he said could be true?"

"There's one way to know. I have a compass in my stateroom."

He left the table and vanished behind the door of his compartment. After a minute he emerged with something in his hand and an odd expression. I could not resist speaking to him.

"Well? What does it say?"

Without speaking, he laid the compass on the table before me. I studied its needle, a mounting sense of dread tightening my throat. The long table at which we sat lay parallel to the keel of the ship. It pointed in almost the same direction as the compass needle.

"Can this be true?"

"It's a good compass," he said. "I won it with three of a kind from a prospector."

"Why don't you ask Mr. Brawney or Captain Haire about it?"

"I never see the Captain. As for Brawney, he doesn't think very highly of me and won't give me the time of day. But he likes you, Miss West."

"The next time I see Mr. Brawney, I will speak to him about it," I said with a sudden resolve. "And about the sickness."

"Don't forget to ask about the disappearing crewmen," he added.

"Yes. I'm sure there's a simple explanation for everything."

6.

Everyone began to initiate their conversation with conspiratorial whispers. All of the passengers avoided casual talk with each other or with ship's officers. Perhaps they were afraid, as I was, to hear of some new and ominous happening. With all my heart I only wanted this hellish passage across the Atlantic to be over and behind me.

Mrs. Sullivan sought me out in the saloon, her eyebrows beetled together with worry. I noted dark shadows beneath her bloodshot eyes, and realized the poor woman had not slept due to concern over her two young girls. I did not want to speak with her, but could not in good conscience shun her, having given her my confidence.

"Alice, did you know that the milk cow is gone?"

I shook my head.

"It's true," she said, as though fearing I would not believe her. "I went to the starboard longboat enclosure, where they keep the cow and some other livestock, to see if I could get some fresh milk for my girls, and it's not there."

"Can it have been moved?"

"I asked Mr. Smalls about it, and at first he didn't want to say anything. Then he admitted that the cow had disappeared in the night. Now I ask you, Alice, how does a cow disappear?"

Forbidden Passage

After doing my best to comfort her, I left the saloon and climbed the steps to the elevated rear deck, where I could usually find Mr. Brawney. To my surprise, the Captain stood with him. He held a shiny brass sextant in his hands, and was peering through its eyepiece. I realized that it must be noon.

I'm not sure why I found Captain Haire so intimidating. He was a clean-shaven, red-faced man of no great height, but something in his manner demanded obedience. He carried himself as if he owned not only the ship, but the ocean and the sky as well. I had seen crewmen wither before his scornful glare and slink away like whipped spaniels, yet he seldom needed to speak more than a few words of reproach in a moderate tone. There is a power in some men, a power of authority and command, and Captain Haire had it naturally. It was not his rank that intimidated other men, but something in his manner, his voice, his cold gray eyes.

Since the beginning of the crossing, he had ignored the passengers as if we were so much cargo. He would speak when spoken to directly, but only a few words before he turned his back and walked away. I had never spoken to him. I stayed close to the rail and watched the Captain finish his sighting of the sun with Mr. Brawney at his side. The first mate's attention was on his captain. He had not yet noticed my presence.

"Sir, you must let me speak."

"Speak, then, damn you, if it will shut your mouth."

"Sir, this course will not do. You know it will not do."

"I am captain of this vessel, not you. I will chart her course."

"I was only suggesting, sir, that you might need help in doing so. You have not been sleeping. You are not yourself."

"My health is not your concern, Mr. Brawney."

"I know you have been taxed by the disappearances of the crew, and the other curious happenings."

"Enough! No more of your feeble quibblings."

Captain Haire left the deck without giving me a glance. Brawney continued to stand with his legs braced, staring out to sea. I allowed several minutes to pass before approaching him.

When he saw me, he gathered himself together and smiled. "Miss West. Have you come up to get some sun on your skin?"

"Perish the thought. The sun gives me freckles."

"Whatever your reason, it is a delight to see you, as always."

I was shocked by the change in his appearance since last I had spoken with him. His bloodshot eyes had the same dark shadows beneath them that I had seen on Mrs. Sullivan.

"Have you been sleeping?"

"Why do you ask?"

"You look tired."

"My sleep has not been as good as it was in the past," he admitted reluctantly.

"Do you get the nightmares?"

He looked at me from the corner of his eye. "You know about the nightmares?"

"It seems everyone has been having them, along with very bad headaches." I did not add that I was oddly exempt from these forms of suffering.

"Yes, I get headaches as well. The damned things make it hard for me to think." He pressed the heel of his hand against his forehead and shut his eyes. "Nothing seems to lessen their severity except laudanum, and I can hardly take that when I am commanding a ship."

"Captain Haire has no such reluctance," I murmured.

"There you are wrong. He never touches laudanum. His pipe is his sole consolation."

"There has been talk among the passengers."

"What sort of talk?"

"About the disappearances. The chanting in the hold. Our altered course."

He studied my face. "What do you know of our course?"

"Only that some of the men believe that it is straying further north than it should."

"I cannot speak of these matters. They are not the concern of the passengers." He fell silent, but after a time he said, "Privately, between the two of us, I believe Captain Haire is not well. He plots a course that takes us well off the usual shipping lines."

His conspiratorial tone made me look around the deck to ensure no others were near enough to overhear our conversation.

"Why is he doing it?"

"I don't know. There cannot be a good reason, but he will not speak to me about it. I am left with only two options."

"And those are?"

"I can remain silent and follow his orders."

"What is the other option?"

"I dare not speak it aloud, not even to you, Miss West. It would be a terrible step to take, one that would certainly end my career, and very likely get me hanged."

I touched my fingers to his lips. "Don't say the word. I understand."

He frowned in frustration. "How can a seaman of Haire's experience suddenly lose his wits? It's not the opium, I know how that affects him. It's something else. It's almost as if this crossing has been cursed."

"Do you know what is happening to the Lascars?"

"They seem to have developed some collective religious mania. Try as I will, I cannot keep them out of the hold, where they sit and chant some gibberish in an unknown tongue. One day Mr. McGee caught them about to sacrifice a chicken down there."

"Can't you just close and lock the hold?"

He shook his head. "Mr. Walther's dangerous beasts require fresh air, and his man, Tim Edwards, must descend every day to clean their cages and feed and water them. Besides this, the leader of the Lascars, who calls himself Jimmy Meercat, came to me and flatly told me that if the Lascars were barred from the hold, they would do no work. I need them to sail this ship, Miss West. What was I to do? I could have ordered Mr. McGee to make an example of this Meercat fellow and a few others, but there is no guarantee they would be cowed into submission. Just the opposite; it might enrage them enough to attack the rest of the crew and the passengers."

My alarm grew with every word. The changes in the atmosphere of the ship had been gradual and seemingly of small concern, but I realized that much had taken place beneath the surface about which the other passengers remained completely ignorant.

"Is there really a chance of an insurrection?"

"I tell you this privately; yes, there is a chance the Lascars might rise against us if I forbid them their religious practices. I have seen it in their eyes. They are a very determined people, and superstitious."

Some of the Pacific islanders were above us, taking in one of the sails on the main mast. They worked in silence, and seemed to lack the energy that had animated them at the beginning of the voyage. Their faces bore the same blankness I had seen in several of the passengers.

"Something has affected them," I said. "Something dark and malevolent."

"Something has affected everyone on this ship, Miss West—everyone, except for you." He stared at me with admiration. "Your hazel eyes are as clear and bright as they were the day we first met."

I left him with a better understanding of the peril we faced, but it did nothing to relieve the weight upon my heart. I dared not share what I had learned with the other passengers for fear that it would send them into hysterics.

7.

The passing days were both dreary in their sameness and terrifying for the unknown dangers they held. The sky became overcast, and the ocean changed from blue to gray. A distinct chill came into the air that had not been there before. I wondered how far north we had sailed, and when Mr. Brawney would find the courage to displace Captain Haire, as it appeared to me he must do if he was to save the ship from disaster. When I looked to the north I could see small white flecks on the horizon. I knew they were icebergs, enormous mountains of ice that would crush the ship to splinters should we run into one of them in the dark.

On the third day after my conversation with the first mate, both the Fieldings disappeared. The passengers helped the crew in their search of the ship, all except the hold which we were barred from entering, but none of us held any hope in our heart of finding them. It seemed obvious that they had gone overboard, either killing themselves from despair, or—the more sinister possibility—thrown over by the Lascars. As to why the Lascars would want to harm so inoffensive a couple, none of us could conceive.

The same listlessness that had afflicted the Fieldings continued to torment some of the passengers. Mrs. Sullivan and both her girls sat by themselves, staring at nothing with faint smiles on their lips, as though listening to distant music. The elder priest, Father Patrick, was the same way, to the great alarm of his young travel companion, Father John. Everyone complained of headaches and nightmares. It appeared that I was the only passenger not afflicted. I could think of no reason why I should be spared while the rest suffered.

On the afternoon of the day the Fieldings vanished, Mr. Smalls entered the saloon with Mr. Walther close behind him. The black-bearded

German carried a rifle. "I have an announcement," Smalls said in a voice that quavered. "A terrible thing has happened ..."

His words trailed off. We waited for him to continue, but Walther, seeing the nervous state of the steward, pushed him to one side.

"My mountain lion has escaped his cage. He is very likely somewhere on the ship, hiding and terrified. We're here to ask that you remain confined to your staterooms and the saloon until I am able to recapture him, or if necessary put him down."

"How did this happen?" Whittier demanded.

"I don't know. The iron bars of his cage were bent aside. I would not have thought it possible that the cat possessed such strength."

"Maybe the chanting of the savages drove it to madness," Mr. Ives suggested with a sardonic smile.

"The Lascars do their chanting in the other end of the hold, where my artefacts are stored," Whittier told him.

"The cat has been well fed," Walther said. "There is very little danger of him harming anyone as long as he is not threatened."

"I feel safe enough," Ives said, drawing his revolver from his pocket and displaying it. "I suggest that anyone who has a weapon keep it on his person at all times."

"If you think that puny thing will stop a mountain lion, you are a fool," Walther told him.

"Fool I may be, but I'm not the one who allowed the beast to escape, am I?"

To this, Walther had no answer. He turned on his heel and left Smalls to attempt in his weak way to comfort us. It was evident that the steward was more terrified than anyone else in the saloon, and in the end it was the young priest, Father John, who comforted Smalls.

We occupied ourselves in various ways to take our minds off the danger. I sat at the table nearer the bow of the ship, which by unspoken agreement had been given over to the ladies in lieu of a withdrawing room, and added to the account of the voyage that was rapidly filling my journal. The men sat drinking and smoking at the other table.

At the usual time Smalls and his assistant brought in our evening meal, and we gathered at the men's table to eat. We had decided among ourselves not to dress for supper on the first evening of the voyage, so we began to eat without formality. I found my portion of chicken disappointingly meager, but would not have said anything.

Mr. Ives felt no such restraint.

"I'm terrible sorry, sir." Smalls bowed his balding head and wrung his hands. "The livestock and poultry are almost gone."

"What do you mean, gone?"

"I mean they ain't in their pens, sir."

"Has someone been stealing them?"

"That's not for me to say, sir."

"Well, damn it, man, are we going to run out of food before the end of this crossing?"

"No, sir, there is plenty of lard, flour, and potatoes. But we may run out of chickens, sir."

This roused a gentle laughter from those not afflicted with the malaise.

The men were finishing their claret, and the ladies had withdrawn to the other end of the saloon, when Mr. Brawney entered. I was shocked at his appearance. I had not spoken to him since our conversation on the deck. His face was haggard, his eyes bloodshot and staring from under disordered hair.

"The danger is over. The cat is dead," he said in an emotionless way.

"Did you have to shoot it?" Whittier asked.

"No."

"Where was it hiding?"

He hesitated for an instant before answering. "In the hold."

"How can that be?" Ives asked. "Didn't you search the hold first?"

"The Lascars are guarding the end of the hold where they chant their prayers. They would not let us pass, so we searched the rest of the ship first, then after finding nothing, returned to the hold. The Lascars resisted us but we forced our way through."

I noticed for the first time that he was cut on the back of his left hand.

"Were they hiding the cat?"

"No. The mountain lion is dead, as I already told you."

"I don't understand. Did the Lascars kill it?"

Again, Brawney hesitated before speaking. "We found it dead. I don't know what, or who, killed it."

We waited for him to continue, but he turned and left the saloon.

I decided to follow and seek a more complete explanation. Night was just falling. On the western horizon the sun had already set, but the sky above it glowed pink. The air was distinctly cold, and I wondered if I should return to my stateroom to get a woolen shawl for my shoulders, then decided it was more important that I talk to Brawney. I saw him walking toward the stern and called out to him, but he did not turn his head. Before I could speak his name a second time, a man abruptly blocked my path.

It was the leader of the Lascars, the one called Jimmy Meercat. I noted that he had changed the skirt he usually wore for gray canvas trousers and a green felt shirt, but he had retained the colorful rag that was habitually tied around his head. The air must have seemed freezing to a native of the South Sea isles. He was an older man of no great stature, with tiny black eyes and a ragged gray beard that descended to a point from his narrow face. His scarred countenance I can only describe as malevolent.

"Let me pass."

"You no go, lady."

"Let me by or I will call an officer."

He grinned a horrible grin that displayed yellow teeth, half of which were missing. "You call, you call, see who come."

I thought about shoving him aside. He was smaller than me and lighter. Then his hand moved in a stealthy way toward the knife tucked in his belt.

"You are insolent. I shall report you to Mr. Brawney."

"Do that, missy."

I turned and returned to the saloon, my heart hammering in my breast.

8.

Something woke me from dreamless sleep. As I lay in my bunk, listening to the darkness, I detected the odor of stale cigar smoke.

"Who is there?" I said, trying to keep my voice firm.

"Don't be alarmed, Alice. My intentions are honorable, I assure you."

"Mr. Ives? How dare you, sir."

He took a step nearer my bed and lowered his voice still further. "Be quiet and listen to me. We all know something strange is happening on this ship."

"This is hardly the time to discuss it."

"I believe the source of the strangeness lies in the hold, and tonight I mean to go below and discover what it is. I want you to come with me as a witness to what we may find."

I realized that he was kneeling beside my bunk with his face quite near to mine. It was impossible to speak above a whisper without our voices carrying to every other passenger, although to some extent the eerie wail of the rising wind concealed our words. I became aware that the ship was rolling more than usual.

"Is there a storm outside?"

"No yet, although it will come before morning."

For several moments I lay in silent thought. "Very well, I will accompany you."

He left my stateroom to allow me to dress. The deserted saloon was lit by a single hanging oil lamp with a low flame that swayed majestically on its brass chains as the ship rolled. I saw that Ives carried a tin lantern that at present was closed to contain its light.

We went silently from the saloon and made our way to the hatch leading into steerage. This was battened down, but with some difficulty Ives managed to knock it open, and we descended, closing the hatch behind us.

There was always the possibility of encountering a member of the crew when walking at night, although the number of men up and about at this late hour was the minimum necessary to ensure the safety of the ship. Half a dozen of the Lascars had reportedly vanished, making it even less likely that we would be interrupted.

Ives adjusted his lantern so that a yellow halo spread around us. Then he opened the hatch to the hold and we descended the steep stairs into the very bowels of the *Caledonia*. The stench almost made me retch, but with difficulty I contained myself. It was a foul smell of bilge water, putrefaction, and dried blood, not the smell I would have expected from the pens of wild animals.

We went first into the forward part of the hold, where Walther's menagerie was kept. The bear continued to sleep in its cage, but the wolves roused themselves at the sound of our entry and began to pace restlessly back and forth, staring at us with their gleaming eyes, which reflected the lantern flame like mirrors.

"This must be the cage where the mountain lion was kept," Ives said in a whisper. "Look at those bars. What kind of a creature could bend cold iron like that?"

One of the bars had been bent to the side, and the bar next to it was both bent and broken, leaving a gap through which the slender cat must have been able to squirm. I noted blood on one of the bars and called Ives' attention to it.

"The poor kitty must have hurt itself wriggling loose," he murmured.

"Do you think the cat bent these bars?"

"No. It would take a sledge hammer to do this damage, or something even more powerful."

"Perhaps the Lascars set it free."

"Why bend the bars, when all they would need to do is lift the lever on the door and open it?"

To this I had no answer.

We made our way into the stern part of the hold, which was piled with crates of various shapes and sizes.

"These must contain Mr. Whittier's curiosities," Ives murmured.

"What kind of things did he collect for his wax museum? I don't recall he ever spoke about it."

"He was probably embarrassed to admit the true nature of his museum."

"Why would it embarrass him?"

"In short, Alice, it is to be a museum of grotesqueries and monstrosities. Whittler has traveled all over the world collecting the most bizarre and horrifying objects from primitive cultures. When I say collecting, I mean stealing, of course—although I suppose it's possible he bought some of them."

"I can see why he might hesitate to speak of it in polite company."

"Exactly so. I overheard him talking to Walther one evening when Whittier was three sheets to the wind, as they say. He actually had the audacity to steal the idols worshipped by primitive tribes in Africa, South America, and Southeast Asia. He spent years gathering them all in a warehouse in New York City, and now he is taking them to be displayed in London for the titillation of bored gentlemen and their ladies."

Something crunched beneath my boot as we went deeper. When Ives played the light of his lantern over it, we saw that it was a bone covered in dried blood. Indeed, the floor of the hold was littered with bloody and broken bones.

The bones surrounded in a circle a large crate that had been pried open, and its sides removed, so that only its lower pallet remained to support a crude carving in black stone that was four or five feet in diameter. The idol was squat and exceedingly ugly. On its front was what may have been a face. It bore a vague resemblance to several squamous creatures without being an exact representation of any of them. There was something toad-like about it, with its broad nose and heavy-lidded eyes, but its body more resembled an octopus with its eight legs coiled around it.

"Is that blood?"

Ives reached out and touched a finger to the sticky brown streaks on the idol, then held his finger near the lantern. "Yes, it's blood."

"The Lascars must worship this stone with sacrifices."

"Look there," Ives said, his voice sharp.

Something lay at the foot of the idol that at first I could not recognize. Then I realized that it was the head of the mountain lion, which had been torn raggedly from its shoulders. The sight sickened me almost as much as the smell had done upon my entry into the hold. Ives bent over and studied the circle of bones with intense interest.

"This is a cow bone, I think, and these are from a pig. All these little bones must be from chickens."

He picked up a large bone that had been splintered on one end. "Unless I am mistaken, this is a human femur. That's the bone of the thigh."

"I know what a femur is," I said in a faint voice.

Something round and bloody gleamed a dull red as the lantern light played across it. I walked over, avoiding the scattered bones as best I could, and nudged it with my toe. It rolled to reveal two empty eye-sockets and a row of upper teeth. The lower jaw was missing.

"One of the Lascars," Ives murmured.

"Or one of the Fieldings."

"Dear God, what have we found?"

While the ship rolled beneath our feet, we stood in silence and stared at the malign, grinning countenance on the black stone. There was nothing human about it. The human countenance, even when it is that of an evil person, has latently in its shape and proportions the expressions of kindness and joy. We are, after all, formed in the image of our Creator. This face, if it could be called a face, expressed nothing but savagery and malice.

The flickering flame in the lantern made the coiled legs of the creature seem to slide over one another. I saw that there were suckers on their undersides, and inside each sucker a single small hook for tearing flesh from bone.

"Why would human beings worship a monster?" I asked.

"Fear. They worship what terrifies them, in the hope that their abject submission will turn away the horror."

"It's evil. I can sense it."

"It's only a piece of stone, Alice. But I agree; there is evil afoot on this ship."

When we emerged back on deck, I was amazed by the change in the weather. We had not been in the hold much more than an hour, but in that time the wind had redoubled its force, and the crests of waves were breaking over the rail and washing the deck, which was angled to an alarming degree. Men shouted from the rigging, their voices faint in the roar of wind. Looking upward, it seemed to me that there were fewer than usual to take in the sails.

Brawney passed us, clothed head to toe in oilcloth. He had to hold onto the rail until a wave passed over us, then he glared at me with wild, staring eyes. "Get to your staterooms, you fools. You'll be washed overboard."

We continued with difficulty toward the bow. Lightning flashed, followed by rolling thunder, and then the rain came down in sheets, instantly drenching any parts of our bodies that had remained dry. Ives' lantern was washed out, but the storm lanterns that had been set burning continued to guide us through the blackness.

Ives stopped at the companionway leading to the saloon. "If we don't die tonight, we must speak to the Captain," he shouted next to my ear.

"I agree."

We entered with difficulty against the blast of the wind and shut the door against the outer world. I found myself to be utterly exhausted both in body and mind, and wanted only to dry myself and sleep.

Ives walked me to my stateroom door. "I will see you on the morrow, Miss West," he said with a slight smile that was almost hidden beneath his moustache.

"We must take what we know to the Captain. Mr. Brawney should know of it, also."

"I suspect Mr. Brawney already knows as much as we do," Ives said.

"Then why hasn't he acted?"

"You must ask Mr. Brawney."

I entered my stateroom and shut the door, my mind filled with unformed terrors that rolled and tossed like the stormy sea.

9.

The storm lasted three days and nights. How the ship did not founder is a mystery on the order of a miracle. Most of the passengers became seasick and kept to their staterooms, except at mealtime. Smalls and his assistant continued to bring our meals, which were poor enough as to be almost inedible. The portions were meager and badly cooked. Smalls himself looked like something that had been drowned and then reanimated. His eyes were dull and he said nothing unless spoken to directly. Indeed, everyone had fallen into this condition except Mr. Ives and Mr. Whittier.

Mr. Ives and I could not venture on deck in the storm, but we took the opportunity to talk to Whittier. At first he would say little about his curiosities, as he called them, but after we gave him a full account of what we had seen in the stern hold, he became more open. Half a bottle of whiskey aided in easing his inhibitions.

"I know that piece." His words were slurred from the drink. "Best piece in my collection. I found it on a little island off the coast of Malaysia. Had to hire natives from another island to steal it during the night. Heavy as the devil, it is. I think it must be mostly iron. It may even be a meteorite."

"What else can you tell us about it?"

He toyed with his glass and stared up at the skylight above our heads, which was battered by sheets of wind-driven raindrops that sounded like hail as they struck it.

"The natives had a name for it. Lakoose … Lakoosa … something like that. In their language it means the Outsider. They said they kept it on the island because it was too dangerous to keep on the mainland. Superstitious fools. They claimed that when it was awakened with chants, it was always ravenous with hunger and had to be fed with sacrifices, or it would eat those who worshipped it."

"Human sacrifices?" I asked.

"It could be. There is a lot of human sacrifice and cannibalism in those lands. It's usually kept below the surface, but it happens. I've seen it."

A shadow of remembered horror passed over his face, and he gulped at his glass, finishing its contents, then refilled it from the bottle.

"The Lascars on this ship must have recognized the idol," Ives said.

"Impossible. The crate was tightly sealed."

"Perhaps they had some other way of recognizing it."

"Don't talk nonsense, woman."

"Perhaps they sensed it."

"I don't believe in any of that mumbo-jumbo."

"Yet they found it and opened the crate somehow," Ives persisted.

"Evidently so. I'll order Tim to close the crate up again."

Ives looked at me and shook his head. Tim had not been seen since before the onset of the storm.

"Won't the Lascars just tear the crate open again?" I asked.

"Damn it all, I'll talk to Captain Haire, then. He'll put a stop to this nonsense."

We left him to his whiskey and withdrew to an empty corner of the saloon.

"I think he's slipping into the malaise," Ives said. "I can see the signs of it in his eyes and hear it in the listlessness of his voice."

"Almost everyone has fallen into it, except we two."

He took my hand. At another time I might have jerked it away, but I let it remain in his grasp.

"Alice, I've been getting the nightmares. Every night they are worse, and I've found it harder and harder to wake up in the mornings."

"What are you saying, Mr. Ives?"

"Please, after all we've been through, please call me Leon."

"Very well, Leon."

"Thank you, Alice." He squeezed my fingers. "I must confess to you that through all this insanity you have become the one constant in my life."

"I don't know why I am unaffected."

"But you are not affected, that is the point. If I go, and Whittier goes, and Mr. Brawney goes, and even the Captain goes, you will be the only one left to confront this rising—" He stopped, at a loss for words.

"Go on; this rising what?"

"This rising evil. I can find no other way to describe it. God knows, I have seen the evil of other men in my time, more of it than I like to remember, but this evil is deeper and more corrupting."

"I know what you mean. I have felt it, also."

"It is an absolute hatred for mankind, maybe even a hatred for life itself," he said, groping for words to describe what he sensed.

"When the storm has abated, we will both go to Captain Haire and confront him with that we have discovered. Surely we can convince him to act."

"Can we?" He smiled sadly. "If the Captain won't listen to his own first officer, why would he listen to a couple of passengers? He will call us hysterical fools."

"Even so, we must try. If we fail, we will go to Mr. Brawney and convince him to take command of the ship."

"Yes, we must try." He patted the back of my hand gently. "Now, if you will excuse me, I must lie down on my bunk. I am exhausted from lack of sleep."

He went into his stateroom and shut the door. I sat on the sofa at the end of the saloon, watching the other passengers. All of them sat listlessly, staring at nothing. Whittier had his chin on his hand and appeared to have fallen into a drunken stupor with his half-filled glass still in his grasp.

A sudden weariness washed over me like a wave. I decided to lie down in my stateroom and try to sleep, if my restless imaginings would permit it. The roll of the ship had reached its greatest extent and the wind howled like some maddened demon seeking entry into paradise, but I had expended the reserves of my care already, and I scarcely noticed these things as I undressed in the darkness and slid my body into bed.

10.

When I woke, beams of light were shining through the louvers of my stateroom door. I lay still, aware that something had changed, but it was several moments before my sleep-numbed brain could place the difference. Then I realized that the storm was over. The ship no longer rolled at an alarming angle, and the wind had ceased its maniacal howling.

Most of the other passengers must still be asleep, was my thought as I emerged into the saloon. Only Mr. Whittier and Madame Volkovsky were there. They sat far apart, their backs to me and heads lowered. The air was so cold, I hugged my shoulders and shivered, then returned to my stateroom to get a woolen shawl.

There was a strange silence throughout the ship. Usually, at any time of the day or night, you could hear voices calling to each other, or the thud of feet upon the decks, but this morning, if morning it was, I heard nothing. It was an eerie silence that spoke of misfortunes and sorrows, which were all the more terrifying for being unarticulated.

I sat at a table by myself and waited half an hour or so, but when Mr.

Ives did not emerge from his stateroom, I went to his door and knocked. There was no response. Opening the door, I peered in. It was a moment before my eyes adjusted to the gloom, and then I saw that his rumpled bunk was empty.

It occurred to me that he had not waited for me to wake, but had gone to speak with Captain Haire alone. I decided to look for Mr. Brawney and try to persuade him to take command of the ship. I did not share Ives' faith in his ability to reason with Captain Haire. Whether the Captain was besotted with opium or had fallen victim to the malaise, he would be in a state unfit to make rational decisions. The northerly course he had charted for the ship alone indicated that his mind was unhinged.

When I emerged onto the deck of the ship, the sight that greeted me caused me to lose my breath. It escaped between my parted lips as a white mist and hung around my head. The storm had passed, leaving the sea like a gray mirror that gently rose and fell. Not even a slight breeze stirred the tatters of sails that hung limp from the broken spars and lax ropes above my head. The top of the mainmast had sheared off completely sometime during the night, leaving only a splintered stump to show where it had stood. Not a single sail remained untorn.

All around, white mountains towered up from the sea. There must have been a score of them, and on the horizon I saw other clusters. One was terrifyingly near. Its broken, icy slope seemed to hang over the very rail. The sky was covered with a leaden gray that was so dense, it was impossible to guess the location of the sun.

Here and there, men milled around. They looked dazed. Some attempted to repair the damage to the rigging, passing ropes through their hands and tying knots. Others merely stood and stared at nothing. I noticed that none of them were Lascars. Faintly, a rhythmic chanting reached my ears in the stillness, and I realized that it came from the open hatchway. All the Lascars must be in the hold, sitting before their stone idol.

Mr. Brawney was not on the upper deck. It took me some minutes to locate him. He stood behind one of the longboats, staring out to sea. His hair was disordered and whitened with dried salt, and his collar unbuttoned. In his hands he held a brass sextant.

I spoke his name. He did not seem to hear. When I touched his arm, he started and stared at me with wild eyes. Instinctively, I took a step backward. His snarling expression was scarcely human. He blinked several times and seemed to recognize my face. The snarl left his lips.

"What has happened, Mr. Brawney?"

"We are lost, Miss West."

I studied his blue eyes for several moments, seeking meaning.

"I know we are off course, but when the overcast clears, can't you take a sighting of sun or stars?"

"Lost," he repeated. "This ship and everyone on her are damned for eternity. I should have read the signs, but I was arrogant and full of sin. Pride goeth before a fall, and we have fallen into hell."

I put my hand on his arm. "You are speaking irrationally, Mr. Brawney."

"How I wish that were true, Miss West."

"There must be something we can do to save ourselves. The Captain—"

His laughter sounded inhuman. It was more like the gibbering shriek of a great ape than the laughter of a man.

"My advice to you, Miss West, is that you end your own life. Do it quickly, while you still can."

Before I could think of a reply to this extraordinary and terrifying statement, he climbed over the side and, without a backward look, allowed himself to drop into the sea. The weight of the sextant cradled close to his chest drew him rapidly downward.

I screamed and leaned over the rail in an attempt to grasp at his collar, but before I could even reach down he had disappeared into the icy water. I saw his shadow slowly descend until it merged with the eternal night of the deep.

Staring around, I ran to the nearest group of seamen and frantically told them that Mr. Brawney had fallen overboard. They did not speak, but looked at me with sullen expressions on their grizzled faces. When I persisted, they turned their backs and walked away.

I saw the second mate, Leaner McGee, standing on the other side of the ship with his back to me.

"Mr. McGee, come with me quickly, Mr. Brawney has gone overboard."

He turned. Dried blood crusted his scarred face where it had run down from his gaping eye sockets. There were scratches on his cheeks and forehead. The horrible conviction came over me that he had clawed out his own eyes. Before I could speak again, he began to titter like an old woman and did a little hornpipe dance, listening to music only he could hear. I backed away, then ran toward the companionway that led to the Captain's quarters.

Forbidden Passage

For several minutes I stood before the Captain's closed door and attempted to compose myself. There was no sound from the other side. I wondered if he was asleep, or dead.

Without knocking, I entered. He sat at his desk with a pen in his hand, peering down intently at a leather-bound book in which he had been writing. His face was clean-shaven, his hair combed, his clothing clean and neat. A pipe rested on a carved, rosewood pipe stand near his elbow. The acrid smoke that rose from its bowl hung heavy in the air.

He looked up without surprise, as though he had been expecting me.

"Miss West, isn't it? Please, do come in."

I advanced timidly, like the mouse who bells the cat.

"Sit down. I'm just finishing up today's entry in the logbook."

There was so much authority in his voice, that even though he spoke in a mild tone, I sat without complaint and waited until he finished his writing. He closed the logbook and turned his pale gray eyes to me. They were bloodshot and underlined by dark crescents that spoke of lack of sleep, but they appeared sane.

"Mr. Brawney is dead. He drowned himself. Mr. McGee has clawed his own eyes out."

My words had no more effect on his composure than if I had commented on the weather. Then I knew what was in his pipe. The opium tar protected his mind from these shocks without inhibiting his comprehension.

"How many men are still working the ship? Not the Lascars—how many Americans?"

"I didn't count them. I would say about twenty."

"Are they all affected by the malaise?"

I nodded.

He took up the pipe from its stand and drew upon its stem, held the smoke in his lungs, then exhaled slowly. He noticed my eyes on the pipe.

"You think me nothing more than a worthless drug addict, don't you?"

"I would never say such a thing."

"No, but you think it. I take the pipe because it is the only thing that keeps my mind from lapsing into this damned malaise that has afflicted the entire ship."

The Captain was correct; I had been thinking ill of him. His words made me reassess my judgment.

"Do you know what is going on, Captain Haire?"

"I know that something—some insidious will—has us in its grip and is guiding us northward. Before I took up the pipe, it had me issuing faulty orders to the helmsman. Since then, I've done everything I can to bring us back on course but the entire crew conspires against me to maintain this northerly inclination, to what end I know not."

"Do you know about the idol in the hold?"

"I have seen it."

"The Lascars broke open its crate and are worshipping it." I hesitated. "I think they are offering blood sacrifices to it."

"That would explain the disappearance of the animals, and the members of the crew who were presumed to have gone overboard."

"Captain, what are we to do?"

"I'm afraid the ship is lost, Miss West. There are scarcely enough men remaining to sail her, even were she in a seaworthy condition. The Lascars have abandoned their duties to sing their songs around that thing in the hold."

My heart quailed at his words, which were spoken in the most matter of fact manner.

"Is there no hope?"

"There is always hope. Say your prayers, keep your faith in God, and go back to your stateroom. Find something to use to brace your door shut so that it cannot be forced inward. Wait for me to come to you."

"What are you going to do?"

"I mean to prepare one of the lifeboats with rations and water, and ready it for launch. I may need your help for that—it's a difficult job for a single man."

"Is there no member of the crew left who will help you?"

"I fear not. If we are successful in launching the boat—and the calmness of the sea will aid us in this—we will take to it and leave the ship to her fate."

Tears started from my eyes. I bit my lip in an effort to contain them but they spilled out. Seeing this, he came around his desk and drew me to my feet with his hands on my shoulders.

"Be brave, girl. I can rig a sail in anything that floats, and can navigate by the sun and stars alone. I'll get us to England."

11.

I made my way back to the saloon, my mind a crazed whirl of fears and hopes. When I came near any of the crew on deck, I shrank away until they passed. For the most part they ignored me. A few cast dark stares at me. I do not believe there was a single man wholly in his right mind, but the malaise had affected them to varying degrees, so that some were gibbering mad while others merely appeared distracted.

Mr. Whittier looked up from his glass when I entered the saloon. The young priest, Father John, sat mumbling prayers on his rosary, and Madame Volkovsky merely stared down at the table as though reading her cards, but there were no cards on the table.

I sat beside Whittier, hoping that his mind was clear enough that I could talk to him. In a low voice I tried to tell him what the Captain planned, but it was no use. His eyes would not focus on my face. They kept wandering up to the skylight. He wore an expression of infinite sorrow, and as he spoke, tears ran down his cheeks.

"It is all my fault, all my fault. I took away their god, and now their god has come to punish me. I've seen him. He walks in the shadows and his arms are long. There is no safe place to hide from his hunger. For long ages he slept, but I awakened him by removing him from his temple, and now he ravens for blood. Even the stars won't shine in these accursed waters. Heaven has covered her face with a caul. We have gone so far north, we are beyond the latitudes of civilized men. Only savages dwell in these cold waters. There is no law here, no justice, no salvation. We are all damned, and it is my fault, for I woke the evil and put the evil aboard this ship."

He continued on in this way for some time, but I stopped listening. I don't believe he even knew that I was sitting next to him.

His monologue was cut off abruptly when the outer door of the saloon banged open. The steward, Elijah Smalls, stood framed in the doorway. His nose was bloody, and the blood had dripped down his upper lip and over his chin and dried there. There was more blood on the front of his white jacket.

He stared directly at me, as though talking to me and no one else.

"There's no more food," he said in a kind of shriek that caused the spittle to fly from his lips. "I'm done waiting on you, I'm all done. You must fend for yourselves, I'm all done."

"But the food can't be gone," I protested.

"It's tainted with maggots and beetles and worms. I can't stand to look at it no more. All writhing and seething it is with white worms and black beetles."

"How can all of it be tainted?"

But he was already gone from the doorway. I got up and closed the door, wondering what to do, and decided it would make good sense to provision myself with a supply of food and water while waiting for the Captain's summons. I did not like to disobey his order to remain in the saloon, but the thought of starving here did not appeal to me. Water was not a problem— the huge cistern between the tables was more than half full.

With great care I worked my way along the deck from the stern to the forecastle, where the cook stove was always kept burning. The fire in the stove had been allowed to go out, and there was no sight of the ship's cook. I took an empty flour sack and rummaged in the cupboards. I found a whole loaf of bread, a large block of cheese, and a piece of roast beef that was cold and hard. In the corner stood an apple barrel that was half-filled with good apples. A dozen of these I put into my sack.

I saw no sign of any taint. There were no maggots, no beetles, not even any mold. All this must have been in the steward's mind.

On my return across the deck with my sack of provisions, Jimmy Meercat dropped from the rigging directly in my path. He must have been watching and waiting for me. There was an evil light in his black eyes. He grinned, showing me his mouthful of rotting and tobacco-stained teeth.

"You not like the others," he said, inching toward me.

"Get out of my way."

"I watch you. There are no dreams in your mind. Lakoosa not speak to you."

"Who is Lakoosa?"

His face took on an almost religious glow. "Lakoosa is great warrior from outside the stars. For long time he dream, but now he is awake and hungry. All will die except those who serve him. Come to hold, serve Lakoosa, save your life."

"Don't be absurd. I'm going back to my stateroom."

I pushed him aside. The unexpectedness of my touch caught him off balance, and the little man fell backward over a coil of rope. He leapt to his feet with his knife in his hand and murder in his eyes. What he would have done, I cannot be certain, but at that instant one of the American crew members began to shriek at the top of his lungs and attacked one of the Lascars. This drew Jimmy Meercat's attention away from me. While he went to intervene in the fight, I turned and hurried back to the saloon.

I looked in despair at my fellow passengers and wondered if hunger would rouse them out of their stupor. They had all gone mad in their own different ways. Whether it was caused by the stone idol of the Lascars or some natural disease, there was nothing I could do to help them. The stark realization that my very life was in peril had a wonderful effect in focusing my mind on matters of my own survival.

Going to Mr. Ives' door, I knocked lightly. When there was no response, I entered it. The room was exactly as I had seen it earlier. With a sick feeling in my stomach I realized that Ives had vanished, just like the others.

The sense of my own aloneness stiffened my resolve. For a moment I thought about what I must do to secure my own safety. Food I had obtained. That left water as the next necessity of life. I carried my pitcher from my room to the cistern and used a glass to fill it with fresh, clean water, then returned it to its place on top of my commode.

Against the wall of the saloon rested a short oaken bench that was not fastened to the floor. I dragged this into my stateroom, for it was too heavy to carry. None of the other passengers even turned to watch. Closing my stateroom door and latching it, I managed to wedge one end of the seat of the bench beneath the door handle and the other end against the base of the wall.

As twilight crept on, the saloon darkened, and the light that found its way through the louvers in my door dimmed. I did not light my own lamp, but lay on my bunk fully dressed and wondered how I could obtain a pistol or at least a large knife. The idea of sleep never even occurred to me. My nerves were wound up as tightly as a clock spring.

When the outer door of the saloon slammed open, I was on my feet in moments with my face pressed to the louvers of my door, but I could see nothing beyond but shadows. I could only imagine what was going on from what I heard. Several pairs of feet thudded on the floor, and I heard the lowered voices of the Lascars.

A man's voice I recognized as Whittier's sputtered protest. The manhandling by the Lascars roused him from his drunken malaise, at least for the moment. "Let go of me, you filthy savages."

The response was titters of laughter and sing-song conversation. I heard a scuffle and the sound of a heavy blow. Whittier ceased to struggle. They dragged him from the saloon.

I held my breath, my heart hammering in my chest, and strained my ears. The saloon had become silent once again, but I had a sense that it was not empty. I heard an exhalation no more than a foot away on the other side of the door, and smelled its sourness.

The door handle rattled loudly and the panels flexed as the man on the other side put his shoulder against them, but the door was stoutly made and withstood this assault. He tried several more times before giving up.

"You clever lady," Jimmy Meercat said through the darkness. "No matter, your time will come. The god is hungry; your time will come."

I heard his footsteps cross the floor, and the rattle of the outer door of the saloon as it opened and shut.

For several hours there was silence. In my imagination I could see the Lascars sitting in a circle around the black stone idol in the hold, performing some barbaric rite that entailed the murder of Mr. Whittier, but I could not hear them chanting. The silence on the ship was almost absolute.

The horrors of the night were not over. After midnight I began to hear screams from different parts of the ship. They chilled the blood in my veins, because I knew they were the screams of dying men.

A kind of slithering noise came across the ceiling. Something was being dragged over the rear deck of the ship. Whatever it might be, it was heavy, for the timbers creaked in protest when the weight of it settled on them.

There was the sound of breaking glass in the saloon. For several minutes I could not imagine what this might be. Then I realized it was the shattering of one of the skylights.

I strained my ears to hear more. A strange and unpleasant odor hung in the air, not like that of a beast, but more like the smell that comes from the body of a serpent, or a toad. There was a slithering on the other side of my door as something felt its way across its surface. It continued on down the line of stateroom doors. I heard an explosion of shattered wood, and a woman's high-pitched scream. Something long and thick seemed to flail against the ceiling and walls of the saloon. It made a terrific racket that sent me cowering to the end of my bed. My heartbeat was so loud in my own ears that I felt certain it could be heard by the monster on the other side of my door.

There was only the single, long and drawn out scream, like the scream of a young child, but I felt certain it had come from an adult woman's throat. Then, shuffling and banging around, and then silence returned.

12.

For two days and three nights I waited in my stateroom for Captain Haire to come and inform me that he was ready to launch one of the longboats. Each night the screams came, but neither Jimmy Meercat nor whatever had slithered across the ceiling returned. On the morning of the third day, I realized I would be forced to leave my room, if only to get fresh provisions.

There was dried blood on the wall in the saloon, and more around the gaping hole in the ceiling where the skylight had been. Beneath the skylight lay scattered Tarot cards.

I checked all the staterooms, and found only one occupied. The door was unlocked. The young priest, Father John, was on his knees before his bed, his elbows on the mattress, folded hands pressed to his forehead. He must have been praying, for I could see his lips move, but he uttered no sound.

He did not hear me enter. I tried to raise him to his feet, but he refused to move. I returned to the saloon and drew a glass of water from the cistern. When I held the glass to his cracked lips, he slowly became aware of the water, and drank it all. A glimmer of reason returned to his eyes.

"It is the Devil, Miss West. I have seen it, and it is the Devil."

"What did you see, Father?"

"It comes in the night and moves like a shadow on the wall. Its arms are terrible in their strength. I saw it rip a crewman into two at the waist."

I remembered the sliding sounds I had heard on the deck above my stateroom on the first night of my concealment.

"You must come with me, Father. We'll go to Captain Haire. He has a plan to escape the ship."

He resisted my attempt to raise him up, shaking his head with wide eyes. "No, no, I must stay here and pray for forgiveness.

"You have no need for forgiveness."

"I let them take Father Patrick, and I said nothing. I did nothing, may God help me. I let them take him to his death."

"You were not in your right mind."

"Let me pray, but save yourself, Miss West. You must save yourself so that the world will know that the Devil is real."

Nothing I could say would move him. I resolved to return with the Captain so that we could carry him to the longboat, by force if necessary.

When I went onto the open deck, it began to snow enormous white flakes that drifted down from a leaden sky. I looked up, and one of them touched my lips and melted into a drop of ice water. I wondered how much longer this unnatural calm would last. I doubted the ship could survive rough weather without a crew, and with her mainmast broken and her sails all in tatters. The cluster of icebergs that had surrounded us was still in plain view, but some distance off the port side. The ship must have drifted through it without incident. All around there was only the seamless zone where the gray sea merged with the gray horizon, broken here and there by the towering bergs.

The longboat on the port side was missing from its place. My heart fell, for my immediate thought was that Captain Haire had betrayed me. He had managed to launch the boat by himself and had not bothered to seek me out in my stateroom.

From the open hatchway that led down to the hold came the monotonous chant of the Lascars. Every so often in the meaningless stream of sounds I was able to pick out the name Lakoosa.

I wandered around the deserted deck, unable to think what to do. There was another longboat, but I knew nothing about how it should be launched, and even had I known, I doubted my strength was adequate to the task.

Behind a barrel of tar lay Mr. McGee, dead. Someone had stolen his boots and cut his throat, probably not in that order.

I searched the Captain's cabin, but as I had surmised, Captain Haire was not within it. Neither was the ship's logbook that he would need to justify his command before a board of inquiry. I wonder what he had written there? Something like: "Struck an iceberg, taking on water, pumps useless." If he were clever and handled himself well, he might even be able to get another mercantile command.

Regardless of what happened, I needed more food. I decided to go to the ship's galley and fill another flour sack with whatever I could find there, then return to the remaining longboat and examine the way it was fastened to its supports. I doubted there was any way I could move it, but I had to try. It was my only hope.

With nervous eyes I scanned the rigging for Jimmy Meercat. There was no one working above the deck. All the remaining Lascars must be in the hold, chanting to their god, who did not appear to venture forth until after sunset. I wondered what relationship the monster that had pulled poor Madam Volkovsky through the broken skylight bore to the carven stone idol? Where had it come from? Where did the Lascars keep the thing hidden during the day?

I rifled the cupboards and drawers of the galley for things I could eat, and ended up taking the rest of the cheese and a dozen more apples. There was a quantity of beef jerky and some hardtack biscuits that I also put in my bag. It was not a food I liked, but I was in no position to pick and choose. More than anything I longed for a cold glass of milk.

Thus far my luck had held, but I knew it could not hold forever. I hurried back toward the saloon with my supplies, which if handled with reason should keep me from hunger for another three or four days.

As I was passing the midsection of the deck where the port longboat had rested inverted on its brackets, I heard an odd irregular tapping. I stopped to listen. It came from the side of the ship. Leaning over the rail, I nearly dropped my sack.

There was the longboat, floating on the placid surface of the sea. From time to time its side drifted against the ship, and made the tapping I had heard. In the middle of the boat lay Captain Haire, face down with his arms and legs splayed, as if he had fallen that way into the boat. The hilt of a knife projected from his back. I recognized it by the red band on its hilt. It was Jimmy Meercat's knife.

I saw that the boat had been provisioned with several kegs of water and a large quantity of the same hardtack biscuits that I carried, along with other foodstuffs.

"You couldn't hide below deck forever."

Jimmy Meercat advanced toward me with murder in his eyes. Two other Lascars blocked my escape along the rail.

I did not pause to think but merely reacted like a wild beast that is cornered. I swung my leg over the rail and dropped into the boat below. The body of Captain Haire in part broke my fall, or I would surely have injured myself. I lay in the boat across the legs of the corpse, stunned. The voices of the Lascars roused me. They were preparing a noose in a rope to swing over the side and into the boat.

Again, it was instinct rather than reason that guided my hand. Pulling the knife from Captain Haire's body with some effort, I used its keen blade to cut through the single line that tethered the boat to the ship, than with the strength of both my legs I pushed the boat away.

Jimmy Meercat glared down at me as I drifted further from the side. Had he held anything in his hands, he would surely have thrown it at me, but his hands were empty.

"You will die slow, you stupid whore," he shouted. "Come back and I will kill you quick like the Captain."

Anger stirred deep within me. In spite of the futility of the gesture, I could not resist putting my hands together around my mouth and shouting back.

"I'll still be afloat when you founder. Where are your sails? Where is your crew? When the weather turns you'll die along with your filthy god."

He continued to shout curses, some in English and some in his native language, but I gave him no attention. The enormity of my situation overwhelmed my senses. I was alone, adrift at sea, and hundreds of miles away from the usual packet shipping lines. I did not know how to raise a sail or work an oar. When the weather changed I would be in a worse situation than if had I remained hidden aboard the *Caledonia*. Despite my boast, we would all end up on the bottom of the sea—me, the Lascars, and their monstrous god.

13.

I lost track of how many days I drifted in that dreaming calm, where the gray sky merged into the gray sea. It was cold, but not as bad as it might have been due to the lack of a breeze. Before throwing Captain Haire's body over the side, I stripped him of his outer clothing, including his hat and boots. Removing my dress and stays with a self-conscious blush, I put on the Captain's shirt and trousers. They were too big for me, but they were warm. I was particularly grateful for his great coat, which was of thick wool.

Forbidden Passage

As I let his body slip into the water, I said a prayer for his soul. It was not his fault that the idol had been brought on board his ship. How could he have possibly anticipated the danger? Not even Whittier could have imagined the plague he was bringing to the *Caledonia*. As long as the idol had remained apart from the Lascars, it had appeared harmless. It was their rites and sacrifices that had stirred it to hellish life.

I occupied much of my daily hours trying to row the boat. It took me a while to understand how the oars were to be placed, and how I was to sit. Even then, my back was not strong enough to pull the oars for more than a quarter-hour at a time, and the palms of my hands quickly became covered with blisters that broke open and bled.

My greatest difficulty lay in knowing which way to row. I had no sun to guide by, no stars, and no wind. All I could do was row, and hope that I had guessed correctly the direction.

One night, while I lay in the bottom of the boat trying to sleep, I was awakened by a soft rustling sound. Opening my eyelids, I saw that the entire sky was lit with bands of color. They had the appearance of curtains that hung downward from the heavens, and they moved like curtains hanging at an open window. I realized that the sound I heard was these bands of color rubbing against each other. I cannot begin to describe the glory of the sight. I had read about the Aurora Borealis, but I had never imagined that it possessed such heart-stopping grandeur and beauty.

It continued most of the night. When it faded, I saw the stars. The sea began to rise and fall with greater vigor, and soon there were waves lapping against the sides of the boat. Either I had managed to row out of the strange calm that afflicted the *Caledonia,* or the calm had dissipated in the natural way.

Then began the greatest battle of my young life. It was me against the sea. Unless I kept the bow of the boat pointed into the waves, they threatened to lap over its low sides and swamp it, or even to capsize the boat. I could only keep the bow into the waves with the oars. I rowed as long as I could remain conscious, and when I felt myself slipping into unconsciousness, I shipped the oars and gave myself and my little craft up to the protection of God.

I lost track of the days. It may have been ten, or even twenty. It was in the early evening that I spied the lantern of the ship. The waves has lessened, allowing me to make good headway with the oars. All the while

I prayed that the ship was not sailing away from me. I had no light and would be completely invisible to anyone manning a watch on the vessel.

The light became stronger. At last the side of my boat kissed the side of the ship. I found a rope that hung down and tied up my boat by its bow. Then I began to shout for attention. To my dismay there was no response. I reasoned that they were all asleep, and taking up one of the oars, I used it to bang on the side of the hull. Still no response.

Having come so far, I was not about to be thwarted. With great difficulty I managed to pull myself up the rope and over the rail to the deck. I could not have done it had my arms not been strengthened by weeks of constant rowing.

There was something oddly familiar about the ship. Only a single lantern burned, and it flickered, showing that it was nearly out of oil. When I listened I heard not a sound. The hatch to the hold was open. It was the foul stench that arose from the hold that triggered my realization. I had been rowing in circles. This was the *Caledonia*.

"I knew you would come back," said a familiar voice.

Jimmy Meercat pulled his way up from the hold with a single hand. His other arm ended in a stump that was wrapped with a bloody bandage.

Holding up his knife, I backed away from him. "Stay away from me."

He started to laugh and ended up bent over in a coughing fit. He looked terrible. His eyes resembled pools of blood, and his lips were swollen and black.

"You got nothing to fear, girl. The others are all dead, all but me."

"You go your way and I'll go mine. But I warn you, if you try to interfere with me I will kill you with your own knife."

He looked at the knife with a brighter interest. "That's right, that is my knife. How did you find it? Give it back."

"Stop where you stand. I'm warning you."

He stared at me and licked his lips, his eyes roving over my body. "I'm hungry. I ain't had meat in four days. The god ate everything, all the livestock and beasts, all the crew and passengers, except for you."

"Why do you call that monster forth with your prayers?"

"No choice, girl. When the god commands, we obey. Everyone obeys, except you. Why are you so different?"

"Where is your god now?"

"Gone back to sleep. It's almost daylight." He held up his bloody stump and laughed. "We had a fine chase around the ship, him and me.

He took my hand. Maybe tomorrow night he'll take the rest. There's no satisfying his hunger."

"Help me fight against it. If we work together maybe we can destroy it."

"The god commands and I obey." He repeated it simply, like a mantra, while advancing with slow steps. He paused to pull a metal spike out of a slot on the side of the ship.

"Jimmy, listen to me. If we work together we can both survive. We can kill this monster. That will end the unnatural calm that surrounds us. You can set a sail or two and steer us south into the shipping lanes."

Without warning he lunged at me with the spike. Instead of falling backward, I stabbed forward with an overhand motion. He did not expect this. He stopped the fall of the knife with his stump, but had to drop the spike to catch my wrist before the blade entered his chest. We wrestled for control of the knife.

Had he been at his full strength, I would never have had a chance, but he was weakened by lack of food and water. I forced him back to one knee. He flailed at my head with his bloody stump, but I continued to push the knife forward until its point entered between his ribs. He gave one shriek and tried to kick me away. Then he was dead beneath me.

I lay unmoving for a time to make sure the knife had done its work before slowly disentangling myself. I left the knife in his chest, for I could not bring myself to remove it. His red-rimmed eyes stared up at me in mute reproach.

A search of the ship in the chill, gray light of dawn assured me of the truth of the Lascar's words. I was alone. There were not even any other corpses beside that of Jimmy Meercat. The galley was a wreck. All the barrels had been overturned and smashed apart. Rotting food littered the floor. The barrels of fresh water were staved in and tipped, so that almost nothing remained of their contents.

I was not as concerned by the lack of food and water as I might have been. There were still ample provisions in the longboat. Neither, however, was I ready to abandon the *Caledonia* for the open sea. Having battled the waves for weeks, I cannot express how blissful it felt to have a solid deck beneath my feet, and not to feel a freezing spray in my face.

If there was any way I could rid the ship of that monster in the hold, I resolved to try it. Intuition told me that the unnatural calm that surrounded the ship was of its making, and when it was dead, the calm would vanish, along with the strange leaden pall that hung over the world. Then the ship would begin to move on the currents of the ocean. With luck they would carry me south into the shipping lanes. Upon sober reflection this seemed my best chance for survival.

A sudden weariness overcame me and caused me to stumble. I had not slept for a day and a night. I went to my stateroom, barricaded my door and lay across my bunk. Sleep took me before my head touched the pillow.

14.

When I woke, I searched the entire ship for a weapon I could use against the idol. The best I was able to discover was an axe. I carried it down to steerage before I remembered that I would need some kind of light by which to work. I confess, my thoughts were not well-ordered. Killing the Lascar had upset me. He was quite literally the first living thing I had ever killed, apart from insects.

When I returned to the hold, it was with an oil lantern in one hand and the axe in the other. The open hatchway made me think of the gaping mouth of a dead giant, the interior of whose body was filled with putrefaction. The air in the hold was unimaginably foul with the stench of death. I went first forward to examine the cages of Mr. Whittier's beasts. They were all shattered, their contents missing. Traces of blood stained the iron bars. It appeared that the beasts had been ripped through the bars by some great force, and that bits of their hide had been sheered off in the process.

It took me some time to find the courage to carry the lantern into the stern part of the hold. To my relief, it was much as I had last seen it with Mr. Ives. The hideously ugly idol, like a head without a body, still rested on its wooden pallet in the middle of a ring of broken and bloody bones. As I looked with greater care, I saw several human skulls that had been staved in among the litter.

"You are a hungry demon indeed," I murmured aloud to give myself courage. "You have eaten all your worshippers."

The eyes of the idol, if indeed those shadowed depressions were its eyes, stared at me with disdain between the loops of tentacles that wrapped so tightly around it. Whatever primitive sculptor had carved this distorted inhuman visage, if indeed it was a carving, had managed to capture with perfect lucidity an expression of hatred coupled with withering contempt. I understood, not just with my mind but with my nerves and my very flesh, that this monster took pleasure in grinding its victims beneath it until not a trace remained of their original shape.

"Very well," I said, forcing my voice to be loud, "let us see what you are made of."

Setting the lantern safely out of the way, I hefted the axe, then swung as hard as I could at the idol. The steel blade clanged and made a bright red spark as it deflected from the snarling face. I struck a dozen times before I brought the lantern close to examine what I had accomplished.

The features of the idol were unmarred. There were not even small chips or cuts where the sharp blade of the axe had bounced away.

Its horrible face seemed to mock me, and I had an impression of a watchful intelligence within its core. It was with the greatest reluctance that I extended my hand to touch it with my fingers. It felt unnaturally cold, and harder than stone. Could it be some meteoric alloy of iron, as Whittier had speculated? That would explain its great weight. How had a savage race managed to carve a face into such a hard matrix? Or was it a carving?

It was some consolation that the Lascars no longer chanted or spoke its name. If they had called forth their god with their prayers from within this unnatural image, maybe it would be unable to manifest without their help. I would soon know, for twilight was almost upon me, as I discovered when I left the hold.

I paused to stare across the sea. The dim glow in the gray sky diminished in what I assumed must be the western quarter, edging the great mountains of ice with silver. There was no sound save for the occasional creak of a rope. The remnants of the sails hung limp. I realized that I had not seen a single sea bird since the end of the storm.

My plan was to go to my stateroom and barricade the door, as I had done earlier. It had served me well the last time the creature had come looking for prey, and might do so again, or so I reasoned. I could think of no other way to safeguard my life except by leaving the ship, which I was loath to do.

I put out the lantern as soon as I had wedged the oak bench under my stateroom door handle, and sat in complete silence with the axe in my hands, straining my ears for the slightest sound.

The fatigue of my body was greater than I anticipated, for I opened my eyes and realized that I had nodded off to sleep. Something had awakened me. I held my breath and listened.

From the saloon I heard the same slithering I had heard before, the night Madam Volkovsky had been snatched through the broken skylight. It came gently tap-tap-tapping on the stateroom doors, and I heard the squeak of hinges as the doors opened one after another. Then the tapping came on my door. I tightened my fingers on the handle of the axe. The tapping stopped and there was silence. The brass handle rattled up and down, up and down.

With a great crash the door was ripped outward in splinters. Something elongated and large entered the stateroom. I could see almost nothing, only a vague shadow, but it reminded me of the questing trunk of the elephant at the New York Zoo. As its end drew near my face, the stench made me gag.

I struck down quickly with the axe. Whatever I hit was not hard like metal, but soft yet tough, like animal hide. The probing shadow quickly withdrew, and from above on the deck I heard a kind of hissing.

I did not wait for its return, but climbed over the wreckage of the door into the saloon. The darkness was filled with probing fleshy tubes that hung down from the ceiling. I could feel them stirring the dead air above my head. I crouched and ran out of the door, then back along the deck toward the hatchway. It was my intention to descend into the hold and try to hide among the jumble of barrels and crates in the bow.

At the last instant, some impulse made me drop the axe and climb up into the rigging of the mainmast. I ascended the rungs of the rope ladder by touch alone, and continued to climb until I reached the crow's nest. The mast had broken not far above it, and a tangle of splintered wood and loose ropes hung over it. I found a place to crouch amid this wreckage and waited.

It was the longest night of my life. The thing was tireless. I heard it drag the body of Jimmy Meercat into the hold, and the tearing of flesh and breaking of bones that followed. One corpse was not enough to appease its hunger. It probed everywhere on the ship as though searching for me. I wondered if it was intelligent.

As the first faint glow of morning paled the eastern horizon, I saw it climbing the rigging of the foremast with its innumerable legs, which were like great snakes. With its round body and slender limbs, it reminded me most of the spider called daddy longlegs that I had watched in fascination as a child. Its strength was astonishing. I saw it snap thick hemp ropes like rotten string, and once it tore off a spar and threw it into the sea. At last, as the light strengthened, it retreated back into the open hatchway.

An intense joy at the realization that I would live another day brought tears to my eyes. Never had life seemed so precious. I descended the rigging with care, my mind strangely calm. Without having thought about it, I knew what I must do.

From the ship's lanterns I collected all the coal oil I could find in a bucket. By this time the sun was well above the horizon, although I could not see it through the overcast that hid the sky. I carried the oil into the hold and poured it over bales of wool that were stacked there. Using my tinder box to set the oil alight, I stood and watched for several minutes to make sure it was burning furiously, then left the hold and went to the rail where the longboat was tied. I dropped into the boat, loosed the rope that held it against the *Caledonia,* and rowed away from the ship to watch it burn.

15.

As I sat and watched the smoke rise, doubt tickled my mind with unanswerable questions. Why had the demon caused the Lascars to bring the ship to this northern longitude? If the demon had created this strange calm to end the storm and preserve the ship from sinking, why had it prolonged it for so many weeks? What was it waiting for?

Black smoke rose from the hatchway like the smoke from the funnel of a steam locomotive. Eventually flames appeared and ignited the remnants of the sails. Each flaming mast collapsed with a crash that sent up showers of sparks, and the fire began to eat at the sides of the ship.

All through the day it burned. To my dismay, when the ship had been consumed down to the waterline, the fire began to go out. Although it was no more than a charred hulk, it did not sink. This filled me with a rage that caused hot tears of frustration to cascade down my cheeks. Why wouldn't it sink?

As I continued to watch into the twilight, something black emerged from the hold. Smoke curled up from its undulating arms as it raised itself into the air. I wondered if the fire had injured it? As if in answer to my question, its arms slid around the charred hulk that had been the *Caledonia,* and with sudden force, tightened. The hull of the ship splintered and broke into two sections that swiftly sank. Where the ship had floated, only gray water remained.

I did not wait to see if the serpentine limbs would reappear, but applied myself to the oars with a will, and ceased not from rowing until daylight.

It is late afternoon. I am writing this in my journal as I lie in the bottom of the longboat. I had the forethought to retrieve my journal from my stateroom and place it into the boat before firing the ship. Whether anyone will read this record, I know not. The strange calm that surrounded the ship has slowly dissipated, and the waves have begun to rise, and along with them the wind.

Captain Haire provisioned the boat well. I have enough food and water for several more weeks. My hands and shoulders have become accustomed to the work of rowing. If I can keep a southerly course, a ship may find me. I will not abandon hope. There must be a reason why I alone of all the crew and passengers of the *Caledonia* was spared.

From time to time I glimpse deep beneath the water a moving shadow. It seems to follow in the wake of the boat. I tell myself that it is the shadow of a shark, or possibly a whale.

There! Just now I felt something touch the bottom of the boat directly beneath me. A gentle tap-tap-tapping on the bottom. Twilight is beginning to fail. I cannot write more. I will try to sleep.

About the Author

DONALD TYSON is a Canadian writer who lives with his wife, Jenny, in a renovated farm house in Cape Breton, Nova Scotia. He is the author of many books on the history and practice of Western magic, including several associated with the *Necronomicon* of H. P. Lovecraft. His fiction includes the novels *The Messenger* (Llewellyn, 1993), about the psychic investigation of a haunted hunting lodge in winter, *Alhazred* (Llewellyn, 2006), about the early life of the author of the *Necronomicon,* and *The Tortuous Serpent* (Llewellyn, 1997), which concerns the doings of the Elizabethan magician Dr. John Dee and his friend, the alchemist Edward Kelley. The short story collection *Tales of Alhazred* (Dark Renaissance, 2015) relates further adventures of the mad Arab who authored the *Necronomicon,* and the collection *The Ravener* (Avalonia, 2011) extends the fictional exploits of Dee and Kelley. Tyson's horror stories have appeared in numerous anthologies, among them the popular Black Wings series edited by S. T. Joshi.

Printed in Great Britain
by Amazon